Strangerland

ALSO BY MONIKA RADOJEVIC

A Beautiful Lack of Consequence
Teeth in the Back of My Neck

Strangerland

MONIKA RADOJEVIC

#MERKY BOOKS

UK | USA | Canada | Ireland | Australia
India | New Zealand | South Africa

#Merky Books is part of the Penguin Random House group of companies
whose addresses can be found at global.penguinrandomhouse.com

Penguin Random House UK,
One Embassy Gardens, 8 Viaduct Gardens, London SW11 7BW

penguin.co.uk

First published 2026

001

Copyright © Monika Radojevic, 2026

The moral right of the author has been asserted

Penguin Random House values and supports copyright.
Copyright fuels creativity, encourages diverse voices, promotes freedom
of expression and supports a vibrant culture. Thank you for purchasing
an authorised edition of this book and for respecting intellectual property laws
by not reproducing, scanning or distributing any part of it by any
means without permission. You are supporting authors and enabling
Penguin Random House to continue to publish books for everyone.
No part of this book may be used or reproduced in any manner for the
purpose of training artificial intelligence technologies or systems. In accordance
with Article 4(3) of the DSM Directive 2019/790, Penguin Random House
expressly reserves this work from the text and data mining exception.

Set in 12.5/15.2pt Garamond Premier Pro
Typeset by Six Red Marbles UK, Thetford, Norfolk

Printed and bound in Great Britain by Clays Ltd, Elcograf S.p.A.

The authorised representative in the EEA is Penguin Random House Ireland,
Morrison Chambers, 32 Nassau Street, Dublin D02 YH68

A CIP catalogue record for this book is available from the British Library

ISBN: 978-1-529-91874-8

Penguin Random House is committed to a sustainable future
for our business, our readers and our planet. This book is made from
Forest Stewardship Council® certified paper.

For Adriana and Željko, and those who came before

Prologue

The hours pass, and still the woman does not know where she is going. She badly wishes that she could speak the local language, and this thought repeats itself over and over, like a prayer. If she could, she would ask someone on the bus where they were all going. It is April, and it should be warm, but it is not. There shouldn't be much snow, but a sudden and unexpected cold snap means temperatures have plummeted to negative double digits. The mountain path is badly lit, with towering snow banks on either side. In this kind of darkness, every shadow takes on a menacing quality. The woman stares out of the window rigidly, as though remaining still will keep her (and everyone on board) intact. This road, which is so potholed and gravelly it is barely a road, must somehow get them safely from one place to another. She shivers. She twists the ring on her hand compulsively. It's not real silver – like almost all the jewellery the woman owns, it is cheap, although that does not mean it has no value to her. It's a child's ring, now only fitting her smallest finger. Her twelfth-birthday present. She decided to take it at the very last moment, though she now feels further from childhood than ever before.

The darkness is so complete it seems to swallow up their surroundings, as if they are driving through an endless tunnel.

She tries not to derive any meaning from it – it's just asphalt and rubble, after all. She tries to ignore the ominous-looking crack in the windshield. Everyone else seems unconcerned. As it pushes through the night towards its destination, the bus rattles alarmingly. Its insides appear fused together from another bus – only some of the windows are opaque, and the seats made of different fabrics are bolted to the floor, which itself is part carpet, part vinyl. She wishes the driver would slow down, but she is a stranger on this bus and has no way of knowing that if he did, the occupants would shout and complain. They are all eager to get to their warm beds and waiting families. They are used to perilous journeys.

Some of the passengers sleep, but the woman simply gazes out at the night, too alert, too aware of the mess she is in. She has never seen this much snow before, and it is blunt and cold in a way that challenges everything she thought she knew about winter – a frightening idea. If she could be so wrong about something as banal as snow, what other mistakes might she be making? Because she has never been the kind of woman to make impulsive choices. Mistakes cost too much; she makes her decisions by attacking the situation from every angle to determine all margins of error. But she did not plan for this, and now her own actions are scaring her. Who gets on a bus in the middle of the night with no idea where it is going, after all? She rakes over the choices she made in the handful of minutes she had before boarding, and comes to the same conclusions over and over again: the cancelled plane, the bus, all this confusion – perhaps it was a by-product of the war marching towards them. Perhaps she would have ended up here no matter what she did. Perhaps this is God's reminder that she has very little control over her own life. She is a stranger in this land, unable even to read the signs at the airport or to ask for help. She thinks about what it means to fall in love in a foreign language, and whether it will be enough. Once, both of his hands enveloping her own, he had told her, 'At the touch of love, everyone becomes a poet.' A quote from Plato that he liked, he explained, with a nonchalance that thrilled her.

But the war? They warned her, all the people who know what she's done, where she's going. They told her it would be unpredictable, dangerous even. She doesn't understand impending conflict the way he does, has never pored over rumours and pieces of information from dubious sources to decipher her country's future. She doesn't know what it means to make, then remake, evacuation plans, to keep the passports by the front door, to hide the money in the mattress. People she knew – people who had no idea what they were talking about – spoke about 'the war' as if the whole country had become one giant battlefield. As if everything had already been obliterated. The weight of her decision bruises her shoulders. She doesn't know war. But he does, and he brought her here anyway. Surely that counts for something? She checks her watch. The instructions had been simple: do not get off the bus. No matter what happens, do not get off the bus.

Eight hours to go.

PART ONE

CHAPTER 1

Uberlândia, October 1990

The sky was angry the moment dawn broke. It grew humid and heavy, warm, fat raindrops thickening the air. It was the kind of heat that could bring out the rage of a man. Toninho stood under the porch and watched the rain turn the narrow pathway outside their home into mud. He was in his mid-sixties, tall, with a light brown, freckly face and soft, tanned arms. It was his day off, but he had an important errand to run and was immaculately dressed for the occasion: a pressed short-sleeved white shirt and crisp cotton trousers. As he listened to the storm and smelled the fresh, wet earth, Toninho imagined himself becoming part of the stone steps, calcification beginning at his feet and creeping up his body until he was immobilised. A statue guarding the only entrance to his home. He reached into his pocket and pulled out a slim packet of cigarettes. Local brand. Then a cheap yellow lighter.

Behind him, through the open metal front door, Adelina paced back and forth in front of a sagging, faded sofa with a large patchwork blanket thrown over it. She was sweating, flapping the collar of her tunic and glancing at the kitchen clock. There was dough underneath her fingernails. A huge rumble of thunder rolled above their heads and Adelina glanced up at the sky nervously. 'Need to leave soon,' she muttered. Then: 'Toninho, my love, put your chinelo on, please. The lightning.' Adelina's own feet were firmly tucked into a pair of rubber-soled flip-flops. He took a few steps backwards until he was in the doorway and nudged the sandals onto his feet as his wife watched, her arms folded. They stared at each other for a moment, waiting. There wasn't much time. 'Have you got the abacaxi?' Adelina asked suddenly. He put a finger to his lips and nodded, glancing up at the ceiling. Above them came the sound of a bedroom door opening, then shutting again. But no one appeared at the top of the staircase. Any moment now, their daughter would be emerging from her room, passport in hand. Her luggage was by the front door. Toninho turned back to observe the rain once again and heaved a long, slow sigh. He was usually not prone to melancholy, but today was a little different.

'Do you think,' his wife asked, voicing Toninho's thought aloud, 'that it's safe to fly in this weather?'

She was looking to him with a kind of exhausted apprehension, as she often did, and so he kept his voice light. 'I'm sure the pilots would never fly if it were dangerous.'

'Yes. You're right.' Adelina sat down heavily on the couch and crossed her pale legs. 'Of course. They would never fly if it were dangerous.'

Adelina tended to consume herself with worry. She had long preferred the indoors, which had given her skin the slightly pallid look of someone who needs more sun than they're getting. A hangover, probably, of being called ugly and dark as a child. Toninho watched her push her hair off her face impatiently and smiled despite his worry. In the rush of that morning – a hasty breakfast, last-minute packing – she'd forgotten to style it her usual way. His wife liked to keep her unruly black hair twisted into a low bun, a ritual she performed in front of the bathroom mirror most mornings. He loved to watch her, often leaning against the bathroom door to observe the way she turned her head to the right – always to the right first – then the left. She wore the same lustrous pink pearls in her ears every day, too, a gift he'd bought her on their second date. Back when he had money.

'Just one more minute!' Alegria's disembodied voice floated down. 'I'm just . . . sorting something out.' Unbeknownst to them, she was counting out her precious American dollars to slip into the top drawer of their bedside table, for emergencies. Not that they would need it, she reasoned. She'd be back in a few months. But just in case. American dollars could undo a lot of damage.

As she waited, Adelina thought of how their younger daughter, Simone, had run around shrieking for her passport just six months earlier, half-packed, frantic and beautiful at the same time. Alegria had lain down on the cool, tiled floor, her arms and legs spread like a starfish, and had fallen asleep despite the pandemonium. Simone left and the house was quieter, lonelier for it. She was headstrong and coquettish, with her haughty face, her small, plump lips and her narrow eyes. Their youngest seemed to have cherry-picked the most hypnotic features of all their ancestors. They should not have worked, all assembled together like that, but they did. Her face was a historical text.

When Simone had decided, on a whim, to follow her

boyfriend to England, she'd arrived via Calais, got off the ferry in Dover and marched straight up to a taxi, his address scribbled on a sheet of paper. In Simone's mind, Dover and London were either the same thing or right next to each other. Halfway through her journey, watching the meter tick alarmingly upwards, she'd realised her mistake and sank back into the furred car seat, wondering how on earth she'd pay him. In the end, she'd arrived at a block of flats in west London, where hundreds of Brazilians had congregated, climbed out of the back seat and turned to face the driver, holding up one hand. 'Please. You wait,' she'd said, and leaned on the buzzer until Ricardo came lumbering down the stairs. 'I owe him one hundred and fifty pounds,' she told him, pointing to the bewildered taxi driver behind her. 'You'll have to pay. I don't have the money.' Poor Ricardo went from door to door, borrowing money from friends until he'd scraped enough together to cover the fee.

Adelina had been horrified by her daughter's recklessness when she'd found out. And the cost? My God! She felt London to be a cold and unforgiving place. And now that Alegria was leaving, their small home would have far too much space in it. They were lucky to have this place, with its high, white ceilings and the large window at the top that directed an imperious beam of light down into the room like a church. Their eldest daughter had painted the living room – which was also the kitchen and the dining room – a buttery yellow, as though they lived inside a lemon. It was cheaper to build the exterior out of stone than with brick, and so great slabs of uneven, multicoloured granite covered the outside of their home. The floor was beige tile. Everything was chosen to give the illusion of a modestly wealthy family. Alegria had managed to buy the plot of land and construct it after years of working as a teacher, thanks to a generous government programme that covered most of the costs. A classic pre-election scheme – but none of them complained. Of course they would vote for anyone who could give them stone exteriors, tiled floors and painted walls, finally bringing a degree of stability to the family they hadn't enjoyed since Alegria was fourteen, when Toninho had lost everything and she began working in the supermarket after school. Every morning when Adelina woke up, she touched the feet of the small Santa Maria by her bedside table and thanked God for the daughter who'd pulled them out of years of struggle.

'I'm ready,' Alegria announced, just as they heard a quick jab of the taxi's horn. Somewhere out there, a driver had pulled up to the gate. Toninho stubbed out his cigarette and the three of them gathered solemnly by the door. Alegria had pinned up as much of her short, dark hair on top of her head as she could. A slight sheen of sweat glittered across her freckled brow. Gold hoops swung in her ears. She was short, with high cheekbones like her mother's, dark and sun-speckled like her father. In her baggy jeans and paisley-print tank top she looked even shorter, almost childlike, even though she was almost thirty. Tucked under one arm was a bulky navy jumper, for when she landed. 'This thing . . .' she hoisted it higher up her hip '. . . is so heavy. So hot!'

'Have you got your passport?' Adelina said immediately, sharply. She reached out to wipe her daughter's forehead with her bare hand. 'All your documents?'

'Of course.'

'And did you pack the Santa—'

'Of *course*.' Alegria smiled at her mother and pulled her into a hug. She was impatient, but Adelina's anxiety hammered through her chest and forced her breathing to slow. 'I'll come back by February – stop worrying. You're acting like it's going to be years, not months.'

'Don't say that,' Adelina mumbled fiercely into her neck. 'Go with God, amor.'

Now that Alegria was about to go, she wanted to find reasons to keep her daughter there. The problem was that Adelina knew she could not trust her gut, because her gut was in a perpetual state of alarm. But something tugged at her, the unfathomable suggestion that by getting on a plane today, Alegria was leaving for good. She tried to think of last-minute necessities that might give them just a few more minutes. But there were none. Alegria had been diligent, she had tied up all her loose ends and done everything she should have done – as usual. It was time to leave. Adelina took Toninho's place by the door and watched as father and daughter dashed along the path to the waiting car, crouching under bags and navy jumpers and old newspapers. They were swallowed by the rain within seconds, but she remained at her post until she heard the sound of a car starting up its engine.

Toninho paid for the taxi. He insisted, gently pushing away his daughter's outstretched hand as she tried to give a fistful of banknotes to the driver. Alegria let him, even though she knew her father could only afford a one-way journey. The taxi rank was just a few metres away from shelter, but the rain was severe, rushing down the hilly streets in torrents and soaking their clothes within seconds – yet he did not quicken his pace. She ran ahead, waiting for him under the grey awning of UDI Airport as he wheeled her suitcase to her, his shirt now semi-transparent. Her jeans were making her sweat. Her flight wasn't for three hours, but Toninho let Alegria check – for the third time – that her passport and papers were where they should be, before asking quietly, 'A snack, maybe?'

'Only if I pay,' she said immediately, but Toninho shook his head.

'Not this time, filha. You pay when you come back.'

She considered slipping some money into his bolso when he wasn't looking. She was stubborn that way, after all. But it was a hard line to walk, dignity versus pragmatism, so she left it alone.

The terminal was dingy and sparse, equipped only for domestic flights, but they found a kiosk selling coxinhas and settled down at one of the tables. Alegria positioned herself as close to an electronic display as she could, even though the gate wouldn't open for a few hours yet. She watched her father converse with the vendor in his usual mild manner and smiled as he bent to look at the fried dough displayed behind sliding glass doors. Toninho had been a fruit seller when she was a child, renowned for selecting the juiciest, ripest produce. 'I never rush,' he always said. 'You have to examine each and every product for as long as necessary – and see if you can smell the sweetness through the skin.' As a child, she'd watched him make careful choices in Uberlândia's open markets. Her father seemed most comfortable in the blur of colour and texture, murmuring as he picked through pink pitayas, golden mangos and papayas flecked with orange and green, their pulp almost bursting through the skin. When Alegria was younger, she'd been convinced that he was actually speaking to the fruit in his hands, willing them to yield soft, sticky-sweet flesh that came away from the peel with no resistance. His abacates were the size of a grown man's hand, green, creamy, never rotten at the centre – the slimy pit slipping right out. And even if they felt empty when you shook them, the green coconuts he'd sold overflowed with water once sliced open. It was an uncommon skill. One Alegria did not possess.

Toninho paid in coins and set down a basket between them, followed by two yellow cans of her favourite carbonated drink. She looked at him in surprise.

'You hate Guaraná?'

'But *you* love it. So today I will too.' He snapped open the tab on his can and took a sip, and she laughed at the grimace he made. 'My love, this is pure açúcar. God help us.'

'It's the best companion for coxinhas, I promise.' Two fat, teardrop-shaped croquettes glistened between them, the napkins underneath soaking up the excess oil. 'What did you get?'

'Chicken, and sweetcorn with cheese.'

'Perfect.' As she spoke, a roll of thunder boomed above them. Alegria glanced up at the windows and felt worry curdle in her stomach. She hated the idea of Toninho getting the bus in this weather, and wondered, again, if she could persuade him to take some money from her.

'You'll be fine,' he said. 'There's no strong winds. A bit of rain won't delay things.'

'Actually, I was thinking about you, Pai.'

'Don't worry about your dad!' Toninho said, taking a small, tight sip of the fizzy drink. 'Focus on your journey. What time do you land in São Paulo again?'

'Seven thirty.'

'And in Amsterdam?'

'Something like . . . ten in the morning?'

He shook off the cotton jacket he wore and tried to push his wet hair away from his face. It fell on either side of his forehead in two perfect little curls. In the gloomy airport light, she thought he looked like a gangster from one of his film noirs. 'Why did you bring a jacket in this heat?'

Toninho ignored her question. 'And after Amsterdam?'

'London tomorrow afternoon. If I get in.' Alegria sighed, reaching for one of the coxinhas and nibbling at it cautiously. She'd had far too many experiences burning the roof of her mouth with an overenthusiastic bite. She blew at the steam rising from the batter, took another small bite and then swapped her own coxinha for her father's. They ate slowly, passing them back and forth until nothing was left.

'These are the first things I'll buy when I'm back,' Alegria said, wiping the grease from her mouth. 'Si said the ones she found were horrible – too oily.'

'Yes, I wonder what the two of you will eat there. I don't think Simone's been eating enough. You will pay attention to that, won't you?' Toninho asked her anxiously.

'You *know* I will, Pai. I'll make rice and beans.'

'Good, that's good.'

They sat in silence momentarily, staring at the people walking past them. Both father and daughter knew what was coming, and they avoided looking at each other. As she worked up the energy to say what she needed to say, Alegria watched a harried-looking woman struggling to push a baby buggy and a large suitcase past them, waiting until she had disappeared around the corner before laying her own hands flat on the table. 'We need to talk about money.'

'Ale—'

'I've spoken to Mum already, and I know you hate this, but you need to know what's happening too – especially whilst I'm gone.'

Without letting him say anything further, Alegria took Toninho through the mortgage, reminding him where important documents were stored, details of payment plans, taxes and the family's health insurance. Even though all this information was sitting in a folder on her bed, it took longer than she'd anticipated. Although he was reluctant, maybe even embarrassed, her father pulled a little notebook and pen from his breast pocket and took notes in his usual unhurried manner, pausing every so often to read an instruction back to her. They had been splitting the household expenses between the two of them for years now, her father's salary as a hotel porter covering utilities and food, and Alegria paying for the mortgage and health insurance. But money was still tight, and she knew the situation was precarious enough that it might be toppled by an unexpected expense – a broken washing machine or damaged roof. And now she was unemployed, with no idea when she'd be earning again. This fact alone made her feel dangerous and out of control, and she was working hard to disguise this from her parents, who deserved to feel safe. She felt like a peach in a market stall with all her bruises turned towards the vendor.

'I have enough in my savings to make the mortgage payments until April,' she said at last, glancing at her watch.

'April? But you're back in February.'

'I know, but it might take time for me to find work when I'm back. Better that we don't worry about it for as long as we can, right?'

'How did you manage all of this?'

'I've been saving for a while. And...' Alegria hesitated. 'And I sold my moto. Rafaela's coming to collect it on Monday.'

'You didn't,' Toninho said, aghast. 'That took you five years to pay off.' He looked away as he said it, down at his hands with their thick knuckles and short fingers. They were covered in sunspots.

'I was going to sell it anyway,' she lied. 'I never liked it as much as I pretended to. The point is, everything's covered, as long as we have your salary, what Si sends and whatever I'll manage to send home too.'

Alegria knew her father was ashamed he couldn't provide for his family the way he used to. She'd been a child when the supermarket chain he had spent two decades growing collapsed into administration. Toninho had sold his business at a loss in order to pay his three-hundred-strong staff a month's salary each, leaving them penniless at the worst possible time. Within a handful of years, Brazil had been plunged into a deep recession it had still not quite managed to shake off. Things had only really turned a corner in the eighties when the collapse of the military regime ushered in a government desperate to win the support of poorer families like hers. Alegria had been twenty-one when she'd enrolled in a government scheme for heavily subsidised housing, twenty-two when she had walked into their rented apartment and announced she had bought them a home. Her father had put his head into his hands and wept like a child.

'You've thought about everything,' he said heavily, sadly. She'd upset him in her efforts to seal up and paint over all the cracks. But it had to be done. That was her role. Toninho took both her hands in his. 'How can I thank you, filha, for always looking after us?' He was so sincere and tender that she had to hold herself there, resisting the urge to make a joke or pull away.

'Just please take care of yourself. And Mãe. She's worrying herself too much – I need you to be the calm one. If Si and I say we'll call and we don't, wait at least a day before you start to worry. Maybe tell her we *did* call but she missed it. For the love of God, don't let her start acting like we're never coming back—' She stopped, guilty at the image she was painting. Acknowledging her mother's panic made her feel as though she and Toninho were conspiring against her. The truth was, Adelina had every reason to fear losing her children in sudden, unexpected ways. Her own childhood had been marked by a series of separations – including from her own twin – estranged family members and premature deaths. Her frantic energy in the days leading up to Alegria's departure had been hard to watch.

'Don't worry about your mother. I'll distract her – you know we haven't lived alone for almost thirty years? Plenty to catch up on.' He winked and Alegria grimaced as she took a large gulp of soda. 'Sure, great, whatever. Just don't break a hip or something. I won't be around to take you to the hospital.'

'I'm sixty-seven, not one hundred!'

Glancing outside, she could see street vendors in their long sleeves and straw hats milling under the airport shelter with their carts and their kiosks. Carts made of cardboard, rope and polystyrene, too fragile for something as dangerous as water. Inside would be all kinds of produce: lychees in plastic bags that often housed dead wasps, green coconuts, condensed milk and burnt sugar in banana leaves, biscuits made of salted, fried dough, palhas – cigarettes made of corn husks that smelled like dried sweetgrass. The palm trees dotting the boulevard were bent under the weight of the rain, and the wind made the carts tremble – even from two storeys up, she could see them shake. But the men and women (mostly men) were there, which meant that the rain was not an all-day occurrence but a temporary inconvenience. They were so laden down with goods they looked ready to set up a small city, right there under the fog of jet fuel. You could always rely on street vendors to understand the weather.

Alegria glanced at her watch once again and then back at her father. She wanted to put space between the men and women outside, and what they symbolised, and herself. She wanted her father to go home and not feel guilty. 'I should go through. There's always a queue.'

'Ah.' Toninho's face grew solemn. 'Before you go, promise me you'll take care of your sister – more than you usually do,'

he added, as she opened her mouth in protest. 'I think maybe she's not doing as well as she says she is.'
'With Ricardo, you mean?'
'With all of it. She never talks about how she's living, or what she's eating. I worry that she's sending us money instead of looking after herself.' This couldn't quite be true, but she didn't bother to correct her father. Simone had sent them money only twice.
'I'll cook feijão every week. Make sure we have rice every day too,' she said, as gently as she could. 'And now – I really have to go.'
'Just one more thing.' Toninho bent down and fiddled with the clasp of his battered briefcase before extracting a small plastic box of fresh pineapple slices. 'For the flight.' He pushed the box into her hands and wondered if he was going to cry.
Alegria pulled him into a fierce hug. 'This is perfect. Thank you.' The pineapple would be gloriously sweet, because he had chosen it for her.
When they broke apart, both father and daughter were openly weeping. 'You know,' Toninho said, still holding her tightly, 'I wasn't afraid when your sister left. We knew if she was ever in trouble that you, my clever, brave daughter, would have gone to help her. But now, if something happens to you, or to both of you, I don't know how we – who we will turn to.' He wiped her damp face with his thumbs and kissed her cheeks. 'That's why you have to take extra care of yourself, and of Simone.'
'It's just three months – that's nothing! I'll be with you

again soon.' Alegria tried to laugh reassuringly as she spoke, but still, her words came out suspiciously feeble.

'I sprinkled fresh mint on the pineapple, just the way you like it. Don't wait too long to eat it, OK?'

'OK. I love you, Pai.'

'I adore you. Go with God, filha.'

They embraced one more time, she breathed in the talcum-powder scent of his hair pomade. Perhaps the rain was slowing now. Perhaps the vendors would soon start their promenade down the streets, tapping on rolled-up car windows and hoping that the driver would see a human being, not a threat. Her father had sold fruit on the side of the road for a few months, a long time ago. The sun had blistered his face.

'You don't need to wait for me.'

'OK.' But Toninho did not move.

'You should get that bus, before it gets dark.'

'I will.' He smiled, he waved, he waited until she had been swallowed up by the crowd before settling back down. 'I'll only bother you for a little longer,' he said mildly as the kiosk worker collected the rubbish from his table. She shrugged, and he pulled a newspaper out of his briefcase. He would not leave until her plane had taken off, just as her mother had asked him to. Just as he and Alegria had done when it had been her sister catching the flight six months before. He would not leave until he knew his daughter was no longer in his realm of protection.

CHAPTER 2

London, October 1990

'Hey, Chef, table eight is asking for two more cosmopolitans. They don't like the way I make them.'

Zivoin glanced up at the bar clock, then back at Lorenzo. Two minutes past seven. 'Where's your cousin? I'm done.'

'Ah, come on! He's coming! Per favore, Chef, make them happy – they've been waiting for their food for almost an hour.'

Lorenzo slapped him painfully in the middle of his back in thanks, and left him reaching for the cranberry juice resignedly. Nico was *always* late, and he, Zivoin, was *always* fifteen minutes early. He liked arriving at Bar Norman with enough time for a cigarette and an espresso, easing his way into his shift so he could then work furiously through it. The best way to endure, he felt, was to constantly keep busy – polishing glasses, refilling jars of pork scratchings, wiping dust off the cluttered shelves. At school he had been taught that some species of shark had to swim constantly to force water over their gills. To stop was to die.

He squeezed a fresh lime into the cocktail mixer and shook it vigorously before pouring the baby-pink liquid into two chilled martini glasses and adding twists of orange. He nodded at Susanna, the Spanish waiter, and she deposited them at table eight with the same wide grin that had prompted Nico to – unsuccessfully – ask her out. Susanna had a smile he liked and two front teeth that were only very slightly crossed over. When she laughed, it charmed everyone. Zivoin felt, privately, that if he asked her out for a coffee, she might say yes. He knew she liked faces like his, ones with thick eyebrows and long noses that looked like they'd been broken at least once. She'd told him. But he had always coloured within the lines. Work was work and everything else ceased to exist when he stepped foot inside Bar Norman.

He checked the time again and sighed. Nine past. If Nico didn't get here by seven fifteen, he'd be out, even if it left his colleagues short for the evening. The first month Zivoin had begun working at the bar, with its smoke-filled interior and sticky vinyl flooring, he'd made a point to count up all the extra minutes he'd worked after his shift ended. There was always something – late staff, blocked toilets, a backlog of orders. But when he'd presented his evidence to Danny, his boss had laughed right in his face. 'Overtime only kicks in if you're doing an extra hour or more, mate,' he'd said, shaking his head as though Zivoin should have known better than to ask. But he suspected Danny was lying to him. When Zivoin had gloomily relayed this information to Lorenzo, his friend hadn't quite met his eye, shrugging his shoulders as if to say, *What can you do?* in a way that made him suspicious. But if Lorenzo was making more money, Zivoin did not blame him for keeping quiet. They were all here because they had families to support, money to send home. He might have done the same.

'Chef!' He looked up to see Nico grinning at him as he slid behind the bar, shrugging a leather jacket off his shoulders and making as if to hug him. 'Come va?'

'You owe me a beer,' Zivoin said lightly, dodging Nico's outstretched arms. 'I'm leaving at seven next time, man.'

'You? You say this every time and you never go.'

He was pulling on his greatcoat when the phone behind the bar rang. Susanna held the receiver out to him. 'For you, Chef.'

'A girlfriend?' Nico asked.

'No, it is a man,' Susanna said, ignoring Zivoin's scowl. They watched him take the phone and lean against the dark, liquid-spattered wall.

'Chef?' Zivoin could hear Darco's grin at the other end of the line. 'I thought you were a bartender?'

'Nickname,' Zivoin grunted. Danny had started it, unable – or unwilling – to learn his actual name. He'd begun as 'Shiv', but when Susanna had mistaken it for 'Chef', the name had stuck. He disliked it. But then, that was the point.

'Well, I like "Big Ears" better.'

'What do you want?'

'Oh, yeah, they fixed the fridge, brate! Your threats worked. I'm on my way out, but I wanted to tell you in case you planned to stop by Nisa.'

'On your way out?' Zivoin asked, distracted. 'Where? With who?'

'Hot date,' Darco said. He said it casually, but Zivoin could hear the tension behind the drawl. He was nervous. 'No need to wait up.'

'Do I know her?'

His cousin sighed petulantly down the phone. 'No. But she's one of us – come on, brate, I'm nineteen. Chill out. I gotta go.' The line went dead before he could say anything further, and although Zivoin felt protective, even paternal towards Darco, he felt a swell of pride as he turned up his collar. His little cousin was finally growing up.

'Going back to base, soldier?' Nico saluted him, sniggering, then yelped as Zivoin flicked a bar cloth at him, catching him painfully on the stomach. The floor-length navy greatcoat, with its epaulettes and stupidly large collar, made him stand out here, he knew. It was sinister and deeply unfashionable, but it was the warmest item of clothing he owned. Army-issue, from his two years of compulsory service, designed for sub-zero temperatures.

The wind barely made a dent as he ducked out of the stuffy restaurant and started making his way down Carnaby Street. There was a mist in the air that charmed things, making the street look like the postcards he sent back home every other month. But the city was thrumming with people and anxiety. Yellow-toned string lights glowed softly, illuminating the faces of fast-paced Londoners and slow-paced tourists swaddled in their winter coats. Susanna often complained about how grey and cold the city was, but to Zivoin the winter here felt mild in comparison to his home town. The snow in Nikšić was knee-high by November, the wind from the mountains far more brutal than anything London produced. Still, it *was* cold – but not raining, to his relief – so he began the hour-long walk back to Queensway. He passed a row of phone booths, their insides stuffed full of flyers of naked women with 0898 numbers. Two young girls were giggling furiously as they pointed a Nikon directly into one of the booths whilst a third posed, pretending she was making a call. He tried not to get in their way.

    If he could, Zivoin walked most places, or took buses. It was cheaper, and he found the London Underground sickeningly hot and loud, full of sweating tourists. It reminded him of the long, torturous train rides home from Belgrade, when he couldn't afford a seated ticket and would stand for thirteen hours at a time, often so hungry he felt nauseous. Even stepping inside the swaying, crowded carriages made his stomach turn. He knew Soho well enough by now, ducking through side streets and cutting through Grosvenor Square until he hit Hyde Park. The most beautiful part of London was the Serpentine in spring and summer, he'd discovered, when the sun properly dried out the grass and he could spend the afternoon under a tree with a sandwich and a book without breaking a sweat. He'd taken Darco there the day after he arrived, but his cousin had merely shrugged and said it reminded him of the lake back home, teeming with silver fish that caught the sun. 'Krupac is better – at least there we can swim.' He preferred the frenzy of the West End – Zivoin would bet his day's wages that Darco and his date would be wandering the busy streets around Leicester Square by the time he got home.

    Spotting Queensway tube station, Zivoin turned right, exited the park and sped up a little as he began to feel the first pricks of hunger. They had been buying a meal at a time lately, thanks to the broken fridge, or ordering cheap gyros from the kebab shops dotting Bayswater. It had burned a hole in his budget. He passed the marble-floored Whiteleys Shopping

Centre and Leroy's record and CD shop, ducking into the Nisa Local. It was time to get back to bulk cooking. The cousins shopped there so often they knew most of the cashiers by name. Judging by how startled the staff were whenever he said hello, he suspected this wasn't very London-like.

Zivoin lifted a hand in greeting as he spotted Margaret, spindly and hunched over the tills, before taking the same route he always took: meat section first, bread, produce, then dairy. He knew the price of a loaf of bread (50 pence), the most cost-efficient toilet-paper brand (Jeyes, single ply), which potatoes were the cheapest (jacket). If the prices went up, Zivoin would stand in the aisle and weigh up what they must leave behind. They rarely made it to the cheese aisle, but sometimes, like today, he would check the discount shelf. The British, he'd noticed, were fond of putting things in cans, from pineapples to cakes to entire Sunday dinners. Occasionally, he looked at the shelves and wondered what items like 'Bovril', so foreign and mysterious, tasted like.

'You all right, love?' Margaret yawned as he emptied out his basket. 'Not on the late shift, then, are you?' She was older than Zivoin by at least twenty years, her coiffed hair always smelling of hairspray and fried fish.

'Not today.'

'I envy you – I've got doubles all this week, with my bad back and all, can you believe it. We're short-staffed.'

'Short . . . ?'

'Not enough people to work.'

Glancing around, Zivoin noticed that most of the tills were indeed shut. 'I thought they were looking for more people?' He could think of several friends who'd happily leave jobs as cleaners and kitchen porters to work in a supermarket, where both the hours and pay were better.

'Oh, they are.' Margaret scanned a head of cabbage and dropped it into a brown paper bag with a thud, making him wince. 'But it's all these . . .' she lowered her voice a little '. . . *illegals* who keep applying, lying about their papers. Dreadful stuff really, and half of them don't even speak English. How are you meant to train them?' She looked at him with her eyes wide and her mouth agape, strongly reminding him of an owl that had once tried to build a nest in one of the oleander trees back home. He wondered what on earth she expected him to say in response.

'I see,' Zivoin said stiffly, pulling out his wallet. 'I hope you find people soon.'

'I hope so too, love. You're not looking for work, are you? You'd get by all right here, probably improve your English to boot. We could have the occasional natter if you worked one till over.'

Zivoin took his time before answering. 'But what if I'm lying about my papers, Margaret? How could you hire me?' He smiled as he said it, but the words came out flat and unfriendly. She laughed nervously, and he watched a flush creep up her neck all the way to her earlobes.

Not for the first time, Zivoin wondered if Margaret even remembered his name. When he and Darco had first started shopping here, they'd introduced themselves to everyone they interacted with, the way they would have at home. But it seemed that most of the locals found this odd, except for people like Margaret, who came from places like Nottingham or Liverpool and seemed friendlier, more at ease with his presence. He'd assumed she'd made the same effort as he had, but come to think of it, Zivoin couldn't remember her ever saying his name. This thought sat with him all through the short walk back to the flat, but the sight of his little cousin sitting gloomily in the shared kitchen drove the encounter from his mind. He dropped the groceries onto the table.

'What happened?'

'She never showed. Waited for twenty minutes at Notting Hill Gate station before I gave up.' Darco's coat was still on, his face set in a scowl. 'Who does that? English girls, brate.'

'I thought you said she was one of ours?'

'I just said that to get you off my back. Can't have Majka hearing that I'm not dating one of our own.' Zivoin could feel his cousin's humiliation oozing out from his leather jacket, and wondered what his role here was. Father? Older brother? Friend? He wasn't sure it mattered anyway. His duties were predetermined by his position in the family – oldest son, only son. He was a rowing boat, carrying everyone through the choppiest of seas. For every wedding, every baby, every fresh member of the clan, he grew a new pair of oars.

'I don't talk to your mother about you. Date whoever you want, just be honest with me.'

As he slipped into Serbo-Croat, Zivoin felt some of the tension leave his shoulders. The words loosened his throat: a glass of water after an entire day in the desert. This was the language in which he could be brilliant, instead of the clunky, dull version of himself English forced him to be. His mother tongue won him debates, charmed women and allowed him to be witty, sharp and inviting all at once. He could feel his mood lighten as he placed a chopping board on the linoleum counter. *Linoleum* was a word Zivoin felt proud to know, and prouder to be able to pronounce. He recently heard the landlord say it in the middle of a complaint about scratched surfaces and had been mesmerised by the long 'o', as in *moan*, as in *groan*, as in *postpone*. It was one of those useless, beautiful words that he had started to collect. He began washing the grime from a kilo of potatoes.

'Did your dad call?'

'Nah.'

'Did mine?'

Darco glanced up from where he'd been inspecting a tiny mark on the leather cuff of his jacket. 'No. Why? Did you hear something?'

Zivoin hesitated for only a moment. 'Of course not. Help me with the carrots.' He did not know how to answer a question like that. Everyone he knew was hearing something – houses abandoned in the middle of the night, weapons funnelled to partisans in Croatia, whispers about cancelled visas, about recalling men like him. About factories quietly taken over by military police. These days he found himself remembering just how cold gunmetal could be in the winter. A neighbour had burned a portrait of Tito in the courtyard, he'd been told. One of their distant cousins had gone to Bosnia last month and no one had heard from him. Yet. But these were just whispers from people who could barely read a newspaper. If things were really serious, he, Zivoin, with his university degree and his command over the English language and all its strange, mysterious words, like *they're, there* and *their*, would realise it. He'd know it in his bones, and his bones stubbornly told him that all of it was village gossip.

They worked in silence, the pile of vegetable peelings between them growing steadily larger, until Darco couldn't hold back any longer. 'Has that ever happened to you? A woman stand you up?'

'Sure,' he said, hands slick from wet, newly peeled tubers. Another lie.

'Did you ever ask why?'

'Not really. I assumed she wasn't interested.' He started dicing the potatoes. 'Her loss. That's how you have to see it, or you'll drive yourself crazy.'

'You always say shit like that – like it's easy.'

'It's not easy, brate, but you have to worry less about what people think of you. Start being comfortable with who you are and what you want, learn to be OK with people who don't feel the same.'

His cousin snorted. 'And you think that's working for you?'

Zivoin ignored him. 'Dinner in one hour. Go shower – you stink of cheap cologne.'

They ate the beef stew in front of the television, a shitty, boxy thing with broken speakers that muffled the sound, forcing them to turn it up to maximum. The old three-seater, covered in a garish floral print, was so sunken that they rolled into its centre when they sat, knees mashing together. The smell of old cat food and boiled potatoes clung to the room.

The BBC was broadcasting footage from Kuwait, showing hundreds of British soldiers taking part in training exercises against sandy, dust-filled backgrounds. A war correspondent, her face partly obscured by a helmet, spoke in a strange, clipped way, her words sharp and fast. It meant something – the same way Zivoin's own countryside dialect had marked him as a peasant amongst some of the students in Belgrade. Despite Darco's complaints, he insisted that they watch the news whenever his flatmates weren't around, convinced it was the best way for the two of them to learn English. He had noticed, a year and a half into his life in London, that people sometimes screwed up their faces as he spoke, as if the way he said words caused physical damage to the fragile bones housed in their ears. The malleus, the incus and the stapes: pushing vibrations through the fragile Anglo-Saxon eardrum to the cochlea. Zivoin knew those words in Latin and Russian and in Serbo-Croat, but not in English, and that was part of the problem. No one on this island knew he could quote Plato off by heart. No one on this island knew he was a poet. 'You do sound a little, well, *aggressive* when you speak, darling,' a puffy-faced customer from Bar Norman with that same strange intonation as the war correspondent had told him once. 'And you forget your definite articles.'

'My what?'

'The articles, darling. "The", "a", "an" and so forth.' Her mouth had barely moved as she spoke.

Zivoin didn't have a clue what she was talking about until he enrolled himself at the Stanton School of English, in Queensway. He had recently become determined to speak as fluently as possible. It wasn't just the quality of English that mattered here, he'd learned, but the way he said things – as well as what he didn't say. This was what he found most difficult – his mother tongue was a language of solid directness, but here words like *mightn't* and *needn't* added layers of potential meanings, until you couldn't be sure if the person saying them was a friend or planning your murder.

'What are they saying? Too fast.' Darco nudged him out of his thoughts and he strained to hear over the muffled speakers. The war correspondent was gone, the images of British soldiers replaced by a journalist conducting a live interview with a panel of experts.

'They're saying the United Kingdom has sent twenty-five thousand soldiers to the Gulf, but America has sent over two hundred thousand.'

'And that's a bad thing?'

'Depends on who you ask.'

One of the panellists was so impassioned his entire face was red, with the exception of a pale, mottled nose. '. . . *with President Bush already seeking congressional approval for the US military operation, America has signalled that once again she does not tolerate bullies. Britannia stands with her – you simply cannot attack, invade and steal from other countries because you feel like it.*'

Darco shook his head in disgust. 'Crazy interventionists. We can take care of our own problems – at least they're ignoring what's happening in Croatia, eh, brate? No tanks rolling into Nikšić anytime soon!' He spoke with the kind of certainty about the world that only a nineteen-year-old could possess. Zivoin envied him for it. 'They won't ignore it for long,' he said, his eyes fixed on the screen. 'You think America will leave us alone just because we don't have oil?'

His cousin started to say something, but Zivoin wasn't listening. Spoon suspended halfway between the plate and his mouth, he was picturing what their home town would look like if the tanks did, after all, roll through it. He thought about the grey concrete buildings flecked with bullet holes, smoke pouring out from shattered windows like blood from a gunshot wound. It was all fragments of memories – memories that didn't even belong to him, but that he had stolen from school history lessons, family stories, old photographs. What would his parents do? The fact that he didn't know scared him. Surely they would follow what their family had done in the last war, when the Nazis had marched in with their knee-high leather boots and their willingness to massacre. They would take to the mountains, hide amongst the trees that were such a dark green they looked black, even in the sun. They would stay there until it was over, until they could return unscathed.

CHAPTER 3

Heathrow, October 1990

One day later

She felt the strange new cold the moment she stepped out of the plane and into the corridors of Heathrow Airport. It wasn't like the cold of back home, that 6 a.m. chill that vanished with the sun, or the toothy bite of a strong wind. This was something that ran much deeper. Unwelcoming. But Alegria was being silly, she knew. It was just nerves, making her afraid of the *weather*. She went to rub her eyes, heavy with sleep, and found that grime had accumulated around them. The discovery alarmed her, and she wondered, for one wild second, if it would count against her. What if she was too dirty and unprepared for this country? What if they turned her away with an ugly stain on her passport to serve as a warning to others like her? There was no visa for Brazilian citizens entering the United Kingdom that would allow Alegria to work and study at the same time. Everyone she knew found illegal jobs, hunkered down and got to work earning valuable British pounds – even a job washing dishes was almost the equivalent of her teacher's salary back home.

Alegria took a slow inhale and focused on the sensation of having a chest full of air. Think about your ribs expanding, she used to say to the children at school when they came in from recess and were too excited to concentrate. For every person who had successfully entered this country, she knew at least two who had been denied entry. Or worse, had been shamefully plucked from their bedrooms, kitchens or workplaces and officially removed, like the time she'd summoned pest control to remove a snake from behind their bathroom cabinet. She had never asked what had happened to the reptile once it left their home.

'Look at this merda,' a voice behind her said gloomily. Alegria turned to the man following her up the corridor, his wife in tow. Luisa and Pedro, semi-strangers who were also trying their luck at the English border. Luisa was a vague friend from her university days – friendly, always smiling, but in only a handful of Alegria's classes. They'd rarely spoken. When Luisa had tapped her on the shoulder before they boarded in São Paulo, it took Alegria a moment to place her. What a happy coincidence! they said. Did such a thing exist? She wasn't sure. The couple wore matching travel pillows around their necks. Pedro gestured to the glass on either side of them. 'Three in the afternoon and it's already so dark.'

'I think it's exciting!' Luisa said breathlessly, jogging a little to keep up. She was a small woman at barely a hundred and fifty centimetres, and had to take two steps to every one of her husband's. Pedro was both holding her rucksack and wheeling her suitcase, but she was still waylaid by a huge puffer jacket that made her waddle like a penguin. 'They said it will be snowing – how romantic! I hope you brought a camera!'

Alegria laughed politely, but subtly tried to quicken her pace. She wondered if they planned to stick with her all the way through immigration. That would be a problem, because they clearly had no idea what they were doing. Like her, they were looking for work – the kind of jobs that needed lies instead of visas. But they were reckless, and now she was worried that she would be pulled into their mess. At first, she'd been grateful for the company – she'd arrived in São Paulo flustered and anxious, her fears now free to run unchecked. Saying goodbye to her dad in the airport had filled Alegria with a sense of finality, like a severed umbilical cord. She couldn't shake the feeling that things would never be the same, now that she had left. But it was all stupid, dramatic – three months was nothing in the grand scheme of things.

'We'll say we're just visiting. Tourists!' Pedro had said breezily as they'd queued to board. 'We're allowed to be tourists!'

'But you don't have a return flight booked!' Alegria had hissed worriedly. 'What about a fixed address? Proof of income?'

Luisa had laughed at her friend's intensity. 'You worry a lot, don't you? We know so many people who entered just like us with no problems at all. And look!' She jangled her flimsy right arm so her pristine leather handbag swayed back and forth. She looked like a tiny, perfect Barbie doll. 'Louis Vuitton! Real Louis Vuitton. They'll know *we* aren't pobre and desperate.'

She'd said it conspiratorially, but Alegria had felt shame roll over her. She said nothing further. They were seated at opposite ends of the plane, giving her plenty of time to wrestle over Luisa's words. Did it make *her* poor and desperate, then, this illicit attempt to seek stability? Brazil's 1980s inflation crisis had become its 1990s inflation crisis. Poverty cost too much, so she'd started to do what she did best: plan.

It had taken her a long time to do it, but she'd finally quit her job as a primary school teacher after four years of waiting for a pay rise that never came, fed up of having to supplement her income with private tutoring every night just to make ends meet. The problem was that her English wasn't good enough – she lacked the fancy foreign-language certificates that the better-paid teaching jobs required. Even the most basic certification from America was worth more than years of study at her local college. She spent her lunch breaks on the chunky library computers researching courses she could take in England or America that would let her into the ranks of the elite private school teachers who taught the children of Uberlândia's richest. She had hoped to go to the United States. Alegria was used to Americanised English from high school and foreign movies, and the curt, flatter intonations of British English made her nervous. But London was cheaper, especially with her sister already living there.

The whole plan had really cemented when her friend, Aline – who taught at one of the city's most exclusive prep schools – had told her about a position opening up the following year, when one of her colleagues planned to retire. 'They're going to be looking for a fluent English speaker, and our Portuguese literature professor is completely useless – you'd be *perfect*!' she'd told Alegria breathlessly over the family landline. 'For the love of God, make sure you're fluent when you apply. You've got six months – you can do it!' The salary would be enough for her to both pay the mortgage and rent out a small flat in the same neighbourhood as her family – to start building a life for herself, at last.

Which was why – Alegria quickened her pace once again – she couldn't let anyone get in the way. Simone had warned her to enter the country alone; a big group would draw attention and make Alegria more likely to be turned away, and she could not allow that. Not after the cost of the journey. She had enough to make it a few weeks in London, maybe, but that was it. She spotted a sign for a bathroom and stopped, turning to Pedro and Luisa.

'I'm going to freshen up – you go ahead.'

'Are you sure?' Pedro asked, glancing at his wife. 'We're happy to wait.' They stood between her and the red border-control desks in the near distance. Already long queues were forming.

'No, no.' Alegria waved her hands at them, shooing them away. 'Haven't you heard how long the lines get? I'll call you when I'm settled – we can go out.'

'We'll go for . . .' Luisa paused to feel out the unfamiliar sounds in her mouth '. . . a pint of Gee-nis!' She gave her an excited wave. 'Good luck!'

They left and Alegria ducked into the bathroom, forcing herself to stand by stalls which smelled faintly of vomit. Underneath the amber bulbs, she looked jaundiced and limp. Her hair was flat, and the navy wool jumper she'd pulled on had turned her figure into a shapeless mass. How did the British seduce each other through all these layers of clothing? She felt anxious and ugly in the grey toilets of this grey airport, but it was too late to rethink her plans now.

Alegria tucked her folder of documents securely under her arm and stepped back out into the crowded terminal, joining one of three long, snaking queues. Once she got through immigration she would find a payphone to call Mãe and Pai, and then Si, too, for instructions on how to find her. Hidden in Alegria's shoe was a scrap of paper with her sister's address on it. Everyone knew that Portobello was the place to go, if you were new. Rent was relatively cheap, and with a large Brazilian and Portuguese population in the area, it was as close to familiar as they could get.

Inching forward in the line, she wondered if she'd overestimated the difficulty of being let into the country. Pedro and Luisa had been so confident, maybe she'd overprepared? Simone had sailed through immigration with a six-month visa and no intention of leaving, because of course she had. Staring down at the (grey) herringbone carpet, she felt the horrible dryness of her mouth. The line moved slowly, because even though there were several planes of people trying to slip through the borders, collect their luggage and melt into the city, only four out of the seventeen desks were open. She wondered if she would be sick, and what Simone would say about that. Alegria listened to the conversations around her to pass the time. She hoovered up information in case it would help her: there was a civil war in Rwanda (she had heard about this); there was a by-election in Kent because the IRA had murdered someone ('by-election' was a strange word); someone's aunt was not well (irrelevant); the football was on (on where?). She hoped that fear did not have a smell.

'Next.' A hand beckoned impatiently and Alegria jerked forward, already fumbling for the plastic wallet. She would be nice and compliant. She took a deep breath, smiled and tried to sound as relaxed as possible.

'Good afternoon, sir.' She slid her passport across the counter and took in the immigration officer in front of her. The desks were low and the chairs were even lower, so it was she who loomed over *him*. That was unexpected. She had not practised looking down.

He flicked his eyes up to meet hers with disinterest. 'Name?' He was slim, with wire glasses perched on a sharp nose, and a neat, dark beard. Most staff in Brazil wore name tags, but not here. She found it a little disconcerting that this man got to know everything about her, but she would never even know his name. At least, Alegria thought, he didn't look particularly unkind.

'Alegria Dias.'

'Reason for visit?'

'Tourism . . . and to speak English—'

'Where?' He had still barely looked her in the eye, his gaze flickering from the screen to her passport.

'Uh . . . the address is – you can see here.' She extracted a sheet from the plastic folder and pointed out the name of her course. He leaned forward, squinting through the glass. 'Oh yeah. Stanton School of English, down by Westbourne Grove?' He phrased it like a question, but didn't let her answer. 'Lots of your lot end up there.'

'You know about it?' Alegria asked proudly.

'Yeah.'

'Is it a good place?'

The man looked at her properly now, seeming both confused and annoyed. 'How am I supposed to know?'

It was a response Alegria couldn't fully grasp – she wondered if she'd offended him. Would he cause problems if she had? She smiled again and said nothing, trying to look apologetic.

'How long is the course?'

'Three months, sir.'

'And why are you coming here to learn English? Not got any teachers there, then?'

She hesitated. He had an unpleasant, nasal voice and spoke quickly, forcing the words out as though he were in a rush. It was taking her longer than she wanted to understand. 'No, no . . . I want to learn, you know, natively? So I can teach in a private university—'

'Here? You looking to get a job teaching?' He raised a thin eyebrow and Alegria pushed past the irritation creeping up her throat. How was she supposed to explain if he kept interrupting her?

'No, sir. I am a teacher – look . . .' She indicated her sheaf of papers, willing herself to look detached and at ease as he rifled through them. Her address, her university degree, her job contract, a letter of recommendation from her previous employer, health insurance – and most importantly, her return ticket. It was all there, she explained carefully. She had a job waiting for her back home, a job she wanted but couldn't get without this qualification. And why not do a little sightseeing on the side? See the Queen's palace, the famous red phone booths Simone swore to her could be found on most street corners. It's a job I really need, she tried to say. 'More salary.'

'A promotion, you're saying?'

'Yes, but for this I need the qualificação. My chief administrator told me.' Her boss's exact words had, in fact, been: *Why would anyone pay you more when your English isn't good enough to teach?*

'Right. And where are you staying?'

'The school has some accommodation for me – you can see the letter. They have a room for me. I have paid a deposit.'

This was it. Her big lie. If this stranger across from her decided to look into it – called the school, or asked for proof of payment – she'd be exposed immediately. It *was* true that Stanton had housing they rented out to students. Unaffordable housing, with full payment expected up front. Simone had laughed down the phone when Alegria told her the price. 'Don't be stupid – stay with Ricardo and me. We can split the rent in three ways and then everyone can save a little bit. Just don't tell them you're staying here, I don't want this address on their system.' But if they caught her now, it would all be for nothing. Her temples throbbed furiously; she badly needed to lie down. She had the urge to apologise and felt pathetic. To her left somewhere, she thought she could hear Pedro's voice cutting through the crowd, sounding annoyed. Alegria ignored it, keeping her gaze fixed on this inscrutable man in front of her rifling through her documents with deliberate slowness. At last, he looked up at her again.

'You've been approved to enter the United Kingdom for ninety days on a tourist visa. Your visa does not give you the right to seek paid employment. If you are caught doing so, you may be deported and fined. You will need to leave the country on or before . . .' He said this all in a flat drawl, looking bored. Alegria nodded furiously to make it clear she had understood. '. . . If you do not do so, you may be deported and fined. You will be unable to re-enter the country.'

The immigration officer stapled a tiny piece of paper – smaller than her palm – to a blank page in her passport. There was a smack of rubber as he stamped a large blue circle on top and scribbled in the dates of entry and exit. He did not smile. In fact, he was already starting to look past her as she stuffed her documents into her bag, feeling light-headed with relief. Si had been right after all – she'd worried too much. She walked towards baggage control, staring down at the image now marked onto her passport in navy blue. A lion and a unicorn on their hind legs, a crown between them, surrounded by words in Latin she couldn't read. The symbol of the royal family. How grand it all seemed, just for her to spend a handful of weeks in this place. She was a little annoyed by his carelessness – the ink was smudged, ruining the unicorn's horn and blurring today's date. Would it be an issue on the way out, maybe? And then she heard it.

'Alegria – *ALEGRIA!*' Luisa sounded like she was crying, her voice high-pitched and breathy.

Alegria turned and everything happened very quickly. Someone asked for her name, and then said something about her luggage. A second voice, unexpectedly close to her right ear, said stiffly, 'Madam, please come with us.' Luisa's face was tear-streaked as she pointed frantically at her, a stream of Portuguese directed at the man now making to grab Alegria's upper arm. Reflexively, she jerked away, clutching her passport to her chest as though she expected the officer to snatch it from her. Pedro stood a short distance away, frozen, as people turned towards the scene, craning their heads. Two more immigration officers were approaching them, and the humiliation made Alegria's legs feel numb. What had they done?

'Yes? Hello? What is wrong?' The words came out forced, high-pitched, and she knew immediately how guilty it made her sound.

'We have a few questions we'd like to ask you.'

'So ask me,' she retorted, too loudly.

The immigration officer by her side took hold of her again. She could see her panicked face in his eyes. The shame curdled in her stomach.

'Not here, madam. Follow me.'

Alegria did not dare look at either Luisa or Pedro as they were silently escorted past the openly staring crowds. The excitement and relief that had blossomed in her chest just moments ago had gone, replaced with shock. All her plans had been thrown up into the air. Where would they land? Luisa was sniffing obnoxiously, and Alegria wanted to turn around and slap the filha da puta across her tiny, irritating face. She might actually have done it, had they been alone. She was shaking with nerves and rage, not just because of them but because of her own stupidity. It was her fault. She should have ignored them completely, told them to stay the fuck away from her – she shouldn't have got on the same plane as them in the first place. *Why* had they singled her out that way?

'In here, please.'

A female border guard whose jumper was stained with a

nasty-looking yellow sauce directed her into an austere, white room. There were no windows. In front of her stood a table and four chairs. A narrow metal bed with a thin mattress had been pushed into the corner, next to a small toilet and sink. The sparseness of the room punched right through her fury. Alegria whirled round, panic setting in. 'Am I . . . ?' She did not know the words to say *under arrest*, and so brought her wrists together as though wearing invisible handcuffs. The woman's eyes flickered down briefly, then back up to meet her.

'We have some questions to ask you.'

As she spoke, a second woman entered the cell. Together, they reminded Alegria of the cockroaches that crawled out of the drains in her family home. When one appeared, others followed. For a moment, no one moved. The two women stared at her as if expecting her to collapse in tears. Perhaps they wanted her to beg for help. Finally, she said, 'I want a lawyer.'

At the same time, the woman on the right, a tiny, bony thing with frizzy red hair, said, 'We're going to need to search you,' and the other laughed.

'Lawyer? This ain't America, love.'

The jumble of words and accents was too much for Alegria. She shook her head. '*Lawyer.*'

The red-haired woman stepped towards her, palms outstretched. 'Look,' she said slowly, obnoxiously, 'we can find a lawyer, or someone from the Brazilian consulate, for you, but you'll be paying for it. We can even get in a translator. But all of that is going to take days. Maybe weeks. You won't be able to leave this room. But if you help us and answer our questions, we'll let you leave. Go and have fun.' She smiled, and though Alegria was certain she was lying, she knew it would be pointless to make a fuss. 'I'm Jenny,' the woman continued, 'and this is Debra.' Debra did not smile, staring Alegria straight in the eye as she pulled on a pair of latex gloves. Hostility crackled between them. Neither of these women were her friends; she knew it. But it wasn't like she had a choice.

The humiliation from earlier was nothing compared to this. Alegria pressed her lips together as she undressed, passing over her clothes for Jenny and Debra to inspect. She felt small and poor and dirty. They ran their hands through her hair, looked inside her mouth with a little light, and examined her underwear as she hugged her arms around herself and tried to seem impenetrable, unbothered. Finally, Alegria slipped off her socks, and the damp scrap of paper with Simone's address written on it came unstuck from the sole of her foot, fluttering to the floor. She froze.

'What's this?' Hawk-like, Debra swooped down and seized the paper. She looked triumphant as her eyes flickered over the neat, rounded letters. Alegria, statuesque, watched her wordlessly hold it out to Jenny. She had forgotten about the address. A wave of horror washed over her. What if they sent immigration officers to that house? It wasn't only Si that she had just put at risk, but at least a dozen other Brazilians renting rooms and working illegally.

'Whose address is this?' Jenny asked, in the loud, slow voice she apparently reserved for Alegria.

'A friend. Of my friend,' Alegria stammered. It was a bad lie, but it was all she felt able to say.

Debra snorted. 'A friend, eh? And you thought your sock would be the best place to keep it?' She tossed Alegria's clothes back at her, and the two women left, taking the piece of paper with them. Jenny held it between her thumb and forefinger like it was contaminated. Alegria heard the loud turn of a lock, and all hope of making it out unscathed evaporated.

She was still shaking when they returned, now accompanied by one of the men who'd surrounded her earlier. Debra was dragging Alegria's suitcase behind her, and she hoped it had been a pain to carry. Numbly, she watched the two women unlock her case and start to go through its contents. She stared at the officer who'd joined them, noticing how his suit was a size too small for him, his hair shapeless and short. The people of England were unattractive. And miserable. His trousers climbed to the middle of his shins as he took a seat in front of her.

'My name,' he pointed at himself, 'is Mark. And *your* name –' he pointed at her '– is Alegria, correct?' He said it strangely, placing the emphasis in the wrong places. *Aleg-riya*. How ugly he made it sound, stripped of the melodic intonation her parents had chosen for her. It felt important to correct him, despite the mess she was in.

'A-leh-gree-yah.'

'Right, yes, Alegria. I'd like to ask you what your purpose here is.'

'I *told* you,' Alegria said tersely, 'tourism and to learn English. Look—' She started to reach for the plastic folder, but Mark cut her off.

'Yes, so you claim. But we've been speaking to your friends and they're telling us something different.'

'They are not friends!'

'So you don't know them? They're strangers?'

'No, no. I . . .' She struggled to find the right words, panic making her clumsy. 'From university. We studied together. But I – I am here alone.' Again, she tried to show him the English school acceptance letter, and again he ignored it.

'The thing is, Miss Dias, they're saying they know you. They were having some trouble communicating with our colleague and told us you'd be able to translate for them. And you were on the same plane – from the same city, right? And then, of course, there's *this*.' He laid Simone's address out on the table, and they both stared down at it. Beside them, Jenny and Debra continued dumping her carefully folded clothes on the laminate tiles.

'You told my colleague you were staying at this language school you're attending. Is that true?'

'Yes.'

Mark looked incredulous. 'You're not planning to live anywhere else then?'

They looked at each other silently for a minute. Alegria knew, of course, what was about to happen next. She glanced from his impassive stare to the mess on the bleached floor, and imagined Si sitting in her place instead. What would her sister do? 'Of course not,' she heard herself say.

'So what is this address?'

'I told you. A friend. In case of emergency.'

'I see.' Mark laced his fingers together, closing in for the kill. 'And why, Alegria, was it in your shoe?'

'I—' she started to answer, but he spoke over her.

'You claim to work as a teacher. What kind of school lets teachers take three-month holidays? Is that normal, where you come from?'

Under the table, Alegria twisted her hands together, trying to conceal her anger. First the condescension, now this? She took a breath. 'I left. To study and explore London. Your laws say I can do this, no problems.'

Mark raised his eyebrows. 'So you've come to live here for three months – unemployed, then? You wouldn't be needing to work at all? I must be in the wrong profession – I didn't know teachers in Brazil were paid so well!'

She glared at him. How else could she have come to stay for such a long time without quitting? She'd never heard of a job that let people take three months' leave. 'I save my money.'

'London is an expensive city to live in, you know.'

'I . . .' What could she possibly say? 'I need to study, I don't need your money.'

'Oh, I think you do. I think you're lying to me. You and your friends have come here under false pretences. A lot of your kind do – we see it every day. You don't have any intentions of leaving in February like you claim – you're here to work, find a nice English bloke to marry.'

'No! I *will* leave in February—'

Alegria was trying desperately to find the words in this language she needed so badly. If she could just make this man understand how much it had taken to become a teacher in the first place – a profession she had only even chosen because it was one of the few evening courses available, allowing her to keep her job in the supermarket. How she would finish class and study until two in the morning, every morning, drinking a mixture of coffee and cola to stay awake. How she'd started working in a supermarket after school at fourteen, her small income bringing some stability to her family's life: no more evictions, no more one-bedroom flats with the windows padlocked shut, no more unpaid phone bills or electricity rationing, or her mother crying into the empty kitchen cupboards. What could this country possibly offer her that was better? Why, she wanted to say, would I give up everything I've worked for, for a country where I'd have to begin all over again? Don't you know how much it costs to be poor? But her inability to find the words hung between them in defeated silence. She could feel the conversation slipping from her fingers. And in any case, Mark was distracted by a packet of flour Jenny was holding out to him, pulled from her luggage.

'What's this?' he asked, examining the yellow and green packaging carefully. He sounded so suspicious that she almost laughed, almost wanting him to make the accusation.

'Cassava flour.'

'Never heard of it. Why are you bringing four packets of this stuff into the country then, eh?'

'To make pão de queijo. Bread. Special bread.'

'I'm afraid I can't let you leave with that. We'll be testing them.'

'Why?' she asked loudly. 'You think it's cocaine? That I have drugs with me, because I'm stupid? Because I come from Brazil?'

Mark rose, the packets of cassava flour in his arms. 'I'd be careful throwing around words like that, madam. I'm just doing my job. Go back to your country and do yours.'

'You're sending me back?' Alegria stood up too, abruptly enough to make her chair smack the floor behind her. She had known it was coming – the second she'd been stopped, she knew it was over – but the shock of it still hit. Her face was burning.

'Oh yes,' Mark said matter-of-factly. 'I have reason to believe you've tried to enter this country under false pretences. You have lied to immigration enforcement officers and intend to overstay your visa to work illegally. That's more than enough grounds to deport you – count yourself lucky that's all we're doing. You came via Amsterdam – that's where you'll be sent. There's a seven-forty-five flight you'll be placed on.' He threw the words at her like they meant nothing at all.

Numbly, she watched as Debra threw her possessions back into her case, making no effort to be respectful. Half of her clothes were still on the sticky, plasticky floor, and she bent down and pulled the huge black coat she'd bought for the English winter around her shoulders. She was still trembling. Mark had her passport clutched in one pale claw. 'Wait,' she called frantically, as he reached for the door handle. 'Please. I need a telephone. To call my family.' She needed to warn Si about how unbelievably foolish she had been.

Mark paused and looked back at her. She watched his eyes scan her, savouring the position she was in. There was a haughtiness to him – to all of them – that told her how much they enjoyed the power they had.

'I'm afraid, Miss Dias, that you should have thought about your family before you tried to take advantage of Her Majesty's generosity.' And with that, they were gone, leaving her standing helplessly in the windowless room, an entire year's worth of planning, hoping and saving now in pieces around her.

CHAPTER 4

London, October 1990

He was daydreaming about sarma. His mother's. He could picture them steaming on the desk in front of him, three or four helpings loaded onto a deep plate with a side of boiled potatoes. Slicing through the sour steamed cabbage to the rice and ground pork inside, soaking up the salty broth with home-made bread. A favourite childhood meal. It wasn't just the taste that was special, it was the significance of the cabbage, the rice – especially the meat. The smell at dinner time meant times were good, and food was . . . well, not plentiful, but hot and available. And delicious. As a boy, he would thoughtlessly pile as many stuffed leaves as he could get away with onto his plate – even if it meant less for everyone else. His grandfather encouraged this habit, often insisting on an extra heaping of potatoes for the 'future man of the house'. He hadn't eaten proper, home-made sarma since he'd left Yugoslavia, and Zivoin was craving it so badly his stomach hurt. He always longed for his mother's food after an argument with his father, as though the two belonged together.

'. . . And so, contractions are best for informal writing and conversation – say, a letter to a friend. You might write "I've been to the dentist" when speaking with a peer, but in a more formal setting it would be more appropriate to say, "I *have* been to the dentist." ' Catherine, their English teacher, wrote both sentences out in chalk, underlining the words *have been*. She was affable, polite, incredibly dull. He often struggled in her classes. 'Today we'll be looking at *would've, could've, should've*.'

Zivoin pinched the bridge of his nose and closed his eyes, willing himself to focus. Apart from being hungry, he had the beginnings of a headache, and his bad mood was making concentration impossible. As Catherine went on, he thought about the phone call with his father earlier that day. Zivoin had bought a fresh phone card to make sure they'd received the two hundred pounds he had sent through. Money often took up to a week to arrive, and he knew all too well the strain of the waiting. He had hoped, perhaps naively, that the money he sent back every few weeks would have softened his father's inability to relax – a survival mechanism born from a lifetime of poverty. And yet, when Drago had picked up the phone, they descended into an argument almost immediately.

'Paja, Bato's cousin, stopped by for a coffee yesterday – you remember him?'

'Of course.'

'Well, he wants to send his son to London for a little while. Boy's twenty. Fighting age. Paja's getting nervous. Things are changing over here, sine. Have you heard what Milošević is planning with his new constitution? Abolishing opposition parties, infiltrating schools, controlling universities – there will be blood in the streets.' He could hear the astonishment in his father's voice. It mirrored his own helpless confusion over the catastrophe of their homeland. Death in slow motion.

'Don't worry,' he said automatically, blankly.

His father ignored him. 'Serbia is going to tear us to pieces,' Drago said. 'We need to prepare. That's why I told Paja you'd help.'

'Me?' Zivoin shut his eyes, feeling the familiar prickle of irritation. Behind him, one of his flatmates, a Russian named Sasha whom he rarely spoke to, clattered around, frying eggs. The kitchen tiles were grimy; he disliked looking at them. Not for the first time, he wished he had a landline in his bedroom.

'He's applying for the visa now. You can get him a job. Have him live with you – Darco will be happy.'

'Live with me? Live with me where? There's no space for anyone else here.'

'Find a new place. You can have your own room – let the two boys share.' His father spoke nonchalantly, as though they were just picking up an old conversation, and it angered Zivoin immediately.

'Do you know,' he said quietly, forcing his voice to remain steady, 'how hard it was for me to find a place I can afford? For the two of us? London isn't like Nikšić. There's more competition—'

'I don't need you to tell me the difference between London and Nikšić.'

'I think you do! It's not the same here. Not everyone wants to rent to me – I was turned down so many times when I first got here. Don't you remember that I spent almost a month in a shitty hostel with twenty people to a toilet?'

But his father didn't want to hear it. 'You're smart, you'll figure it out. Get Darco to look for places. Tell him I'm the one asking.'

'Darco works. Every day, pretty much. The both of us do. The kid can come, and I'll keep an eye on him – he can come for dinner a few times a week. But I'm not finding him a job or somewhere to live. It's too much.'

He could feel his father probing at him, poking for the holes in his armour. They both knew what was coming – all their fights were just the same one over and over. He fought the impulse to tell Drago that the weight on his shoulders made him feel breathless. That the expectation of having to care for not only his parents but his aunts, his cousins, his cousins' children, had pushed him into a state of constant panic. That he couldn't sleep, and he shouted at Darco in the same way Drago shouted at him. But they did not have a shared language for this sort of conversation. 'It's too much,' he repeated, and the words were inadequate.

'I gave Paja my word that my son would help out.'

'Then you'll have to take it back!' Zivoin snapped. 'I've told you before not to make promises on my behalf, Tata.' Behind him he heard the scrape of a chair on kitchen tile as Sasha sat down to eat and he cringed, knowing that Russian was similar enough to Serbo-Croat for his flatmate to grasp what was going on.

Drago was silent for a moment, his displeasure radiating through the receiver. 'You're the only son in this family. This is your duty.'

At this, Zivoin lost his temper. 'My *duty*?' he shouted.

'My duty is to provide for my family, not your friends! What do you think I'm doing here? Sitting with my feet up on the sofa, getting fat? There are only so many people I can support – at this rate, you'll be sending half the village to my door.'

The instant he'd raised his voice, Zivoin regretted it. Without another word, Drago hung up on him, leaving him swearing in the kitchen as Sasha chewed stoically, feigning intense interest in the piece of bread in front of him. The morning was ruined. He knew what his father had been getting at: why did you leave in the first place, if not to help? The injustice of it burned his throat. There was nothing to feel guilty over – he was doing everything right. And yet.

As he stared down now at the blank sheet of paper in front of him, a memory guiltily clawed its way to the surface. Zivoin at twenty-one, newly released from two years of compulsory, unpaid military service and less than a month away from starting university in Belgrade. Tuition there was free, student hostels were too, but there was no money for food, let alone the books he needed. Zivoin couldn't even afford the train ticket out of Nikšić. Together, he and his father had spent three weeks hiking to the mountains and chopping wood, then hauling the logs – cut down to the size of a man's arm – into neat piles in the courtyard of their building to sell to neighbours. Every morning before setting out, they would dismantle and rebuild the pile, turning the logs over to ensure they dried out and would not rot. It was back-breaking, blistering work. For days afterwards, neither had been able to walk, or even stand, from exhaustion. Drago's help hadn't been discussed, a mutual understanding between them: if this was what it took to get Zivoin to Belgrade, this was what he would do. They'd sold all the wood. His father gave him every cent. And he, Zivoin, had just shouted down the phone because Drago refused to ignore someone who needed his help.

He suppressed the urge to rest his pounding forehead on the table. This building was bright – far too bright. Fluorescent bulbs, white-painted walls and large windows with mould in the corners meant too much light was pouring into the room. Zivoin glanced at the clock and was immediately exasperated with himself – the lesson was almost halfway through and he hadn't taken in a single word. Christ, what a waste of money. He stared at the teacher through narrowed eyes, determined to extract something of value from the remaining half hour.

'So now what we'll do,' Catherine was saying, the palm of her hand splayed against the blackboard, 'is write three sentences – informally, this time – on what we *should have* done, what we *could have* done, and what we *would have* done. For example: I *should've* gone to the dentist, but I mixed up the dates and missed my appointment. What I *could've* done is write down the date and time, instead of just trying to remember it. And if I could go back in time, I *would've* called to double-check I had the correct details. Any questions?'

There was a quiet rustle of paper and shuffling of chairs as most of the adults bent over their desks. The intermediate English classes typically held fifteen to twenty students at a time, and Zivoin, who took weekly morning classes, had grown to know most of the faces in the room with him. Almost all of the students came from countries like his own, where learning English was less of a priority. Zivoin had grown up learning to read and write in the Cyrillic and Latin alphabets for both Serbo-Croat and Russian. All the children in his village who had gone to school were taught Latin, considered essential for grasping Serbo-Croat's complex grammatical infrastructure. Of course, they were taught the basics of English too – almost as an afterthought. He had noticed the difference this had made in his first job working as a kitchen porter. His Nigerian and Indian colleagues had navigated the barked orders of a dinner rush far quicker, whilst he lagged behind trying to unpick garbled phrases like 'get a wriggle on' or 'He's from the arse end of nowhere, that one.' But he also noticed the ease with which the owner, a Greek man who resembled one of Zivoin's university professors, sacked them, even when they were better and faster at the job than he was. Called them names under his breath – names Zivoin had later learned were slurs. Slurs he had repeated in the first few weeks of arriving in London, ignorant of the weight they carried. He did not like to remember that.

Zivoin grabbed his pen, translating mentally, like he always did, then writing: *I should've listened to my father.* Immediately it felt silly. He crossed it out, feeling both impatient and frustrated – a whiny adolescent instead of a man who was almost thirty. This was ridiculous. He knew the difference between all the contractions already. In fact, weren't they all basically interchangeable? *I should've stayed home, I could've stayed home, I would've stayed home.*

Catherine was slowly moving between the desks, glancing over shoulders and occasionally pointing out errors. As she approached, he covered his words with a hand and stared out the window, as if immersed in thought. They were too high up – the seventh floor – and all there really was to look at was the sky, clear and bland. Below them, a bus trundled past and the windows rattled slightly from the vibration.

Catherine walked past him without comment, and Zivoin once again forced himself to stare at the page. He knew what he wanted to write – the thought had been plaguing him since he'd arrived in London. *I should've studied something that would've guaranteed me a job. Medicine, maybe. Then I could've stayed and worked as a doctor, supported them all and been happy.* But this wasn't quite true. The priority had been to secure the fastest degree possible and start earning money for the family. And he had been desperate to leave, in the end, fed up of the inflation and seemingly endless corruption that made securing a well-paid job surprisingly difficult. Three times he had applied for a research position at the University of Belgrade after graduating with a degree in history and politics. Three times he had failed, and assumed it was just bad luck – until he'd discovered all posts were taken up by the sons of department professors. Eventually, he'd found work in a factory, loading concrete bricks onto delivery trucks. A job he could have had four years earlier; no degree or chopped wood required.

And then, at last, just before the class ended, he wrote: *I should've enjoyed myself more.* That felt like the most truthful thing he had said all day. It solved nothing, of course. But at least, Zivoin thought, as he screwed up the paper and threw it in the bin on the way out, the reminder made him feel a little less guilty for disappointing his father. What was one 'No', anyway, after years of doing what was needed, rather than what was wanted?

CHAPTER 5

Amsterdam, October 1990

One day later

Four a.m. The curtains were open and street light invaded the room, bouncing off the walls. It was too bright for her to sleep. Since midnight, she had been lying on the hotel bed fully clothed, staring at the reflections of car headlights on the ceiling. Her bladder was so full it ached, and still Alegria could not bring herself to get up. The room was small and austere, like a prison cell. The plane deporting her to Amsterdam had left almost two hours late, giving her far too much time to comprehend the enormity of what had just happened. The dark green of her passport stood out as it lay on the duvet beside her, a large red stamp with the words ENTRY DENIED now invalidating the visa, forever marking her dishonesty.

Shame curled through Alegria's abdomen, giving her the bizarre urge to crawl under the covers and hide, like a child. What would happen now? The only reason she wasn't truly spiralling (yet) was because of the conversation she'd had with her sister the second she'd landed. Simone had listened silently as Alegria sobbed down the phone, apologising over and over for having written out her address – out of everything, this was what devastated her the most. In that moment, their roles in the family had switched. Simone, perpetually the family's baby, took charge.

'Enough,' Si had said sharply, when she'd grasped the situation. 'Here's what we're going to do. Are you listening? You have to stop crying and listen.'

'But what about the house—'

'Forget the house! I'll sort that out. You need to focus on what happens next, because when you get here, I might need to borrow some money—'

'*When* I get there? Si, they've deported me. That's a ten-year ban. Forget it.'

There was a rush of static as Simone sighed in exasperation. 'No, no. There's still a way. I can't fully explain now, I need to get things moving. But, Ale, I need you to trust me. Do not buy a ticket home. Promise?'

At first, Alegria did not respond. It was clear to her that things were well and truly over – all she could do now was go home and try to beg for her job back. 'Promise!' Simone had insisted. And so she had promised. And now she was in a hotel room, unable to sleep and wondering what on earth was going to happen in the morning. She had not managed to buy a phone card to tell Adelina and Toninho. She had not spoken to anyone else, in fact, aside from the kind woman at the hotel front desk who had checked her in. Thirty dollars for a single night! She would have to find somewhere cheaper tomorrow. If she would even be here tomorrow.

Ignoring the pressure in her stomach, Alegria forced herself to sit up and drink water. She was too shocked to eat and too numb to cry. There was only the bed, the pain in her abdomen, and the thickness of failure. The hours were sticky; they dragged and stretched in front of her like the condensed milk her mother cooked on their stove for brigadeiro. Si had told her to call back in the morning. Eventually, the urge to use the bathroom forced her to her feet. This small move seemed to trigger – at last – a wave of profound exhaustion. When she fell back onto the bed, she sank into the paralysing kind of sleep that meant she awoke in the exact same position, her neck twisted to her right and aching in protest. She showered and washed her puffy face, staring at herself in the mirror as she brushed her teeth. She looked the way she felt: tender, defeated. Even her hair, usually so curly and voluminous it haloed around her head like a dark, fluffy cloud, lay limp.

The suitcase was still a mess from the search. Alegria sighed loudly as she picked up a white blouse, now crumpled from being hastily crammed back in with her other possessions. Most of her clothes were like this, but she could not bring herself to wear any evidence of the past twenty-four hours and settled instead on a square-necked minidress in midnight blue, sheer tights and, of course, the cumbersome wool jumper. The dress had been a parting gift from her best friend, and although it was heavy and dated, with its shoulder pads, it was the warmest one she owned. When she paired the look with knee-high black boots, she didn't think she looked too bad. But Simone was the dazzling, fashionable one – it was hard to trust her own judgement without her sister there to approve.

The sun was strong, the sky huge and empty, and

Alegria decided it would have to be a good omen. She could wait no longer. Si answered on the second ring, sounding breathless.

'Entaõ,' she said, the second she heard Alegria's voice. 'Paul's coming to get you.'

'Paul? Who's Paul?'

'He'll land by midday – where's your hotel?'

'It's the Novotel, terminal two. I never left the airport. But who's—'

'Oh, *perfect*! He lands at terminal two! You'll need to wait for him there – I've given him your foto, so he'll come to you. I have to go—'

'Wait!' Alegria barked. 'Just wait! What's going on? Who's Paul? Why is he coming?'

But Simone was barely listening. 'That's not ours!' Alegria heard her say to someone in the background. 'I don't have time to explain, irmã, we're packing up.'

'Oh.' Another wave of guilt hit her. 'Have you found some—'

'Just be there for midday. You can trust Paul – he's our friend. I'll see you soon.' And before Alegria could say anything else, the line went dead. She held the receiver suspended in the air for a moment in disbelief, then glanced at her watch. It was close to ten. She couldn't think of anything else to do but make her way back to the airport, tucking her passport and wallet into a money belt around her waist.

Alegria chased the smell of warm, sugary dough to a cheerful-looking coffee shop, near the airport's exit. Amsterdam was another city that she had always wanted to visit.

London, Paris, Rome, Barcelona and Amsterdam – those were the places everyone she knew talked about. Europe was so far away and unattainable for most Brazilians that the entire continent had a glamorous, romantic sheen to it. Miracles happened here.

As she waited for Simone's mysterious friend, Alegria bought a black coffee and an apple pie that was so delicious, she immediately bought another slice, and then a third, making her way through them slowly. Already, this place seemed more welcoming. She hadn't even needed a visa to enter – at the border, they had simply waved her through. Though she knew it was a fantasy, Alegria let herself imagine staying here until February, walking along the famous canals, exploring the museums – maybe even finding a job in a bakery. That wouldn't be so bad; she was used to early mornings.

She wondered if Pedro and Luisa were somewhere here, too. Or were they on a plane right now, Luisa's useless designer handbag tucked under her seat? Savagely, she hoped they felt as desperate as she had last night. The three of them had been kept in separate interrogation rooms until the very last moment, so her only glimpse of them had been in the cold, narrow corridors that led them to the plane once everyone else had boarded. The couple had tried to speak to her, but Alegria had stared past them expressionlessly, her rage clenching her stomach. *I am a stone, I am a stone, I am a stone*, she thought, jerkily shaking off the hand Luisa had laid on her arm. Luisa had been crying, Pedro shocked into dazed silence, nodding desperately at whatever his wife said. It had not softened her. Ordinarily, she forgave and moved on quickly, but this felt different. The stupidity, the betrayal was too great. The sense of opportunities she would now probably never have haunted her, and she did not notice the man hovering by her table.

'Erm. Miss?' a hesitant voice asked.

Alegria looked up in surprise, and saw her own face staring glassily back at her. A photo of her and Simone at her graduation, held out at arm's length by a stocky, nervous-looking man. It was awkward right away – he tried to shake her hand right as she automatically moved to hug him. Paul immediately flushed pink as she laughed uneasily. 'Sorry, sorry.' They both waited on the other to take charge. In the silence that followed, Alegria suggested ordering more coffee – or in Paul's case, something he called 'breakfast tea'. She watched him pour milk into the brown liquid and wondered what to say. The way her sister had talked about Paul had made it seem like he would have arrived filled with confidence and solutions. But although he was nice enough, he lacked urgency – asking about her and her family and actually listening as she stumbled through her answers. He looked into her eyes when she spoke. He had evidently spent a lot of time with Simone, because his communication was measured enough for her to catch every word of his lyrical accent, but not so slow as to insult her.

'Here's what I think we should do,' he said eventually, glancing around the terminal. 'You're going to tear that page with the cancelled visa on it out of your passport. Do it carefully so the rip isn't visible. Then we'll try going in again – through Glasgow this time, pretending to be a couple.'

Alegria stared at him for a long moment, dismayed.

Neither of them spoke. She couldn't believe this. Simone had sent her an idiot. 'I . . .' She leaned forward and tried to find the right words to convey just how terrible an idea this was. 'No.'

'Nervous, are we?'

The man was insane. 'I can't mess with my passport. That's fraud – that is *more* illegal than what I did!'

'Other Brazilians have done it,' Paul responded with a shrug, fiddling with a toggle on his cargo pants. 'It worked for them. But you can just go back home if you want to. I'm not making you do anything.'

'I *know* that,' she said irritably. 'It's easy to tell other people to be brave when it's not your life.'

Paul seemed unfazed. 'Well, you wouldn't be here if you weren't willing to take a risk, would you? You'd be halfway back to Rio.' He leaned back and took a loud, nonchalant slurp of tea.

In the silence that fell between them, her suspicion began to mount. Who was this man? Alegria tried to remain polite. As though they were having a normal conversation and not conspiring to commit a crime. 'Look . . . I just need some time to—'

'Digest?' Paul offered. He smiled, and despite how annoying she found him, it felt kind. 'Your sister said you'd need convincing.'

'It's just a bit crazy, this idea,' she said, with a weak laugh. 'How do I trust . . . how do you know Si?'

He shrugged again. Alegria was getting the sense that this was Paul's default response. 'Through friends.'

'When?'

'A few months ago.' When Alegria continued to stare at him, he added casually, 'At a bar. She was with some of her friends. We all got talking.'

'*Mmm.*' She suppressed the urge to roll her eyes. 'Let me guess – her boyfriend was working at the bar.'

'Maybe.'

Now things made sense – he was here because he was in love with Simone. Almost all her sister's male friends were – and rightly so. Her sister had more charisma in a single finger than most people had in their entire bodies. Alegria scrutinised the man in front of her. 'Why Glasgow?'

'Different system there, isn't it? Only updates every week or so.'

'How do you know that?'

'And you'll be with me,' he continued, ignoring her, 'your fake boyfriend, so that will help. We'll take a coach – they don't check passports at the Scotland–England border. But you'll never be allowed back in with that red stamp in there. People do it all the time. But if anything happens – if you get stopped – it's nothing to do with me.'

They went back and forth, but Alegria was resolute, and Paul grew more irritable. He laid both his palms flat onto the table and asked, with the air of someone fighting to remain polite, 'You realise I could be back in London right now, instead of sitting here trying to convince a woman I've never met to come with me? Why don't you just book yourself on a flight back to Brazil, if this is all so impossible?'

Despairing, Alegria sank back in her chair, tipping her head up to the ceiling. 'You're right,' she said reluctantly. 'I'm sorry, I know I am being difficult. But what you and Si are asking is stupid. It could get me in trouble in both countries. If I get a criminal record in Brazil, I will never work as a teacher again.'

'So go home.'

'I can't.' To her horror, Alegria felt tears welling up and furiously blinked them away. She would *not* cry in front of this man.

'Why not?'

'Money.'

'Ah, that old devil,' Paul said as she buried her face in her hands, trying to keep it together.

The past twenty-four hours felt surreal. She knew this man was trying to be kind – she knew he *must* be kind, because he was right. Who would drop everything and fly to another country with just a few hours' notice? No one normal, surely. He had to be nice – or insane, or infatuated with her sister. Alegria wanted him to both leave her alone and solve the mess she was in, and she disliked this new, helpless side of her. She was used to doing whatever needed to be done to survive – so why was she lounging about, waiting for someone else to solve her problems?

Alegria sat up and willed herself to be more appreciative. 'That old devil,' she repeated, carefully, sounding out the unfamiliar words. She recounted the story she'd tried to tell during her interrogation, about her family's struggle, exacerbated by Brazil's most recent economic crisis. Paul listened quietly, nodding when she described how her mother would take the bus to pick her up at 11 p.m. when her shift ended, a young Simone asleep in Adelina's arms. He probably knew all of this, she realised – had probably heard Si tell this story a dozen times already. 'Sorry . . .' she said, trailing off. 'It's just . . . in Uberlândia, I support my whole family. Going back now – no job, no money, no English. It's not an option for me. I have to think of something. I have to go, even if they don't want me.'

At this, Paul laughed again – a real laugh, a cutting one this time. 'I know that feeling. You should try being Irish – they *really* don't want us.'

Alegria laughed too, but not in the same way he had. 'Impossible.' How could this white man possibly understand what it meant to be made to feel so unwelcome, with his powerful British passport? He had shown it to her in a clumsy gesture before they sat down – 'So you know it's really me' – and she'd felt a surge of longing so powerful it had temporarily silenced her. The dark burgundy, the golden crest, the right to travel wherever he wanted – not just through Europe, but most of the world. People back home would give up everything they owned for that kind of power – he had no idea how lucky he was. She wondered if he was patronising her. 'I don't think that can be true if you have this passport,' she said.

Paul gave her a tired sort of smile. 'You know, Simone said the same thing.' The incorrect way he pronounced her sister's name reminded her of Mark from immigration, ruining something beautiful. *Si-moan*.

'Si-mo-nee.'

'Sure, sure. Well, she said it too, but you're both wrong there. England doesn't like people like me, either. We're in the same boat – might as well trust me. Tear the page out. Nothing else for it.'

Alegria shook her head and stared past Paul to the table behind him. A little girl – whose hair was not so much blonde as it was white, like silk – sat with her mother devouring a custard-based pastry with intense dedication. Her mouth was covered in icing sugar and yellow puree. Some of the custard had dripped onto her striped pullover, but the girl was oblivious, too busy enjoying herself. Her mother was next to her, frowning down at her Walkman as she fiddled with the headphone jack. She also hadn't noticed the mess – or perhaps she had simply accepted it as part of her daughter's commitment to true pleasure.

Paul was still watching her expectantly. 'I will not touch my passport.' On this she was firm. Whatever he said about being disliked, Alegria knew he couldn't possibly understand the gravity of what he was suggesting. But if there were Brazilians who had done it before, if Si had done all this work, spent all this money to get Paul here . . . perhaps there was a different way. She'd been toying with an idea since last night – a dishonest idea, sure, but not an idiotic one. 'Maybe I can report it as stolen?' she offered, tentatively. 'There is an embassy here. I could pretend it was stolen – or maybe that I lost it, so I don't have to go to the police. What do you think?' She watched him frown, thinking it through.

'But don't you need some kind of ID to do that? A birth certificate or something?'

'I have this . . .' She rooted around in her bag, pulling out a wallet and showing him her laminated ID card. Everyone in Brazil carried one of these – it had all the same details as her passport, alongside an address and an inky-black thumbprint.

Paul took it from her outstretched hand and examined it, looking doubtful. 'Never seen one of these before – are they nationally recognised? Like a driver's licence?'

'Yes – but I have that too. Look!'

'I reckon this will work,' Paul said slowly. 'But I'm not sure we'd manage to get you a new passport in the next few hours. Might take a day or two—'

'I'll pay,' Alegria said pleadingly. 'I can pay for food, for your hotel room. I think we need two days, maximum. I can pay for the emergency passport – it's very quick. If you can please wait.'

'Well . . . if it gets your sister off my back,' he said slowly. Then he grinned.

She laughed and the tension between them eased a little. Alegria felt hope pumping through her veins again, washing away the lack of sleep and the bitterness. How could she ever have thought this man across from her deranged? She could have kissed him – he was cute enough, with his full beard and blue eyes. Instead, she reached out to grasp his forearm with both hands. 'Thank you,' she said earnestly. 'I would *never* do it – break the law for someone else.'

'Ah, sure you would.'

'I'm not brave – I like rules, I like knowing exactly what will happen. No risks, no stupid decisions.'

'Is that what this is, then?' Paul asked lightly as he drained his cup. 'A stupid decision?'

'No, no, this is an aventura – I'll make it fun. We should go straight to the embassy,' she said, already halfway out of her chair. 'It's in Rotterdam. I hope that's near, I don't know . . .'

'About half an hour away from here. We can probably

catch a train right here, from the airport. If we get this wrapped up by tomorrow, we could even land in Glasgow in the evening and take a night bus.'

'You're a good man, Paul!' she said gleefully, suppressing the wish to throw her arms around him. 'And look!' She pointed to the sky outside the glass walls. 'The sun! Look how strong she is. I *knew* today would be a good day. I knew it.'

Alegria wheeled her suitcase towards the exit, her brain whirring, already thinking about where they'd stay, what she'd say at the embassy – would they still need to file a police report? As Paul scrambled to catch her up, she realised that for the first time in her adult life, she was being as impulsive as her sister. She hoped it would be enough.

CHAPTER 6

London, October 1990

Two days later

When Simone opened the door of the flat on the north-west London housing estate and saw her sister's exhausted face staring back at her, she screamed theatrically. 'You made it!'

'Si!' Alegria gasped as she was pulled into a passionate hug. 'Your hair – what did you *do*?' Simone's wild, hip-length hair, always worn loose and pinned with flowers, was gone. She'd chopped it into a short, sharp bob and looked stunning, of course. The length brought out her high cheekbones and slender chin, making her hooded eyes appear even larger.

'Do you like it?' Si asked happily, holding Alegria tightly. 'Don't I look chic?' she added over her sister's shoulder to where Paul stood, awkwardly holding on to the suitcase.

'I love it.' Yet Alegria felt a little sad as she touched the new locks, thinking of how many years her sister had grown it. 'But your hair was so long and beautiful . . .' Unlike Si, her own hair did not grow down. It grew outwards, whorling around her head. Her maternal grandmother's hair, apparently. The one neither of them had ever met, who'd given away Adelina like a sack of flour at the age of four. Or five.

Or six. There were no records kept about poor, dark-skinned families like her grandmother's.

'Pois é.' Simone waved her hand dismissively. 'It'll grow back.' She ushered Paul and Alegria inside from the narrow, dark stairwell, and the sisters gave in to the urgency of catching up. Was the bus OK? Had the police shown up to the house? Where was her passport? Was everyone safe? Was Ricardo angry with her? Did Mãe and Pai know? Was she cold? Hungry? Tired? Afraid? Trading rapid-fire Portuguese, they piled into the kitchen of the unfamiliar new flat that Simone had somehow managed to rent at such short notice. It was claustrophobic and cold, with a layer of grime across the surfaces and mould growing up the sides of the single-glazed windows. But it was safe. And affordable.

Alegria gazed around the bare walls, full of guilt once again. 'Si, how did you find this place? It's been three days – you're a miracle worker!'

'I'm a bruxa,' Simone grinned. 'It wasn't too hard – I found it through a friend of a friend who was looking to move out. You know Donna Maria from back home?'

'Mmm.'

'Well, it's her cousin's friend's son, you've never met him. He's going back to Brazil in a few weeks. The only downside is that this place stinks – he's a smoker. So that part was easy. It was breaking the lease on the old place that was tough.' As Simone opened the fridge door, she glanced behind her apologetically. 'Sorry, Paul – we should speak in English. Who wants coffee? Or . . .' She straightened up and twirled dramatically to face them, a gold bottle in her hand. 'Blue Nun, anybody?'

'What's that?' Alegria asked as Paul said, with a shudder, 'Jesus Christ. It's half eight in the morning.'

'But she's *here*! Thanks to you, Paul, my darling!'

'I wouldn't be here without him, Si. At the border in Scotland, they let me in like *this* . . .' Alegria snapped her fingers. She'd been shocked at how things had turned out. A new passport, a maxed-out credit card and Paul's presence meant she'd walked through border control with a fresh visa and no one had looked twice. 'We got a – what was that thing again?'

'Coach.' Paul was still lingering by the doorway, his eyes following her sister around the kitchen.

'We got a coach from Glasgow and they didn't even stop us when we got to England.'

'I bet she was hysterical in Amsterdam.' Simone grinned, leaning against the fridge. 'Did she cry?'

'As if you wouldn't if you'd been deported,' Alegria retorted, before Paul had even opened his mouth. 'I'm never going through that again. This country isn't worth it.'

'What are you talking about? Paul will come meet you any time, won't you, darling?'

'I was planning on leaving her at Victoria Coach Station,' Paul said, a red flush creeping up his neck as Simone noisily kissed his cheek, 'but it seemed a bit cruel in rush hour.'

'You're our hero. We need to celebrate – will you stay and join us?'

'You're grand, actually,' Paul said quickly, already backing into the corridor. It seemed like the two of them together was more than he had the strength for. 'I'll be heading off home – got work tomorrow. Plus, a proper bed, a shower that needs me, all that.'

'Of course!' Si said warmly. 'But don't be a stranger, OK?' Alegria had to hide her grin as her sister thanked Paul – now redder than she'd ever seen him – one last time before he left. Simone locked the door behind him, then spun round and let out another scream. 'I can't believe you're here! I thought for sure he'd never get you to agree to the passport thing.'

'He didn't,' Alegria said indignantly. 'As if I would ever do something like that. Idiota.'

'You know how many Brazilians have done it? Ale, I think you just have terrible luck – coffee? Or shall we start celebrating your arrival?' Simone waggled the gold bottle as though that might tempt her. 'It tastes like nail polish remover and sugar!'

Alegria took the bottle and looked at it suspiciously. She had no intention of drinking, especially after the long night she'd had on the bus, drifting in and out of sleep. 'Si, this merda looks corrosive. I mean,' she added with a laugh, 'I'll drink it! For you, I'll drink anything, but maybe tonight instead?'

'Deal!' Simone shoved the Blue Nun back into the fridge and flopped down at the kitchen table, her arms folded. She looked thinner, Alegria realised suddenly. Her sister's wrists were bonier.

'Have you been eating, Si?'

'I had a whole party planned,' Simone said sorrowfully, ignoring her, 'for your arrival. People were going to come, I bought English party food – you'd like these little sausages wrapped in pastry – I had balloons, everything! I wanted to make you feel welcome, so you could relax in this city – unclench that asshole a bit.'

'Si!' But Alegria was only feigning outrage, a huge grin spreading across her face. In that moment, she realised how much she'd missed her sister's sense of humour. When the two of them had lived with Toninho and Adelina, the house had constantly rung with Simone's loud, sonorous laughter, inevitably followed by her mother, her sister, or both. Every neighbour and friend knew that the Dias women sounded identical when they were happy – even Toninho struggled to distinguish between the laughs of his wife and daughters.

'Oh, come on, irmã – you had to know about your asshole already.' They settled at the kitchen table, nudging cardboard boxes and bin bags aside. Simone made coffee on the gas stove: strong, black and with half a teaspoon of sugar. 'Now, you're not allowed to feel guilty any more, but I have to tell you – the old place was really nice,' she said, sliding Alegria's cup over. 'Portobello is much prettier than Wembley – there are more Portuguese there, unfortunately, but the streets are so majestic. Our bit wasn't as nice, but if you walked about twenty minutes, there's this place called Notting Hill – oh, it's so beautiful. One day, I'll marry a rich man and have him buy me a house on Portobello Road. And then I'll divorce him. There's a street with a huge market, where every house is a different colour. Blue, orange—'

'Orange? For a house?'

'Yes! And all kinds of people on the street, in these big fur coats that stink of cigarettes, leather trousers, sunglasses on, even though there's no sun – you need to see it to understand.

There are boom boxes outside the cafés – you go from Bob Marley to Jon Bon Jovi to Billy Idol to Prince, it's so exciting. *Oh* – and there's a bakery, Lisboa Patisserie, they sell boxes of linguas de gato for almost as cheap as back home. I'll take you there . . .'

As Simone described this part of London Alegria had never heard of before, she looked around their new home, trying to be subtle. Si had told her to focus on getting here. And now she needed to know how much her blunder had cost her sister.

'. . . and sure, we only have one bedroom here, so you and I will share it and Ricardo will take the sofa – it makes sense because he gets up *so* early for the newspaper delivery work most of the week, and anyway, it's one of those sofa beds, and between you and me, I think there's a part of him that would like to share a bed with the two—'

'Hey,' Alegria said gently, interrupting Simone mid-ramble, 'irmã. Thank you for the party. For stepping in, for sending Paul, for not giving up. I wouldn't be here without you – but the whole point of you coming here was to have fun, to travel around Europe for a bit. And now I've taken all your money, haven't I?'

Simone did not meet her eyes at first, and took a long, slow sip of coffee. She made a face as she set the cup down. 'Urgh. Bitter. It's fine, Ale. This was more important – and anyway, fun is not the only reason I came. I want to help too.'

'What did the landlord say?'

'Him? We didn't have time to tell him!' Simone waved a hand dismissively. 'You know there were seven of us in that house, right? The only two people that didn't panic were this

Spanish couple. They stayed, and everyone else packed up and left.'

'And the depósito?'

Simone sighed, looking serious for the first time. 'Of course we never got that back. That was the hard part, to be honest. I was counting on that money. Everyone was.'

Alegria covered her face with her hands, shame oozing from every pore. 'How much was it?'

'Two months' rent.'

She was horror-struck. In British pounds, a currency eight times stronger than their own, that was a staggering amount of money. 'Oh God. I'm so sorry, Si. I wish I could apologise to everyone – I wish I could go back in time. Were they angry at me? Was Ricardo?' This was what she felt guiltiest about, out of everything – how could she have been so naive? How could she have put her sister – and others – at risk that way?

'Angry? No, they were thrilled! The whole house celebrated,' Simone said sarcastically, prodding her arm. 'Uncover your face – don't be boring. Of course they were angry. Mostly scared, though. Why didn't you just memorise the address?'

'I know, *I know*. It was so stupid of me. I never thought they would actually search me the way they did.'

Once again, she went through the mess at Heathrow Airport. Simone was the perfect audience, gasping and interjecting at exactly the right moments. When Alegria mentioned the way Luisa had waved her designer handbag in the air, her sister's eyes narrowed and her lips pursed, making her look reptilian. 'Conceited little cow.' By the time she got to the part where Mark confiscated her cassava flour, Alegria was laughing at the absurdity of it all. Especially now, when she was safely with her sister, the venom no longer stung as much. But Simone was outraged. 'That's theft!' she screeched, slamming both hands on the table. When Alegria finished, Simone looked at her, stunned. 'So you actually made it in, and *then* they deported you? If that idiot woman had just kept her mouth shut—'

'That's exactly how I felt! I was *furious*—'

'I would have slapped that puta right across the face. Why the hell did she drag you into—'

'And the most frustrating part – they tried to apologise *as we were being deported*—'

'Guess her precious Louis Vuitton couldn't save her!'

As Si spoke, the front door opened and Ricardo walked in, a hat and scarf blocking off most of his face. Though they both stood up to greet him, Alegria hung back guiltily. She had met Ricardo – a tall, blue-eyed Brazilian with broad shoulders and a visible beer belly – many times before, but never knew what to make of him. He was different to the type of man Simone usually dated, reserved, preferring not to speak unless it was necessary. She had no idea how he and her extroverted, theatrical sister had managed to stay together for this long. As Simone threw her arms around his neck, standing on tiptoe to kiss both his cheeks, Alegria waved nervously. She had expected Ricardo to resent her – and for good reason – but he hugged her and gave her a genuinely warm smile.

'It's good to see you, Ale. You should have seen how stressed this one has been, waiting for you to get here.' He nudged Si, who rolled her eyes.

'Me? I never get stressed. How was your shift, paixão?'

'Eh, like always. It's too early for a beer, isn't it?'

'Without a doubt.' Simone pointed to two black bags on the large, L-shaped sofa. 'Those are your clothes, by the way. Unpack today.' They bickered playfully, back and forth, Alegria's eyes flickering from her sister to Ricardo in astonishment. Their domesticity surprised her, as did her sister's satisfaction in bossing him around. Simone tended to fall for men who doted on her, treating her like a glittering, easily breakable object they could put on a shelf and admire. It was sweet to see how comfortable they were with each other.

As Ricardo sank into the sofa, suppressing a yawn, Alegria said, 'I'm really sorry, by the way. About the deposit, and leaving Portobello and everything.'

'Don't worry about it – we can't let these gringos divide us. When I first got here, the guy who let me in said something about "people like you" taking all the jobs. And not a single person on the delivery rounds is English, you know that? Half of them are Lebanese refugees, and the rest are Indian, or whatever. Whose fucking jobs are we taking?'

'Still,' Alegria said awkwardly, 'I've made a mess. I can't get you the money back, but I can take you out to dinner tonight, to say thank you.' Her credit card had one more use out of it, before she hit the limit.

'I'm working tonight – but tomorrow?'

'Tomorrow.'

Ricardo raised an imaginary bottle of beer in salute, then nestled back between the two bin bags. 'So, you came in from Glasgow? It worked?'

'Oh, yes!' Si rounded on her, curiosity written across

her face. 'What happened with you and Paul – you have to tell me.'

'It was so easy – the complete opposite of England. You picked the perfect person to send, Si. He was so calm.'

'You know,' Simone said thoughtfully, 'I think he'd be good for you.'

Alegria snorted at the suggestion. But in front of Ricardo, she wasn't going to point out the fact that Paul was so obviously infatuated with her sister. 'If I'm going to date, it will be with someone I can speak to without having to translate every other word.'

'Really?' Looking unimpressed, Simone pulled Alegria out of the kitchen and onto the sofa, sandwiching herself between sister and boyfriend. 'You'd limit yourself to a Brazilian man in a place as international as this one?'

'Worked for you.'

'No, no.' Simone held up one finger and waggled it under Alegria's nose. 'I was already in love with this *idiota* before I came here. You're alone. Too alone – how long has it been since you kissed anyone?'

'Shut up.'

'I'm serious! It's been, what, two years since things ended with Marcio?'

Alegria tipped her head back against the leather and shut her eyes, saying nothing. She heard Ricardo ask, in an obvious whisper, 'Is that the one who broke up with her via a mixtape?'

'I broke up with *him*,' she said loudly, before Simone could answer, 'and it doesn't matter. I don't want some guy who doesn't know the places I know, who doesn't feel like home.

I don't have time for romance, anyway – I didn't come here to fall in love.' There was more to it than she could say to her sister. But the truth was also that Alegria was tired of looking after everyone else – ex-boyfriends included. She wanted to be the one who was taken care of. 'I want stability,' she added, and immediately felt ancient.

'No one comes to London looking for love,' Ricardo said. 'That's Paris. People come here for opportunity. What if you find a nice Englishman, one of the ones that doesn't look like he could be snapped in half? This colourless city could end up being your home.'

'Never. That will never happen. Not to me.'

At this, Simone let out a self-satisfied laugh. 'Ohhh, irmã – be careful what you say. You can't plan your way out of love, if that's what the universe has in store for you.'

Alegria suddenly remembered an overwhelming sense of finality she'd had on the plane leaving Uberlândia. The feeling that she was leaving her home for ever. The memory, its potency, made her feel uneasy. But, no – it was just Si and Ricardo messing with her head. 'That's not me,' she said firmly.

'Just make sure you fall for a rich one, OK? Love is much more fun when there's money to go round.' Simone nudged her boyfriend with one sock-covered foot. 'Come on, paixão, sort your clothes out before you forget and then I end up doing it.'

As Alegria watched Ricardo amble through one of only two doors, something Simone had said earlier finally registered. 'Wait – there's only one bedroom?'

'I already told you, Ricardo will go on the sofa. Don't try and argue – we decided on it before you even got here.'

'I will argue!' Alegria said indignantly. 'It should be me on—'

'No.'

'I—'

'*No!* I'll call Ricardo back here and tell him about that break-up mixtape again in front of you. Remember how embarrassing that was? You really gave him a *mixtape*.' She grinned as Alegria covered her face with her hands and groaned in resignation.

'You're a devil. An actual devil.'

Simone gasped dramatically, a hand on her chest. 'I'm a saint. And I'm going to get you laid – look at you. You *need* it.' Alegria aimed a kick at her, which she dodged with a yelp. Then Si made a gesture with her hands like a flower blooming. 'Unclench, irmã. Unclench.'

CHAPTER 7

London, November 1990

Bar Norman had managed to survive the chaos of Carnaby Street for years. It was a small place, a few too many tables crammed into the poorly lit interior, forcing customers to squeeze past each other with mumbled apologies on their way to the bar. It wasn't uncommon for a stray elbow or hip to send wine glasses crashing to the ground, often accompanied by enthusiastic cheers from surrounding guests. In the summer, the tables would spill out onto the pavement, crowds sometimes growing so large they took up half the street. The food was cheap – for Soho – and the cocktails weren't watered down. It wasn't the worst place in the world to be a bartender. Zivoin mostly worked nights, coming in at five, when the bar would slowly start to fill up with suited men and high-heeled women trickling in from the surrounding offices. By day, Bar Norman was more of a pit stop for the tourists wandering around central London, often stumbling in after hours of walking in the rain, disposable anoraks dripping everywhere. But, at night, it transformed into a smoke-filled, sticky-floored frenzy that made the hours pass blessedly fast. This time, though, he was on the dreaded double shift, and time was dragging its dead body across the floor.

Things had gone downhill from the moment he'd woken up, when Darco, avoiding his eye, muttered that his own mother – Drago's youngest sister – was asking after him. Zivoin hadn't called home since the argument. The longer he waited, the harder it became. Duty. The word hissed and sparked like a live wire. During the final, dying gasps of their relationship, Ina had warned him this would happen. 'This pressure you've taken upon yourself to carry is going to eat you alive,' she'd said, and he'd retorted that she couldn't possibly understand, not when she'd grown up the way she had, with money freely available to solve every problem. That had been the big, yawning gap between them. Poverty had chipped Zivoin around the edges, whilst his ex was smooth, untouched. 'There's no pressure like not having a safety net. Like being homeless, your entire family living out of a single hotel room and sharing a toilet with fifty other people,' he'd wanted to say. But he hadn't, because it upset Ina when he threw her wealth back in her face like that, and he had loved her.

And she had also been right. Lately, he had started to grow sour. He could feel bitterness creeping over everything, from conversations with his family to his job to his dating life and turning Zivoin into a cynic, a version of himself that he despised. It felt like he was trying to run forwards with his head twisted backwards – staring so hard into the past that the future dissolved in front of him. He'd ruminated sullenly on this all the way to Carnaby Street, his shoulders hunched against the relentless English rain. And the day had been dull, his mood leaching the colour from it. Work was the same as it ever was. He'd unlocked the place with the set of keys attached to the same ring as his own. Opened up the canopy. Hauled tables and chairs out for the smokers. Switched on the lights. Warmed up the coffee machine, turned on the kitchen extractor, fired up the ancient till, placed menus on the tables, on and on and on.

    By afternoon, the rain had slowed to a drizzle and the footfall had decreased. Susanna had finished her shift, saying something about a big night out, and Lorenzo had taken her place. Only a handful of tables were occupied. A group of German tourists hunched over pints of blonde beer, a sleepy-looking woman nursing a pot of tea, and a grey-suited man having a murmured conversation with a woman in a cropped red leather jacket. They appeared to be on a first date, and not a particularly successful one. She was keeping up a conversation, but kept glancing around, as though bored. From behind, she looked a lot like Ina: tall, blonde, fine-boned. Ina had been close to six feet, almost as tall as he was. He could still remember the peachy smell of her shampoo, which often lingered on his clothes long after she'd left to go to class or work. Zivoin didn't think he actually missed her – it was more the familiarity, the routine of being with her, that he still thought about. As painful as it had been, he wasn't surprised when their relationship imploded. He had been desperate to leave, whilst she could only fathom staying. By twenty-three, his ex had wanted to get married and have children right away, and at the start of their relationship, he'd wanted that too. Zivoin probably would have married her, had his time at university not changed him as profoundly as it had. For the first time in his life, he'd been rewarded for critical thinking, not punished, and it had awakened a deep hunger to understand his country. He might be a peasant, but no one would ever know Yugoslavia better than he would. He read Trotsky, Marx, Lenin, Tolstoy – and then Dostoevsky, Pushkin, Kundera, Andrić and Crnjanski. He joined a debate club for extra credit, discovering he had both a knack for remembering dates and quotes and a formidable talent for wielding political theory into winning arguments. And then, slowly at first – then all at once – he had got involved with the student union and local politics. But as his interest in intellectual debate and ethics grew, so did his disillusionment. There was a secret behind everything. It took Zivoin seven attempts to pass his driving test, because he did not know to leave a bottle of whisky in the examiner's seat. Students bribed the professors for the highest grades; when he found out, he felt extraordinarily naive, but a little heartbroken too. The only thing Zivoin could rely on was his ability to work harder than everyone else. Yet if degrees could be bought, then what was his worth? He joined the Communist Party and then left when he realised the student branch was full of members who insisted that 'Yugoslavia' really meant 'Serbia', and anyone who disagreed might find themselves struggling to get a graduate job. He looked behind the curtain, and in place of a functioning system found a stunning mess. Glancing again at the blonde woman, Zivoin saw that she had twisted around in her seat, her gaze flicking expectantly between him and Lorenzo.

Lorenzo had seen her too. 'Should I—' he began, but Zivoin was already sliding out from behind the bar, notepad in his hand.

He could sense something was off before he even reached

the table. The couple both seemed hostile, eyeing him as though they were expecting him to break into song, or jump up onto the table and tap-dance. The grey-suited man was curt as he ordered a pint, his face growing surlier when his companion asked for tea. It looked like she wasn't planning to extend their date into the evening.

'Anything else for you?' Zivoin asked.

She opened her mouth, but the man interrupted. 'You know she means proper tea, right?' he said coldly. 'Not Earl Grey, not coffee, yeah? *With* milk. Cold milk, but on the side, with a spoon.'

Zivoin stared at him, wondering if the man was simple. 'Of course,' he said slowly, trying to sound reassuring. He took fifty requests a day for tea.

'Oh, need to hear it again, do we?'

To Zivoin's surprise and confusion, the customer repeated himself in an unnecessarily loud voice, causing heads to turn towards them. The blonde woman covered her mouth with her hands, but it wasn't enough to stifle a snort. At last, understanding bloomed in Zivoin's chest. He felt anger creeping up the back of his ears and he lowered the notepad. 'I know what tea is.'

'You do? Gosh – lucky us, then.' The man smiled unpleasantly, and made a dismissive motion with his right hand, as if shooing him off. As Zivoin was turning away from them, he heard it: 'Foreign prick.' Instinctively, he swung back round.

'What did you say?'

For a few seconds, they stared at each other, the stranger's face carefully blank. 'Dunno what you're talking about, mate.'

Zivoin knew he'd heard correctly, even though it had been

quick and muttered. Back home, he'd have punched the guy. Back home, that would have been acceptable, expected, even. The rules were simple: you insult me, I hit you. But here, it would have cost him a job – branded him a barbarian. British etiquette was by far the most perplexing thing about this place; rudeness had to be shrouded in politeness, insults implied, or whispered, rather than directly spoken. The man was a coward. He walked robotically back to the bar, his gaze fixed on a spot on the wall. He was certain Lorenzo had heard everything, but felt too humiliated to check. It didn't matter, anyway. He was used to this. *Foreign prick* was the same as *your name is bloody difficult to pronounce*, which also meant *I can't possibly understand what you're saying with that accent*, and that inevitably led to *I've never heard of Yugoslavia*, which, really, was code for *well, this is England, and you're not English*. But it all meant the same thing: *fuck off back to where you come from. Fuck off, fuck off, fuck you.*

The phrases were so recognisable they blurred into each other, a meaningless grey churn of disdain. He should be immune by now. He *was* immune. All he had to do was sink back into his quiet mourning – for his country, for himself – and a veil fell between him and everyone else. Lorenzo, Danny, Susanna, the suited man – they were all on the other side, unable to touch him. He knew how to work on autopilot, his eyes never quite meeting anybody else's. *Foreign prick*. Maybe Ina had been right when she'd told him that he'd never be happy here. They had been good together in some ways, her solemnness balancing out his idealism, his resilience cushioning her fear of change. Zivoin really *had* thought he would marry her – so had everyone else, even his parents. As he stood there, his hands resting on the wooden bar, unsettling memories resurfaced.

The two of them in Belgrade that final summer, Ina's hands tense around her cup of Turkish coffee. Placards bearing the face of President Slobodan Milošević. Rumblings of what was to come. She'd upturned the cup when she'd finished, waiting for the coffee dregs to crawl down the porcelain so she could read the future. Just like his mother and grandmothers did. He remembered queues to watch *Scarface*, *Back to the Future*, *Aliens*, *Top Gun* at the DKC on Kolarčeva Street. Student halls plastered with posters, old Tito propaganda intermingled with warnings – lies – about untrustworthy Croatians, Bosniak fundamentalists, unreliable Montenegrin allies. He'd once been offered $15,000 for his Yugoslav passport on a student trip in Poland, still felt the agony of turning it down. Fifteen thousand American dollars. 'Thriller' overtaking the radio, snippets of the famous dance re-enacted in nightclubs. Summers in Kalemegdan Park.

The woman he had once thought the love of his life sat across from him, waiting. Zivoin tried to push some words out, but found nothing more to say. Ina angled the coffee cup towards him, pointing to a desperate smear of black grit. 'See this? That's us. With a child.' The devastating feeling of collapse – of all kinds – gathered on the horizon. Putting his hand on hers and saying, 'I think it's over. I'm sorry.' The growing demos, the crowds getting angrier, chanting, 'Serbia bleeds for a false republic!' Silence. Ina leaving, eyes hard and angry. A dropped glove, trampled by muddied boots. His mother's face when he broke the news. 'Serbia bleeds for a false republic! Serbia bleeds for a false republic!'

Since coming to London, his time in Belgrade had become kaleidoscopic, tension and joy intermingled until he couldn't always tell them apart. The happiest, most painful years of his life. Zivoin forced himself to think about his family for the rest of his shift. It was easier to revisit an old, familiar wound, and when 4 p.m. rolled around, he left without a word, a club sandwich from the kitchen tucked into his pocket. He had an hour – well, fifty-eight minutes now – to shake off the stink of that interaction before he had to be back. Fifty-eight minutes – well, fifty-seven now – to be less of a foreign prick.

Enough, Zivoin thought suddenly, aggressively. It had just dawned on him that he was on the verge of becoming unbearably boring. Enough with the self-indulgence. Enough with the yearning. It was time to leave. Six more months, and that was it. He'd stop paying for the English classes, start picking up every double shift – or find a second job – save up as much as he could, and go home. Home was on the brink of war. But still, he convinced himself that it probably wouldn't happen. And if it did, it would never reach his family's village in Montenegro, safely nestled in the southern tip of Yugoslavia. If it did, they'd run to Greece. His closest university friend had offered to take them in, if things really got bad. He'd stash some money aside to pay for everyone's tickets. He'd make it work. Tonight was the last night he'd let himself be seduced by the possibilities of the past. *You get tonight*, he thought. *One more chance to wallow.* And then, fuck it. He'd start looking ahead to his future. Stare straight down the barrel of the gun.

CHAPTER 8

London, November 1990

Two weeks later

Alegria caught sight of herself in the reflection of the shop window and adjusted her skirt. It had been two weeks since her dramatic arrival, and things were at last going well. She hadn't missed a single English class and – most importantly – she had found a job as a shop assistant. As ever, Si, the woman who could befriend Margaret Thatcher herself if she wanted to, had come to the rescue. She had found a friend of a friend who had an aunt looking for help running her shop in Queensway. Bryson's was (as had been drilled into Alegria) a family-run business that had operated for over thirty years selling luggage and travel accessories. Linda Bryson hired her after a brief interview and a tacit agreement that Alegria would be paid under the table, in cash – 'Saves us both a little visit from the taxman, doesn't it!' And she had agreed, scarcely believing her luck.

Both Simone and Ricardo had told her to lie about everything. 'Whatever experience she asks about, say you have it. If she asks for your passport, tell her you'll bring it next time, and don't mention it again,' Si had said when they were on their way to Bryson's for the interview. 'Apparently, this family is obsessed with the royals – now you are too. And pretend to be religious, they like that.'

'I *am* religious.'

'Just push the Catholicism, OK? Not the spiritualism. Here, wear this.' Si hung a small, gold-plated cross around her neck and nudged her into the store.

The first thing Alegria saw – it was impossible to miss – was a framed, gilded picture of the Queen, which was hanging by the entrance. Bryson's was large, but the space was so full of bulky luggage, strip lighting and mirrors that the whole room was an assault on the senses. The shelves were decorated with tiny porcelain houses and trees covered in snow, with various Santa Clauses hoisting themselves in and out of chimneys with sacks of presents, and the entire shop floor was, inexplicably, red carpet. Over by the counter, a large sign pinned to a corkboard read 'FRIENDS OF BRYSON'S!' above newspaper cut-outs of Rick Astley, Christian Bale, Craig David and others she did not recognise. They were all men. Trying not to stare too much at a figurine of a particularly fat Father Christmas stuck head first down a chimney, she introduced herself to Linda, a pink-cheeked woman with carefully pinned hair.

'So whereabouts in Italy are you from?' Linda had asked, her eyes raking over Alegria's coffee-coloured brown skirt suit, red lipstick and small hoop earrings – the same ones she'd worn since she was eleven. She'd thought she looked pretty good when she'd got dressed that morning. At the very least, good enough to pass for an Italian.

'A small town – village – near Milano.'

'And your experience with shop work?' Linda was wearing a pink blouse with enough ruffles to make at least two more, and matching capri pants that clashed horribly with the carpet. Alegria would have wondered how her ankles weren't frozen from the cold if there hadn't been a portable heater by the till, making half the room a little too warm.

'Many years. I worked in a supermarket, in a clothes store, in a shoe shop—'

'But not in a luggage shop?'

'Also a luggage shop. Near Milano Airport.'

And this, apparently, had been enough. She'd been told to turn up the next day with 'neat hair and a big smile!' It was Alegria's third shift, and she was finally starting to relax. The job was easy, sometimes bordering on dull, but she didn't mind. Money was money. Most people who came in were in a rush, needing a last-minute suitcase before catching a flight. So far she'd dusted shelves, reorganised racks and rewritten the 'Special Offer' board the Brysons insisted on changing daily in neat, rounded letters. Linda spent most of her time sitting by the cash register – 'keeping the books', as she called it. Her new boss smiled often and made a point of thanking her, but Alegria had noticed that she was constantly being watched. She didn't want to give Linda the impression that there was nothing to do, in case her hours were cut.

It had been a slow day. She'd already dusted the shelves once, but she decided to do it again anyway, grabbing a yellow dusting cloth and heading over to a rack of leather luggage tags. As Alegria carefully picked up a porcelain Father Christmas – a particularly chipper-looking one that reminded her of Linda – she thought back to the conversation she'd had with Si the day before, which had been worrying her. They had gone to one of the most fascinating places she'd ever visited, a huge, multi-floored department store called Harrods. A place so lavish, Simone had explained, it had a dress code and suited men in white gloves who opened and shut the doors for them. And two kinds of people would visit: the rich women in their fur coats and kitten heels, with winter sunglasses perched on immaculate blow-dries – 'Em sério, who wears heels *shopping*?' – and then the gawking tourists with their Nikons or Minolta Maxxums who looked anything but rich. No matter where they came from, the wealthy ones didn't count as tourists in Harrods.

The experience had captivated Alegria – she'd never seen so much concentrated, historic wealth, the kind that not even the richest people she knew from back home possessed. They walked through a maze of luxury – watches, bags, perfumes, sweets that looked like jewels – coming to a stop in the bridal section on the fourth floor, a dazzling array of designer dresses, overflowing with lace, silk and tulle in every possible shade of white. The room had been decorated to look like an enchanted forest, with seemingly real moss-covered trees growing out of the marble, their branches adorned with glittering stars and ornamental butterflies. 'This is beautiful,' Alegria breathed, wishing she owned a camera to capture the large chandeliers dripping with crystals, each one catching the light and throwing out a shower of reflective golden beams. The whole room looked like it was bathed in sunlight.

'It is,' Simone agreed. 'And so repulsive.'

'Repulsive? What are you talking about?'

'All this stuff to buy, like that's the most important thing in the world. Like you need it to be happy. All this money for a wedding to someone you might end up leaving anyway.'

Tearing her gaze away from an ivory-coloured silk cape, she tried not to roll her eyes. 'Si, people *do* need money to be happy. You know that.'

'Not this much money. We're happy enough with what we have back home.'

Alegria had said nothing in response. It was easy, she felt, to say that when you were not the one responsible for putting the food on the table. Si had drifted from occupation to occupation since leaving school, unable to commit. First it was nail art, then dressmaking, and then beadwork, Alegria paying for it freely, happy that her baby sister could figure herself out without the pressure to make money. It was an opportunity she'd never been given, but now she wondered if Si truly realised that the more Alegria spent on her, the less she had for her own dreams. But that was not a conversation she planned to have that day.

They'd climbed to the very top floor, in search of a French café that Simone had been told Princess Diana *herself* frequented, settled onto one of the plum velvet sofas and split a box of four macaroons. And there, as they passed the little French biscuits back and forth, each taking tiny bites, Simone said casually, 'I thought I was pregnant, last month.' Alegria had almost choked on a mouthful of lavender-flavoured buttercream.

'You thought? You're not?'

'I got my period the week before you came.'

'Graças a Deus.' She slumped back against the plush sofa in relief. 'You're too young.'

'I know. But I've been thinking about it a lot.'

'About a baby? Right *now*?'

'No, no.' Si sighed and rested both her elbows on the table, her eyes downcast. 'About Ricardo and me. And what a baby would bring to our relationship. It's made me realise that I'm bored. He wants to stay here for God knows how long, but I think I'm done. We're poorer here than we were at home!'

'Oh.' Her sister's declaration took Alegria by surprise. Simone had seemed so comfortable, so content in domesticity when she'd first observed her with Ricardo. She had yet to witness an argument between the two of them, unlike Si's previous, more tumultuous relationships. 'So you're going to end things?'

'Eventually. Maybe.'

'You know it might end naturally, if you come back with me like you planned.'

Simone's eyes finally met hers. 'Irmã, if I go back I don't think I'll ever leave home again. I just feel it, here.' She tapped the base of her throat miserably. 'Sometimes I feel like I'm just delaying the inevitable. You'll end up leaving us, but I'll end up staying.'

'That's—'

'Já sei, já sei, you disagree. It doesn't matter whether or not you believe it. I've had this conversation in my head a thousand times.'

She spat the words out, and Alegria didn't know what to do. Part of her marvelled at Simone's ability to leap from extreme joy to complete anguish. Another part of her felt exhausted, unsure if she had the energy to walk her sister through this latest crisis. Alegria glanced around the café. Heavy curtains cut off the view of the street below, making it hard to gauge the time of day. 'This place is a little depressing,' she said, without really thinking about it. She was surprised when her sister laughed.

'Only for those without any money.' Simone finished off the last bite of macaroon. She pressed her finger down onto the paper doily sitting atop the plate, scooping the final sugary crumbs up to her mouth. 'I already know. You're thinking about how complicated I am.'

'No,' Alegria lied. 'I was actually thinking that Pai was right. He told me before I left that you weren't happy.'

Simone frowned. 'I'm not unhappy, though. That's why I feel so conflicted. I love Ricardo, but it's not the kind of love that makes you crazy – you know, makes you want to tear your life apart for them. It's – it's *fine*, but it's not, you know, a move-to-the-other-side-of-the-world kind of love.'

At this, Alegria laughed. 'Irmã, I'm not so sure that's love. It shouldn't be that dramatic – that's infatuation.'

'That's just something people say in the aftermath, when they have forgotten what life-changing love feels like.'

'I'm not sure that's true, Si. In my experience—'

'What experience? You've never been in love before. Your great loves are your family and your career.'

Alegria felt stung by this, even though she knew there was no malice intended in the words. 'That's not true,' she said quietly. 'You're wrong to think I don't know what I'm talking about, Si, just because I don't feel things as intensely as you do. I loved Marcio. And I was in love before him too.'

Even as she spoke, she could see that her sister was determined to disagree. Simone couldn't have sounded more dismissive as she asked, 'Go on, then – what did it feel like?'

'It was tender, it was safe. I think real love is peaceful.'

'No! No, it isn't. Sorry, irmã, but if that's what you think, we haven't felt the same kind of love.' Simone was shaking her head vehemently. 'Love *isn't* peaceful. It makes you so vulnerable that it sets you on fire, and the burn is what makes you feel alive and more connected to the world than you have ever been before! Like everything painful that has ever happened to you no longer hurts the same way, because it got you to where you needed to be, to your person. Love cracks your chest open, and suddenly the whole world can fit inside you like it's nothing – and still you could make room for more. It's the thing that makes every other thing in life bearable. Haven't you ever been so in love that you would . . . I don't know, risk everything?'

Alegria had found herself unable to respond. She didn't know which one of them understood love better, but her own version of it felt weak by comparison. And now, wiping nonexistent dust off the shop's gleaming surfaces, she couldn't get her sister's words out of her head.

A bell chimed as the door opened and both Linda and Alegria straightened up. A harried-looking man walked in, unbuttoning his coat and pulling his scarf away from his neck. He checked his watch and immediately moved towards a line of large suitcases, muttering to himself, clearly stressed. She would have preferred to wait until he turned and asked for assistance, but feeling Linda's eyes on her back, Alegria smiled and stepped forward. 'I can help?'

'Eh?' The man looked at her blankly and said something too swiftly for her to understand – it was definitely not English – before turning back to examine a grey case. Alegria frowned. She heard Linda grunt as she got to her feet. The words he'd said were familiar – perhaps a dialect of Spanish she'd not come across before. As she stood there, trying to work it out, Linda appeared at her elbow.

'Welcome! Looking for something in particular? Off on holiday? Hope it's somewhere nice and sunny – the weather's been all sorts, hasn't it?' She chirped all of this quickly – too quickly.

The man looked slightly panicked, holding up both hands as if he expected Linda to leap at him. He shook his head and said, 'Scusi.'

'Oh . . . is that – are you from Italy?' Linda asked brightly. Alegria froze, knowing the second the words were said that it was true. Of course it was true. He had spoken to her in Italian. She felt as though she was about to be sick.

'Sì, sì, Italiano,' the man said impatiently, and pointed towards the carry-on. 'Quanto costa?'

Linda beamed. 'Well, it's your lucky day – my assistant is from Milan! Alegria, why don't you help this gentleman with his purchase?' She nudged her forward, and stood looking at both of them expectantly.

The customer had clearly not picked up a word of this, and if her heartbeat hadn't surged its way into her eardrums, if she didn't feel faint with anxiety, Alegria would have laughed at the look of frustrated bewilderment on his face.

'Quanto?' he said again, louder.

Alegria knew what he was asking, and she tried to say

something back, she really did. 'Sessenta,' she said, praying that the Italian word for sixty was close enough to her mother tongue. Miraculously, he nodded. And then let loose a stream of words that was too fast for Alegria to even begin to make sense of it. God, this was awful. She wondered if she should simply grab her bag and coat and run out of the shop. The customer repeated himself, and she shook her head helplessly. 'I don't know, I don't know. I'm sorry,' she mumbled in Portuguese, backing away from him. 'I'm sorry.' In English this time.

Linda's eyes flicked between the two of them in confusion. 'What's he saying?'

'I don't know,' she whispered, and felt her boss stiffen as she finally understood.

The next few minutes crawled by. Alegria stared at her shoes as the man bought the suitcase, wordlessly handing over cash. Linda counted it carefully, loudly saying 'Gracias!' as she handed him his change. She felt feverish with embarrassment, and fought back a nervous giggle. It was too much to hope that Linda would find it funny. If the roles had been reversed, Alegria knew that she'd be furious. The yellow duster twisted between her fingers.

Linda waited until the customer had left before she turned and looked at her again. When she spoke, all the syrupiness had gone from her voice.

'You lied to me.'

Alegria nodded. There was no point in denying it. 'Yes.'

'You're not Italian.'

'No. I am sorry.'

Linda was breathing heavily, her face slowly turning purple. 'What are you, then? Where've you come from?'

'Does it matter?' Alegria said desperately. 'I am doing the job, no problem! I have a visa, I just need—'

'Get out,' Linda spat. 'Get your things and leave. I will not have criminals in my shop!' She pointed a trembling finger at the door, and once again, Alegria's feeling of shame flickered with anger. The nerve of this woman, with her plans to pay her under the table, to shout that in her face. The suitcases were overpriced anyway, the shop too gaudy, too loud.

'I am not a criminal,' she said, making an effort to sound calm. 'I just need a job.'

'Well, you won't be finding that here. Out!'

Alegria did not move. 'What about my salary?'

'You're not getting a penny from me!'

Trying to keep her voice even, Alegria took a deep breath. 'I have worked for you for three days. Are you not going to pay me for this?'

Linda's eyes started to pop, and her hand, still pointing at the door, shook even more. 'How *dare* you!' she shouted. 'If you don't leave right this second, I'm calling the police. And if anything happens to my shop, I'll call them! I have your face on the camera. Get out. Get OUT!'

CHAPTER 9

London, November 1990

Zivoin hurried along the street, preoccupied. He was sweating a little despite the sharpness in the air, but he didn't slow down. Unease had become a hand between his shoulder blades, pushing him forward. It was the third day of Darco's fever, and his cousin was getting worse. That morning, he'd hallucinated that their flat was flooding, crying out as he saw the ceiling swaying and buckling above them. Neither of them had health insurance, or had bothered to register with a GP, suspicious that there might be hidden charges. No one they knew used England's health services – Zivoin wasn't even sure what would happen if he took Darco to a hospital. He worried about leaving his cousin alone with doctors he'd never met. The hallucinations had been bad enough, but by the afternoon, Darco's face was a chalky grey, his eyes glittering and unfocused. The concern that had gnawed at him over the past few days grew more forceful, and Zivoin had made up his mind. 'I'm cancelling my shift and going to Nisa.'

Darco groaned weakly. 'No, brate, please – give it another day before you bring out the village shit.'

His pleas went unheard. Potato and cucumber were what Darco needed, even if he didn't want them. Zivoin would cut them up into thin slices and place them in the fridge in a large bowl of water until they were dense and cold, then lay the pieces across Darco's shivering limbs. The result was unpleasant but effective – he'd never known it to fail. This was how Zivoin's mother had broken the fevers of all the village children, ignoring their cries of discomfort as their beleaguered bodies registered each slice of raw vegetable as a slab of ice pressed against burning skin. He remembered the ordeal – it felt like being branded. But it worked, and that was what mattered, he thought, hurrying through Nisa's automatic doors. The supermarket was busy, lines already forming at the tills. Going straight to the produce section, Zivoin picked up cucumbers and an armful of loose potatoes, inhaling their earthy, nutty smell. In later retellings, he would claim he knew from the moment he entered the shop that his life was about to change, but for now, he was preoccupied with thoughts about Darco. In the queue, his eyes danced over newspaper headlines, the same woman's smiling face – more like a grimace – plastered over them. 'WHAT HAVE THEY DONE?' screamed one paper. 'BATTLE TO HALT THE USURPER', another declared.

Margaret Thatcher had resigned yesterday. It had taken him by surprise – Zivoin had been watching her slow decline with detached interest for over a year now, but he had not expected this woman, who seemed to enjoy the ruthlessness of politics, to back down from a fight. Politically, she was the polar opposite of Milka Planinc, the only woman Yugoslavia had ever elected, back in '82, after Tito's painful fade into irrelevance. But there was a similarity in their steeliness that intrigued Zivoin, despite his disgust at Thatcher's anti-communism. He'd been on the bus, wondering why the crowd around him seemed strangely energised, strangers talking to each other animatedly. Eventually a cry broke out near the front. 'She's OUT!' a man in a flat cap, nose red from the cold, had shouted. The crowd around him had burst into applause and cheers, and he'd witnessed something remarkable from the usually guarded Londoners – unrestrained emotion. Joy and hope for the future – he yearned for that feeling again. Stories had begun trickling out of Kosovo, rumours of mass beatings, demonstrations, police brutality against the Albanian population there. Rumours that had been met with jubilation by too many in Belgrade. Thinking about Yugoslavia these days felt like gripping a knife by its blade.

Zivoin was so distracted by the newspaper headlines, he didn't notice the woman until it was almost his turn to be served. It was her voice that pulled him from the wreckage of his thoughts – he could hear the smile in her words. When he looked up and saw her, he found that he could not look away. It wasn't just that she was beautiful – though she was, with her freckled face and high cheekbones – it was the warmth radiating from her, as though she'd swallowed the sun. Several seconds passed. Zivoin knew he was being obvious, knew that she could probably sense him staring, but every time he glanced away, it was impossible not to look back. He wanted to commit her to memory, and as soon as he realised this he stumbled into a new and terrible thought: what if he paid for his groceries and then never saw her again? It was an intolerable idea.

He caught sight of a name tag on her white shirt. *Alegria*. An unfamiliar name. He tried to sound it out. Would it be split into two – Aleg-ria – vowels cut short, like the English did with his name? Or did she pronounce it melodically, like the Italians? A-le-gri-a? It had to be the second – it matched her unusual intonation. When she spoke, it almost sounded like a song. He wanted – needed – more time to figure her out, and felt a rush of gratitude for the stranger in front of him, the woman who had a week's worth of food piled on the conveyor belt. He listened to their back and forth eagerly, trying to soak up any information he could. But she gave very little of herself away, asking questions with what sounded like genuine interest whilst revealing nothing in return. He wanted to know where she came from – he would have guessed Portugal, or Spain, but that accent ruled it out. It wasn't staccato enough, her vowels too soft and elongated. He noticed that she cut the endings off some of her words: 'pepper' became 'pepe', 'orange juice' was 'orange joos'.

There was a lull in the conversation. For God's sake, he wished the customer between them would ask her a question, any question. And then the woman was turning to him and chiming 'Hello!' as if he were an old friend. It was rare that Zivoin found himself tripping over his words, but her wide, open smile disarmed him. Before, he had struggled to look away from her, but now that she was the one watching him, looking directly into her eyes felt too raw. She had a small brown mole at the left corner of her lips. He discovered it as he placed the vegetables on the counter, and stood there silently as she weighed and bagged them. His arms felt stiff, his army coat too warm. She did everything methodically, purposefully. It was mesmerising. A single potato was lifted with care, turned over once or twice as she checked it for blemishes, and then gently placed into a brown paper bag. He wished he'd bought more, much more, to lengthen the time they had together, to give him the chance to know her. She saved the cucumbers for last, stacking them on top of the potatoes and folding the lip of the bag once, twice. 'Here,' she said, sliding the bag to him as if it was a gift. 'For you.'

'Thank you,' Zivoin said at last, aware of the man standing behind him. 'You are new?'

'Yes,' the woman smiled. 'I started this week.'

She was on her feet, he realised, not sitting like some of the cashiers chose to do. At that height, she could probably fit perfectly under his shoulder.

'That's excellent,' he said stupidly, handing over a five-pound note. When she said nothing in response, he introduced himself and continued, 'I come here a lot – I live near here.'

'Then I will see you again soon?'

There was that glowing warmth again. Later, in a moment of weakness, he would describe himself as a moth to a flame to Darco, who would proceed to mock him relentlessly. Zivoin wanted to ask this mesmerising woman out right there and then. He would have, if there hadn't been a line of strangers watching their interaction. He would have, if he had been his usual assured self, instead of the clunky, awkward man he had suddenly turned into. He would have, if he wasn't running out of time, and if her dark eyes weren't already sliding away from his, counting the people behind him. He could have, he should have. By lingering this way, Zivoin knew he was keeping her from doing her job. He despised it when customers did this to him. But he couldn't bring himself to leave just yet. He needed one more minute. 'Your name, I've never heard it before. Where are you from?'

'Italy.'

If Zivoin hadn't been so focused on her answer, he might have noticed the smile slip from her face or the tension in her shoulders. But in that moment he knew it wasn't true, and all he saw was a way for them to keep talking. Without thinking, assuming it was a joke, he laughed and said, 'Italy? No way. I know it well, I went many times as a student – you're not—'

'Do you want to see my papers?' Alegria snapped, cutting him off. Her fingers were twisting together, her knuckles pale. 'I'm from a small village near Milano.' All her sincerity had disappeared, replaced by a horrible, unnatural stiffness. Later, much later, he would tell her, 'The sun vanished – the clouds had blocked them out.' And she would roll her eyes and smack his arm playfully. He was a poet, after all. But for now, Alegria picked up the brown paper bag and pushed it into his arms as he stared at her uncomprehendingly. Then, as though remembering where they were, she gave him a quick, tight smile, her lips pressed together. The mole half vanished. 'Have a good evening. Sir.'

He tried to speak, to extricate himself from whatever offence he had committed, but she motioned for the next customer to come forward, and it was clear that she was done. He'd screwed it up, the warmth between them extinguished. Zivoin had no choice but to turn around and leave, confusion surging through his chest.

A few hours later, Alegria slammed the door behind her, a yell of frustration escaping her mouth. She was furious and afraid. She'd blown it. She knew she had. What if the man had followed her home? What if he knew where she lived, and Simone would be forced to move, yet again? Could they even afford to?

'Ale?' Simone's alarmed face appeared from the bedroom. She was wrapped in a thick pink bathrobe. 'O que foi?'

Alegria didn't answer at first, struggling to remove her coat. She'd jumped off the bus and walked home so quickly she was now boiling and clammy, her face slick with sweat. At last, she tore it off her and collapsed onto the sofa. 'What is *wrong* with this city?' She watched her sister pull two bottles of Bass from the fridge and hold one out to her.

'What's wrong with *you*?'

Alegria groaned, rubbing her face with her hands. She was so tired, yet so full of adrenaline. She took a long sip of beer before saying, 'I think it's happened again.'

'What has?'

'I think they know. At work.'

Simone frowned. 'What do you mean? They asked for your visa?'

'Not exactly.' Alegria told her about the man in the queue. She had noticed him watching her. To be looked at by an attractive man the way he had looked at her – openly, hungrily – had given her a thrill at first. In retrospect, though, it no longer felt exciting, but threatening.

'He asked me where I was from – he was watching me the whole time.'

'And then they asked for your papers?'

'No one asked me for my papers!' Alegria said impatiently. 'But what if *he's* Italian? He had this rich, dark hair . . . and said he knew the country well – he could tell by my accent that I was lying. What if he tells someone?' As she spoke, she saw her sister's expression change from concern to amusement, and her irritation grew. 'I knew you wouldn't get it,' she snapped as Simone started to grin. 'But he had a *military coat* on, for God's sake. What if he's a – a—'

'A what?' Simone asked, feigning horror. 'A government *spy*?'

'Well, maybe!'

'London is filling you with paranóia. Did he sound Italian?'

Alegria shrugged. 'I don't know. You know every accent sounds the same to me.'

'OK.' Simone leaned back and crossed her arms, still sounding, Alegria felt, far too calm. 'Describe him – what did he look like?'

'You know what was odd – all he bought was potatoes and cucumbers. Nothing else.'

'Pelo amor de Deus, fuck the potatoes, Ale, what did he *look* like?'

'He . . . he was good-looking, I guess. Ish. Tall, olive-skinned.' She ignored the grin creeping across Si's face. 'A bit too skinny, but he had these big eyes. I think they were brown, they must have been brown – or black. Big eyebrows . . . sincere eyebrows. His nose, it was strange. Quite ugly, but it suited him – it looked like it had been broken—'

She didn't even finish her sentence before Simone pointed at her triumphantly, cackling with laughter. 'I knew it, you paranoid little puta. I know you so well, Ale – you're acting this way because he's hot! You liked whatever it was he was doing. I don't know if you can call it flirting, but it was something, anyway.'

Alegria shook her head incredulously. 'That's crazy. I was afraid – why would he ask unless he's trying to get me in trouble—'

'Ai, come ON!' Si shouted, flinging her hands up in the air. Immediately, as though waiting for a cue, a loud banging came from the ceiling. They had disturbed Priscilla, the elderly Jamaican woman who lived above them and always filled the hallway with the tantalising smell of fried sweet plantain. She was particularly sensitive to noise. 'Sorry!' Simone called, with an eye roll. She dragged her hands down her face, pulling her cheeks into a grotesque expression. 'Irmã, sometimes I struggle to believe that you're six years older than me and *this* dumb when it comes to romance. He was flirting with you. And you liked it!'

'He definitely wasn't flirting with me. He wasn't even that hot. Apparently, he knows all the people who work at Nisa. All the women. He knows their names and speaks to them when he comes in.'

Simone smiled, looking smug. 'So you asked around about him?'

'I needed to know more about him,' she responded abruptly, feeling defensive. 'He could be dangerous, questioning me like that . . . it was scary.'

'You were scared because you knew you liked him, and he could maybe come along and mess with your careful little plans, your desperate need to prove yourself—'

'Enough,' Alegria said sharply. The words stung. 'Enough, Si.'

'Sorry,' Simone said, sounding utterly unapologetic. 'But you know you do this with every man you want, don't you? You did it with that teacher from your school, when he asked you out—'

'It's unprofessional to date at work—'

'You did it with Rodrigo, our neighbour,' Simone interrupted, her voice drowning out her sister's. 'Didn't Marcio have to ask you out three times before you said yes? You're like this, irmã, you never let anyone in.'

'I do!' Alegria responded reflexively. She took a gulp of beer, knowing what was coming.

Simone leaned over and swapped Alegria's half-empty bottle for her barely touched one. 'You push them away and make up some insane justification because you aren't willing to take a risk on someone, even if they're the last biscuit in the packet.'

'That's not true.' But she knew that her sister was right. Alegria had always been too rigid, too unwilling to bend. It had taken her months to even get here, always frantically running to catch up. She pushed the thought away and closed her eyes, her head feeling heavy as the beer churned in her empty stomach. 'I feel old. And tired. And hungry.'

'Don't forget cowardly.'

'You know,' she said later, after Simone had forced her to eat and shower, 'I used to have this recurring dream when we were little.'

They were back on the sofa again, a single lamp lighting the room. Simone was unscrewing a jar of coconut oil that Alegria had brought from home. She handed it to her and settled between Alegria's knees. Simone was a big believer in deciphering dreams.

Using a comb, she parted Simone's hair and tried to divide it into six even chunks. It wasn't easy – Si's hair was as thick as hers, though nowhere near as curly. She could run her fingers through it without catching them too much. 'In this one, I was walking on that street by the Beach Club—'

'Avenida Uirapuru?'

'Yes, the one with all the fancy bungalows on it.'

'And two cars per house – sometimes *three*.'

'Yes!' Alegria dug her fingers into the coconut oil, hard and solid from the cold, and gouged out as much as she could, rubbing it into her sister's scalp. Back home, they had done this for each other every week – or, more accurately, she had done it for Simone every week, trying to ease the pain of the chronic migraines her sister suffered from. She'd missed this ritual. 'So I'm walking on Uirapuru, looking at all the houses, and then in front of me I see a person on the ground. A man.'

'On the ground? He's a beggar?'

'I don't know. It's not important, what matters is that he's lying on the ground, and I know something isn't right. And I keep walking towards him, but it's like time doesn't work properly – like I'm walking through jelly.'

'Urgh,' Simone groaned. Alegria felt the vibration through her hands. 'I hate dreams like those. So you're walking towards him . . . ?'

'But the closer I get to him, the more I know something isn't right.'

'Like . . . he's dead?'

'Yes, maybe, I think so.' She kept rubbing the oil in, trying to massage the tension out of Simone's temples. 'And then I finally walk past him, and I don't even look at him – actually, I start running. And when I get to the corner of the road, I look back before I turn, and he's still there, alone, nobody to watch over him.'

'And then?'

'And then . . . I would wake up,' Alegria said lamely. She didn't know how to describe how she felt in the moments between leaving the dream and fully waking, a mess of panic and guilt that she couldn't make sense of.

But her sister, the one who knew her best, understood. Simone placed both hands on Alegria's feet and started to knead them gently. 'You felt like it was your fault.'

'Yeah. Because I didn't intervene – I wasn't courageous enough – he died. I'm scared of doing anything in case it goes wrong – and sometimes in life I get that same feeling of deep fear, that something bad is coming and I won't be able to stop it.'

They spent a few minutes in silence, Alegria braiding Si's hair as much as its new length would allow before wrapping it into a headscarf. She stretched out, and Simone nestled in next to her, spreading the robe over them like a blanket. 'Ale, that dream was just a dream. I shouldn't have called you a coward earlier. And whatever part of you that feels guilt . . . I don't even know what to say to that. You're the best sister, you've been the best daughter – literally their miracle child – whilst I've been the crazy, unpredictable one.'

'Well, maybe I want to be crazy and unpredictable.' At this, they both laughed.

'OK,' Si said, her voice taunting once again. 'Ask out

the spy from the supermarket.' Alegria gasped, and Simone mirrored her, placing a hand over her mouth mockingly. 'Why not? What's the worst that could happen?'

'I told you, he wanted to—'

'He wanted to *fuck*! That's all!'

'You're covering me in oil.' Alegria shoved her. 'Anyway, it doesn't matter. I'm here to make money, not go on dates.'

'And that's why you don't actually want to be crazy and unpredictable,' Simone declared. 'Irmã, all you want is to know where you're going. That's who you are.'

'But that's so . . . boring.'

'How can anything that brings you contentment be boring?'

Alegria sighed, feeling her sister's words settle uncomfortably. 'I mean, to other people.'

'Most other people are tiresome, their brains full of little monkeys all saying the same thing. You're fine.' As Simone spoke, the single lamp lighting the room spluttered and flickered a few times before plunging them into darkness.

'I'll change the bulb later,' Alegria said, and the two of them lay there, waiting for their eyes to adjust to the moonlight trickling in from the kitchen window. They were lying side by side. The room smelled like coconut. She wondered where this sofa had come from, who had used it before their arrival, and whether her sister had cleaned it. She suspected not. Outside, the noise of the cars was a constant churn of sound, rising and falling in vaguely predictable rhythms. Alegria suddenly felt very small, and very helpless. She was a fish caught in someone else's net, blindly pushing her way forward without noticing the mesh around her. It would be nice, she thought, for someone else to step in and hold a little bit of her life for her. Not all of it – but enough for her to feel taken care of, instead of being the one taking care of everyone else. 'I'm so tired,' she announced.

Si wormed her way closer so that their bodies were squeezed together even tighter. Alegria rested her chin on her sister's shoulder, breathing in the smell of washing powder, lemons and the sour, unmistakable smell of old sweat. Simone had stopped using deodorant years ago.

'I love you, my dear, beautiful sister, my soulmate. But you're like a robot. A stressed-out little robot. You need to mess around a bit, have an adventure. It doesn't need to be with this government spy, but, you know. You're only here for a few months. Fuck a guy! Make the mistake! Or . . .' Alegria could feel Simone's face stretching into a grin '. . . make two mistakes at the same time.'

CHAPTER 10

London, November 1990

Three days later

The same week he met her in the supermarket, he thought he saw her in one of Stanton's corridors, rounding the corner. Instinct told him to go and look for her, but the hallway had been crowded and he was already running late. That day would've been his last lesson, if he'd actually entered the classroom. But Zivoin had done something uncharacteristic: he'd turned and walked in the opposite direction. Away from her. Or the person he'd thought might be her. He'd walked all the way out of the building and down the street before he stopped to think things through. What was he doing? He couldn't answer, he just knew he couldn't walk back into that building. Anticipation gripped his muscles like a coiled spring.

Once, when Zivoin was ten, he'd been sent up the mountain to bring his father and the other workers food. This wasn't unusual – he did it every day in the summer. He, his cousins and the other children in the village would get up at five thirty and then take the cows out to graze in the fields shadowed by the mountains, whilst the men would climb up into dense forest to chop and carry lumber. By midmorning, he'd be home again and his mother, Milenka, would hand him a parcel of bread, cheese and dried meat, sometimes with sour cabbage and potatoes. It was the children's job to undertake the ninety-minute journey to their fathers, uncles and grandfathers, eating their own meal along the way. The climb was always subdued, rushed. If they took too long, their fathers would be angry and beat them. But on the way back, they would chase each other and play, picking tiny wild strawberries the size of their fingernails and threading them onto stems of wheat for later. Or they would catch grasshoppers and pull their legs off, leaving behind twitching, limbless bodies.

This particular day, he had spotted a large yarrow bush growing on top of a sheer boulder face, and had drifted from the other girls and boys to pick some of the flowers. He knew his mother made yarrow tea, knew she would be happy if he handed her the stems. Milenka smiled so rarely that it felt well worth the climb. So Zivoin had scrambled up, skinning his knees, and cut a handful of stems with the small home-made knife he carried to pick stones out of the cows' feet. And then he had seen her. The bear. A medium-sized brown one, staring right at him. It was the biggest animal he had ever seen, and he knew it was only surprise at his sudden arrival that kept her still like that. It wasn't mating season, which was why the bear seemed so docile, and it wasn't winter, which was why he was still alive and not halfway down her throat. Boy and bear stared at the other, both unable to move. Zivoin had known what he should do: shout with all the force of his little body, wave his arms, throw stones. But he simply remained crouching there, clutching his useless knife in one hand and the plant in the other. Her black eyes were unblinking. The sun started to burn the small of his back, exposed from where his shirt had ridden up. He felt the sting of sweat in one eye, but did not dare move to wipe his face or break eye contact. In that moment – which felt like hours, he would later brag – he felt something he could not explain, even to this day. He was limp with fright, and yet he almost *wanted* the bear to attack him. Zivoin had not wanted to die, quite the opposite. But he could not take being frozen that way, his fate suspended in another creature's hands, an animal he could not understand or communicate with. In his young mind, he could see only two options – be eaten or be spared – but the fact that the choice was not his to make felt so utterly terrifying, so paralysing, it was almost worse than the bear itself. So be it, he had thought. Go on then. *Attack*. But he had been lucky, unbelievably lucky. The bear had turned and lumbered away. It did not look back.

As soon as it was a good fifteen metres from him, the urge to flee took over. Zivoin ran, his limbs so weak that he kept falling, grabbing blindly at rocks and plants to keep himself from descending too far. He moved faster than he ever had before, unable to even glance over his shoulder. Twice he grabbed stinging nettles, painful welts rising on his hands and wrists. Of course he told the other children once he rejoined them, and they had accused him of making up the whole thing. But Zivoin had always been known to tell the truth, and his scratched-up limbs, his damaged hands and grey, bloodless face presented as evidence. For one glorious summer, he had been Zivoin lovac na medvjede: the bear-slayer. His only regret was the yarrow; in his panic, he had abandoned it somewhere. But he did not ever go back to the ridge, or tell Mama and Tata about the bear.

Since meeting the woman in the supermarket, Zivoin had felt that same curious feeling. A strange sort of impatience – a powerful, instinctive recoil from the agony of waiting. He knew he had to speak to her again. After their meeting that day, he'd become convinced a fork in the road had opened up: a life with her, and one without her. It felt urgent. She was radiant, but the shock of her beauty would fade eventually, and what then? He didn't know how he would ever explain this, but it was the earnestness with which she'd picked up and examined each vegetable that had moved him. She was so unwilling to let a stranger walk away with something as inconsequential as an imperfect potato, he could only imagine the kind of love she reserved for the people in her life. He wanted to be one of them. Once again, the situation felt out of his hands.

It was unacceptable, Zivoin thought, pulling out a cigarette. Twisting away from everyone, he lit it and exhaled a long, slow breath. He offered the packet to Marta, the Polish girl Nico had been casually seeing for a few weeks and the other smoker of the group. She shook her head with a smile. There were seven of them, seated on the low leather sofas in the far corner of Bar Norman, which had shut an hour ago. It was past midnight. Occasionally, someone – usually Lorenzo or Nico – would convince everyone to stay behind for a drink or two. The radio was on, the impossible falsetto of A-ha in the background, and they were four bottles of wine in. To

Zivoin's left was an old university friend, Feki. Susi was on his other side, and to her right sat her friend Janice, who was off a late shift at St Thomas' Hospital. It was the first time he'd stayed behind to drink with his co-workers – the first time he'd brought a friend. It was lazy of him, but Zivoin found it far easier to surround himself with people who knew his home, who understood him culturally as well as linguistically. So he'd never strayed beyond a polite sentence or two with the people he worked alongside. Apart from the Italians, because they were familiar enough. And the Bulgarians, because they could understand each other quite easily. And the Russians, because there was a powerful cultural connection. And, of course, the Serbs, because they were from Yugoslavia, and he loved Yugoslavia.

Janice was British. Zivoin had heard a firmness in her voice when he'd asked her where she was from, and he had not broached the topic again. She later told him her parents were from St Lucia and had come to the UK in the fifties as part of what she called the 'Windrush' generation. He found the story astounding – the idea that one country could decide to absorb the people of another, granting them the right to live and work as if they had belonged there all along. No wonder Janice's family had made that journey. His own process of securing a work visa last year had been complicated and expensive, and had his country not been on the edge of violence – according to the British government – he doubted he would have been successful. A 'political refugee' was what an official at the embassy in Belgrade had called him, and Zivoin had not bothered to correct her, though the suggestion had seemed laughable. The separatism now raging through Yugoslavia's politics had been a fringe movement at the time.

He reached out and topped up both Feki's and Janice's glasses, finishing off the last of the wine. They were part of two passionate conversations – Feki, Nico and Lorenzo were furiously arguing about the World Cup that had taken place in Italy that summer. To his right, Janice was talking about her job as a nurse in the National Health Service, complaining about the government's attempts to cut costs. 'The competitive tendering is now so ingrained, it's completely dominating our hospital – you know they're contracting *private* nurses who earn twice my daily wage . . .' Susi was definitely bored, her face blank as she nodded every so often, her eyes flitting around the empty bar. He did not feel like joining either conversation, staying silent until Feki nudged him.

'Seen that woman again?'

'Who?' Zivoin asked, though he knew exactly who he meant.

'The Italian.'

'What Italian?' Nico had heard them. He leaned forward, his interest piqued. 'Chef – you have met an Italian woman? Ma ovviamente – of course you have! Italian women are the best.' He did not notice Marta's eyes flicker towards him as he spoke, though her face remained expressionless.

'She's not Italian – that's sort of the problem.' As Lorenzo uncorked another bottle, Zivoin told them about meeting Alegria in the supermarket and her strange behaviour, the speed with which she'd shut him down.

'She was probably shocked at your ugly face, brate,' Feki

said, grinning. He tapped his nose with two fingers. 'Took a look at that lump and screamed.'

'She didn't *scream*.'

'Ma, of course not,' Nico said seriously. He seemed to find the idea that a woman would dislike a prominent nose like his own deeply concerning. 'What did she do?'

'She basically told me to fuck off.'

'She actually said that?' Janice gasped, looking slightly impressed. They were all listening now.

'Uh... well, she said "goodnight", or something.'

'Oh.'

Zivoin could tell from her voice that Janice found his response dissatisfying. He leaned forward to make his point. 'But it was the *way* that she said it – she was angry. Like a snake.' Truthfully, she had been polite, and he had been the one asking her the same kinds of questions he probably would have bristled at too. Now that he thought more about it, maybe her defensiveness had been a natural, even expected, reaction.

'She sounds crazy,' Nico said matter-of-factly, flopping back in his chair and pushing his hair off his face. 'Lucky escape.'

'And you are sure she's not an Italian woman?' Lorenzo asked curiously. 'She sounds like one.'

Sandwiched between the two Italians, Marta frowned. 'Perhaps she just comes from another part of the country.'

'Or one of the border towns? Trieste, maybe?'

'No, that accent was definitely something different. It was unusual – when she spoke her voice sort of went up and down, like she was singing.'

This seemed to momentarily stump them. The conversation circled back to football, and Zivoin ended up being drawn into a heated debate with the men as Janice and Marta sipped their wine in silence. Occasionally, he caught a look between them, as if they were having a second, secret conversation. It seemed obvious that Marta probably wasn't going to spend much more time with Nico. She appeared bored, whilst he came across as totally indifferent to her, even though he'd admitted to Zivoin that he in fact liked her a great deal. He toyed with the idea of warning Nico, who still had some growing up to do. The blunder was so clear, he itched to meddle, to fix things for his clueless friend. But Zivoin was increasingly feeling that he could not be responsible for everyone's well-being. He picked up his half-empty wine glass, angling it away from the table to discourage anyone from filling it up, and suppressed a yawn.

'We're getting old,' he muttered in Serbo-Croat to Feki, the only person at the table his age. 'All I want to do is sleep.'

'Speak for yourself.'

But his friend looked at least a decade older than he was, his temples greying from stress. Zivoin noticed that his eyes were bloodshot. 'Everything OK?'

Feki shook his head and reached into the back pocket of his jeans. 'I'm returning this.' He handed Zivoin the borrowed paperback of *The Satanic Verses*.

'You finished it that quickly?' Zivoin asked, surprised. He took the book from Feki's outstretched hand. 'What did you think?'

'I couldn't – I didn't finish it.'

'Why?'

Again, Feki shook his head, like their conversation was a mistake. He'd forgotten that no one around him could understand them. 'I'm leaving. It's not safe here.'

Zivoin stared at him. 'Bar Norman? What—'

'I'm leaving England, brate. This shit in Iraq, *that* . . .' He gestured towards the book in his friend's grip. 'Some of the papers here are calling for all the Muslims in the country to be rounded up and sent back to the "Middle East". Can you imagine? Me, in Baghdad!' He forced out a laugh. 'You haven't noticed?'

'Čekaj, čekaj.' Zivoin shut his eyes momentarily, the words ricocheting around his head. 'You think that going back home is safer than staying here? Are you joking?'

'Are *you*?' Feki hissed, glancing at the group across the table from them. Zivoin could hear the frustration in his voice, like he couldn't believe he had to spell it out. 'I've been here for almost five years now. Every year it's worse. They call us mad mullahs, radicals, terrorists. I haven't even read the fucking book, man.' He sighed, staring down at the dark blue cover. 'I flipped through the first chapter. It's not bad, you know . . . it just doesn't matter. It's not real. I'm going home, inshallah. Mirjana and I are going to stay with her family in Bosnia. Her father's a mechanic, he'll give me work.' He drained his wine glass and set it back on the table, looking exhausted.

Zivoin didn't know what to say that would help. He fought back the urge to point out the damage Serbian nationalism had done to Yugoslavia's political climate. That home was more hostile than this place could ever be. He wanted to ask, 'But what about Kosovo? What about the killings?' But who was he to tell Feki where was safe, when he did not even recognise the poison his friend was running from?

'If you need anything,' he said, and held out his hand. They shook.

Feki nodded. With great effort, he smiled and asked, 'So. What are you going to do about this woman?'

'Nothing, probably.'

'But you like her.'

'I . . .' How to answer a question like that. He was a poet; the word 'like' wasn't enough. 'I'm captivated by her.'

Feki laughed, a real one this time. He clapped his friend's shoulder and said, 'Then you have to at least try again. You're an only son – only truly happy when a woman's taking care of you. Speak to her again.'

'No point.'

Feki switched back to English. 'At least find out where she's really from.'

'I bet it's Sicily,' Lorenzo interjected with a grin. He raised a glass as if toasting Zivoin. 'If she's Italian, marry her. One day, you'll be telling the children this story, and she'll be there, laughing at you.'

Though he began stopping by the Nisa regularly, Zivoin did not see her again that week. It took another four days before he walked in and spotted her fussing with the rack of newspapers by the till. Even though the store closed in ten minutes, Darco had insisted on meeting him there after work, keen to see Alegria in person. The last thing he wanted was his cousin watching him trying to flirt with a stranger, but he fought the instinct to turn and walk out. She met his eye and then looked away quickly, pretending to read the paper in her hand. Aside from a security guard, the store was deserted. Zivoin picked up a basket and moved through the aisles, forcing himself to go slowly. He had assumed he'd just know what to say to her, but now he'd seen her all he felt was panic. He lingered for a moment near the canned goods. Alegria had settled back into her chair and was now flicking through the pages of a book in such a conspicuous way, he was suddenly sure that she felt as uncomfortable as he did. That helped.

'Good evening,' he said. A little too loud, a little too formal. Alegria folded the corner of the page she was reading and slipped the book under the counter before Zivoin got a chance to see the cover. Goddammit. That could have been a conversation starter.

'How are you?' She sounded polite, even as she roughly pulled the basket towards her and began to unload it at speed. She wanted him out of there.

But he had to try, didn't he? There was a loud rattle of metal as the security guard pulled the entrance shutters down to hip height.

'I'm sorry if I upset you, last time,' Zivoin said quickly, trying to match her pace. He handed her a head of broccoli. 'I didn't mean to. I was just curious – immigrants like us tend to stick together.' The words sounded ludicrous and he regretted them as soon as they left his mouth. Around this woman he seemed to lose all his cool, all usual feelings of detachment.

Alegria's eyes flickered over him briefly. 'Who says I'm an immigrant?' She said it solemnly, but he could see the beginnings of a smile on her face.

'Just a guess – too fiery to be English. They're like extremely polite ghosts.'

At this, she burst into laughter, shaking her head as she scanned a packet of ham. 'Do you talk to all cashiers like this?'

'Only the ones that intimidate me.'

'I see.' To his relief, she began slowing down, and even leaned back in her chair a little. 'So . . . what is all of this? What are you cooking?' Alegria waved a delicate wrist over the slightly random assortment of vegetables. She looked genuinely interested now, watching him intently. There was no way he was going to admit that he'd picked up whatever was in front of him. 'Stew,' he said moronically. She was trying not to laugh, he could tell.

'Oh. It's a lot of stew for one person?' Alegria phrased it like a question as she scanned through the single carrot he'd bought. Was she trying to find out if he was single?

'It's for me and my cousin,' he said quickly, glancing back to where Darco waited by the exit, a huge grin on his face. He waved. They ignored him.

'That's nice.' Eyebrows raised, she held up a single courgette and said, 'This seems a little small. For the stew, I mean.' And then held his gaze for a second too long, her face impassive. And then she winked and moved on so swiftly, Zivoin had no idea how to respond. She gave him the powerful impression of a cat, playing with its food. And he kind of liked it.

Was it wishful thinking, or was she slowing down? Was she pausing to give him a way in? She was hard to read, so wide-eyed and blank-faced that he felt completely unsure of himself. The only way out was forward. He took a breath and tried to sound casual. 'I'm a good cook. I could make you dinner some time.'

Alegria took her time answering, waiting until everything was bagged up before she said, carefully, 'I'm not sure.'

'Coffee, then?' He hated how desperate the words sounded coming out of his mouth. Regardless of whether she said yes, he'd never felt more uncool. Darco was going to tear him to shreds.

'Maybe it's not the best idea . . .'

'OK,' Zivoin said quickly. 'That's OK.' He smiled at her like it meant nothing even though his face felt too hot, too big, too shiny. 'No problem.' He wondered how long it would take for her to forget he'd ever asked her out. He glanced around the shop as she rang up the total, fiddling intently with his watch, which felt too tight all of a sudden.

'Sorry.' Alegria handed him a receipt. 'It's not because I don't—'

'Don't worry about it.' She looked confused, upset even, but Zivoin was done trying to figure her out. All he wanted to do was get out of there. He couldn't believe he'd misinterpreted things so badly.

'It's just—'

'Have a good night!' Giving her a tight smile, he grabbed the brown bag of produce – just a little too roughly. It tore all the way down the edge and, to his horror, the courgette tumbled out onto the counter where it lay sad and limp between them. Too embarrassed to look at her, Zivoin forced himself to pick it up, then turned and walked away before she could say anything further.

CHAPTER 11

London, December 1990

Four days later

On the morning Alegria turned thirty, she woke up an hour before her alarm to a black sky. It wouldn't lighten for another hour and a half, and even then, the sunrise would be timid, slow, as if the sky itself was surprised at what was going on. Lying in the gloom, listening to the sound of the rain, she found herself feeling profoundly lonely. And she was still squirming over last week's interaction with that good-looking man from the supermarket – *why* had she done that? She'd been so obvious in her flirting, hoping that he'd ask her out. When he suggested dinner, it had thrilled her. She'd wanted it, she really had – and then she'd pulled back. That had been a mistake. Underneath her excitement was the truth, and its voice was loud: she wasn't going to be here long. What if she really liked him? What if she gave away too much of herself? What, she'd asked herself as he waited nervously for her to answer, would be the point of baking a cake she couldn't eat?

Next to her, Simone stirred and Alegria held her breath. She knew what her sister would say when – if – she told her.

There was no way Zivoin would ask her out again now, not after how embarrassed he'd been as he left. Making the most of her staff discount, she and Simone now shopped there often enough to bump into him, but he barely acknowledged them. It was foolish of her to be disappointed at this, but that was how she felt. She needed to get a grip.

Careful not to disturb her sister, Alegria sighed. She found the winter darkness melancholy. In Brazil, you blinked and there was the sun. When she had been very young, five or six at most, she had sometimes stepped out onto the inner patio of their old home – a large house, back when they had money – to look up at the night sky. As Uberlândia was still a small town then, masquerading as a city, the light pollution hadn't yet impacted the view. She would tilt her head back until her neck ached, her mouth open, and stare at the freckled sky, unable to tear her gaze away from its terrifying beauty. All those billions and billions of stars, the sheer vastness, made her feel small and very scared, as if she were being watched by something out there. To her, the pinpricks of light made it seem as if the entire world was wrapped in tin foil, and someone much bigger and more powerful than all of them had poked all these tiny holes in for everyone down on the ground to breathe. That was where the light was coming from, these things everybody else had mistaken for stars. And the real world – real life – was beyond, but she was the only one who knew. The problem was: no one would believe her if she tried to explain it. That realisation was a sudden and lonely one. It had frightened her and made her dizzy, torn between wanting to run inside or stay out there, staring at fragments of this other life.

Even thinking about it now made her uneasy. Alegria squeezed her eyes shut and tried to go back to sleep, but it was impossible. Once again, she felt deeply alone. Yet she wasn't unhappy. How could both of those feelings sit together at the same time? She couldn't go down that rabbit hole. Simone lay beside her, facing away. Her breath was quiet and even; Alegria knew exactly when the next slow inhale was coming. As she listened, she felt paralysed with love for her sister. She would do anything, take any risk, if it meant Si would be all right. She wished she could channel that bravery towards her own life.

The air was stale, but Alegria didn't want to risk disturbing anyone by opening a window. She lay there with her eyes shut, trying to focus on the weight of her body on the mattress, until Simone whispered, 'Are you awake, irmã?'

'I am.' The bed moved as her sister turned to face her.

'The end of your twenties,' she said solemnly. 'Happy birthday.'

For some reason, this made tears well up behind Alegria's eyelids. Again, it was that strange blend of happiness and sorrow that she didn't understand. It scared her a little. She opened her eyes and looked at Simone, saw her confusion mirrored back at her, and laughed. 'I'm a mess!'

'You're not a mess.' Simone reached for her hand under the covers. 'Old age can make people emotional.'

'I'll remember that for when you're my age, you little cow.'

'Eh, you'll be thirty-six – I'll be young by comparison.' Simone squealed as her sister poked her in the stomach, then shuffled closer, her warm body pressing up against Alegria's.

'I need to tell you something.' She paused, and from the next room Ricardo gave a loud snore. 'I'm not staying in London. I've decided.'

'Oh.' Alegria tried to keep her voice neutral, sensing more news was to come. She seemed nervous. 'You made the decision just now?'

'Last night.' Simone took a deep breath. 'I'm coming home with you. Same flight, if I can.'

'*Oh.*' This time she failed to keep the surprise out of her voice. 'So you and Ricardo . . .'

'He doesn't know it's over yet.' As she spoke, Simone's voice cracked. She gave a sudden gasp and her eyes filled with tears. 'It's over, Ale, it's really over. I don't know how I'm going to tell him.'

Wrapping an arm around her, Alegria kissed her head, and the sisters lay quiet for a while as the room gradually got lighter and lighter, a pinkish hue filtering through the window and reflecting off the full-length mirror opposite. 'You don't need to tell him yet,' Alegria said finally, her voice soft. 'Tell him before you go. A few weeks before.'

Simone pulled away from her then, looking shocked. She propped herself up on her elbow and stared at her. 'Isn't that cruel? I couldn't – I would be lying to him.'

'I'm not sure it's cruel. He loves you, and you already know it's going to end. Why not make these last few months here beautiful, instead of being sad and apart?'

'That's not a good enough reason.'

'Is it not? Do you think he would come with you if you told him you were going?'

Simone sighed, rolling her eyes up to the ceiling. 'Já sei, definitely not. We've talked about it.'

'Então. You going home would be a natural end to the relationship. You might as well enjoy the time you have left together.'

'Ai, I can't believe it.' As Si spoke, she wiped her face with the duvet. 'I still love Ricardo, but I want to be alone for a while. I'm too young for this sort of life, living glued to someone's side. I want to go home and eat fresh fruit every day, wake up to the smell of Mãe's cooking. I miss going to people's houses and spending the whole day there. I miss the *sun*. I miss the sun so badly, irmã, it's like the corners of my soul have grown dark.' She sighed again and buried her face into her pillow, exhaling loudly. 'I don't think I love him enough to stay here.'

Alegria's alarm went off, and though it was on Simone's side of the bed, her sister did not move, and neither did she. The clock beeped and beeped, and they simply lay there until they heard Ricardo shouting in protest from the sofa, followed immediately by Priscilla's furious thumping from upstairs. Without lifting her face from the bed, Simone fumbled around and finally yanked the cord out of the wall. The silence was exposing. Alegria felt as if Ricardo was standing on the other side of the door, holding his breath and waiting for them to speak. Finally, Si lifted her head and whispered, 'I won't tell him yet.'

Alegria nodded, and reached out to wipe the traces of tears off her sister's cheeks. 'Just make sure you give him time to find somewhere else to rent.' And they did not speak about it again.

*

Back home, Alegria would have gone to a boteco with her friends – one of the ones still untouched by gentrification, with a tiny menu, filthy bathroom and live music that spilled out onto the street. They would have danced all night. But today, everyone was working. Everyone she knew needed money too much to take the day off. Alegria's double shift finished at nine, and she had been reluctantly convinced to meet Simone, Ricardo and a few mutual friends afterwards for a celebratory drink. She could have easily gone home, tired and broke as she felt, but when Alegria glanced out of the Nisa window at the end of the day and saw the newly white-dotted ground, she was elated. Snow, on her birthday! It had to be a good omen.

Though the air outside was so raw from the cold it hurt her throat, Alegria was too excited to wait indoors. She huddled under the protective entryway of a nearby office building, bouncing up and down to stay warm. The flakes fell weakly, and it soon became clear that it wasn't cold enough for them to settle the way she hoped. But snow was snow, and it was romantic, even if the flakes on the ground were rapidly turning to sludge. She observed people walking past, interested in their reactions. Some – most – were blank and detached. Either they hadn't noticed or this was as normal to them as the tiny geckos running across the living-room floor back home. But others were stopping, holding their hands out to catch the crystals and witness their passage from solid to liquid. A child across the road lagged behind his father, a huge grin on his face as he stuck out his tongue to eat the falling flakes. She had only ever seen people do this in films. London was, in fact, beautiful, she thought. She could find happiness whilst she was here. This was a place where, along a single street, she could find ten restaurants from ten different countries, and the bus was always filled with unfamiliar languages. Where the entire world lived just beyond her doorstep, in areas with names like 'Shoreditch' and 'Camden' and 'Chinatown', their streets filled with people spilling out of bars, theatres, galleries and restaurants late into the night, without fear. Where people stopped to catch snow in their hands. And the city had reached out and absorbed her: she was part of it too.

The moment felt weighty and important, and she was still enjoying her newfound sense of awe when Simone and Maria joined her. Maria was a child psychologist who, like Alegria, had found it harder and harder to make ends meet back home. Her parents had once worked with Toninho – the three of them had known each other since they were children. Alegria had been surprised when she'd first arrived by how often she came across Brazilians she knew from back home. Everyone and their cousin, it seemed, was trying to work their way out of economic stagnation. She hugged Maria affectionately and kissed her sister's cheek. 'Is this everyone?'

'We need to wait for Ricardo,' Simone said, burrowing into her coat apprehensively. 'But let's just go now instead of staying outside?'

'We can't – Pedro's coming too. I told him we'd meet here.' Maria lit a cigarette and offered one each to the sisters. Both shook their heads.

'Pai uses that same lighter,' Alegria said, nodding at the yellow plastic with a smile. 'He always says it's proof that expensive doesn't always mean better.' The lighters never cost more than twenty cents, and were sold in the green, blue and yellow shades of the Brazilian flag.

Maria handed it to her, nodding as she exhaled. 'Keep it – your birthday gift! I brought so many with me – that's the thing about being in a foreign place, isn't it? Things from home become almost sacred, even when they're cheap.'

'Terrible gift,' Si said teasingly. But she reached out to examine the lighter anyway, and handed it back to Alegria with great care.

'Better than what you got me.'

'What did she get you?'

'Nothing!'

They laughed as Si shook her head. She was distracted, gazing intently at a man far across the road from them, standing underneath the red and blue Underground sign of Bayswater station. 'Irmã, when I find a gift worthy of my brilliant sister, you'll be the first to know.'

They stood shivering under the office portico as the snowfall gradually stopped. The wind began to pick up. 'Can't we just meet your boyfriend at the bar?' Alegria asked Maria, as her teeth began to chatter. She was getting sick of watching her own breath.

'He doesn't know where we're going,' Maria said fretfully, craning her neck as she peered down the street. 'I told him not to be late – Si, what are you looking at?'

'I'm observing this city at its best,' Simone said, pointing at the man across the road. If Alegria hadn't been so cold – if she had been paying attention – she might have caught the dangerous smile playing on her sister's face. 'Look at that bird directly above his poor head. Perfect positioning.' They stared at the man. Busy smoking a cigarette, his face was obscured by a turned-up collar.

'I don't understand.'

'She's messing with us, Maria.'

But they went along with whatever Simone was doing. She pulled Maria and Alegria closer to her, looking like she was struggling to hold in a laugh. 'We might witness something magical,' she whispered dramatically, still strangely fixated on the stranger. The pigeon was perched precariously above him, its head tucked into flecked, black-grey wings.

'Do you think she's going to take a shit?' Alegria asked, almost reverently. She kept her voice low, even though there was no way they could be heard from where they stood.

'It's bad luck,' Maria said immediately. 'Don't sound so hopeful.'

'It's *good* luck.'

'That's just what they say to make you feel better about having merda in your hair. If you wish it on him, it's gonna happen to you.'

'You're right!' Simone exclaimed, as though the thought had just occurred to her. She turned to them with sudden urgency. 'Ale – don't you think that man looks familiar?'

'Er . . .' Alegria squinted, but the distance was too great for her to tell. 'You know I can't see that far without my glasses. Is it Pedro?'

'I wish – he's not that tall,' Maria muttered, frowning. 'I can't recognise him.'

'We should warn him – we wouldn't want that ridiculous navy coat to get ruined.' And before anyone could stop her, she started waving both her hands in the air. 'HEY!' Simone shouted. 'Hey! Come here! It's an EMERGENCY!'

'Simone!' Alegria grabbed at her arms, alarm coursing through her. 'Shut *up*.' She had just realised who was now walking towards them, and was mortified. 'What the fuck are you doing?'

'I'm giving you your birthday present.' Simone dropped her arms and was struggling to hide her grin. 'Irmã, just try him out. One night of good sex – and you don't have to see him again.'

'Si, I'm going to *kill* you,' Alegria snarled, doing her best to look as composed as possible as she tried to drag her sister away. In a few seconds, Zivoin would reach them. She could already see the confusion on his face – he was slowing down now, as though reconsidering getting any closer. And he looked different, she suddenly thought. Under the unforgiving lights of the supermarket, he'd mostly come across as tired, a little dishevelled. But out here, Zivoin was commanding. He was freshly shaved, which emphasised his sharp jawline, and he'd cut his hair too. It made his ears stick out a little goofily. Had he always been this good-looking?

'Ai.' Maria was wide-eyed. 'He's the guy you turned down? You never said he looked like *that*.'

'Shh,' Alegria hissed. Briefly, she considered running back into the supermarket, but abandoned the idea almost immediately – that would be the only move more pathetic than staying here, frozen and silent.

Simone beckoned him closer. 'Hello! I thought it was you!'

'Hello,' Zivoin said cautiously. He looked from Alegria's

flushed cheeks to her sister's wide smile, his own face carefully blank. 'Something wrong?'

'No—' Alegria started, but Simone cut her off. She kept a tight grip on Alegria's arm, her fingers digging in warningly.

'Thank you *so* much for coming to help us. We have a serious problem. You know Alegria, right?' Grinning maniacally, Si finally let go and pushed her towards Zivoin.

Alegria stumbled forward and forced her numb lips into what she hoped was an attractive smile. He nodded at her politely but coldly, and she felt as if she was going to be sick. The whole thing was so bizarre, she would have laughed if she weren't so mortified. No one spoke. Alegria looked at Maria – who was staring at Zivoin open-mouthed – for help, and then back at him. 'I'm so sorry,' was all she could manage. 'She's not normal.'

'It's her birthday today,' Simone continued loudly over her, 'and we don't know where to celebrate. Maybe you could show us a place?'

'Ave Maria.' Alegria buried her face in her hands. It was catastrophic – what if he thought she'd engineered this somehow? She heard her sister pointedly inform the group that they needed more cigarettes, and Maria's protests as she was shepherded into the supermarket. There was nothing she could do except get through the painfully awkward conversation unfolding in front of her. Alegria took a deep breath. 'Hi,' she squeaked, feeling her curls trembling around her. 'That was my sister. Sorry.'

Zivoin – she couldn't believe that he was still standing there – laughed in a bewildered sort of way and said, 'I've seen you both together.'

'She's much younger than me.'
'You look similar.'
'We're very different.'
'I can see that,' he said coolly. 'Happy birthday, by the way.' He looked so calm and unbothered, standing there in a cream wool jumper and brown corduroy trousers – she liked the way he dressed, even if the military look was a little eccentric. She twisted her hands, trying to figure out what to say next, but he got there first. 'I'm busy tonight, so I can't celebrate with you. And your sister.'

'Oh.' A fresh wave of embarrassment hit her – how desperate he must think she was, inviting him out on the night of her birthday. 'No – of course.' She couldn't bring herself to explain. Standing in front of him, Alegria found herself fed up with her timidity. An adult woman with so little self-possession that she had to rely on her younger sister to propel her forward. She said quickly, 'Look, Simone just called you over because she wanted us to have a conversation. We have plans already.' She winced – it sounded like a lie – but ploughed on. 'Anyway, I owe you an apology.'

'An apology?' Now she had his full attention. 'What for?'

'For the . . .' Alegria waved her hand vaguely in the direction of the Nisa, 'the way I reacted when you asked where I'm from. It's complicated . . .' In a low voice, she tried to explain, but was so flustered and unsure of where to start she found herself going further and further backwards until she was almost shouting at him about teaching salaries in Brazil. Her feet had now grown so numb she had to do a stiff little march on the spot. Nevertheless, as she spoke, Zivoin seemed to relax, listening to her with a concerned look on his face.

'And like I said . . . I've been deported because of my situation, and I've already lost one job, I can't lose another. And that's . . . that's the story,' she finished, feebly.

'I'm sorry to hear that,' he said, and she could tell he meant it.

But still he did not smile, did not open up to her the way she realised she'd been hoping for. She could tell he was about to make an excuse to end the conversation – and of course he was, when all she was doing was dumping her baggage on him. Alegria found that she did not want him to stop looking at her. She pressed on. 'I mean, it was scary when you could tell I was lying – I thought I was about to get fired.'

As confusing as the explanation was, she thought it had at least softened him a little – it was hard to tell through the coat. 'We're in the same boat,' he said.

'What, you're also pretending to be Italian?'

It was a feeble joke, but he laughed politely anyway. 'I mean, I also need my job. This is not an easy place to live.'

'Amen,' she said, and he nodded, looking down at his shoes and shifting his weight back and forth. Alegria wished that things hadn't become so complicated between them. 'I'm sorry,' she said again, in a sudden rush, 'I'm not a perfect person. But I promise you, I'm not crazy, and I'm nice – and, and I'll prove it to you.'

'You don't have to do that,' Zivoin said kindly.

He seemed moved by her words, and when he smiled at her, it felt sincere. Alegria could see he'd let it go. But that was it. He would walk into the Nisa tomorrow and be perfectly nice to her, but he wasn't going to ask her out again. She'd taken her axe and hacked away at that bridge, and suddenly it felt very important that she find some other way to get him back on her side. She wanted to make him laugh – properly, not out of courtesy. She wanted him to look at her with the same intensity as the first time they met.

'Would you like to come for a coffee with me?'

'Coffee?' Zivoin repeated, and she nodded, pushing her hands into her pockets so he couldn't see her fingers nervously clenching and unclenching.

'Or dinner. I'm a good cook.'

He laughed, but shook his head. 'I don't need you to keep apologising, don't worry.'

'That's not why I'm asking. Sorry – I should have just said yes the first time you asked me out. Sorry.' The idea of him rejecting her made Alegria want to melt into the pavement, but she forced herself to stand still and wait.

He looked surprised. Surprised, but pleased. 'When?'

'Tomorrow? I can meet you back here at seven?'

Zivoin smiled at her, a genuine, soft smile that opened up his face. 'I know exactly where we can go,' he said, and gave her a nod. 'See you soon.'

She watched him walk away and felt flushed with pleasure and anticipation. This was braver than anything she'd done since leaving home. A round of applause broke out. Alegria turned to see Simone and Maria huddled by the automatic doors, whooping and cheering her on. Si ran towards her, shrieking so loudly that Alegria just knew Zivoin would hear. But it didn't matter. She found that she could not stop laughing.

CHAPTER 12

London, December 1990

One day later

She had asked *him* out! In the strangest way possible, yes, but Zivoin had found Alegria's panic yesterday charming. It had diffused all the confusion between them, until all that was left was a slow, pleasant build of excitement as he waited for the evening to roll around. He was halfway to the supermarket before he realised that he'd chosen the same clothes he'd been wearing the night before for Feki's leaving dinner. There was no time to change – he hoped she wouldn't notice.

Zivoin arrived outside Nisa at seven exactly, bouncing with nerves. He was certain that if tonight didn't go well, there was no chance that whatever fledging feelings that existed between them would recover. He tried to figure out what to do with his hands – whether he should keep them in his pockets – and considered lighting a cigarette. His main worry was the language barrier. Already, they sometimes struggled to communicate, and he wasn't nearly as smooth or as confident in English. He'd never dated in another language before. He'd never dated anyone like her before.

Zivoin felt himself relax when Alegria arrived a few

minutes later, looking incredible in knee-high boots and a miniskirt that showed off her legs. She was clutching her huge jacket in her arms.

'Oh, thank God!' Alegria said, when she spotted him. Before Zivoin could say or do anything, she handed him her little leather bag and pulled on the jacket, zipping it all the way up to cover her mouth and nose. She gave a full-body shiver. 'I wanted you to see what I looked like first. This thing hides my best features.'

'Your best . . . features?' He stopped himself from asking her which ones she meant, not wanting to come across as crude.

'My smile,' she said, and pulled her collar down to flash him a grin. 'Why, what were you thinking?'

Zivoin was careful not to look anywhere except her face as he answered, 'Your customer-service skills.' He was profoundly grateful that none of his friends were around to hear him. It wasn't funny – it didn't even make sense – but he was lucky. She appeared to find it hilarious, and her laugh was loud and uninhibited, the kind that made him laugh too; he couldn't help it. She seemed so different from the polite, uptight version of herself she presented at work. He felt a flutter of nerves in his stomach – he already liked this woman. A lot.

'So, what are we doing?' Alegria asked as they fell into step. They were a little clumsy with each other, smiling too much, laughing too loudly – and she was nervous too. She hated uncomfortable silences – so much so that she had a bank of questions in her head ready to deploy if they struggled for something to say.

'It's a surprise.' He was leading her to Bayswater station. 'How do you like London?' he asked.

She considered saying something bland about how pretty it was, or something about the snow, or the cold, or the rain. But what came out instead was, 'I saw a crushed mouse a few days ago. I was walking from the bus stop near my home, past a huge building with pillars and white walls, big windows – I think people live there – and I looked down and saw it. It was so tiny – the head had separated from the body, and most of it was smeared into the pavement. But the head, the head was stuck to the . . . to the . . .' She pointed to the grey kerb, not knowing the right word for it. 'That thing. Like someone had stepped on it and then wiped it off there, assim.' She mimed scraping something off her shoe, and then, slightly perplexed by the disgusting image she'd just created, said, 'Anyway. That's London – beautiful homes for beautiful, rich people, but outside their doorstep there is a dead mouse. Most of the time I think I like it here, but I'm never sure.'

Zivoin was nodding. 'I see dead pigeons all the time – not even their bodies, just a wing, sometimes. I've never seen a city with so many dead animals.'

'Why is that? Are all cities like that?'

'I come from a small town. A village, actually. So I wouldn't know.'

'Me too!'

They caught the Circle line, talking about where they'd both grown up. Brazil sounded unbelievable to Zivoin. Alegria talked about it as if it was a work of art, describing colours and smells and sounds so vividly that it filled him with curiosity. He couldn't think of anywhere more different to home, and when he told her that, she asked question after question about Yugoslavia, leaning forward to grasp every word. Gradually, the awkwardness between them dissolved. Looking each other in the eye was getting easier.

They exited the tube near Westminster Abbey, and she pointed to the illuminated face of Big Ben against the navy sky. 'There are three hundred and thirty-four steps to the top, where the bell is. I went on a tour inside with my sister – you can walk behind the clock!' Alegria stopped suddenly, looking worried. 'Is that what we're doing?' she asked. 'Have I ruined it?'

'Definitely not,' Zivoin told her, trying not to sound smug. 'But if you like that sort of thing, you'll like this.' He checked his watch, then led her to a queue that had formed by Westminster Pier. 'We'll be boarding in five.'

'Boarding? We're going on a boat?' Her eyes widened and she looked excited – adorably so.

'Do you like it?'

'I've always wanted to do one of these!'

Alegria gave him a smile that transformed her face, her cheeks pushing her eyes up into little crescent moons. It was so joyful and genuine that he felt a sudden pang of alarm, as though his body had only just realised he was on a date with the woman he had been thinking about endlessly since he'd first laid eyes on her. What if he fucked it up?

'Did you just think of this today? Or is this where you take all the girls you date?'

Zivoin laughed at this. It had been so long since he'd fielded that kind of question. 'I haven't dated anyone in a while. But I've been wanting to take you here since the moment I saw you.'

'Now I know you're lying,' Alegria said. She was gazing out at the black water lapping at the sides of their riverboat.

But she was wrong. Zivoin had known this is where he would take her from the moment he'd resolved to ask her out. After convincing Lorenzo to cover for him earlier, he'd gone straight to the pier to get the tickets and reserve the table at the very front, with the best view. What was more romantic than a cruise down the Thames at night, when the water reflected the city lights? First dates had to be memorable, after all. It was obvious from the way she was looking at him that he'd hit the nail on the head, and something within him eased.

'It's true,' he said, resisting the urge to pull her towards him. 'I only date women I want to spend the rest of my life with.' As soon as the words left his mouth, he wished he could take them back. He was a poet, but she didn't know that just yet, and it was too much – it was an insane thing to say to her.

Alegria stopped peering over the side and said: 'I think that's beautiful.'

After a moment, she slipped her hand into his, and Zivoin had to fight the huge grin spreading across his face. He felt a surge of adrenaline and hoped his hands wouldn't get clammy. It was too soon to kiss her, of course it was. But now he was sure he could, when the right moment came.

As they were shown to their table, she spoke over the sound of the radio blaring through the speakers above their heads. 'I don't want to tell you this, but I'm leaving in February.'

'Oh,' he said. 'Well, that's months away.'

'But—' Alegria could see that he didn't understand what she was trying to explain. She'd spent the day obsessing over whether she should introduce this definitive end point to whatever was happening between them right away. Si had told her to stop overthinking – but she couldn't help it. 'Once I leave, that's it.'

'What do you mean?'

'I told you yesterday about the first time I entered the country, right?' She took a deep breath, pushing past residual shame. 'When they sent me to Amsterdam, they told me that I faced a ten-year ban.'

'But you're here now,' he said, as if it were that simple.

'Once I go, I'm not coming back.' Alegria found it hard to look directly at him as she spoke. He made her feel too much, too fast. His gaze felt like pressing a lighter to her skin and she feigned interest in the view to get away from it.

She should have kept things light. The tour had started. In the speakers above them, Vanilla Ice's confusing tempo was replaced by the pitchy voice of a man standing a metre away from them, wearing a captain's hat. He was speaking into a microphone as the boat set off on its journey down the Thames. They both ignored him.

'We shouldn't waste any time, then,' Zivoin said suddenly. He got to his feet. 'The bar has opened.'

He joined a growing queue at the other end of the boat whilst Alegria sat there uncertainly. She was thinking about the time she'd gone to her cousin's farm when she was fourteen or so, and had waded a little too far out into their pond. She'd emerged with a leech suckered onto her leg. It hadn't hurt when it bit her – she'd only realised when she'd felt its slimy body writhing against her calf. 'It's best to let it fall naturally or the teeth can get stuck in you and get infected,' Toninho said when she'd run onto the porch to show him, dry heaving in disgust. 'After about twenty minutes it should let go.' But Alegria couldn't wait twenty minutes. She was a teenage girl with a fear of bugs, and now one was stuck to her body, slowly feeding off her – it was too much. So they had burned it off with a lighter, and as predicted, some of the leech's teeth had stayed in her skin, giving her a fever and a permanent scar that looked like a cigarette burn. Maybe she should just wait to see what would happen now, instead of rushing through it and trying to burn herself free.

Zivoin came back with two tumblers of red wine and Alegria tried to nudge the conversation elsewhere.

'What do you think of this place?' she asked abruptly, gesturing vaguely at the shore. 'This city?'

'You go first.'

'It's . . .' She hesitated. 'It's good, I think. I'm not always sure.'

'What do you mean?'

'I have seen so little of it, you know?' Alegria turned away from the oily water and rested her back against the seat. Her nose was scrunched into a frown. 'I've seen so little. I think this is maybe the fifth time I have gone out . . . between work and school, and work. Sometimes, for extra money Si and I step in to do cleaning jobs, if our friend needs more people. So, I barely know this place. London is so special, but it's like I'm always looking at it through glass. This city is for people with money.'

'And time,' he said, and she nodded quickly, relieved that he could understand. 'I know what you mean.'

'Because everything I earn here in one month, it's what I would earn in two, even three months in Brazil. But then it's so expensive here too.'

'Sometimes when I leave the house, I feel like I'm suffocating from the effort of trying not to spend any money.'

'Exactly! It's exhausting. Yes.' She flicked her eyes to his, and asked, 'And you?'

Zivoin had thought he had an answer ready. Yet when it came to it, he hesitated just as she had. 'It's different,' he said after a moment. And then, 'It's beautiful and it's ugly, like most cities, but at least here I'm free.' It wasn't quite the right word, but he did not know how to say 'unburdened'. 'It feels good sometimes to just worry about myself, instead of my whole family,' he said finally. He'd never said that out loud before, and cringed as the words left his mouth. 'Sorry. I—'

'Don't be,' she interrupted, eager to put him at ease. 'I know what you mean. No one needs you here apart from you. It *is* freeing.'

'Yes.' Zivoin could feel the weight of what he wanted to tell her in his throat, pushing against his Adam's apple. He wanted to tell her how being here had solidified his sense of who he was, where he came from. Yugoslavia had become so much more than a country – it was part of his soul, part of the fabric knitting him together. What a glorious feeling it was, but a lonely one too. Back home, everyone seemed to be going in the opposite direction. Montenegrin, Bosnian, Croatian – people were desperate to be anything except Yugoslavian. All this heaviness required a command of English that he simply did not have. No class Zivoin had ever attended had taught him how to talk about grief. Aware of his date staring at him expectantly, he shrugged helplessly and shook his head. 'Very freeing.'

'It's complicated,' Alegria said gently. 'I know.' She tried to subtly inch her hand forward, hoping he would take it. Her hands were always cold. She wanted him to reach out and envelop her, but she was too shy to ask. After all, *she'd* asked *him* out, *she'd* taken *his* hand out there on the docks. Wasn't it his turn?

The tour guide rattled off facts about the landmarks they were passing – Shakespeare's Globe, HMS *Belfast* – none of which meant much to them in that moment. Later, Alegria would look back at their two-hour boat ride and call it the best date of her life, but she would not remember the colour of the boat, the gleam of rain on the windows, or the scenic view. All she would recall was the need to be close to Zivoin, the desire to drink up every word he said. She told him things she hadn't spoken about to anyone, even her closest friends back home. The relentless, stomach-twisting pressure to support her family, like a drill in her ear. The constant fear of losing her home.

Zivoin said, 'Sometimes I'm just walking along the street, or sitting somewhere, and I get this horrible feeling that everything could crumble at any moment, if I let my guard down. And I have to flick through all the bills that need to be paid, all the money coming in and going out, before I can relax again.'

Alegria hit the table with her hand a little too hard and said, '*Yes!* Yes! That's it!'

They bought more drinks and slipped into wine-soaked euphoria. When he talked about the ways people pretended they couldn't understand him, she nodded and said, 'The worst is when they talk to you slowly, loudly, like they think you're a fucking idiot.' He loved, *loved* the way she said 'fucking', the way her lips curled around the 'f' and how she then threw the word away from her. She inched closer until Zivoin finally took her hand and looked at her perfect, freckled face with her slightly large front teeth and the little smudge of red lipstick on her chin. He considered reaching out to wipe it off gently, a perfect excuse to touch more of her. He asked her to say something – anything – in Portuguese, and she obliged, the mesmerising words tumbling from her lips like a stream trickling over rocks.

'What does it mean?'

'It means, darling, for the love of God, don't ask me that again.' And they both dissolved into laughter. He would have watched only her mouth when she spoke, if her eyes weren't so tender, reflecting the lights strung up above their heads. She reached into her bag, saying, 'I still feel bad about what happened,' and pulled out childhood snacks she had brought from Brazil: first, small yellow rectangles called Paçoquinha – paste-like candies the size of a baby's fist, made out of ground peanuts and sugar. Then something she referred to as mini mel, tiny sachets of honey strung together like golden pearls.

'What are you supposed to do with these?' he asked, confused.

'You just pull one off the string and bite into it like this.' Alegria demonstrated, showing him how to suck the honey out of the plastic sachet. 'I always carry some of these with me,' she said, as though that was a completely normal thing to do.

'Why?'

'In case I need something sweet!'

Zivoin found the whole thing both weird and deeply alluring, and they ate the snacks together between a third, then a fourth glass of wine. They were way too sweet for his taste, but nothing in the world would have compelled him to tell her that, not when he could sense her longing for her home country pouring out of her like sweat. He liked that she seemed genuinely curious about Yugoslavia and that she could recognise his hurt. Her empathy was a balm. At some point, she had moved to sit next to him, rather than across from him, and her fingers delicately stroked the inside of his wrist in little figures of eight. It made him shiver, distracting him to the point where he had to keep asking her to repeat herself.

Alegria's cheeks were flushed, a little tipsy, and as the boat started to make its way back, she said, looking crestfallen, 'I can't believe two hours have passed, just like that. I don't want this date to end.'

'I'm starving,' he said. 'We could get something to eat?' And then, just to make sure she wouldn't get the wrong impression, Zivoin added, 'I'll walk you back home. And take a taxi back to mine.' And she agreed, tremors of excitement – from the wine, from the thrill of it all – setting her cheeks ablaze.

'It's so hot in here,' Alegria declared. 'Shall we go outside?'

It was much quieter, much colder, out there on the deck. They no longer had to shout over the soft jazz or drunken conversations of other, more boring couples. Zivoin pulled a cigarette from his pocket and turned to offer one to Alegria, but paused at the look on her face. 'Not a smoker?'

'I don't like the taste,' she said, and he wondered if that meant she wanted him to kiss her. He had been thinking about it all evening. But he couldn't kiss her whilst holding a cigarette – it had to be better than that. He did not smoke. They leaned over the guardrail, made jokes about falling in, brushing up against each other the way people do when they're trying to figure out when to touch, and how.

A while later, he found himself talking about Darco. 'I brought him with me just after he turned eighteen, before military service. I wanted to protect him – he's not like me. He's just a baby. And I think he doesn't really understand how tense it is right now. I keep telling him that Yugoslavia is covered in petrol, and *everyone* is holding a match. But I don't know if he believes me . . . Sometimes I don't believe it either. Maybe the idea of a civil war is just too strange for him.' He cleared his throat, aware still that he might be coming across too strong. 'Sorry – he's just important to me.'

'Don't be sorry. I like how you talk about your family,' Alegria said. She was so close now, he could count each of her eyelashes if he wanted to. He found that he did want to. 'My family is everything to me. The best thing in my life is when everyone I love is in one room together. We talk, we laugh, we eat, we dance. We marinate in joy. That's who I am. I know it's simple – not exciting, not sexy.'

'It is to me,' Zivoin murmured. He looked down at her

and this time he was sure that she was waiting for him to do it. He didn't want to rush, he didn't want to scare her, but it was hard to make himself go gently when all he really wanted was to be as close to her as possible. In the end, this is what happened: Zivoin took the glass of wine from her, and placed it on the decking. Alegria went still, watching him, waiting. There were people around them and normally Zivoin would have been self-conscious, but not this time. He took her in his arms and felt the warmth of her there, and he liked it. And then he cupped her face with his hands, and she gripped the collar of his coat, and *she* pulled *him* in and it felt incredible to be wanted like that by someone as electric as she was. He kissed her softly, lightly at first, her eyelashes fluttering against his cheek. And then, because she tugged him even tighter towards her, as if to say *More! Now!*, he kissed her with a ferocity that surprised him, and she kissed him back just as hard. All of this to say, the first time they kissed, it was visceral, intuitive, delicious. After some time, their mouths dry from the wine, they pulled apart. She gingerly wiped red lipstick off his lips, holding his gaze, and then they embraced, standing there in glorious, heart-thumping silence.

How does it happen so quickly? How does a stranger move from the periphery to the centre so fast there is no time to prepare any cushioning in case things break along the way? It doesn't make sense – but then, a lot of things in life don't make sense, even after they've been explained. Fax machines. Vinyl. Whatever goes on inside a caterpillar's cocoon. The fact that the stars we see in the sky are mostly gone, their dying light crawling its way towards us from the future. The length of time it takes to fall in love. None of these things should operate the way they do, but they do. And, yes, there were steps that were supposed to happen. Conversations about Thatcher, about life's biggest fears, about what kind of holidays are best and what a typical Sunday looks like. There were meant to be family introductions, first arguments, sweaty nights in bed, questions about the future, yes, all of that. But the thing is, sometimes all it takes is a few hours. That's just the way it goes.

Everyone looks for similarities when choosing a partner, and sure, those matter. But at the end of the day, what could be more romantic than sinking deep into the strangeness of another person, all guns blazing? She uses bookmarks and can never keep track of her glasses. He folds down the corner of the page he's on, and never loses a thing. Her favourite colour is yellow, he doesn't understand how anyone gets attached to one colour more than another, but fine, if he had to choose, it would be brown. She likes to sleep with the blankets over her head, a small hole, like a tunnel, for air. He likes to sleep with the windows open. He can drink all the coffee he wants; if she doesn't stop at two, she bounces off the walls. He smokes and she hates the taste of cigarettes. She gathers up all the information she possibly can before she makes a decision, he follows his gut. She can get up early without any trouble, he struggles to fall asleep. His head hurts when he's exhausted, hers only hurts if she's dehydrated. She cries all the time and forgets about it afterwards, but that does not mean the tears weren't important. He never cries, and cannot be pushed to, but that does not mean he doesn't know the immensity of sorrow. All these little parts of a soul that yearns to be attended to. They have so much to learn and not all of it will be easy, but it is intoxicating nevertheless.

None of this is known to them yet.

CHAPTER 13

London, December 1990

Two weeks later

'. . . so I might be staying for longer, if things go well.' Zivoin said down the line. He could feel his mother's breathing getting more agitated as he spoke, but she said nothing. He fingered the phone card in his hand, making a tiny rip in the corner. It was almost out of credit anyway.

'Remind me where she's from?' Milenka asked eventually.

'I've told you that three times,' he said evenly. 'You know where she's from.'

He could picture them now in the narrow, dark hallway, his mother clutching the receiver, Drago standing silently beside her. This had been a loud fear of hers, that he would fall in love with some strange Englishwoman and decide that he wasn't coming back home after all. But this was possibly worse. At least England was somewhat of a known entity – but Brazil? The little Milenka knew about a place like that came from grainy television footage of half-naked women parading through the streets of Rio wearing feathers on their heads. She couldn't envision anything beyond bare skin. 'Paul McCartney played a concert there this year,' she told him, because she wasn't sure what else she could say.

'Did he?' Zivoin was amused. 'I didn't know you were a fan.'

'He's no Ljubomir Đurović or Safet Isović, but I saw it on the news because it broke records – largest paying audience in history.'

'I see.' He glanced at his watch. 'I've only got a few minutes of credit left.'

'What does she look like?' Milenka asked cautiously. She meant: how dark is her skin? But he pretended not to know that.

'She looks like a normal woman,' Zivoin replied, a note of warning in his voice. 'She's beautiful, and wonderful.' Neither of them said anything. He gritted his teeth and continued. 'Just wait until you meet her – you'll love her, I promise.'

'You're planning on bringing her here? With all this talk in Belgrade about secession? And all the tension in Croatia? You know a few Serbian paramilitaries have started blockading some of the streets over there?' Drago said, taking the phone from his wife. He sounded incredulous, and Zivoin had to fight to keep his temper in check. Did his father really think him that ignorant?

'None of that is happening in Montenegro. It's safe.' He heard the sharp intake of breath and braced himself for what was coming next. He knew what his father would say. It wasn't as if Montenegro was staying out of the power struggle. If push came to shove, everyone knew it would follow in Serbia's footsteps.

But all Drago said was, 'Does she even want to come?'

'Of course she does!' Although as Zivoin said this, he realised he'd never actually asked her. He could do that tonight.

'She wants to . . . live here?' Now his father sounded sceptical. He couldn't imagine a foreigner living with him and Milenka. 'You're going to marry her?'

He heard Milenka mumble something in the background. It was unintelligible, but she was clearly unhappy. He wished they could have had this conversation in person. Zivoin tried to keep his voice light. 'Tata, it's only been a couple of weeks. No one's talking about marriage.'

'Well, if you're saying she's coming here—'

'I mean, one day. Maybe. Not right now. We have time.' This wasn't true, and Alegria loved to remind him of it. Though they'd seen each other every day – almost every night – since their first date, she kept saying how little they knew each other, how little time they had. He hated hearing it, but he could tell that Alegria was saying it defensively, like she could see the heartbreak coming and was trying to build a wall high enough to stop it.

Drago was talking again, and Zivoin willed himself to try and be patient.

'You shouldn't be wasting your time if it's not serious, it's disrespectful to her. This is Ina all over again—'

'I didn't say it wasn't serious,' Zivoin said, his temper rising.

Sensing danger, Milenka took the phone back and said quickly, 'Of course not, hajde, hajde. We're proud of you, working so hard for your family. You deserve to be happy – if you're happy, so are we.'

She must have said something to his father, because after a

small pause, Drago said, 'Of course.' His voice sounded a little breathless, as though he'd just been elbowed in the stomach.

'OK,' Zivoin said, and glanced at his watch. 'I should go. I'm meeting Alegria. Her Christmas is next week and she wants to see the lights.'

'All right, sine. Enjoy.'

Zivoin tried not to stew over the conversation as he made his way to central London, but it wasn't easy. It was always this way, the loop of resentment, impatience and then guilt he cycled through most of the times he spoke to them. Even Alegria, who understood on a visceral level just how hard it was to have nothing, had a family who seemed much less preoccupied with every decision she made. He envied her and then felt guilty for the envy, because she had her own burdens too. At least he was free to come in and out of the country, earning money with relative ease. He tried to shake off the mood; he didn't want to bring his shit to Alegria, who would no doubt spend the evening trying to make him feel better. And then he'd feel guilty about that too. His problems weren't her problem, but it felt almost instinctive, the way he leaned into her warmth. She made him feel calm. He loved all the ways she made it clear that she did not need him, yet constantly let him take care of her. Who said it wasn't serious?

Zivoin realised his jaw was clenched. The closer he got to Piccadilly, the more people jammed their way onto the tube: older men in flat caps and leather jackets; women in wool blazers with gold-finished buttons, teetering in tiny skirts and heavy boots; teens in slouchy parachute pants and bomber jackets, making him feel both old and deeply grateful to be thirty. It had been incredibly cold lately – the snowstorms had been rough, snow falling thick and fast, icing over the pavements. Everyone around him was sweating, peeling off hats and coats and scarves – getting progressively pinker in the face if they tried to brave it out.

These days, the city was buzzing with optimism. Ever since Thatcher had gone it was as if a temporary friendliness had taken over Londoners – they smiled at each other more, smiled at Zivoin more, too. Even though, to him at least, the man who had filled her shoes seemed exactly the same. Even though prices were creeping up. He and Darco had started timing their showers, because topping up their electricity and gas meters was quickly becoming difficult. Just a few weeks ago, a shower had cost them fifty pence. Now it cost a pound. But other seismic things seemed to be happening. A newly reunified Germany had just held its first election, and Zivoin had been gripped by a powerful longing for his own country to find some semblance of unity. Soon, Slovenia would hold a referendum on whether it would leave or stay part of Yugoslavia. Even though he was certain the Slovenians would vote to leave, and other republics might too – Croatia, for sure, maybe even Bosnia – the thought of secession horrified him. What was a country with half its people missing?

Zivoin emerged, blinking at the unexpected brightness. It had begun snowing heavily whilst he'd been underground, and the streets were blanketed in white. He squinted towards Regent Street to see if he could spot her. They had arranged to meet by Lillywhites, but, as usual, it was pandemonium. The Piccadilly lights spotlit ads from Panasonic, Foster's and Sanyo as buskers playing the Smashing Pumpkins and Duran Duran drew in large crowds, adding to the chaos. The roundabout was a sea of umbrellas and dirty snow. As Zivoin crossed the street, he saw her, half-concealed underneath a hat and scarf. 'Hey!' He ducked under Alegria's umbrella, a huge grin on his face, but she drew back, shaking her head.

'No, no! Stay far away.'

He could barely hear her through her scarf. 'What?' He peered down at her in confusion and realised she was trembling. 'What's wrong?'

'I'm – I came to tell you that I can't make our date today. I'm sick,' she rasped, trying to lean as far away from him as she could whilst under the umbrella. 'I have a temperature.'

Looking at her more closely, Zivoin could see her eyes were glassy, her face a little puffy. She looked totally miserable. 'Peach,' he said, concern overriding disappointment, 'you shouldn't have come all the way here – why didn't you call?'

'I tried – I called three times, but the line was busy. I didn't know if you were at the bar or not, so I thought I would just wait here for you.'

'So you came all the way to central London just to tell me you couldn't see me tonight?' he said incredulously.

Alegria squinted up at him. 'Yes.'

'But . . . why? Why didn't you just leave me a message?'

'I told you, I tried—'

'But I would have just gone home and listened to it later,' he said, taking the umbrella and drawing her into his arms. 'It's snowing, and you're sick.'

'I didn't want you to think I stood you up – I thought it would make you sad.' When Zivoin kept staring down at her, she grew annoyed. 'What?' she asked defensively. 'I care about your feelings.'

'I can't believe you did that for me.'

'Yes, fine, I won't do it again. I'll go now. No need to look at me like I'm stupid,' she said crossly and tried to take the umbrella away from him.

But Zivoin didn't budge, tightening his grip. 'Just wait a second, wait a second, OK?' He bent down and kissed her gently, one, two, three times. Soft, light kisses. When she protested, he did it again, and then said, 'I don't think you're stupid. No one has ever done anything like that for me before. It's . . . it's really kind. It's more than kind.' He was trying to find the right way to tell her how adorable he found her in that moment, but the only words that were coming to mind felt far too quick, far too intense. He couldn't say it. He couldn't.

Alegria rested her head on his chest and sighed, and he felt her relax against him. It was an incredible feeling. 'OK, good,' she said feebly. 'I should go now. Can you wait with me at the bus stop?'

'Wait – you came here by bus?' he asked, astonished. 'You're joking?'

'Like I would pay for a taxi.' She sniffed loudly and started digging in her pockets for a tissue.

'OK – *that* was stupid. Come on.' Ignoring her protests, Zivoin pushed through the avalanche of people, led them to the relative calm of Lower Regent Street and hailed the first black cab he could find. As it slowed, he could feel her pulling away. 'What?'

'No, no, not this one, it's too expensive,' she mumbled, not wanting to look him in the eye. 'I'll take the bus halfway—'

'Don't worry about it.' Zivoin pulled out his wallet, giving her all the cash he had. He would have to ask Darco to top up the meters this week, but it didn't matter. He could not let her get on a crowded bus for an hour when she looked so unwell. When she baulked, he kissed her again. He had to fight the urge to pull her to him, to grab her face with both hands and kiss her hard. But she looked – and sounded – so unwell. There would be time for that later. The words hovered in his throat like a trapped insect. Just because it was quick didn't make it untrue. Still, he couldn't say it.

'I'll pay you back,' Alegria said, lingering at the door of the cab. She looked so charming with her flushed face and wide eyes, he wanted to keep her there, just for another moment. 'I'll pay you back,' she repeated.

'Say it like you mean it,' he said, and she laughed, closing her eyes as she leaned back against the seat. The driver was looking at them a little impatiently, but Zivoin ignored him. Now that she was leaving, the thing he had to say was becoming urgent. It would torment him if he didn't. She was still looking at him. Waiting. The window was wound down. He leaned halfway into the cab and tenderly cupped her cheek, and she pushed her face into his palm. 'I'll see you soon.' And then, with a slight ringing in his ears, he said, 'You know, I've never met anyone who cares so much about other people.'

'I'm sure you have,' she said immediately, but he shook his head and spoke over her.

'No. You write down people's names so you don't mispronounce them. At work, you open cartons of eggs when you scan them, just to check they're not broken. You took a bus to come and tell me that you were too sick to see me.'

'I just—'

'I love you.' It came out rushed, maybe a little bit too loud, but all that mattered was that he had said it.

He heard the driver mutter something like, 'Oh, for fuck's sake.' They ignored him.

Alegria was beaming, her eyes black and glittering. 'I love you too,' she exhaled, like she was letting go of a heavy weight. 'Oh, thank God you said it.' Her hot, sweaty hand found his and squeezed it hard, and she closed her eyes, murmuring, 'I feel terrible, but that was worth the journey.'

'I love you,' he repeated, and she laughed. She let go of his hand and he made himself step back up onto the pavement.

'I hope this is real and not something my fever has created. When I get home, call me and tell me again, OK?'

Zivoin stood there and watched the cab drive away, euphoria racing through his veins. *I love you. I love you too.* He was invincible: he could pick a fight, he could lose his job, a war could break out, and it wouldn't matter at all. He felt, with a sharp and sudden clarity, that everything that had happened to him since arriving in this city, with its grandiose beauty and its shabby underbelly, had to have happened in order to push him into her path. In the coming weeks, they would repeat the words to each other endlessly, adoringly, gleefully. *I love you. I love you too.* Snow fell down the back of his neck and ran under his collar, but he didn't care, he didn't care.

CHAPTER 14

London, December 1990

One week later

Was it a bad thing? A good thing? The start of something that might destroy her? She couldn't wrap her mind around the idea after just a few weeks. Hours were spent agonising over the difference between infatuation and adoration. But this wasn't her first time, she knew what it meant to love a man. What else would it be? She feared nothing when they were together. In front of Zivoin, Alegria became funnier, fiercer, self-adoring. She saw her reflection in his eyes and was astounded by the woman looking back at her. He had started calling her 'Peach', because he said her ass reminded him of the peaches back home – perfectly ripe – and she began calling him 'Cricket', because of the way he rubbed his feet together as he fell asleep. In bed together, after they made love – and she had to call it that, because 'fucking' was too vulgar, and 'sex' felt too mundane to encapsulate the way time collapsed when they touched each other – she often lay on his damp chest, black hair feathering her cheek. They would talk for hours and hours, telling each other the most minute details about themselves, hungry to see and be seen by each other.

Occasionally, Alegria found herself noticing small things about him: tiny nuggets of incompatibility, possible inklings of disagreements to come. The way he seemed to only ever speak about his mother in the context of what she did for the family: cleaning, cooking, fussing. The way he grew visibly agitated and terse when she spoke about God, as though he suspected her of trying to convert him. His tendency to get sucked into the Russian novels he was obsessed with, emerging melancholic and hopeless. She had the impulse to explore these moments, the way a tongue probes around a cavity, but backed away from the impulse every time. Their love was still flushed with newness. And there was so much more of Zivoin that was alluring, making him so easy to love. She admired how he cared deeply about the world around him and its problems (which was *especially* why the impact the Russian novels had on him irritated her so), drawing neat arguments that would begin at British imperialism and end at the Balfour Declaration of 1917. She loved the way he reached for her the second he woke up, just for the pleasure of holding her in his arms. She loved that he wasn't shy about how much he wanted her. On the inhale, it intoxicated her, the power she had over him. On the exhale, it was terrifying. And every feeling he elicited in her was heightened, every moment between them poignant.

There were uncomfortable moments too. On their third date, in an effort not to spend money, she'd invited him to her home for a picnic. She'd laid out the table with homemade pão de queijo, fresh baguette, cheese, beef jerky and liver pâté – her favourite – as a treat. Everything had been fine until after they'd eaten, when she leaned forward to kiss him and he'd pulled away.

'What's wrong?'

'I *really* hate pâté,' Zivoin said awkwardly. 'I can smell it on your breath. Sorry.'

'Oh.' They weren't even close to the stage of acknowledging things like that, and she'd drawn back embarrassed.

'It's for a good reason. I grew up really poor. We didn't have a home a lot of the time.' Zivoin stumbled over his words as he explained that his family had a little house made of concrete in a village in the mountains, a village so remote and small there was no electricity, no running water, no roads. In the summer that was fine, and all the siblings and cousins and uncles and aunts lived off the land, making it work. But in the winter and spring, when the snow was two or three metres high, it wasn't possible. The entire family had to move to the city and disperse, finding work, renting rooms, going to school. 'My cousins – they're my brothers and sisters because they always lived with us when my uncles and aunts had to leave. Sometimes they found work in Titograd, sometimes it was further away – in Bosnia, or Serbia. There was never enough money. Sometimes I just . . . didn't have shoes,' he said. 'Do you know what we used to eat as a treat?'

'What?'

'Lard smeared on bread, sprinkled with sugar.'

'Lard? What is lard?' she asked, wrinkling her nose.

Zivoin scooped some soft cheese onto a slice of baguette and popped it in his mouth. 'Pig fat.'

'*Oh.*'

'Yeah,' he said, nodding. He could read the shock and

disgust in her eyes. 'That's what I mean when I say I grew up poor.' He told her about the years they spent living in a single hotel room, and the suffocation of not having any space to call his own, sleeping on the floor or head-to-toe in a bed with his cousins. The toilet shared by the entire floor, mouse droppings in the corners. Always moving: never much to pack, yet somehow always stuff to carry. And then he told her about the flat. 'It was the best thing that could have happened – after years on a waiting list, we were finally given a home, a home we could live in during the winter *and* the summer. No one could take it from us – that was the most important part. They called it a small flat – two bedrooms – but to us it was a castle. My parents still live there now.'

'So . . .' Alegria said slowly, 'your family own two houses. One in the mountains and one in the city.'

He grinned. 'That's right. Two worthless houses. One day you will see them and you will understand.'

'I understand already.' And it was true, she did know what he meant. Homes were expensive, homes fell apart. Homes owned by poor people were bought in the middle of nowhere because a mortgage was cheaper than renting, built on land that had often been discarded by someone richer because, say, the marshes were slowly pulling the foundations down into the earth. Homes were not assets to be sold for cash – not when anyone who would ever be interested in buying them was as poor as they were. 'But . . . none of this has anything to do with the pâté, Cricket.'

'Oh, that. When my parents got the flat, we moved right away. But for the first time we had more rooms than we knew what to do with – and no stuff to fill them with. No sofa, no table, no beds. My parents made a bad choice. They bought all this cheap pine furniture on credit, quickly, without really thinking about it. I think they were as excited as my cousins and I. But then they had to start paying it back.'

'Ai.' She winced, and Zivoin nodded, staring down at the pâté between them.

'Yeah. So then we had this flat, and all this furniture, water and electricity. But we had no money for food – really, nothing. For seven months, all we could eat was bread and liver pâté. This disgusting, pink shit that we squeezed out of a tube like toothpaste. My aunt worked in the factory that made it – she would bring us all the faulty tubes and we'd slice them open. Three times a day. By the end, my hair started falling out, and I would have to force myself to eat it and then go stand outside with my eyes closed, breathing slowly so I didn't vomit. Once that winter ended, I never touched it again.'

He spoke matter-of-factly, as though this was something every child experienced, but the story was awful to her. It seemed excessive – offensive, even – to cry on his behalf when Zivoin himself seemed hardened against the pain. But she'd cried anyway. Who wouldn't?

To mark Christmas Eve, the four of them – Simone, Ricardo, Alegria and Maria – had decided to attend midnight Mass at the Catholic church in Willesden, off Dudden Hill Lane. It was popular amongst Brazilians, and sat amongst coloured-brick-and-blue-glass apartment blocks, homes with pointed roofs and chimneys – actual chimneys – and council flats. It was the kind of area that had one street full of ornate houses with more bedrooms than occupants right next to a street filled with laundrettes and carpet shops, a Supersave on every corner. As they approached the church, the smell of weed and urine hung in the air. The church, though, was nice enough, all stone and elegant windows with cross-hatching on the glass. High ceilings, too, with a beautiful wrought-iron chandelier in the centre. Alegria liked how old the churches here were – they felt much more spiritual in comparison to the bigger, flatter, newer places back home. The church wasn't full, though, the way it would have been in Uberlândia. A few hundred people were seated in the pews, listening to a priest conduct the Holy Communion in Latin. Two screens on either side of the altar provided both English and Portuguese translations, but the crowd was fidgety all the same. Alegria's head hurt. She was still recovering from the flu and had felt nauseous at the idea of dinner. But now her stomach kept grumbling, her tongue was furry from hours of not eating. Her jeans dug into sensitive places, and she was irate about that too.

'It's not like I thought it would be,' Simone whispered as she jiggled the plump little prayer cushion with her foot. 'I was hoping there would be more . . .'

'Energia?' Maria said out of the corner of her mouth. 'It's true, his delivery is kind of lifeless.'

The communions they knew at home were less formal. Colour was everywhere, especially in the clothes the churchgoers wore. Neighbour held hands with neighbour, people sang and shuffled in and out of the hall, toddlers wandered down the aisle. Often they would sit on the ground instead of on stiff wooden benches. Though she was nodding in agreement, Alegria said nothing, her eyes fixed on the English lettering on the screens. She had spent the last half hour astonished at how her comprehension had improved, until Si had pointed out that she was probably just reading both languages simultaneously. *Make holy, therefore, these gifts, we pray, by sending down your Spirit upon them like dewfall.*

'I'm still surprised you wanted to come, irmã,' Simone said softly, nudging her. On her other side, Ricardo sat with his eyes closed. It was unclear if he was praying or napping.

'Why wouldn't I come?'

'Spending the night at the igreja isn't normally your scene. Are there any sins you're trying to repent?'

Alegria glanced over at her and had to suppress a smile when she saw the mischievous glint in her sister's eye. Simone was in the mood for chaos. She reached out to still Simone's knee with her hand. 'If you knock that cushion down, people will look.'

'Where's Zivoin?' Maria asked, over on Alegria's left-hand side. 'Surely he's not working?'

'Probably not.' She wondered briefly if she could use the events of the previous day to explain his absence. The night before, Slovenia had overwhelmingly voted to secede from Yugoslavia. Both Zivoin and Darco had talked about it numbly. It seemed they simultaneously knew it had been coming and couldn't have imagined it. But this wasn't even the truth about why Zivoin wasn't there and she certainly wasn't about to lie on holy ground.

'So why didn't he join us?'

Alegria gave a (quiet, respectful) sigh and glanced at her watch. 'He's not religious like we are. It's a . . . cultural thing.'

Under her breath, she told Si what Zivoin had said when she'd tried to persuade him to come: 'I was raised by communist parents in a communist country,' he'd said shortly. 'Religion has no place in my life. After the war, the church was shunned in Yugoslavia because it collaborated with the Nazis. To many, it's a source of national shame.' Her attempt to persuade him had quickly fallen apart after that.

'You should have told him how important it was to you, and he should have come.' The whisper came, somewhat unexpectedly, from Ricardo. His eyes were open now, though he kept his gaze fixed ahead as he spoke. 'Church is important.'

'Don't be an idiot,' Simone said impatiently. Alegria said nothing at first. It wasn't that she disagreed, but Ricardo was religious in a way that she wasn't. It was tradition and community she'd come here for. Back home, they preferred congregating in the kitchens and patios of aunts and uncles to mark the death of Christ. Candle-lit Virgin Marys would watch over steaming aluminium vats of arroz and galinhada as the family gathered, hands clasped, in a circle to pray. The backdrop of their worship was the low whistle of the pressure cookers on the stove, their plastic release valves jiggling frantically as the steam cooked the rich black and brown beans. Feijoada for the adults and feijão for the kids. Solemnity never lasted long – the beer and Guaraná Mineiro would come out, someone would find sertanejo on the radio and dig out a football, and very occasionally her uncles would set off fireworks. Only *then* would they go to the Missa do Galo to see the nativity scene and listen to the hymns. Alegria had heard things were more sombre here, but she'd never expected it to be so dull. 'I miss the way we do it back home,' she whispered.

'It's probably good he didn't join us,' Si muttered. 'When he comes to visit, we'll show him the real church – he might like it.'

'Mmm.' Alegria did not want to think about things that weren't ever going to happen. 'I wanted him to be here.' She and Zivoin had argued when she first told him about the Mass. 'It's just a few hours!' she'd insisted. 'I told my friends you'd be there – they'll think it's rude if you don't come.'

'I can meet you afterwards, Peach, but I'm not going to sit through something I don't believe in just so you can show off how obedient I am to your friends. Maybe your Brazilian boyfriends did that, but I won't.'

'It's not about that!' Alegria lied. 'It's about sharing something, about community.'

'You mean *your* community.'

'Which I want you to be a part of.'

'And that's kind of you, but I have no interest in it.' When she'd protested, Zivoin had frowned at her and said, 'How would you feel if I told you I didn't want you to go to church, Alegria? What if I said I wanted you to be a part of what *I* believe?'

'I wouldn't like it,' she'd snapped, knowing exactly where he was going with this. 'But—'

'Exactly – which is why I will never say that to you. I'm not interested in changing or controlling you, but it has to go both ways if this is going to work.'

'What about compromise?'

'I'll compromise with you on many, many things. But not this. Religion isn't one of those things you force on people.' And he was right, she had to admit that he was right, even if it annoyed her. The truth was, Alegria hadn't actually cared about whether Zivoin would feel comfortable in the church with her. She'd just wanted him to be there. But she apologised, and made her peace with it. They could disagree about religion. It wasn't like they were going to spend their lives together.

'But he believes?' Maria probed. 'He's a Christian at least, right?' She was already looking affronted. Alegria could tell her friend was trying not to sound self-righteous. She felt that Maria could try harder.

'He's an atheist,' Alegria said shortly. No one spoke, but she could feel the judgement rolling off them like steam.

Si gently pressed her knee against Alegria's. 'He's a very good man,' she whispered. 'I can always tell.'

'Sure, sure,' Ricardo said quickly, resting his arms on his belly. 'But there's a lot of value in tradition.'

Maria was nodding vigorously. 'Have you talked about what happens in February? Is he going to go back to Brazil and live there with you?'

'As if you two care about tradition – you're talking through Mass!' Simone said suddenly, forgetting to whisper. The woman in front of her, dressed in a red coat and matching hat, turned around, frowning, and Simone hissed, 'Can I help you?'

'It's fine, Si,' Alegria murmured, reaching for her hand. 'I'm OK.' But her sister just shook her head, looking like she'd swallowed a lemon. They stood for the Communion Rite, and the church rumbled with mutterings of English and Portuguese. The congregation meandered through the 'Our Father', and Alegria shut her eyes, enjoying the vibrations she could feel in her bones. Since meeting Zivoin, she'd been feeling strange. Restlessness rattled around her chest, but she couldn't figure out what it was she was impatient for. It was like having an itch that couldn't be reached. What was it she wanted? For now, she wanted Zivoin, and all the things he brought with him that put her so at ease. The way he let her fall asleep on his chest before turning on his side – his preferred sleeping position. He found out what brand of coffee she drank (Nescafé) so she could have it in his kitchen in the mornings. She'd discovered a notebook in his jacket pocket that had a list of her favourite films that he had not yet seen, books that he had not yet read. He saw her and the little things that made her happy in ways that no one else did.

She wanted to pick up this part of her London life and deposit it back home, like slotting in the final puzzle piece – it was all too much, too good, to lose. Maria and Ricardo had been right, in the core of what they were saying. Zivoin couldn't possibly understand the way it felt when a room full of people took each other's hands and prayed together – the joy of it, the poetry of it. He had never seen a room full of aunties commanding a family dinner – plates of beef kibe crowding the table, competing for attention with clay bowls of gleaming banana da terra, Alegria's favourite. Sharing plates piled with white rice fried in oil and garlic before boiling, dipping bowls of farofa, and terrines of oily sausage chunks glistening amongst black beans. In the centre, a sizzling slab of fillet steaks sitting on a bed of onions, drenching all of them in the scent of fried food. Rectangular parcels of steamed pamonha, tied neatly with twine; perfectly cooked rice; succulent, juicy meat that soaked up the feijão broth and melted in her mouth; crispy, earthy mandioca that crunched between her teeth – all of this was a kind of love he *had* to know in order to know her. She didn't need him to believe in the same things as she did, but she needed him to recognise the way her people loved each other and looked out for one another.

Zivoin would never experience Brazil the way she could, on her skin and in her mouth. It would never be home for him – and she already found that Yugoslavia loomed large and foreign in their conversations. She was curious to see it, but the thought of living there felt impossible. Not just because of the threat of civil war that lurked constantly on its horizon, or the language barrier – far more impenetrable than English – or the chasm of cultural differences between them, but because they both knew she'd never earn enough to support her family. Yugoslavia's economy was as catastrophic as Brazil's. All they had was here, and now. So what was the point of falling in love as quickly – and as deeply – as she had if she was just going to go back home, alone and starving once again? She was impatient for the answers.

The service was coming to a close. Once they had risen for hymns and sat back down for the final time, Simone said, 'Tell us about that second date you had.'

'I've already told you, irmã.'

'Tell me again – I can't remember all the details.' Simone glanced at Maria, checking she was listening. 'I've been thinking about this date since she told me about it.'

'Ooh . . . então I want to hear it!' Their friend leaned closer eagerly.

In between prayers, Alegria whispered the story to Maria and Ricardo as Simone nodded along, looking smug. 'We were walking back from Camden – it was late afternoon – and Zivoin kept saying he wanted to show me something in the flat, so he invited me to come up for coffee—'

'Ai, oldest trick in the book!' Maria breathed, rolling her eyes. 'Obviously you knew já já what he wanted to show you.'

'No, actually—'

But Ricardo interrupted her now, his cheeks reddening. 'I hate to puncture your tyre, but that's *definitely* what he wanted. How do you think I first got Si into bed with me?'

Simone gave a little 'Ha!' of laughter. 'Typical man, thinking *he* was the one getting *me* anywhere. Go on, Ale.'

'Well, he did mean coffee,' Alegria said quietly, carefully. She could sense the red-coated woman in front of them listening now. 'At first I was suspicious too, and disappointed. Because . . .' She trailed off, realising this wasn't to be said out loud, given where they all were. Of course she'd wanted to sleep with him. From the moment he saw her in the supermarket, he'd looked at her like he wanted to unwrap her and then wrap her back up – just so he could do it all over again. Alegria knew that look; the men in Brazil were capable of giving it to anything with a pulse. Sex was in the air, back home. Everyone walked around like they were having it at that very minute, all loose-hipped, flexed muscles and curling laughter. So it never felt personal when men looked at her with their eyes dark and deep. Until Zivoin had looked at her that way. Thinking about it sent little spasms down her thighs. Deeply inappropriate. 'Anyway, I thought, Oh, he's the same as the rest of them, but I decided to go, just, um, to see what would happen. And he did actually mean coffee. But actually, he makes it very strong, different to how we do it, so I said I didn't want that stuff so late—'

'He was clearly making coffee to get you both hot and hard!' Maria breathed, holding in a giggle. She looked scandalised and delighted.

Ricardo glared at her. 'You. Are. In. A. Church,' he hissed, but the women ignored him. Simone absent-mindedly patted his knee, as if he were a stray child.

'Anyway, what he actually wanted to show me were all these fotos. He had a whole album of his family, all his cousins, and their children. It was his way of trying to introduce me to them all.' They had sat on his bed together as Zivoin flipped through the album and slowly brought his family to life for her. He could name all his nephews' favourite football players, and knew what his nieces' favourite games were. He told her what everyone did for work, what they liked to do in their free time, when their birthdays were – details of their lives that he cherished and wanted to share. It was clear how much he missed them, as well as how much they depended on him. In Zivoin, Alegria saw herself: the constant pressure to push forward, to care for everyone, and all the guilt this generated. She could sense his inability to relax, too, the way he was always having to think two steps ahead of everyone. She also saw the kind of love he was capable of. They did not talk about children. But he would be a devoted father. He really would.

'It was special,' she said. 'It moved me.' Alegria glanced down and saw a spider scuttling out from underneath her pew. It was one of the ones with a tiny, round body and long, spindly legs. Instinct told her to crush it under her foot, but as soon as the thought hit her, she knew she wouldn't. The spider crept into the shadows of the bench in front of them and she soon lost track of it.

'Of course it moved you,' Maria whispered. 'It moved you right into his bed!'

'Shh!' she whispered, though she was holding back a giggle. 'God might hear you.'

'Oh, God would be thrilled to know the sorts of things we're getting up to down here,' Maria said. 'Why would He have created the orgasmo if He didn't want us women to enjoy them?'

Simone let out one of her cackles, mouth pressed into the crook of her elbow in an effort to stay quiet. They heard the woman in front of them clear her throat loudly, pointedly, and that only made them laugh harder. Maria had tears in her eyes. Even Ricardo was fighting back a smile. Alegria pictured telling Zivoin about this conversation later that night, all the ways it would amuse him, what he might do in response. 'Amen!' she grinned, pressing her hands together as though in prayer.

CHAPTER 15

London, December 1990 – January 1991

One week later

'Just a few more minutes,' Alegria whispered into his ear, and he jumped as the words tickled him, sending prickles down his spine. She laughed, stretched closer and kissed the hollow underneath his earlobe.

'I can't feel anything from the waist down,' Zivoin muttered, and she raised her eyebrows.

'We can fix that later. But this could help for now ...' From her bag, Alegria took a silver hip flask and then pulled off one of her gloves with her teeth to open it. 'Whisky.'

They were stiff and frozen after two hours of standing in Trafalgar Square, sandwiched in amongst an enthusiastic crowd. Fireworks would go off when the clock struck midnight, and people had gathered in their thousands, becoming rowdier as time passed. Every so often, drunken carol singing would break out, people raising their voices to join in. But neither of them knew the words. Simone and Ricardo had disappeared a while ago, saying something about a New Year's Eve party in Croydon. 'You should come!' Si had said to Alegria, and she had nodded, pretending to memorise the address. But they weren't going anywhere, not when all they wanted was to be left alone.

Zivoin took a sip from the flask and winced. With effort, he swallowed. 'Christ, why is it so sweet?'

'I mixed honey in.'

'Of course you did.' He shook his head in disgust. 'I don't know how I'm still in a good mood.' Even though Zivoin had every reason to be grumpy – it was cold and they'd been milling about the square for hours – he couldn't find it in himself to be. He couldn't even smoke to stay warm when he was with her. But she was so excited, almost childlike in her glee, that it kept him smiling. Around her, he was always smiling. Things were going so well between them, it sometimes felt too easy. They spent every single moment together that they could: nursing a single pint each at the Dublin Castle as bands they'd never heard of played indie pop all night, for free; wading through the ripped jeans and acid-green mohawks on Brick Lane, past the Bengali sari shops, the curry houses and halal butchers to try the tender salted beef bagels from the Beigel Shop, mustard smeared across their lips. Through her, the city had been transformed from his adversary to more of a distant friend. Zivoin yearned for home less and less, and instead began to look at London more appraisingly. Could he stay here, with her? Where would they live? Did she think about it as much as he did? They'd been together for little over a month, and normally that meant it was too early to know, too soon to tell, but not with her. He had become quietly convinced that this was it, and once the realisation had gripped hold of him, so too had the knowledge that their time together was running out. Something had to be done.

Alegria was checking her watch. 'Eleven fifty-eight!' She offered him the flask, but Zivoin shook his head. He wasn't about to make that mistake again. He moved even closer and wrapped his arms around her as the crowd pressed forward towards Nelson's Column. Earlier, stressed-looking security guards in neon vests had tried to keep people from climbing onto the plinth, but now they appeared to have given up. People were huddled on each of the great stone steps and perched on the backs of the bronze lions. He saw fathers with children on their shoulders.

'I can't wait,' she said, for the twentieth time that evening.

'I know, Peach.' He kissed her lips, quick, little kisses that made her grin but did not stop her from talking at a rapid pace.

'In Brazil, we would always watch the fireworks from my friend's house – she has a balcony that overlooks one of the biggest parks in the city, and it was always a good show.' She told him about the tradition of wearing white at the start of the new year, to symbolise peace, then listed off the other colours and what they meant. 'Gold and yellow are for wealth, green is for health, pink is for love and red is for passion – the only colour you can't wear is black, of course. The symbol of death.' She glanced down at her black winter jacket and grimaced. 'The rules were made for hotter climates, I guess.'

'What colours did you choose?' Zivoin asked, and she unzipped the parka to give him a brief flash of a red jumper before quickly zipping it back up again.

'More of this,' she said, and pressed against him, finally kissing him back. He held her and rested his chin on her head, and she wound her arms around his waist, leaning into him. The solidity of it felt so good. They clung to each other as the crowd rippled with excitement, suddenly alert. 'Fifteen seconds to go,' someone said cheerfully behind them, and Alegria's grip tightened. They counted down together, their voices rising to join the crowd, and as the clock struck midnight, a huge cheer erupted. 'Happy New Year!' Alegria breathed, looking up at him.

Zivoin held her face with both his hands and wished they could stay in this moment for longer. As her eyes bore into his, he felt like she was slipping away. 'Happy New Year,' he said into her mouth.

They watched the fireworks light up the square, illuminating their faces. Golden Catherine wheels, red and blue rockets and multicoloured peonies mingled terrifically with the snow, and the city looked dramatic and seductive and overwhelming all at once. At first, Zivoin found himself laughing helplessly at the way Alegria was startled by every single whistle and bang, jumping without fail. She laughed, too, delighted by his amusement. But as the fireworks went on, the mood between them slowly grew more solemn. Zivoin stopped laughing. It was now January, and that small shift suddenly made her departure feel much sooner. Alegria was no longer going back 'next year' but in a few short weeks. Their time together was now made of glass. By the time the final firework dissolved into the blackness, they were both silent. The acrid smell of gunpowder lingered. As the crowd began to disperse, they looked at each other, a new weight settling in. Alegria was about to speak, but he cut across her quickly and said, 'Let's walk home?'

'Walk? Now?'

'It's only about an hour.'

She glanced around at the falling snow and the drifting crowds, and then shrugged. 'OK.' Hand in hand, they meandered through the streets, Zivoin leading them west. Alegria had always found it incredible that he could navigate that way. 'All the streets look the same to me,' she'd once said, showing him the pocket *A–Z* atlas she carried with her at all times. He'd laughed, taking the book from her and flipping through it in amusement.

'I was taught to navigate in the army,' he told her, 'using the position of the sun.'

'But what if it's dark?'

'Then you rely on the stars – the North Star, and so on.'

As they walked, Alegria wondered if he was looking up at the sky for guidance, or if he just knew the city well enough by now. He had gone quiet and introspective, and she pretended she didn't know why, choosing instead to keep up a stream of chatter. All around them, drinkers stumbled in and out of pubs, made their way to parties, shrieked in the street. They watched two women dressed as angels, complete with yellow halos, pick their way through the ice and she pointed out how cold they must be, bare-legged like that. Zivoin nodded, but said nothing. She talked frantically, barely pausing, laughing too loudly at her own jokes and being careful not to look at him too much. But it was coming, of course it was. She'd sensed the change as they'd watched the fireworks. She wondered what he would say about her leaving, and whether he would tell her it was over, and she wondered if she would be able to hold herself together if that were the case. She wondered if he was going to be cruel and ask her to stay, even though he knew she couldn't.

'I've never done this before,' Alegria said, as they made their way down Edgware Road, passing the Lebanese restaurants, the shisha bars and the Turkish coffee shops, their windows overflowing with baklava.

'Done what?'

'Walked around a city so late – we could never do this in Brazil. And I would never do it alone.' Though it was past one in the morning, the street was filled with people eating, smoking shisha pipes and drinking cups of fresh mint tea. She looked intently into each of the cafés and restaurants they walked past, as though a solution to their heartache was lying on one of the tables.

He watched her search for things to distract them both, watched her pretend everything was all right, and couldn't take it any more. 'Are you still leaving at the end of February?' The words came out harder than he would have liked, but it pained him to see that the expression on Alegria's face didn't change at all.

She hesitated briefly, but kept walking and said calmly, 'Yes.'

'You haven't even considered staying?'

'No.'

'I see,' he said, anger now creeping into his voice. 'Well, that's good to know. I'm glad it's such an easy decision for you.'

At this, Alegria rounded on him with a scowl, and he realised – belatedly – that she was as upset as he was. 'Easy?'

she repeated, sounding hurt. 'What the fuck are you talking about, Zivoin?' The intensity with which she spoke surprised them both. 'I *have* to go back – you know this. My visa expires, my flights are booked. I don't have the option to consider anything.' Alegria had stopped walking now, and stood on the corner of Praed Street. She had wrenched her hand from his. 'I will never go through the humiliation of being deported again,' she said quietly. 'Never. I refuse to spend the rest of my life just waiting to be caught, never able to relax. You saw the way I reacted when we first met – I never want to live that way again. I refuse to stay in a country that doesn't want me here. How dare you tell me it's easy.'

'I'm sorry,' Zivoin said quickly. 'You're right, that was unfair. But you seem so at peace with the decision. It hurts to see that.'

'It's not like that – there's no decision to make. But of course I'm sad. I'm . . .' Alegria searched for the right words. 'I'm devastated, I don't know what to do. I wish we had more time.'

'What if you came to live in Yugoslavia?' he asked desperately, knowing before the words had even left his mouth that it was a terrible idea. Not to mention a dangerous one.

She shook her head and said gently, 'I can't start all over again somewhere else. Could you? Would you come to Brazil?'

'I couldn't,' he said immediately. 'I can't leave my family without any money – it feels too risky. I'm sorry.'

'You don't need to apologise to me. I have the same problem – and it would be a terrible idea. You wouldn't be able to work.'

'So we'd have to stay here—'

'We *can't*—'

Round and round they went, repeating the same suggestions over and over again, as though a solution might occur if they both just made it clear how desperately they wanted to find one. The snow fell thicker and faster than it had before, but they kept going, marching past Paddington Station and through Cleveland Square. Later, she would try to think of this walk back home, and this conversation, and find herself unable to remember a thing. It became a messy blur of cold feet, frozen tears and stiff, frustrated questions flung at one another with secret accusations behind them: *Don't you love me enough? Won't you upend your life for this?*

By half one, they were at Zivoin's kitchen table, tense and exhausted. Alegria thought about the party her sister was at and wondered if she should have spent the night with her instead. The flat was lonely and far too empty. He had chilled a small bottle of Prosecco in the fridge, but it sat there, untouched, as he brewed coffee and she tucked up her feet on the chair, his duvet wrapped around her shoulders. He sat across from her. Then, like scavengers picking over a carcass, they went through yet another version of the fight they both kept losing. Zivoin could see she was miserable, trying not to cry, but he couldn't stop poking at this growing wound. It had become an obsession. For the past few days, every time he'd felt her relax into his arms, any time she threw her head back in laughter or smiled so widely her eyes vanished into her cheeks, he would remember that soon she would leave him and he felt himself yanked out of the moment to grieve silently. He could not stand the waiting, he could not settle under the pressure of the unknown.

Alegria held a mug of coffee between her hands for warmth. He knew she wouldn't drink it. 'Earlier,' she murmured, pressing the mug to her chest, 'you said, "What if you came to live in Yugoslavia?"'

'Yes,' he said miserably, 'I know. Stupid suggestion.'

'Putting how I feel to the side for a moment . . . is it dangerous? Could we live there?'

'I don't know.' Zivoin could hear the kitchen tap dripping behind him. It had been leaking on and off for weeks now, and it had never bothered him until this very moment. He wondered if he should take a look under the sink—

'How can you not know?'

'It's complicated.'

'So?' She sounded impatient. 'We aren't going anywhere else tonight.'

'It's . . .' Zivoin exhaled and massaged the tension in his jaw with one hand. 'You know some parts already. Yugoslavia is—'

'Six countries in one. I know.'

'Yes. That's how I grew up – as a Yugoslavian first, a Montenegrin second. But not everyone wants to live that way – even in my own family, we can't agree on whether Yugoslavia should fight to exist or just break up. The problem is that we're all over the place. We're mixed up—'

'What do you mean?' Sensing his agitation, Alegria put down the coffee and began kneading his hands with her own, stretching out his fingers and pressing down on the flesh between thumb and forefinger. 'Does that hurt?' she asked.

'Yes.'

'You might be stressed,' she said earnestly, and despite the strain between them, they laughed.

Zivoin closed his eyes and leaned back in his chair. 'It's not like all Croatians live in Croatia, and all Bosnians live in Bosnia, you know. Everyone lives everywhere – most people are a mix of different ethnicities. If one country became independent, what would happen to the other people living there? Who would they belong to? Where would they vote?'

'And everyone is, what, arguing about it?'

She still didn't get it. 'I wish it was just arguing. There are paramilitaries being formed, riots in the streets, politicians calling for the army to be mobilised against the partisans . . . people are starting to go missing. Some of my friends are vanishing – we don't know if they're hiding or going to fight. Families are being torn apart – brother against brother, sometimes. The army is calling in the reserves.'

'Wait.' She stopped massaging his hands. 'The army? The one you were conscripted to?'

'There was no conscription at the time – but, yes, that's the army I trained with.'

'So they can't call you to fight, if there is a – a war?'

'Actually, they can now. The law changed last year. They won't,' he said quickly, seeing her eyes widen. 'So much would have to go wrong first . . .'

Alegria stood up, the duvet falling from her shoulders. She began to pace around the small kitchen with renewed vigour. 'Is there going to be a war?'

'How could I possibly know?' Zivoin asked, exasperated. He reached for her. 'Come back – you'll get cold.'

She ignored him. 'But what would you bet on?'

'I . . .' He could see that she would not come back to him until she had a concrete answer, something she could measure against and calculate with. Alegria was breathing hard, her hands twisting together like they always did when she was stressed. 'I really don't know,' he said again, gently. 'Every day I hear different, contradictory things. Some weeks I think, this is it, it's really happening. And then nothing, things calm down again. But Yugoslavia is a big country – Montenegro is still safe, still stable. I was planning to go back in January, before we met. Come here . . .' Reluctantly Alegria let herself be pulled onto his lap. He kissed her neck. 'It's complicated, remember.'

'But you were a machine-gunner,' she said. 'Isn't that a valuable position? Wouldn't you be one of the first ones they call back?'

'I wouldn't go,' Zivoin said firmly. 'So it's irrelevant. I would never fight against my own people.'

'What if it was a war with another country?'

'Then I would, yes.'

Alegria shook her head and muttered something in Portuguese. She sounded angry. 'So even if I decided I could live there, it's not even an option.'

'No.'

'So *why* would you—'

'Because I can't keep loving you without knowing where it will go,' he said into the stillness of the kitchen. The sound bounced off the tiles. Alegria did not flinch. She peeled herself off his lap and went to the sink to pour herself water.

'Love is *all* not knowing where it will go, Cricket.' He was surprised to see that she was smiling, despite how sad she looked. 'You know, once, Si and I talked about what we thought love was. She said it was this wild thing that sets you on fire. And I said it was the opposite – I said love should bring you peace.'

'She was right,' he said immediately, and Alegria laughed despite her frustration. She reached out and took both his hands again, laying them flat on the table. She ran her fingers over each knuckle, then bent to kiss them, and Zivoin, in his anger and hurt, wanted to push her away. But he closed his eyes, stayed still, wondered how to hold himself together.

'She was, but so was I. We can't torture ourselves, or other people, and call it love.' Alegria saw him frown, a retort already forming, but she pressed on. 'In my life I have always, *always* done what was safe, and what was best for my family. Years of thinking about everyone else, constantly working, putting money away like a disaster was just around the corner – I'm so bored of it. I'm bored of myself.'

'That's not your fault,' he said quickly, 'that's what being poor—'

'I *know* what being poor does, amor, I know. I'm thirty, and I have no idea what I actually want for myself, or if all the choices I have made will save me the way I once thought they would. That's OK. You don't have to try and make me feel better about it. But I am tired of myself. I almost didn't let myself fall in love with you – just imagine that!'

Tears were running down Alegria's face, but she ignored them. It filled him with a sense of dread. He knew she was going to end it right there, in his grimy kitchen, on New Year's Eve, and he wanted to launch himself towards her and cover her hands with his mouth. But he did not move. He could only sit there, feeling the hard slats of the wooden chair digging into his back.

'Maybe you're hoping for – no, I mean, expecting me to be the one that breaks us up, because I'm the one leaving. And that would make the most sense. But I won't do it, Cricket. I won't end this, even though we probably should, even though it's probably going to be so painful that I can't even think about it. But I won't deny myself what I want. If our relationship is going to end, it's going to be because you chose that, not me.'

'Well, I won't choose that.' In his relief, the words tripped over themselves.

'Good. There we are.' She stood up, looking at him with heavy eyes. 'I'm tired. Come to bed with me.'

She wore one of his T-shirts like a dress, his wool socks on her cold feet. They lay in the bed like they always did, Zivoin by the wall with his arm around her stomach, her back pressed up against him. He inhaled the coconutty smell of her curls and whispered, 'But what do we do if we can't be together and we refuse to be apart?'

Alegria took so long to reply, he thought she'd fallen asleep. The world outside was already beginning to yawn and stretch and open its eyes. He wished they could remain untouched here for a while longer, just the two of them. In a few hours, he would have to wake up, drag his body into work and pretend that everything was all right. Then Alegria moved unexpectedly. She found his hand, cupping the softness of her belly, and brought it up to her chest, cradling it with her own. 'We find a way around,' she said into the stale darkness. 'It's what we do, isn't it? We find the way around.'

What do you think happens to time when you fall in love? Does it slow down, or speed up? They argue about this through the depressing gloom of January. For her, time is a collapsed lung. She feels perpetually short of breath, convinced that everything is moving at double speed. They see each other every single day, and still it is not enough to ease her panic. She rests her head on his chest, closes her eyes just for a moment, and suddenly it is one day closer to the day she must leave him. But he cannot see it the way she does. He feels as though time has settled into his limbs, expanding who he is and what he wants. Their moments together are slow and sweet, a daily epiphany. The world falls away when they're together and he feels that he's changing all the time, all the time. They talk about it all the time, all the time. How do they know which path to take when all options are unacceptable? January becomes February and she thinks about how little room visas and borders leave for love. He talks about war and disintegration in the present tense and she starts to dread the sound of the words as they leave his mouth. This is the thing that gnaws at them: after all the trust it took to fall in love the way they did, hungrily, impatiently, is it enough to just wait and see what will happen? There will be so much courage required in the months ahead, and so much they must be willing to lose.

None of this is known to them yet.

CHAPTER 16

Uberlândia, March 1991

Too many days later

These days, she woke up alone. She had grown used to making herself as small as possible – look, here she was on the very edge of the double bed with her arms hugging herself. Alegria shifted her weight into the middle and starfished, feeling the light cotton sheet lift as she moved. It was nice, all that space. But soon the bed would feel too big again. Back in London, she would sometimes wake up in the middle of the night, shivering. Zivoin had a single bed where they slept body to body, hair caught underneath shoulders, legs entangled. Yet somehow, he turned and turned in his sleep, forehead sweaty, until the duvet was wrapped around him like a joint and she was left shivering. She would prod at him, sleepy, grumpy, and without properly waking up he always knew what the matter was. He'd shimmy around to her, pulling her back into his armpit. She liked to sleep half-buried in there, breathing in the scent of yogurty lotion and off-brand deodorant and pepper – he always smelled a little bit like peppercorns. Sometimes, Alegria would wake to his hands already tucking the blanket up around her shoulders.

This was the secret to a good, uncomplicated life. She yearned for it so much that she had absorbed the wanting into her body – her foot twitched constantly, her hands were restless.

Yet at the same time, she was home. Alegria realised how much she had missed Brazil the moment they walked out of the airport doors and she took that first, hedonistic inhale. Everything was exactly right, the wetness and greenness of it, the creamy, floral smell in the air, layered with gasoline and rotting vegetation. She loved how little restraint her country had, how it was bigger, juicier, sweeter than anywhere else. She loved that the raindrops were warm and left as quickly as they came, she loved that the sun dried the pavement in minutes, she loved that the weather was the same in the morning as it was in the evening, and if it looked like rain, it would rain, and if it looked like sun and blue skies, there would be sunshine with blue skies. This was the world Alegria knew, and it sank back into her skin with satisfying speed. How could anywhere else mean as much as Brazil did?

She found her parents in the kitchen that morning. Adelina was rolling meatballs. A large silver bowl was held steady between her hands as she plucked and rolled, the raw mince and diced onion oozing between plump fingers. Toninho sat at the kitchen table with his glasses on, reading her the newspaper. 'One of our research institutions has just been given access to something called "the Web",' he was saying when Alegria strolled in.

'What?' Adelina said, distracted. The radio was also on, and she found it hard to listen to two sounds at once.

'The ABC,' Toninho called, still squinting at the paper.

'The what?'

'The Brazilian Academy of Sciences. They've got the World Wide Web there now!'

'I don't know what any of that means,' his wife said impatiently. 'Read me something that I can understand!'

'Filha.' Toninho had spotted his daughter and a large smile that looked exactly like hers broke over his face. 'Come sit with us – do you know about this Web? This . . .' he looked down at the words again '. . . this World Wide Web?'

'Not really.' Alegria dropped a beijo onto his forehead and went to hug her mother, resting her cheek on Adelina's shoulder. She listened fondly as they bickered, and wished, not for the first time, that Zivoin were here. She wanted to show him everything – their little kitchen with the sliding pantry doors that popped off their hinges if you didn't open them at exactly the right angle, the concrete veranda with the large stone basin and ribbed counter that her mother washed clothes on, honeyed with sunlight.

'. . . read me something about Rock in Rio – is there anything about that?' Adelina was saying, dipping her hand into a cup that contained a single, beaten egg.

The counter had a crack running up it that had grown longer since Alegria had been away. She wondered how much it would cost to replace, and how long they could go before the whole thing fell apart. It hurt to look at the crack, it hurt her that she couldn't quietly walk over to her mother, take the raw meat mixed with alho and sal and pimenta and finish it for her. She wanted to pull the silver bowl out of her hands, corral her towards the table and say, 'Relax, Mãe, pelo amor de Deus, have a coffee with your husband and rest. Let me.

Let me.' But her mother was the kind of woman who couldn't stand to sit and watch other people work.

'That was a month ago, paixão,' Toninho was saying, all salt-and-pepper hair, all heavy-eyed. 'I don't think we're going to find anything here about that.'

'But the Queen was there?' her mother asked.

'Queen the band, not the little English rainha with all the diamonds.' Toninho's and Alegria's eyes met, and they had to hold in their laughter so as not to offend, because Adelina was a little sensitive when it came to mishearing what the radio said.

'I know what I heard!'

'I'll make us coffee?' Alegria cut in quickly, trying to hide her grin. She would tell Si about it later, whispering through her laughter. Moments like that, Adelina's little slip-ups, her stubbornness, elicited such affection from them both that they would descend on their mother, pull her onto the sofa and drape themselves on top of her so she could not escape. They would kiss her and fawn over her until she was too weak with laughter to stop them, and their father would watch with quiet satisfaction and say what he always said: 'I'm a rich man, a rich man indeed.' If he weren't a little fragile, already a little unsteady on his feet, they would have pulled him down with them.

Alegria dragged the chairs out onto the shady part of the veranda and served them coffee in the little ceramic cups made by her cousin, Daniela. Adelina's mustard-yellow shift dress caught the sun and her hair shone like polished walnuts. 'There are sequilhos in the cupboard.'

'Your sister,' Toninho said, when Alegria had laid down a

plate of the condensed milk biscuits, 'could sleep through a thunderstorm. The morning is almost over!'

'You should have seen her in Londres when it was seven thirty in the morning and still dark outside.' Alegria had been back for over a week, yet it was the first morning her father had not needed to work the early shift. There was still so much to tell them, she was unsure where to begin. The problem with five-minute phone calls was that they left no room for anything but the basics: are you all right? Are you safe? Have you been eating? Is the money OK? She hadn't been able to tell them about the small but essential things, like the way snow actually hurt because of how cold it was, and how quickly it melted, or about the tantalising smell of warm, honey-roasted peanuts, or how painful the screech of the Piccadilly line was when it ran through High Street Kensington. There was no metro system in their state, and her parents found the idea of travelling below the surface bewildering. They watched a small blue-winged butterfly explore the yellow mimosa flowers Adelina took such diligent care of. The colour contrast was vivid and perfect.

'You don't see many of those in the city,' Toninho remarked. 'It must have travelled far.'

'No, they're always here in the mornings,' Adelina said. She was already glancing back into the kitchen, thinking of the work that lay in front of her. 'Usually there's two – I think they travel in pairs.'

'In pairs?' Toninho leaned forward in his chair to get a better look, moving out of the shade as he did. Alegria watched the way the sun lit her father's wispy, delicate hair. He had lost even more of it since she'd been away.

The top of his head resembled an adolescent chick losing all its baby feathers. With an anxious twinge, she realised her parents were old. Hardship had prematurely aged them, and this frailty was what Zivoin couldn't see, what words didn't convey whenever she insisted that she could not leave them behind. The foundation of her life was a unit of four; her family were her framework, her purpose. Her triumphs were their triumphs, their pain hers. The furthest Alegria had ever imagined living from them was down the street.

'I didn't know butterflies travelled in pairs, paixão – how romantic. But she's all alone,' her father was saying, clasping Adelina's hand in his free one. 'What do you think happened to her mate?'

'I need to talk to you,' Alegria interrupted, 'I need . . .' She stopped then, because she wasn't sure what she needed, or how to finish that sentence. Zivoin had been a ghost in the house. He lingered behind every anecdote from London, every memory, every conversation they had. 'I met someone,' she said, finally. 'We're still together.'

Her parents glanced at each other as though confirming some secret conversation between them. 'But why do you say this so sadly?' Adelina asked, at the same time as Toninho exclaimed, a little too brightly, 'That's wonderful, filha! A Brazilian?'

'Actually . . .' She gave them vague details about Yugoslavia without alluding to any of its issues. When it came to Zivoin, though, she was meticulous in her descriptions. Alegria could not resist showing him off a little, telling them how he had called her a taxi when she was sick and came to check on her the next day. He had insisted on taking her to the airport with Si, even though she'd told him she was fine. 'If you think I'm going to pass on the opportunity to spend time with you, you're an idiot,' Zivoin had told her, and so she'd relented. He'd carried her suitcase for her all the way to Heathrow, getting slower and quieter the closer they got.

Standing by security, when they really couldn't put it off any longer, Simone had cleared her throat and looked at both of them. 'I'll go through first,' she'd said, her eyes red-rimmed, her whole body drooping. Ricardo had not come with them, having found out that morning she wouldn't be coming back from Brazil after all. Simone had taken her sister's advice a little too seriously, electing not to break up with him until the very last second. Her guilt had followed them all the way to the airport. Now, she sniffed loudly, reaching out to hug Zivoin. She muttered something in his ear and then left them alone to say goodbye.

Alegria was crying before she even opened her mouth. 'What do we do?' she'd wanted to ask. But she didn't, because they'd had a version of that conversation a thousand times already. So she just gave him a wobbly smile and told him everything would be OK. What a useless thing to say. It was easier for her; she was the one going home. The thought of Zivoin in his empty room, the smell and touch of her all over it, made her feel desperate. But he had not cried, not even a little. His face was set, determined. 'I'll see you soon,' he said, and made it sound like a promise. 'We'll write letters. Maybe we'll each get one of those mobile phones – the ones you can take anywhere. We'll carry them around and call each other all the time.'

'I don't think they would even fit in your pocket – they're as heavy as bricks, aren't they?'

'I'll get a briefcase,' he said.

'Can they even call other countries? Wouldn't it be expensive?'

Zivoin ignored this and said, 'Portable phone or not, I will call you every day.' And then: 'Don't forget about me.'

'Don't be stupid.'

'I'm already stupid,' he said, looking at her, wide-eyed, eyebrows contracted goofily to make her laugh. 'Look at me here, in love with a woman who lives on the wrong side of the world.'

'*This* is the wrong side of the world.'

Their goodbye had been too quick. It should have been special; she should have planned it better. Alegria had thought about it in her head over and over again, trying to think of what to say to make it perfect, to make their time together feel real. And she was certain Zivoin had been doing the same – too often, in the days leading up to her departure, she'd caught him staring, like he was trying to commit all of her to memory. But in the end, there had been no space and not enough words. Or too many words, but no way to say them in ways that felt meaningful. All she could think of in that moment were overused, trite statements, and those were no good in the face of the biggest love she had ever known. They held each other and her body heaved with sobs. 'It's all right, it's all right. I'll see you soon,' he murmured over and over, stroking her hair, cupping her cheeks, kissing the tip of her nose. But they had at last run out of time. He let her go, and looked so twisted with the effort of holding himself together that Alegria had simply nodded and turned robotically to walk through the sliding doors. She had not looked back, and had regretted it immediately.

Now, in her family home, she felt her father's arms around her and realised that she was crying. 'It's nothing, it's nothing,' she gasped, but of course they did not listen. They were her mother and her father, and they held her as she wept. They held her until the sobs became gasps and the gasps became hiccups, and then Adelina crouched beside her, took her daughter's hands in her own and said, 'You're in love, querida.'

'I know.'

'But you came back.'

'I did.'

'But you are still together.'

'We are.'

Adelina nodded and stood up, wincing as her knees cracked loudly. Toninho planted several little kisses on top of Alegria's head. They both looked so concerned that she forced herself to smile, shaking her head as though sloughing off all her heartache. 'It will be fine,' she said automatically. 'Don't worry.'

'But what are you going to do?'

'I really don't know.' Needing to move about, to disperse some of her feelings, Alegria dragged her chair away from them a little, into the sunshine. It scraped loudly over the concrete and she flinched. She'd probably just woken up Si. 'Zivoin keeps insisting that everything will work out.'

'That's very steadfast of him,' Toninho observed. He was looking at his daughter with immense tenderness. She sat with her head tipped up towards the sun, her eyes closed, arms dangling beside her. 'He sounds like a good man.'

'Or,' Adelina said, 'he's in denial.'

'Mmm. Sometimes I worry about that too, but I don't think so. I think he just really believes we'll find a way through.'

'Do you believe it?'

'Most of the time. Sometimes it's hard – there's no *plan*.' She groaned in frustration and rubbed at her eyes furiously. 'I hate not knowing what to do.'

The mimosas trembled a little as a weak breeze lifted the edges of their petals. The butterfly had long since flown away.

'I wish we could meet him.' Her mother got up, went into the kitchen and came back with more coffee, more biscuits, and Alegria accepted them even though she could not find any pleasure in their taste.

'I've never seen you like this before,' Toninho said as she forced herself to take a sip. 'So stuck. You always know exactly what you want, or what needs to be done. It's why we always know you're going to be OK.'

'This time feels different.'

'What's going on?' Simone had appeared at the kitchen door, blinking sleepily at them. She was wearing nothing but one of Ricardo's old T-shirts, her face puffy and her hair all messed up on one side. Her eyes flickered from Alegria's deflated posture to her parents' worried faces. 'So you've told them.'

'She has.'

'Have you told them he says it's going to be OK?'

'I have.'

Si nodded and then cracked a smile. 'So stop looking so gloomy! We can't *all* be sad today or it's going to start raining.' She pointed accusatorily at the plate of biscuits. 'You have breakfast together out on our veranda and don't wake me up to join you? What kind of merda is this?'

Zivoin's breast pocket, March 1991

Cricket,

There's this old telenovela I used to watch with Mãe that had the most unlucky couple – no matter what they did, nothing ever went right for them. Whenever they had to part ways, the woman used to say, 'Ten hours away from you feels like ten days, which feels like ten years.' I always used to find that stuff embarrassing, but I think I understand now. Today makes ten days since you left me at the airport – how has it only been ten days? The mood in the house is sombre. Si is still sad from her break-up. Pai goes to the market every morning to buy us pineapples or graviola or mangos, and Si and I have to force ourselves to eat them with a smile, even though all she wants to do is lie in bed and all I want to do is go outside and keep moving so I don't have to think about this miserable heart of mine. Ten days and I still don't know what to do. The job I told you about – the teaching position, with more money – opens soon. I tried to gather my papers to prepare for the application and my arms suddenly got so heavy, my eyes closed and I woke up when it was dark – I fell asleep in the middle of the day! I'm used to waiting, but I'm not good at doing nothing. It feels wrong to have no job to orient myself around. There's a folder in my room full of my payslips – going back all the way to the seventies! I took them out and looked at them yesterday. They map half my life spent stacking shelves in supermarkets, or working the register, or teaching. I looked at them and I couldn't recognise the person who did those jobs any more. So much has changed.

I'm jumping about all over the place, because my thoughts won't stay still. They're like the lagartixas that run in and out of the house, too fast to catch, too slippery to see properly. Before I took out the payslips and sat there like an idiot, I went to my friend's house – Xiomara. I've known her since we were seventeen. She came as an exchange student and never left – we used to ride my moped to class together, first to school and then to university. She taught me how to curse someone out in Spanish – you'd like her. She has this beautiful little balcony overlooking Sabiá Park – when I say park, I don't mean like the ones we walked through in London together. Ours are much bigger, full of wilderness and giant monkey trees with their branches stretching up like hands emerging from the earth. Our lakes are bigger, deeper, snake-filled, our sun is stronger, our earth is richer, our colours more alive – these days I walk around making lists of places I want to show you, so you can understand why I love it here so much. Sometimes I think if I focus hard enough on the good parts, the bad ones won't be so bad. But I'm getting distracted – I was telling you about Xiomara, and I've just remembered that I've already talked so much about her that you already know all the things I wrote earlier. I don't want to cross it out, though, because it will look messy, so just pretend it's all new information, OK?

So, we sat on this balcony and Xiomara rolled a joint. Since I'm not working, I joined her. It was a perfect kind of heat – the kind that lets you sit still without getting itchy and damp – and all we could hear was the sound of crickets echoing through the trees. Of course it made me think of you. I haven't smoked in about a decade – it went straight to my head, and after a while I started creating this fantasy world where you and I could live and make things work. So here's what it looks like: we have all the money we could ever need, of course. So, you and I buy a big plot of land somewhere. It depends on where you'd like to go. Maybe by the ocean – our waters are warm, so you can swim there any time of the year. And there we can build houses, one for my parents, one for yours, one for us. Homes for everyone. And, yes, we have all the money we need, but we'll still want to work, right? What would we do if we had too much time? So I thought about what we could do – I never wanted to be a teacher, to be honest. I like it, but it was more for the stability. The more I thought about it, the more I thought about how nice it would be to run our own business – a restaurant! A Brazilian–Yugoslavian restaurant by the sea, so popular we take reservations six months in advance, and all the celebrities could come visit. Rita Lee would perform there twice a year, and Gilberto Gil would too, and maybe even Caetano Veloso, and people would sit outside the restaurant even if they couldn't get a table, just to hear them sing. We could get some good beef in and do a churrasco for them, set up a bar at the edge of the water. You could run it, I could do the accounting and keep the books, and then for six weeks every year we would close it down and go travel the world together with our children.

I know you wanted five, but even in a fantasy, that's never going to happen! We can have two, or three, maybe. Twins run in my family, you know, just like yours, so maybe we'll have twins, and we will take them with us and let them learn about life by seeing the world. Our home would be three floors and made of dark wood, only wood, and glass. We'd be surrounded by palm trees and grow our own fruit, so that every morning I could eat papaya by reaching out of my window and taking it straight from the tree. There could be a pool on the far edge, for the days we're too lazy to get to the ocean, and a jacuzzi so that at night we can lie in the warm water and look up to see the stars. Brazil has the most incredible night sky – you have to see it one day. I got so sucked into this fantasy that I stopped paying attention to everything else. After a while, Xiomara said something like, 'Wow, that sounds like paradise.' It turns out I'd been talking the whole time, not just imagining it all like I thought.

Of course, this is my fantasy, not yours, so it was always going to be set here. I'm sure if you could, you would bring us all back to Yugoslavia. I like to think I could be happy there too. I like to think you and I can be happy anywhere. We'll talk on the phone soon after I finish this, but it won't ever be the same. I spend all day having conversations with you in my head. Writing that makes me want to cry. Be safe, be careful, be happy.

I love you,
Ale

Alegria's bedside table, March 1991

My love,

I tried calling last night and the call couldn't go through. I don't know if the problem was at your end or mine. Of course, by the time this letter reaches you, I think we will have already spoken, and I will have explained it all to you and felt better for hearing your voice. Forgive the repetition. Forgive it all: I'm a man stuck underneath a cloud. Sometimes, I translate expressions from my language directly, impatiently, hoping the meaning will come across. You know one of them – imate putera na glavi – 'you have butter on your head'. This is the one I said that time in bed, late at night, trying to make you laugh. You choked on your tea and spilled it, pulling the bed sheets up across your bare body to protect it from the hot liquid – you thought I was insulting you. But how could I have known that my word for butter sounds like your word for whore? By the way, you were right when you said there was an equivalent in English. It's 'butter would not melt in his mouth'. I asked a customer – a native speaker – at work if it was similar and she said it was. Another one is: Ja sam kao muva bez glave. 'I am like a fly without a head.' This one also has a translation: 'to be a headless chicken'. That's how I feel these days.

Peach, on the phone, when you told me what the immigration lawyer said, I should have made more room for your feelings instead of rushing past them. I felt so helpless listening to you cry down the line, hearing your parents in the background trying to comfort you. That's my job. But we didn't have enough time and I didn't want to spend it being sad. It is torturous, only being able to speak for a few minutes at a time, but who knew calling Brazil was so expensive! My bin is full of used-up phone cards, but I will call you every single day until we reunite, whatever the cost. In other news – I'm no longer buying cigarettes, to fund my new international habit instead. I bet that makes you happy. Look, I still don't believe that lawyer. The ten-year ban can be dealt with, we just haven't found a solution yet. Things back home are bad once again. Nothing official has happened yet, but things are deteriorating fast. Rumours are circulating that the People's Army could take away the weapons of the Croatian territorial defence force – effectively, a coup. There have been riots in the streets over this possibility, and even though Serbian leaders have come out to say that this would never happen, I'm not sure Croatia believes them.

These days, every Yugoslav I know is walking around with a pit in their stomach. You know the feeling you get when you miss a step? That's how I feel all the time. I call home and my mother cries, and I make emergency evacuation plans for everyone and think about where I can take them. I call my friend Kajo, and he says the same thing. I can't even get hold of Feki. Montenegro has a beautiful coast – one day I will take you there. Whenever I think about it now, I think that it would be an eleven-hour boat ride to Italy, across the Adriatic. Or an eight-hour drive to Greece. That's how I would try to get them out, if the war ever reached my family . . . and then I think I am overreacting, that the international pressure will force Serbia to back down, and actually, we'll find a peaceful way through. Yugoslavia will emerge shaken but unbroken, and we won't be looked at with pity by the East and West. Is that hope? Is this feeling coming because I am dating you?

I have got carried away again – when I write to you, I pretend we're having a conversation. It takes me hours, but it feels like minutes. I'm saying all the nonsense I can think of, because as I write, I imagine your face reading this and it is too pleasurable to stop. Have I ever told you that I'm a poet? I'll say all the terrible, funny, stupid things possible if it will make you smile that huge smile I love so much.

So. Yugoslavia can't have us, London won't have you. What's left? Would I move to Brazil for you? Of course I would, if I only had myself to worry about. We've talked about this before – it would be almost impossible for me to make enough money there, even just for the two of us. But my family needs me. I'm their only child, their son. They have always needed me, and they will always need me. I cannot leave them behind. I know you know this, which is why you have never asked me to come to you. I am sorry. I wish I could. But what kind of man would I be if I abandoned my family? Not the kind that you would love.

Where does that leave us? Somewhere in the middle, I guess? I will keep thinking, and I will find a solution for us. Please do not give up hope. I know you think love should be peaceful, but I still think you're wrong about that. Love should make the impossible feel possible.

What else . . . Work is the same. A few days ago someone spat at me, actually spat at me. The spit landed at least a metre in front of my shoe. First I froze, and he told me to go back to where I came from. I forced myself to laugh in front of him and his friends, but I would have fought them. I was ready to fight them.

Here the radio is playing an old song over and over – it's called 'Should I Stay or Should I Go' by a band called The Clash. Do you know it? It's because of a Levi's ad that everyone's talking about, the one where two men play pool. The guy in the Levi's wins, of course. It's everywhere. Have you seen it? Is the song playing on the radio there? If it is, listen to the lyrics. They make me think of you every time. Also, Darco has been seeing someone! I know – the same boy who could barely look you in the eye is dating. He seems happy. It's nice to see him happy.

I have to stop here, or I will run on to a fifth page and it will get too expensive. One day, Peach, we'll speak each other's language. We'll raise children with three mother tongues. If you die before me – and you won't, because you are the smarter one – I'll carry all your letters in my briefcase so that in the hard times and the impossible times I can hold them in my hand and know that we were real. We are real.

Stupidly,
Zivoin

CHAPTER 17

Uberlândia, the first day of April 1991

The phone rang. Everyone knew who it was for. Her mother was in the kitchen making pamonha, there was the faint whiff of pineapples and beer, meaning her father was in the house somewhere, and there was Simone, who was probably lounging on Alegria's bed right at this moment. Then there was Alegria, of course, looking stunning in a white shift dress with green and yellow bangles at each wrist, made of smooth, painted wood. A gift from the love of her life from the time they'd walked hand in hand through Portobello Market and the smells – of bodies, of food, of sewage, of cigarette smoke, of old meat – had made her nauseous. She was dozing; the afternoon heat had made her sleepy. She'd worn one of her favourite dresses to do nothing but lounge about. At any rate, the phone rang and everyone knew who it was for, and Alegria got up off the tiled floor she so loved to lie on and scrambled for it, her entire body trembling. She didn't know why her entire body was trembling. And then it happened fast, as if they'd rehearsed it enough times to know the conversation off by heart and were delivering lines from a play back and forth, rat-a-tat-tat, rat-a-tat-tat—

'Alô?'

                                              'It's me.'

'Of course it's you. How are you, my love?'

                    'Fantastic. I am fantastic, Peach. I have figured it out!'

'Figured what out?'

                              'You *know* what.'

'I just like to hear you talk. I like to distract you into spending more time on the phone with me.'

                    'I spend all the time I can afford on the phone with you.'

'I wish I could be the one to call you. If it weren't so expensive—'

                    'I take great pleasure in calling, please don't take it away from me.' Laughter. A pause.

'So . . . you have an answer?'

> 'I do, but first let's talk more. I have missed the sound of your voice so much.'

'How is Darco?'

> 'He thinks he's in love.' More laughter. 'His first love – it's going to be brutal.'

'Oh, poor Darco. I hope you aren't teasing him!'

> 'Just the normal amount. Of course, if he needs me, I will be there for him. But before I tell you about my solution to our problem, let's be silly, let's pretend we can go anywhere.'

'Why?'

> 'Because sometimes you have to let your imagination take a leap of faith, Peach. So, where shall we go, then, if we can go anywhere?'

'We can't go anywhere.'

    Rush of static, sigh. 'OK, but if we *could* go anywhere, if money and family weren't an issue, where would you go?'

'... I don't know, Zivoin.'

    'I'm sure you can think of somewhere.'

'Where would you go?'

    'I've always wanted to visit Russia. Leningrad, maybe. Japan too.'

'Oh, yes, Japan would be amazing. I'd buy a Sony Walkman.'

    'Where else?'

'Well... probably Peru. I would like to see Machu Picchu. And I've always wanted to visit Paris, the city of love.'

MONIKA RADOJEVIC

> 'Well, I don't think I can manage
> Peru, but I can definitely
> take you to the city of love.
> Would you like that?'

Silence. 'Zivoin, don't joke
about things like that.'

> 'You know, Peach, there's an
> expression where I come from,
> for people like you.'

'Oh really?'

> 'Yes, if I translate it . . . you
> are like a thirsty person who is
> always busy refusing water.'

'What?'

> 'I'm trying to say that you deny
> yourself all the time. Even when
> it's just a game. Even when it's
> things you want – especially
> when it's things you want.'

'I'm not den—'

'You are. You're so afraid that
this might be exactly what you
want, and what you need, that
you would rather close every
door and walk through the one
you *know* you don't want. I
know you, Alegria—'

'You don't know me as well
as you think you know me!'
Shouting now. The house fell
silent under the weight of this
unfamiliar anger.

'Yes, I do. I know everything I
need to, and you do too.'

'You're crazy.'

'Yes, I am! And so are you!
But you go in the opposite
direction – you're the kind of
crazy that starts to tidy up *before*
the party's over.'

'That's not nice.'

'Come on, Peach, I've told that
exact joke to you before and
you laughed.'

'Well, if I were with you, I
would laugh. But I am not with
you and so everything that
should be funny isn't funny.'

        'That's why I'm calling. Come
        back, Alegria. I never beg, and I
        won't beg, so I'm only going to
        say it today.'

Silence. A bangle clinked
against the receiver. Just do it,
she thought, just say it. Go on,
deep breath.

        'Come back here and we'll
        make it work.'

'I want to, but my visa—'

        'Ah! Your visa – OK, this is the
        thing I have figured out. Are
        you ready?'

'. . . Yes.'

        'Come to Belgrade and—'

'I don't have the *money*,
Zivoin—'

        'You will have the money, because I will buy the ticket for you, OK? Now can you please stop interrupting? I can tell you're angry, but because I know you so well, I know that you're not even angry at me, you're angry at yourself. And I think I can fix that too – so can I finish, please, Peach?'

'Fine.'

        'Good. So, here is what we do. You come to Belgrade, we'll sort out your visa over there, and then we both return to London.'

'To London?'

        'Yes – it's not my home, it's not your home, but maybe together we can make it our home. We've talked about it so much, it's worn holes in my trousers—'

MONIKA RADOJEVIC

'Ugh, what does that even mean?'

'It's a translated expression, but you get what I'm saying?'

More laughter, curt, angry laughter. 'I do not.'

'I'm saying, marry me, love of my life. Come to Belgrade and marry me, and we'll change your passport and get you added onto *my* visa, and then you and I will be together, and the rest won't matter.'

'Marry you?'

'Marry me. Yes, we've only really known each other for three months—'

'Four months!'

'Can you relax? I'm not counting the time we've spent apart. Let me finish my speech – sure, we don't speak each other's language, yes, you have never met my family, but so what? So fucking what? I love you, and we can't live this kind of half-love, where we spend all day working to pay for a five-minute phone call. I won't do it. I know your family is everything to you. So is mine. But if we cannot bear to be apart, we are going to have to be together. So. Marry me?'

Silence. Bangles clinking against the receiver, sliding down a shaking arm. *Just do it, just say it.* Long, slow breaths from the other end of the line, her family gathered behind her, watching, waiting.

Once, when Alegria was a child, they had gone on a family holiday to Pirenópolis, a mystic city with almost a hundred sprawling waterfalls open to the public. On the third day they had walked through dense forest to get to Corumbá, one of the widest, largest waterfalls on the trail. You could stand on the very precipice of a huge rock, peering over the edge to the long drop below – signs were plastered everywhere warning people not to jump. Adelina, clutching a baby Simone to her chest, had refused to go near it, so Toninho and Alegria went together, heel-toeing the path, edging forwards carefully. Toninho's hand hovered by Alegria, ready to grab her if she tripped. When they were half a metre away, Toninho stopped her from going any further. 'If you stretch your neck out like this,' he said, 'you can see some of the bottom.' And so she had, craning her neck and her shoulders forward whilst keeping her feet firmly planted on the slimy rock face. She had always been such a careful, well-behaved girl. Looking down into the waterfall's mouth had elicited a feeling Alegria could not, to this day, explain. A powerful, almost overwhelming urge to pitch forward. Every nerve in her body sang, every muscle clenched; she had known with an eight-year-old's utter certainty that if she were to jump, she would not plummet. She would fly.

And so she had made an involuntary movement. A sort of lurch forward, except not really a lurch – her feet, she insisted later, had never left the ground. But in the space between one moment and the next, her little body twitched as though she were about to run, full speed, and throw herself off the cliff with every ounce of her energy. Adelina screamed, Simone, frightened by the sound, began to cry, and Toninho let out a yell and grabbed his daughter's arm so hard, she slipped, slicing open her knee. The wound had scarred. She could see the scar now, the rippled, puckered skin. Alegria stared down, clutching the phone and feeling her entire body thrumming, gearing up for the leap. What an offer he'd made. What an urge he gave her, to fly off the cliff edge – this time for real. No hand on her arm to stop her, or save her.

'OK.' She pushed the word out from her mouth in a way that some might mistake for reluctance. But not the man at the other end of the phone, no. He recognised it for what it really was. Faith.

PART TWO

CHAPTER 18

Ljubljana, April 1991

Day 1

After the phone call in which she agrees to marry Zivoin in a country she knows nothing about, Alegria begins the process of dismantling a life of thirty years in a city she knows like the back of her hand. It takes her far less time than she assumed it would, systematically moving her belongings between piles labelled 'Take', 'Leave' and 'Donate', which grow and shrink each day as she changes her mind – or as Si convinces her that she will definitely miss the sheer leopard-print top she hasn't worn in years, because it goes *so* perfectly with her black skirt and her boots.

On the third day of this, Adelina, fed up, bans Simone from the bedroom and takes charge of packing with the brutal practicality of a mother who knows she will be the one dealing with whatever gets left behind. Together, she and her daughter set aside school exercise books, beloved travel guides, a stuffed toy toucan, CDs, photo albums and letters from friends. They neatly pack them away in labelled boxes, ready for the day she will come back to claim them. Alegria puts roughly a third of her life into two large suitcases she will take with her, and donates or bins the rest. She marvels at how methodical she is able to be despite the gaping hole that seems to have opened up in the centre of her stomach. Less than six months ago, nothing in the world would have torn her from her family. And now she is putting an ocean between them. How can that be true? It fills her with an exquisite kind of pain, but it does not make her stop. She ties up loose ends, she calls old friends and meets them at their old haunts, drinks endless coconut waters and repeats a memorised script, stopping at the appropriate moments to make room for gasps, for astonishment, for alarm. She fields the repeated questions about where Yugoslavia is, what it is, why there, why London, why a man from this cold, exotic place – and what about money? And her visa? Is he rich? Does he have a British passport? Is he beautiful? Does she have a photo? *Aren't you afraid? I would be!*

She hugs her parents endlessly, relentlessly, and they stop whatever they're doing to hug her back, sad, nervous, excited, worn. She starts spending every morning in their bed with them, sometimes right as the sun is rising, brewing sugared coffee and carrying it in on a little tray. They learn to associate the smell of coffee with her arrival. Simone often joins them in the bed, sleepy and placid. They lie there and talk, laugh, until Toninho heaves his body up, the grey hairs on his chest worrying them all, and gets dressed for work. At dinner one night, when her father unexpectedly reaches out to grasp her hand, his eyes blurred with tears, her heart swells with expansive, aching love for him and for everything she will lose when she leaves. And they sit there eating in silence, grief taking its place at the table.

She navigates all of this with an unexpected sense of calm. She is fairly certain that this process changes her profoundly. This calmness surprises them all. It begins the moment she agrees to marry Zivoin and makes the decision to go to him. It is with her as she catches the plane with the ticket he bought for her, draining his bank account, she is sure. It is there throughout the turbulence over the Atlantic Ocean, when the seatbelt sign flickers on and the in-flight meal service is temporarily paused. It does not waver when she catches sight of herself in the airplane bathroom mirror, the artificial lighting making her look sickly and dull, and she sees that grief has sunk in around her eyes in the form of dark circles.

All this to say that when she begins the journey, Alegria does not anticipate anything difficult unfolding on the path in front of her. The hard things have already been completed and ticked off. She has arrived in Germany, and her flight from Frankfurt to Belgrade will take off in a couple of hours. All she needs to do is collect and then check in her luggage all over again. She detaches herself from the crowd of Brazilians, heaves her suitcases onto a trolley and walks absent-mindedly through to international transfers, not paying much attention to her surroundings. She's thinking about her wedding dress. They could not afford to buy a new one, of course, but after she announced the news, Adelina had emerged from her bedroom with a cream cardboard box and beckoned Alegria over. She and Simone had sat cross-legged on the floor, watching curiously as their mother removed the lid and protective plastic wrapping, revealing tissue paper layered over a luxurious-looking, peach-coloured fabric. On top of the tissue paper sat a pair of cotton gloves, which she put on before carefully lifting the dress from the box and holding it out in front of her. It was both simple and exquisite, a floor-length slip dress that shimmered slightly in the light.

'This was my wedding dress. You should take it with you,' she said, as Simone and Alegria gasped and bent closer to look at it. 'Don't touch it! It's silk, handmade – the grease from your hands will ruin it.' She held it up to Alegria's shoulders. 'We can get Daniela to alter it in case it doesn't fit you.'

'It's so beautiful, Mãe,' Alegria had said tenderly. 'Thank you – but are you sure you don't want to keep it?'

'Does it look like it would fit me any more? Just make sure that when you touch it you use the gloves.' Her mother's voice was full of longing as she added, 'And take lots of photos, so I can see you on your wedding day, OK?'

But the trouble begins shortly after landing in Frankfurt – of course it does. Alegria is still thinking about what pair of shoes she could possibly wear with a dress so elegant when she is informed that her ongoing flight has been cancelled. She joins a long queue at the customer service desks and watches as other people are issued with tickets to wherever they need to go. It seems like things are running smoothly and she is not particularly worried. Flights get cancelled all the time, and there are always plenty of replacements. It's like missing a bigger, more expensive bus, she thinks. Another should be along soon. And then she gets to the front of the queue.

'There will be no flights to Yugoslavia this week,' the German woman behind the desk informs her. She says this incredibly casually, almost cruelly, as though this isn't news that anyone might be bothered by.

Alegria stares at her for a little too long, trying to catch up. 'I'm sorry?' she says, and the woman repeats herself, adjusting her thin wire-framed glasses with a delicate pinch of forefinger and thumb.

'But – but why?'

'Well . . .' The woman sucks in her breath and stares down at the computer for what feels like an unreasonably long time. Alegria watches her tap on the keyboard half-heartedly, and then lean over to mutter something in German to her colleague. She turns back to Alegria and says, 'There has been an incident in Croatia. All in all, there are now no flights to Yugoslavia at all, and you cannot get where you need to go, yes?'

'But how long until there are flights?' Alegria asks, uncomprehendingly. 'Tonight? Are there any tonight?'

'We think it will be at least a week. Maybe more.'

'A week?' she gasps, the shock of it making her eyes water. 'But . . . but . . . that's impossible. I'm supposed to be getting married in a few days.'

'I don't think so.' The woman who is meant to be helping her wears an all-black suit, has her brown hair in a severe ponytail. It waggles as she talks. Her name tag says *Ana* and she is detached, matter-of-fact. She is unmoved by Alegria's distress. 'We would only be able to cover your first night in a hotel, yes? After that you will need to file a compensation claim with the Frankfurt office. Make sure you keep the receipts, because you will need to produce an itemised—'

'I can't afford to stay in a hotel for a week – and I don't even have a visa,' Alegria pleads, impatiently brushing away tears of frustration. 'Can't you put me on another flight?'

'As I said, all British Airways—'

A mother who is queuing behind her with a small, fussing child in her arms, and who looks as frustrated as Alegria feels, has been listening to their conversation and promptly joins her at the desk. She heaves the baby onto the counter and starts arguing with Ana in a mixture of German and heavily accented English, pointing first at her son, then at the bewildered woman next to her. The baby starts to wail furiously, his fat hands tugging at her hair.

'What about different airline?' the mother demands, wincing as she tries to disentangle a strand that has become wrapped around her son's fingers.

'Excuse me?'

'Yugoslavia national airline still flying, yes?'

'JAT Airlines does have *some* planes, yes, but—'

'So we go with them. You give us tickets.'

'It would be a matter of—'

'No time to argue – where is the gate, please.' The woman is stoic, hammering away at Ana with the same kind of blunt stubbornness as Zivoin. They must be from the same place, Alegria thinks. Even the way she pronounces 'Yugoslavia' feels familiar and safe. She watches the woman push and prod until finally things go their way.

'OK,' Ana says at last, reluctantly. 'There's a direct to Ljubljana Airport leaving now, if you *insist* on going today.' She repeats this in German and Alegria's new friend nods enthusiastically, her fingers drumming on the counter.

'Is that in Yugoslavia?' Alegria asks.

Ana sighs at the question. 'It is. Once you land there, you will have to make your own way to Belgrade. We are not responsible for you once you transfer airlines.'

'Yes, yes, fine.' Because it all happens so fast, because everyone seems so uncertain, because she is so eager to get to Zivoin, it does not occur to Alegria to ask certain questions. For example: do I have time to make a phone call? For example: how far away is Ljubljana from Belgrade? For example: is it easy to get to Belgrade from Ljubljana? And then there are other questions she doesn't know she should be asking, such as: what has happened in Croatia? What about the border? These are all things she will think about later, astounded yet again at her own naivety. But because she is in love and the idea of waiting is unbearable, all Alegria can do is plough forward.

Ana prints off their new boarding passes, looking sour. 'You will need to be quick. The gate has already closed. You probably need to run.' She repeats herself in German.

The woman with the small boy looks at Alegria, and Alegria looks at the woman with the small boy. Without speaking, they launch into action. Alegria takes the woman's suitcase and heaves it onto the trolley, next to her own. She grabs the boy's little red backpack and sets it on top; he screams and protests at this development. Together they run, the woman's son bouncing on her hip. Her cornflower-blue skirt flaps around her ankles as she shouts people out of the way. The terminal is not far away, but it is far enough for people carrying a bad-tempered, squirming child or pushing a heavy trolley. By the time they arrive, Alegria's back is uncomfortably wet, and heat rises off her in waves. The woman places the child down and searches for her passport, her chest heaving. They *just* make it. There is no time to stop and buy water, no time to use the bathroom, no time to call Zivoin and explain that she will not be arriving in Belgrade after all.

By the time Alegria lands in the minuscule Ljubljana Airport at 10.37 p.m., hope is the only thing that keeps her going. Or perhaps that's a lie she's telling herself, and what keeps her going is the simple fact that she cannot turn back now. Her heart and her wallet will not allow it, and maybe this is truly what propels her forwards.

Either way – she's lucky. She is lucky, for example, that only a single plane has landed there that evening, at this small airport with only two terminals. She is lucky that she is waved through by immigration with a two-week visa casually stamped in her passport, because by the time she walks out of the arrivals gate it is 11:09 and the airport is shutting down for the night. Alegria did not know this was something airports could do, but there is no other explanation – there are security guards escorting them out of the building, shutters are coming down and lights are being turned off. They are ushered outside, where a single, powerful light illuminates the snow-covered road. The contrast between the night sky and the bleak terminal – beset by creatures that are either enormous moths or tiny bats – is poetic. Though she knows it's ridiculous, Alegria has the powerful impression that they are floating in outer space, because beyond their building, there is only complete and total blackness. She can see nothing beyond where the street light reaches. There is no moon tonight.

Alegria looks around, hoping to spot the woman from Frankfurt. Olga. They had ended up sitting across from each other on the plane, each with a row to themselves. The boy had stretched out on the seats and fallen asleep with his thumb in his mouth and his head in his mother's skirt. The women looked at each other and shared that slightly clumsy smile of two strangers thrown together by events beyond their control. Alegria had tried to talk to her across the aisle, but after a few minutes of stilted conversation, she gave up and stared fretfully out of the window as Olga chain-smoked menthols, making the entire cabin smell like a burning forest. Eventually, Olga had pulled out a miniature chess set and waved it at her with a raised eyebrow. A tiny game of chess on a plane! How surreal! She wasn't particularly good, but they played anyway. With one hand protectively on her son's forehead, Olga lowered the tray table and placed the board on it, and Alegria would lean forward gingerly whenever it was her go, taking care not to knock the little pieces. She suspected that her new friend played badly on purpose to prolong the game. It had been a helpful distraction.

But she'd lost track of mother and son at immigration, and now she glances over the heads and shoulders of other people, trying unsuccessfully to spot them. She thinks about the panic her parents tried to conceal from her when she sat down and informed them of her decision.

When she'd put the phone down, her whole body surging with energy, she had turned to find all three of them,

Toninho, Adelina and Simone, gathered behind her solemnly, like mourners at a funeral. She had to explain – properly this time – where exactly in Europe this strange country called Yugoslavia was, the language spoken, the region's instability as she understood it. As she spoke, her parents seemed to shrink before her eyes, perhaps fully grasping the enormity of what she was saying, and how helpless they would be if she needed them. Unable to reach her. Unable, even, to attend their daughter's wedding.

'How can you marry if no one will give you away?' Toninho had asked quietly.

'They don't do weddings in churches there,' she'd said, although everyone knew that wasn't what he meant and that, really, the detail of being given away, or even of getting married, didn't matter at all. What mattered was that she would have to do it alone. There was no money to do it in Brazil, no money to take them to Yugoslavia, no money to do it twice. The family had celebrated, in a shell-shocked kind of way, by going out for ice cream and eating it in silence.

Now, Alegria blinks her eyes dry and strains to hear the noises of a city – cars, trains, people – but there is nothing, only expansive silence. The crowd stands out there in the cold and the darkness, and panic grips her by the throat. What has she done? She obviously cannot stay here, but where on earth can she go? And with what money? There are no taxis anywhere, and the airport has been locked and shut down. And although she is not the only person waiting there, everyone else seems to have somewhere to go. The thought of spending the whole night on the concrete bench beside her, in this freezing and unfamiliar place, makes Alegria's heart beat so fast she feels light-headed. She twists around to look at the airport, as though a clue might appear. But it is just a small building. Grey concrete and tinted windows, nondescript. Alegria wonders if the people who work there are still inside, and if they have their own exit. How do they get home after their shifts? It must be their cars parked out front – perhaps one of them would give her a lift? Being in a car with a stranger makes her uneasy, but surely it would be safer than staying out here all night. She'd freeze to death if she did that, or at the very least lose a few fingers. Or her ears, or the tip of her nose. Would Zivoin still want her if she were disfigured?

The other thing she cannot stop worrying about is the peach-coloured dress. Her wedding dress. Zivoin had warned her that it is unseasonably cold at the moment, that some parts of the country are still experiencing snow. This does not feel like snow, it feels like she's stumbled into a brutal, remote part of the earth. If all of Yugoslavia is like this, there is no way she will be able to wear the dress. She doesn't own anything else remotely as beautiful, nothing that makes her skin glow like that dress. She shivers violently and glances around. The crowd doesn't seem panicked. Some of them are getting into cars, but most are simply standing there, lighting cigarettes or stamping their feet.

A hand suddenly grips her elbow, and Alegria jumps. Olga is by her side, chocolate-brown strands escaping the scarf loosely tied around her head. The child is asleep again, drooling down her shoulder. 'What's going on?' Alegria asks her helplessly in English, knowing it is fruitless. 'Is there a hotel? A taxi?'

Though they can barely communicate, Olga recognises Alegria's fear, and gives her a thumbs-up. 'Is OK. You go. Autobus,' she says loudly, pointing to the crowd of people. Her voice is thin, a little nasal. She says something unrecognisable in her own language, and then points to the payphone attached to the wall behind Alegria.

'Telephone?' she asks, and Olga nods vigorously, jabbing repeatedly at the phone. She's becoming more impatient. Alegria shakes her head. 'No money,' she says, pointing at herself. When the woman keeps pointing, growing insistent, Alegria almost begins crying in frustration. 'No money,' she repeats, and opens her wallet to show the woman her American dollars. Olga lets out a low whistle, her eyebrows raised, as if to say, *Wow, how unprepared you are.* If the situation didn't feel so desperate, she might have laughed, but she can only nod – and then, adding to the humiliation, she finally starts sobbing.

Her new friend makes a clucking noise, and waves her hands as if trying to dismiss the tears. She turns to say something to a man who has been standing quietly behind her, holding her suitcase. The man nods, goes to his car and returns with a handful of coins. 'Autobus, Beograd,' the man says, pointing again to the gaggle of people. 'Beograd, OK?'

She nods, feeling a small gasp of relief – so there *is* a way to get to Zivoin after all.

The man holds up both his hands, showing her ten fingers, and then holds up his left index finger. They both look at her expectantly. Are they telling her the time the bus will arrive? But it is already well past eleven. Confused, she points to her watch, and he nods enthusiastically, then repeats the gesture. 'Big motorway,' he says, indicating the road. He opens his arms as wide as he can.

She stares at him for a moment, until something clicks into place. An eleven-hour bus ride to Belgrade, that's what they're trying to say. In that moment, she wouldn't care if he told her it would take a hundred hours. She nods again, thanks him and gives him a weak smile. The gesture feels inadequate – she'd hug him, if Zivoin hadn't already warned her that people here aren't as affectionate with strangers as they are in Brazil. Olga takes Alegria by her arm and steers her to the phone. She inserts the coins, punches in the Belgrade extension and then holds the phone out to Alegria. As she takes it, Olga grabs her shoulder and nods once, her eyes boring into Alegria's, and then she lets go and is gone before Alegria can say thank you, or even fully comprehend what is happening. In the days to come she will think about her often, wishing there had been time to express her appreciation for all this effort, all this kindness. But there's a flurry of activity from the small crowd of people, and she senses, rather than sees, that a bus must be on its way. So she dials the only number she knows, the one Zivoin gave her in case of emergency. It belongs to an old friend of his, a man called Kajo she's never met. She doesn't know the sound of his voice, but prays that someone – anyone – will pick up. By now Zivoin will know about the cancelled flights, surely. He must be worried, wondering why she hasn't been in touch. Her decision not to stay in Frankfurt for a few extra days feels incredibly short-sighted.

She can see the bus coming now, yellow headlights like two exploding stars. Someone picks up on the first ring.

'Molim?'

'Hello? Zivoin?'

'Eh! Alegria!' an unfamiliar voice shouts. There's a brief rush of static, and the sound of yelling.

The bus trundles into view now, coming to a halt a few metres away. Panic bubbles in her stomach. There aren't many people waiting, not more than fifteen or so. Alegria has to get on that bus – but she badly wants to hear his voice first. What if he thinks she's changed her mind?

'Kah-Kah-Kajo?' Her teeth begin chattering so hard she can barely spit the words out. 'Can you hear me?'

'It's me.' Zivoin is on the other end now. She's so relieved she almost begins sobbing again. He is urgent, asking too many questions. 'Where are you? What's going on? The flight—'

'No time!' she says wildly, trying to keep her voice steady. 'Listen! I'm in Ljub-Ljub—' In the chaos and the cold, she stumbles again. Her mouth has never had to make this sound before, this 'l' that tips into a soft 'j'. Her lips move but only gibberish comes out – it's like being trapped in a nightmare. People are boarding the bus now, and Alegria knows she has barely a minute left. No one has realised she is still there, no one will wait for her. She tries one more time. 'Ljub—'

'Ljubljana? But how—'

'No time!' she cries. 'The airport has closed, I have to go – there's only one bus. I think it goes to Belgrade, I don't know. They said it takes eleven hours.'

'OK, go – I'll find you. Stay until the last stop.' She can

tell he's making an effort to sound calm and reassuring, as though he has known all along that this would happen. It fills her with a powerful, aching wish to see him, a renewed sense of fear at everything that has gone wrong. She wants to say something about it being a bad omen, she wants to explain that she's flailing, ill-equipped for this journey, she wants him to step in and come to find her. There is no plan, there is nothing she can rely on except the person at the other end of the phone. Zivoin makes everything seem less frightening. 'Whatever you do, don't get off the bus.'

'OK!'

'I love you.'

'I love *you*.' She slams down the receiver, grabs her suitcases and runs out into the darkness, apprehension building in her chest like a hurricane about to hit land.

CHAPTER 19

Belgrade, April 1991

Day 1

Zivoin's eyes are strained, his neck and shoulders aching from hunching over a map of the city. He has temporarily taken over Kajo's apartment, now a makeshift command centre. As he rubs his eyes, Svetlana, Kajo's wife, disappears into their bedroom without saying goodnight. She is fed up now, irritated that the evening has been upended by a call from Zivoin's foreign girlfriend – unable to catch a simple bus. The timing of the journey confuses them. It usually takes six hours to drive from Ljubljana to Belgrade, so why has Alegria told them it will take eleven? Can she have misunderstood? Is she even coming here at all? Zivoin and Kajo go back and forth, until Svetlana interrupts and reminds them of the checkpoints. And the recent events with the soldiers. Events that Alegria knows nothing about. How would he even explain it to her? Zivoin can't answer, and all three of them fall silent. The soldiers have nudged everyone into a state of uneasy, unspeakable tension. Zivoin, who has not visited Yugoslavia in six months, is shocked. He had expected change, but this is different. People do not look at each other in the streets. Many Croatian bars and restaurants have their shutters down, their owners nowhere to be seen. There are no more jokes about spying on your neighbours, or burning your draft papers, or dating the wrong kind of girl. Yugoslavia has been plunged into icy water, the country collectively holding its breath. And no one is untouched – even the three friends in the room. Svetlana, a Montenegrin with a Croatian father, married to Kajo, a Serbian with nationalist parents who bemoan their union. And then Zivoin, Montenegrin to the core, even if his mother insists that she, too, comes from Serbia. All of it bears so much weight, and yet all of it is meaningless, identities cobbled together by myth and incomplete family trees. It is the custom not to record the births of women, their marriages or the children they go on to have. Anyone could be from anywhere.

Surely, Svetlana eventually suggests, the bus will have to go around Croatia, maybe even crossing into Hungary? And then she announces that it has become late and she leaves the room, a sourness in the air. The door clicks shut behind her. Kajo sighs. Zivoin has known him since their army days – a fellow trained machine-gunner. They both ended up at the University of Belgrade, even living in the same student dorms. He's always known his friend to be a jokester, the life of the party. But this time around he's subdued. Zivoin can't stop looking at Kajo's hair, which has turned completely grey.

'Sorry for ruining her night,' he mutters, still focused on the map. 'And yours.'

His friend shakes his head. 'She's on edge – everyone is. Nothing we can do except drink.' Kajo rests his hands on his generous stomach and nudges him. 'Are you going to sleep anytime soon?'

'Not until I know where she's going.'

Only now does he appreciate how large and sprawling Belgrade is, and how little he knows beyond the city centre and one or two neighbourhoods. Kajo makes a dismissive noise in his throat and shakes his head. 'Women. Even when they're not here they're causing trouble.'

Zivoin ignores this. He's worrying about Alegria being alone out there. It's almost one in the morning and he has no idea where she is, or how she's feeling. He's afraid that the missed flights, the strange bus route, the subtle signs of decline will scare her into changing her mind. Sometimes, Alegria reminds him of the skittish horses from the village, easily spooked by loud noises, prone to bolting. He feels like he has to manage the situation around her carefully. She keeps her cards close to her chest – or, maybe she's so afraid by the depths of her feelings that she pushes them away. He can't tell. He loves her, but she can be a mystery to him. Zivoin considers himself to be as transparent as a man can be. He says what he's thinking, he tells her he loves her, he asks her to marry him, and although she said yes, and he knew in that moment she truly meant it, Alegria has a tendency to dance around the edge of something, flirting with the idea of leaping off but never quite committing. So what if she has changed her mind? What if she arrives in Belgrade tired, frightened, hungry, and says, 'We are too different for this to work'? He loves her, but he will not beg her to stay. Zivoin is too proud to beg for anything.

'Let's start over,' he says, and returns to the map. He pours Kajo a glass of wine from the bottle he brought as an apology – a bottle that Svetlana did not touch – and they resume their work. The problem is that Yugoslavia is a large country – over two hundred and fifty thousand square kilometres – with an advanced network of buses and trains. There are dozens of routes Alegria's bus might be taking, even after ruling out Croatia. Which means there are several bus stops she could end up at. He is determined that her first experience of Belgrade should be a good one. He must be the one to find her, just like he promised during her panicked call. They bend over the map again, and his temples start to throb.

'Let's assume it *is* Belgrade, then?' Kajo says after a moment, and Zivoin does not know what else to do, so he agrees. 'If it's not, we'll spread further out when we have more information. But this is all we can do for now, yes?'

'OK.'

'So, for long-distance buses, the most likely place is the central bus station off Nemanjina Street.'

'So that's where I will go,' Zivoin says, circling the station with a black marker.

'But it depends, because if the bus goes through Novi Sad it sometimes terminates at a stop in Zemun – that's tricked me a couple of times. What's that municipality again . . .' Kajo bends over and traces his finger north from Belgrade's centre. Zivoin works his way forwards from Ljubljana Airport with the black marker whilst his friend goes backwards with a red one, until finally they trace out the routes that make the most sense and circle the four most likely bus terminals Alegria could end up at. Kajo sits back and drags his hands down his face, massaging his jaw. 'You can't be in four places at once,' he says. 'You go to Nemanjina, I'll go to Dušanova?'

'Yes,' Zivoin nods. 'Good. Thank you.'

'But the other two—'

'Don't worry about that.' By now it is early in the morning, but this cannot wait. He pulls out his address book and calls two of their mutual friends from university, choosing them primarily because he knows they can be trusted (but also because they have cars) and explains the situation to them. And because it is Zivoin, the kind of friend who never asks others to do something he would not do for them, they agree to help. When he hangs up the phone, yawning, he turns to see Kajo leaning against the kitchen door, rubbing the back of his head. He's so big – at least a head taller than Zivoin – that his hair skims the top of the door frame. He looks intrigued.

'What?'

'You must really like this girl.'

'I wouldn't be here if I didn't.'

Kajo drains the last of the wine in his glass. 'All this effort – maybe that's why my wife was annoyed. You're showing me up, brate!'

He claps Zivoin on the back and bids him goodnight, leaving him perched on the sofa bed with the map and his turbulent thoughts. Tonight was meant to be spent in a hotel, but knowing that Kajo and Svetlana's home is the only way Alegria can reach him means he cannot risk leaving. Zivoin washes the wine from his mouth, drinks a glass of cold water and tries unsuccessfully to will his nervous system into sleep. The kitchen, which overlooks the living room, is a horrible shade of mustard. It clashes with the salmon-pink velvet sofa he's lying on. The flat feels overwhelming and cramped. The ceilings are too low. When he stares up at them he feels like he can't breathe properly. Zivoin considers perusing their bookshelf for something to flick through, but feels too lazy to stand up. He isn't sure he'd be able to concentrate, anyway. Pulling a yellow lighter from his pocket, he half-heartedly lights a cigarette. Twirls the cheap plastic in his fingers – he can't even remember where he got it from. He cannot sleep. Svetlana has left him a pillow and sheets, Kajo has lent him pyjamas, but Zivoin opts to lie fully clothed on the unmade sofa, in case he must leave in a hurry.

When he does at last drift off, it is uneasy. An imaginary phone keeps ringing. He jerks awake multiple times, convinced someone's shouting his name. Eventually, Zivoin gives up. He turns on his side and thinks about the moment she said yes. The jubilation in his chest, the triumphant yell he made as he slammed down the phone. It had been loud enough for Darco to come running from his room, alarm morphing into shock when Zivoin pulled him into a bear hug and broke the news. They'd celebrated with beers and doner kebabs, his cousin cracking jokes at his expense, insisting that Alegria must be suffering from concussion. But when Zivoin explained that he'd be returning to Yugoslavia, the excitement left Darco's body like a deflated balloon. 'You can't go home,' he'd said slowly, 'you have a job here.'

'I'll find another one.'

'What about me?'

'I'm not going for long – don't tell me you'll miss me after just a few weeks?' Zivoin clipped him playfully around the neck, but Darco had shrugged him off. He was frowning. 'It's dangerous.'

'Who cares? I'm engaged! Let's drink!'

'But, brate, what about the military police?'

Zivoin, who had been leaning into the fridge, digging out fresh bottles of beer, pretended not to hear him. But Darco wouldn't let it go. 'You've heard the same stories as I have. They knock on our doors, send men like you and me to Croatia, and we never hear from them again.'

'My papers—'

'Oh, come on!' Darco had exploded. 'You know half the men they arrest have exemption papers – you think those mean anything any more?' He slammed his fist down on the kitchen table, which shuddered ominously. 'What the fuck are you talking about – why do you have to go back?'

'You *know* why. She's banned from this country. Without a Yugoslavian marriage licence, we can't apply for an international one, and without that she'll never get a visa.'

But even as Zivoin spoke, Darco was shaking his head, his face twisted with fear and anger. 'That's not a good enough reason.' His rage had momentarily ruptured their dynamic of older and younger cousin, pushing him to speak to Zivoin in a way he never had before. He seemed much older than nineteen. 'Alegria's great, brate. But she's not worth your life.' There was a plea in Darco's voice as he spoke. They both knew he couldn't go back, having skipped out on the draft. He would have to miss the wedding. Zivoin had said nothing, finishing his beer in two large gulps and leaving his cousin alone in the kitchen. The next day, he'd handed in his notice.

Outside, a cat yowls suddenly and Zivoin jumps. His thoughts have now turned to death. He would rather not think about it, but sometimes these things can't be helped.

He pictures the bus skidding on the road, the driver nodding off, the shriek of metal and fracture of glass, bodies and limbs entangled, crushed, burst, burnt. He feels a swooping sensation in his stomach, the kind he gets when the serrated edge of a knife is dragged across a plate. He worries about Alegria dying alone and afraid – this is a familiar obsession he reserves exclusively for the most important people in the world.

He punches his pillow a couple of times, quietly, forcing the thought away. If he ever has children – and he very much hopes he will have children with her – he wonders if he will pass this fear on to them. This kind of terror is primal, after all. It lingers in one's DNA. Only now does it occur to him that maybe his great fear of losing the ones he loves might not come from an internal source, but an external one. War, or the promise of it, for example. Shoeless winters. The quiet emaciation of some of his friends in the village school after a poor harvest, seeing more of their ribs than he should have. The house fire that almost killed his uncle as a newborn – would have killed his uncle had Zivoin's six-year-old father not run into the bedroom and grabbed him as one side of the infant's body caught fire, burning off his ear. The membrane between life and death is stretched so thin, he constantly waits for it to rupture.

He sits up, too hot, too unsettled. Thinks about drinking more wine. Opts for water instead, so cold it makes his teeth ache. By six, the living room is bathed in light. Zivoin parts the white crochet curtains and looks at the city spread out in front of him. Kajo's apartment is located in Dedinje, a wealthy residential district about half an hour from the city centre. The roads are still, iced over from a brief snowfall the night before. He slips out, walking deeper into the neighbourhood in search of an open flower shop, then buys fresh krofne and poppy seed rolls from a local bakery. They are still warm. Before the grease can seep through the little paper bags, Zivoin presses them to his nose and inhales the scent of fresh dough and sugar. He walks back quickly and arranges the pastries on two separate plates. When he thinks he can hear movement from the bedroom, he makes a large pot of Turkish coffee and hopes Svetlana will take the gesture as a peace offering. By seven, Kajo has joined him, chain-smoking as they wait for Marko and Andrija to arrive.

Kajo is subdued. 'Spoken to Feki recently?'

'I haven't heard from him since he left London. He said he was going to Bosnia – I don't know where to reach him.'

'What about Bato? Anything from his family?'

'Not since the day before yesterday. You?'

'Nothing.' Kajo glances at his friend. 'Aren't you worried it will happen to you?'

'I don't have time to be worried,' Zivoin says lightly, batting the question away. 'Anyway, they don't even know I'm in the country.'

'Yet.' Kajo nods at the kitchen counter. 'I see you bought flowers.'

There had been very little to choose from; in the end he had settled on two identical bouquets of dried lavender and fresh cherry plum blossoms, their soft white and burgundy petals blending well with the wiry purple stems. Zivoin stands and throws open the windows to clear some of the cigarette smoke.

'These are for Alegria.' He points to one of the bouquets.

'And the other one?'

Zivoin sips his coffee and raises his eyebrows. 'What do you mean? You bought that one for your lovely wife.'

Kajo laughs. 'So I did! So I did. And I bought these pastries too?'

'Nice try. You're not that thoughtful.'

The doorbell rings. Svetlana emerges from the bedroom dressed in jeans and an oversized white blouse. Her blonde hair is swept up into a bun, making her look even taller than her husband. Leaving Kajo to give her the flowers, Zivoin awkwardly welcomes his friends into a home that is not his. They gather around the kitchen table, eating, drinking, smoking, and he explains the plan one more time. He is unable to keep still. He hovers around them busily, barking orders.

'Marko, you'll go to Surčin airport. We don't think the bus will terminate there, but she might get off if she hears someone say Belgrade.'

'Can she speak our language at all?'

'No.'

'How will we talk, then?'

'Who says you need to talk?'

'To get her to come with us, brate,' Andrija says around a mouthful of krofne. 'We don't even know what she looks like.'

'You'll be able to tell.' But Zivoin removes a handful of photographs from the inside pocket of his jacket and passes them around. 'Take these with you. And . . .' He rips a piece of paper in three and scribbles identical notes on each.

Marko holds up a photo of the Dias sisters sitting on their old black sofa. Simone is in the middle of speaking, her lips curled into a satisfied smile as Alegria clutches her stomach in laughter. 'Which one is she?'

'The one with curly hair, on the left.'

Svetlana pulls the photo out of his hands with renewed interest and points to Simone. 'Who's this?'

'Her sister.'

Marko lets out a low whistle. 'Man. If they all look like this, maybe I need a Brazilian woman for myself. She single?' He sees the look on Zivoin's face and holds up both his hands. 'Come on – it's a compliment!'

'Shut up. She doesn't know this country, she doesn't know you, and she's coming here completely alone, without her family. She's scared. You can't do that shit in front of her, OK?'

The men stand in silence for a moment. Then Andrija grins and turns to Kajo. 'He's really in love with this girl, isn't he?'

'That's what I said last night!'

They leave, Svetlana bidding them goodbye at the door. 'Bring her here for a coffee once you find her,' she says. The photographs have piqued her curiosity – she's looking forward to telling her friends she's met a woman from this strange and exotic country. 'Too short,' she plans to say in an aloof voice, 'too dark – she looks like she's been left in the sun for too long.'

'OK. Thank you.' But Zivoin does not plan to return there that day. They will check into a hotel as soon as Alegria arrives. He is restless with longing for her, impatient for the two of them to be alone so that he can hold her.

Andrija gets in his car. He has the longest drive out of all of them, going south, past the city centre to a bus stop that no one really thinks is a realistic option. But Zivoin isn't taking any chances. Marko leaves with a wave, Alegria's photo on the passenger seat next to him. As Kajo is about to get in the car, Zivoin stops him. 'She might be nervous,' he says. 'Don't talk about what happened in Croatia, OK? I'm not even sure she knows, but if she does, just reassure her.'

Kajo stares at him. 'She's not made of sugar, man,' he scoffs.

'It's just – she's already had a rough journey . . .' Zivoin hesitates and then says, 'I don't want her to look back at this moment and only remember the bad parts. I don't want her to think that our life together is always going to be this hard.' He looks away as he speaks.

'You should trust her,' Kajo says. 'Anyone who would agree to marry that ugly face doesn't scare easily.' He pats his friend's arm reassuringly and wishes him luck before driving away.

Zivoin watches him leave. The flowers are clutched tightly in his hand, his backpack is in the other. Just a short walk and a bus ride, and then he will find her. His heart beats and beats and beats.

CHAPTER 20

Somewhere between here and there, April 1991

Day 2

She occupies a window seat, hunkered down as if trying to hide. Her knees are drawn into her chest. She stares at a non-existent view. Her body aches from the uncomfortable position she has forced it into, and Alegria considers lowering her legs or stretching, but she does not. An exhausting routine has been established. She looks through the window and occasionally drifts into sleep, until her forehead touches the glass and its great, juddering rattle immediately startles her awake. It may not even be sleep, this thing she's doing; after a few hours, Alegria is unsure if her brain is tricking her to make the time pass. There is very little to see anyway. The darkness is a chasm, punctuated only by the infrequent headlights of a passing car or by a solitary, feeble street light. The disorientation reminds her of a game she used to play with Simone and her cousins: Old Man Anchovy. One blindfolded child cautiously edges around a room, looking for a mass of warm, solid flesh to grab as the others climb furniture and squeeze themselves into hard-to-reach crannies. If the blindfolded child needs a clue, he or she shouts, 'Old Man!' and every contestant has to shout back, 'Anchovy!' Alegria still remembers the unsettling feeling of navigating a room blindfolded, inching forward with her arms straight out in front of her, unsure of where she was going and afraid of getting hurt.

A line of grime is smeared into the silicone around the window frame, and patches of moss grows on the frame outside. She catches a brief glimpse of it whenever there is a sliver of artificial light. There is no moon, just snow falling, thick and heavy. The bus navigates only with its headlights. There's a crack in the top left of the windshield, large enough for her to notice – and she is seated in the fourth row. Alegria finds herself thinking about that crack excessively, to avoid thinking about other things that are worrying her. At every bump she closes her eyes, expecting to hear the sound of glass shattering. She wonders how the driver can possibly feel safe enough to drive at this speed, and imagines him rounding a corner too sharply, tyres losing their grip and hurtling the bus off a cliff edge or directly into a rock face. She imagines dying in the most unfamiliar place she has ever found herself in. No one in the bus wears a seatbelt that she can see, not even the elderly man next to her. This is a mountainous region – are they on a mountain right now? What if there is an avalanche? Does Yugoslavia have avalanches? If she dies, they will not even know who to call to collect her body. Would she be buried here?

To calm herself, she takes a deep breath and regrets it right away. The air inside the bus is unpleasantly stale. Alegria coughs, then licks her lips, which feel chalky and dry.

The entire day has been so adrenaline-fuelled, the last time she had the chance to eat was a few hours before landing in Frankfurt. That had been early in the morning – she is now so hungry and thirsty, her head has started to pound. She checks her watch. It is almost three a.m. Seven or eight hours to go. She will arrive in Belgrade – if she even makes it to Belgrade – a shrivelled husk, her skin rough and patchy from the air conditioning and the cold and the cigarettes. The smell of body odour is powerful: a mixture of sweat, onion and fertiliser. Every so often it wafts towards her like a small electric shock, making her exhale forcefully out of her nose and shrink further back into the seat. At the start of the journey, she tried fiddling with the oval-shaped buttons next to the filters above her head, hoping for a little fresh air. Nothing had happened and the man next to her shook his head and said something that vaguely sounded like, 'Ne radi.' Alegria assumed that meant 'It's broken.' She'd lowered her hand and turned back to the window. Now, a small patch of grease marks the spot where her forehead keeps touching the glass. She swallows and feels the dryness of her throat. She will endure it. She will.

Most of the occupants have, at some point, discussed her presence. At times they stare at her, talking amongst themselves with undisguised interest. At least the old man by Alegria's side seems indifferent to her presence. Across from her, two elderly women sit, talking and smoking and occasionally glancing at her. In front of her is a young couple, and the man has once or twice twisted in his seat to look back at her, turning around quickly when she catches his eye. She pretends not to notice. What else can she do? She cannot communicate, cannot even begin to formulate a sentence. Earlier, Alegria had tried to say hello in English, and no one responded. She has only managed to remember a few words that Zivoin has taught her: ne, meaning 'no', da, meaning 'yes', and hvala, which she knows means 'thank you'. Though yet again, she struggles with the double consonant, inserting an extra vowel so it becomes ha-vala. And, unhelpfully, the word for 'pepper', from one silly afternoon with Zivoin when they were both in that playful haze of new love. They had been in his kitchen when he'd pointed to the pepper grinder and said in a deep, oddly serious voice, 'Biber.' She had let out a burst of laughter, more like a cackle, which had startled him, and set them both off. She loves to hear him laugh. She loves to hear him speak his own language. People transform when they're speaking their mother tongue. Zivoin often murmurs to her in Serbo-Croat when they are alone together, cupping her face with his large hands. It's always much softer than she anticipates, the consonants tender and flirtatious. She wants the version of him his friends and family get: the debater, the reader, the poet. Zivoin struggles with Portuguese because of how many vowels lie next to each other, and she struggles with Serbo-Croat for precisely the opposite reason.

As she sits on the bus, this niggles at her – in the short time they have been together, they have not learned their more subtle differences. In so many ways, Zivoin is a stranger, one for whom she has upended her entire life. And she will be the outsider at her own wedding, alone amidst a sea of family members she has never met before, committing herself to someone in a language she cannot even speak. The enormity of what she's agreed to do unfurls and stretches out in front of her. Alegria's entire body feels heavy, her arms like concrete blocks by her side. Time – which really means money – and circumstance have robbed her and Zivoin of the opportunity to fall in love slowly. They have not been afforded the luxury of travelling, of living together, of sinking into each other's lives, of really arguing – of sleeping in a double bed together! To her, it feels like their entire relationship has been a fight against time. She is ready for things to slow down. She picks at her bottom lip until fragments of old, dry skin start to flake off.

The bus stops abruptly and the driver flips on the lights, surprising her. They have pulled into a small petrol station. He stands and announces something to the passengers, opening the door and stepping out. Cold, crisp air cuts through the sourness of the bus and Alegria takes a deep, appreciative breath. She sits up, abandoning her cramped position, and peers through the windshield. There is only a single pump that appears to be working, and behind it a modest shop and a public toilet. Men and women file off the bus, but Alegria hangs back. She has no way of buying anything anyway, and the threat of being left behind whilst using the toilet feels all too likely. Zivoin told her not to get off the bus, no matter what.

The two old women across from her are the last to leave, along with the man seated by her side. She watches as he stiffly manoeuvres himself off the seat, groaning as he does so. The older men and women here do this, she has noticed. If they are in pain or discomfort they do not hesitate to inform everyone in their vicinity with moans, heavy sighs, muttered curses or even wails. For the first time, she understands what

Zivoin meant when he'd once told her that his country and its people were overly familiar with pain.

The man finally stands and turns around to lift his jacket off the seat. Almost all the hair from his head has gone and the remaining fluff around his ears is white. His moustache is stained yellow from tobacco. The women are looking at her expectantly again. One of them wears a knitted bonnet that covers some of her face, two watery-blue eyes peering down into hers. The other has dyed her hair a strong yellow, her long face framed by a fringe. When Alegria does not move from her seat, they speak to her, pointing to the shop through the window.

She smiles politely and shakes her head. They seem unsatisfied by her response, and the man takes over, repeating the same action. He points to the little kiosk, and then pats his stomach and mimes drinking. When she again refuses, all three of them speak amongst themselves. One of the women frowns and gestures towards her in a way that strikes Alegria as maternal. Caring. Once again, understanding slots into place. They are worried about her. That's why the women have been watching her, that is why the three of them are wasting their precious time on this bus, trying to convince her to eat and drink something. The knowledge flushes through her warmly, and she smiles, placing one hand on her heart and bowing her head gratefully. But she does not move, so neither do they. Finally, she opens her wallet again and shows them its contents. They leave her be.

As soon as she is alone, Alegria stands up and stretches. The door has been left open. She tries to soak up as much of the fresh air as she can to ease her aching head. Pacing up and down the bus, she checks her watch. Five in the morning. They have been driving for almost six hours. She should feel tired, but adrenaline has been coursing through her body since she landed in Frankfurt, and she feels hyper-vigilant, straining her ears for the sounds of – what? Some unidentified threat? Picking up her coat, she places it around her shoulders and hovers near the entrance, taking deep breaths. Simone would have been the perfect companion. By now, she would have befriended everyone on board, cracked jokes, found them a meal somewhere, somehow. Her sister is so much better suited for this journey than she is, she can't believe that she's the one to leave and Si's the one who stayed. She wishes the driver would hurry up.

Alegria waits like this for twenty minutes, both feet firmly in the bus. When, at last, she sees the driver walking towards her, she returns to her seat and pulls her coat over her head, hoping the other passengers have eaten before boarding. The smell of food would be too much – she's so hungry, she's light-headed. The bus sways as passengers board, and Alegria closes her eyes. She listens to the sounds of people fussing with their belongings, rustling plastic bags, talking amongst themselves, and feels both impatient and lonely. When she feels a tap on her shoulder, she pulls the coat off her head and looks up wearily. What now? To her surprise, her neighbour is holding out a plastic bottle of water and a small packet of crackers, nudging them into her hands. 'For me?' Alegria asks, hoping she hasn't misunderstood. He nods, and the two women peer around him eagerly, waiting. She gulps down half the bottle gratefully, not caring about how cold it is against her throat. The ice water slides down her chest to settle in her stomach, leaving her short of breath. But it feels fantastic. She's a plant on the edge of death, slowly being infused with life again. 'Hvala,' she gasps, trying to thank them. But the women have settled into their seats, no longer looking at her, and the man appears not to have heard. She is too self-concious to repeat herself.

The bus starts, lurching them forward. The crackers are bland and powdery, barely touching the edges of Alegria's hunger, but it does not matter. She is so depleted that her hands shake as she shoves them into her mouth, her cheeks tear-streaked. The camaraderie is as much of a relief as the food and water. Wiping the crumbs from her mouth, she relaxes back into the seat. Perhaps it is not such a dangerous country after all. She holds the plastic bottle, half-empty, to her chest and resumes her stare out of the window. It is a good omen, she decides. God, or fate, or love – or perhaps all three – was nudging her along the path she was always meant to have taken.

Her companion falls asleep and starts to snore. Alegria sleeps too – or maybe she does not. Who can be sure? She thinks about Zivoin, the man who must be the love of her life. It's an alarming thought – once you have met the love of your life, does life not, in fact, get worse? Rather than the possibilities of a great, life-changing love, there is the reality of it, which means a slow, maddening descent into mundanity. Like brass, the shine slowly rubs off, no matter how hard you polish it. And then, Alegria thinks, you are resigned to the knowledge that the person you have picked is not perfect at all, and people are human with strange habits and systems of putting things away or not putting things away, systems that are so obviously wrong or inefficient, but which they stubbornly will not change. She has already noticed that with Zivoin, even though they have not lived together. He and Darco drink a lot of coffee – she has watched him drink three, sometimes four cups a day, then sleep like a baby. He makes it in a coffee pot, like they do in Brazil. And yet, for some reason, he chooses to keep the pot in a cupboard on the other side of the kitchen, far away from the gas stove. And the coffee itself in a different cupboard altogether, and the spoons in the incorrect drawer, not the one closest to either the pot or the stove. She thinks this is annoying and inefficient, and she has not told him. Should she have told him? Isn't that what you do with the love of your life? Show them your raw, exposed self, like peeling back the skin of a blister?

Once, about a month into dating, she opened all the cupboards – just to observe how he had (incorrectly) organised the dry food and the utensils. She must have been there for longer than she realised, because he had left the bedroom to find her, a blanket wrapped around his shoulders like a cloak. She hadn't explained what she was doing, and Zivoin didn't seem to require her to. She likes – no, she loves – this about him, his neutrality to other people's quirks. It feels like acceptance, not indifference. Around him, Alegria can switch off her brain and stop worrying, because he makes her feel safer than anyone else can. Which is why the second she sees him, she will relax. She will stand on her tiptoes and bury her face into his warm neck and close her eyes, leaning into him the way she always does: with all of her body, her way of telling him that she's in his hands completely. If he were to take a step backwards, she would fall. But he never does that.

He pulls her to him tightly, one hand behind her head, the other on the small of her back; his way of telling her to lean on him even harder, trust him even more. Give me more of you, he'll say, without saying it, and so she will, and all of this will just be a story they both can laugh at, time smoothing out the wrinkles of anxiety and unease.

Four hours to go. Once she finds him, things will be all right. She can take tiny little sips of the water, rationing it out until daylight. And finally, *finally* the view is beginning to lighten. If she cranes forward, she can see the outlines of a horizon at last. Soon the sky will flush with pink and deep purple, indigo will dissolve into a brighter shade of blue and there will be clouds, fragmented and frayed at the edges, as if they'd been dragged there by a large, omnipotent hand. Daybreak will wipe away fear, giving her a glimpse of this new, curious world she has agreed to be a part of. At last, she will see the sun.

CHAPTER 21

Belgrade, April 1991

Day 2

Zivoin waits anxiously in front of the Metropolitan Hotel, shifting the flowers from one hand to another. The hotel and the bus station share the same plaza; he has determined it to be the best vantage point for him to see her. If he waits round the front in the arrivals hall, he will miss the moment the buses park and the passengers file out. The space will become congested, she might walk past him, alone, into the city and he wouldn't spot her. Their reunion should be perfect, romantic and tender. It should erase any and all tension.

His heart speeds up whenever a bus pulls into its docking station, even though he knows she will not be on board any of these. They're all local. And it is still a little early.

As usual, daylight softens everything. The landscape no longer feels impenetrable and unknowable to her. Pine trees, maples, chestnuts are scattered across mountains on either side of the motorway. They gleam in the sun, the melting snow on their branches catching the light. Green patches of earth poke through white – another good omen, she decides. Houses start to dot the scene and the road is smoother now, asphalt patchworking the holes in the concrete. Belgrade looms ahead of her. People start to wake, shifting and bustling about with coats and bags. Soon the journey will end, and yet the bus seems to have slowed to a crawl, inching forwards infuriatingly slowly.

This new impatience unnerves her. Alegria has always been the kind of person who finds the waiting as delicious as the moment of relief. But now? She wants to grab the cushioned headrest in front of her and crush it beneath her fingers – until it is disfigured, until her nails break with the force of her grip. But of course, Alegria doesn't do this. Instead, she drains the last few drops of water and stows the bottle in her bag, subtly trying to sniff herself as she bends down. The heaters kicked in at five, as the witching hour dawned, and now it is too hot. Layers have been peeled off, necks and collarbones and armpits exposed. The air is marshy with sweat and morning breath. She worries that she stinks and can no longer tell. She worries that soon she'll see Zivoin and instead of looking glamorous and brave and also a little mysterious, she will look helpless and dishevelled. And smell like unwashed bodies and tobacco and stomach acid. She drums her fingers on her thigh, her jeans feeling stiff. The crack in the windshield is the same size as it was when they began the journey. Another good omen. She fidgets with excitement.

At ten thirty, the long-distance bus enters the square.

It is not the only long-distance bus to pull into Belgrade's central bus station at that moment, but it is the only bus that has Alegria on it. This bus has, in fact, stopped at one other station. Had she been looking out of the window, she might have seen a man standing there awkwardly, holding up a small photo of her and her sister mid-laughter. But Alegria is not looking out of her window any more, she is busy staring straight ahead of her trying to find Zivoin. Her coat is on, she is ready.

Zivoin, however, is busy thinking about three brown moles that fall between Alegria's breasts. They are perfectly aligned, right in the centre of her sternum. He'd mistaken them for tattoos the first time he saw them, and she had fallen about laughing at the idea. Now he can't remember if it was three moles or four – he knows it is definitely not two. Funny how memory works that way.

Zivoin sees Alegria before Alegria sees Zivoin. She steps off the bus, squinting against the sun and biting her lip. He starts forward, stumbles a little, then finds his footing. As he approaches, their eyes meet and her whole body visibly relaxes, her smile touches her eyes. All the things he had planned to say, the way he had planned to greet her, fall out of his head. To his embarrassment, he gives her the flowers *before* he embraces her, so now they are crushed between them. She smells like smoke and deodorant. 'You found me!' Alegria says excitedly, burying her face into his neck. He doesn't think he's ever seen her this euphoric.

Zivoin is overwhelmed by the way she looks at him, and without thinking about it, he kisses her deeply, lifts her up and spins her around. She gasps, squeezes him a little too tightly round his neck, and when he sets her down he realises people around them are watching. He suddenly feels self-conscious and lets her go, taking a step back. 'Sorry. I got a bit excited.'

But she is grinning up at him, her cheeks flushed. 'Do it again!' So he does, laughing. Her weight on him feels incredible.

He insists on taking both her suitcases and dragging them back to the Metropolitan. This is not where they are staying – it is too grand and expensive – but the taxi rank is there. They catch up as they wait, tripping over their English, a little out of practice. Alegria fills him in on everything that happened, tells him about the strikes and the cancelled flight, and he says, 'Do you know what? I had a bad feeling that something like this might happen.' And she says – although she's unsure if this is true or if it has become true retrospectively – 'Me too!' Then, quietly, seriously, he tells her that this shared premonition is yet another reason why they belong together. Alegria laughs. The love of her life is always doing this, finding meaning in coincidences and patterns in the random, scattered facts of their lives to declare how perfect they are for each other. She loves it.

A queue has formed at the taxi rank. Alegria unzips her coat and yawns, says something about needing a shower. Behind her, Zivoin sees two things: a silver car turning into the taxi rank, and a man, his face bloodied, eyes wide, rounding the corner towards them. 'They stole it!' he's screaming as he stumbles forward. He's been badly beaten up, blood gushing down his left temple from a head wound, one side of his face already swelling. He clutches his side as he runs. 'The military police took my car! Help me!'

The crowd shrinks backwards, alarmed. Any moment now, he will run straight past them and onto the steps of the Metropolitan, and she will see the blood spotting the pavement and the crazed fear in his eyes. The silver car is pulling up beside them. Alegria is busy talking, and does not hear the man over the noise of the traffic. 'Excellent!' she says, pointing. 'The taxi is here.' In the second between her turning and the man crossing her path, Zivoin pulls her tightly into a hug, pressing her into his chest and wrapping his arms around her head so she cannot hear or see.

The man runs past them and vanishes up the steps of the hotel. He lets her go. 'The taxi is here,' Zivoin says, distracted. 'You get in. I'll handle the luggage.' Through the car's back window, he can see she's registered that something strange has happened. She has a hand covering her face.

Alegria slides into her seat and smiles hesitantly at the driver. She knows something is a little off. In the enclosed space of the taxi, she catches a whiff – just briefly – of her sweaty body. In the joy of seeing Zivoin, she has completely forgotten how she must look and smell – she hasn't brushed her teeth in twenty-four hours. Was that why Zivoin hugged her like that? To stop her from talking? She claps a hand over her mouth and resolves to be quiet until she's had the chance to clean herself up.

'We'll go to the hotel first – have you eaten?' Zivoin gets in beside her and nods at the driver, gives him instructions.

He glances back at the Metropolitan as the taxi pulls away, but the injured man doesn't reappear. As the car takes them through Belgrade, he quietly points out parts of the city he knows: the cinema, the public library, the English-language bookshop, the coffee shop/bakery hybrid with the best burek – 'Have you ever had burek? No? We'll go there to eat, then. And later tonight, we can see some of my friends – they're all keen to meet you!' She nods again, smiles at everything he says. Her hands are folded tightly across her body. She must have seen the man with the broken face, he thinks.

'This feels a little bit like a first date, doesn't it?' Zivoin says, trying to make her laugh.

'Oh! That reminds me . . . this is for you, a wedding gift from my parents.' Alegria speaks quickly, her jumper half pulled over her chin as she hands him a hand-wrapped jar of guava jam. 'It's a small thing, but my mother made it . . . she said she hopes it will tempt you to come visit.' She laughs nervously. 'But if you don't like it, don't worry. I'll eat it.'

He kisses her again, thanking her. He will eat the whole thing, he promises. He takes her for burek and sour yogurt, trying not to overwhelm her in his eagerness to introduce her to his country. Alegria compliments Belgrade as much as possible, but she cannot help it – she catches herself comparing everything to Brazil, the public transport, the food, the people, the coffee shops, as though determined to prove her loyalty to her home. Zivoin listens and nods because he can see this is a way for her to grieve, and he wants to be as helpful as possible in this process. As they eat, she talks about the cafés she used to visit with her friends on Saturdays, all outdoors, or roofless, or surrounded by coconut trees, about the açai bowls covered in honey and peanuts and Leite Ninho, how they turned her tongue purple and made her too full to eat dinner at home. She talks about the cafés in Sérgio Pacheco Square with their red plastic chairs, selling hot, sweet coffee in little disposable cups and pão de queijo still warm from the oven, fat, golden, delightful. The kind that leaves a layer of grease on the lips like a gloss. She talks about the greenness and the lushness, the smell of wet earth and the intensity of colour, and how bleached Europe feels by comparison – even the sea here, she says, even the sea.

'You haven't seen the Montenegrin sea.'

'I'm not saying it to complain,' Alegria says. 'I'm saying it because I need you to know that nowhere will ever replace Brazil for me. It will always be home.'

'Home can be many places at once, Peach. I'll take you to the sea here – it will change your mind, I promise.'

'No.' She shakes her head. 'No, no. It's beautiful here, but it's never going to be more beautiful than my backyard.' He promises her they will visit the second they can, and she nods and smiles with wet eyes. The bureks are hot and delicious. She orders a second plate.

Zivoin asks, 'Where is Sérgio Pacheco Square, anyway?' as though he's intimately familiar with her big city, her Uberlândia, and she says, 'It doesn't even matter, Cricket, you don't need to know where it is, you just need to know that it exists.' They go back and forth in this lazy, easy way, saying lazy, easy things to stay calm and pass the time. Alegria reaches for his hand under the table and Zivoin strokes her thumb with his own. And because they are in love, because they have finally reunited, they make a foolish mistake. They assume that from now on everything is going to be all right.

CHAPTER 22

Nikšić, April 1991

Day 4

They end up spending a single night in Belgrade. Zivoin had planned for her to meet as many of his university friends as possible, but the cancelled flights condense their time into one brief dinner with Svetlana, Kajo, Andrija and Marko and a day queuing at Belgrade's municipal office for a marriage licence. There is barely any time – Alegria and Zivoin have a week left before their flight back to London.

It is past midnight when they catch the sleeper train to Montenegro. Kajo and Svetlana – who will act as best man and Alegria's witness respectively – are with them. At first, she's excited at the prospect of spending a night on a train, but the bubble bursts as soon as the four of them board the carriage. It's cramped, unpleasantly so. Two bunk beds bolted to the walls with mattresses that are so thin she feels the metal slats poking through from underneath. There's no room for more than one person to stand at a time, so they have to enter one by one, awkwardly shuffling onto the mattresses. Alegria is the shortest of everyone, and even she cannot fully stretch out. She and Svetlana opt for the bottom bunks and the men take the ones above, where they cannot even sit up. The only good thing about it is how comical the Yugoslavians look, as though they're lying in children's beds. It makes Alegria laugh so hard that the others laugh too, easing some of the tension that has made its way into the carriage with them. They lie on their sides as the train creaks and sways its way out of the city, and it is here that Alegria finally remembers to ask the question that's been nagging at her since Frankfurt.

'What is happening in Croatia?'

There is silence in the cabin for a second, as both Svetlana and Kajo look to Zivoin. Alegria cannot see the expression on his face, but it's obvious that he doesn't want to tell her. She repeats the question, and this time it's addressed directly to him, giving him no choice. 'It's nothing to worry about,' Zivoin says at last. 'But there was a . . . problem with two Macedonian soldiers. By the coast.'

Svetlana snorts derisively. 'A problem? Is that what you're calling it?' She switches to Serbo-Croat. 'She's here now, she needs to know these things. You tell her – my English isn't good enough.'

Zivoin turns over onto his stomach and peers over the metal railing at Alegria. She's frowning up at him.

'A problem?'

'A murder,' Kajo explains. 'Two Macedonian soldiers from the Yugoslav People's Army were attacked.'

'By who?'

'Croatian paramilitaries,' Zivoin says, reluctantly. 'And some civilians, too, apparently. The soldiers were patrolling one of the busiest streets in the city when the paramilitaries surrounded their tank.'

'Oh my God.' Alegria is wide-eyed, alarmed. 'And then what happened?'

Kajo sighs heavily and shakes his head. 'It is shocking. One of them was thrown off the tank and beaten, and the other one was suffocated under the weight of the crowd.'

'The cameras,' Svetlana says. She nods up at Zivoin. 'Tell her it was caught on camera.'

Once again, he peers over the bed to check on Alegria. It is so difficult trying to tell her about this when he cannot see her face, cannot monitor her reactions. 'Someone filmed it happening – there was a television crew on the ground at the time. It was broadcast all over the country.'

Kajo is staring up at the train's ceiling. He's so large, it is just a few centimetres away from his nose. 'You know,' he says, shifting clumsily onto his side, 'we were always taught that we were all brothers. But some of these people – our people, their people – have a way of turning brothers into enemies.'

'And now we don't know what it means for our country,' Svetlana finishes, her voice tight. 'Translate it for her – now that Croatia's borders are semi-closed, and with this tension between the People's Army and local paramilitaries, everyone's saying it could be all-out war—'

'It's not war,' Zivoin says suddenly, firmly. 'Nothing has been declared. The only people who are talking about war are old people and separatists.'

'And the papers.'

'Not all of them.'

'Sorry,' Alegria interrupts quickly. She can almost taste the animosity between Svetlana and Zivoin, with Kajo suspended somewhere in the middle. 'I picked a bad time to ask—'

'No, it's fine.' Zivoin reaches his hand down to briefly squeeze hers. 'I wasn't sure if you already knew about it or not. That's why it never came up.'

But that isn't the full truth. Once again, he finds himself unable to taint her view of his home. Though he knows it may be unwise, Zivoin decides to say nothing about the rumours that the national government will soon declare a state of emergency. Or the risks of arrest. Or the problems at the border. And of course, he does not mention what the military police are doing. He does not want her to think of his country as a lawless, violent place. It isn't, it *really isn't*. Yugoslavia is beautiful; the people are rugged and reserved, yes, but they never hesitate to help a neighbour or assist a stranger on a long-distance bus. He wants this version to be the one she knows and remembers. So when they arrive at Nikšić train station early the next morning, he does not linger to show her the abandoned old church at Trebjesa Park, or the summer palace of King Nikola, Montenegro's last monarch. He bids Kajo and Svetlana a quick goodbye and bundles Alegria into a taxi. She twists in the back seat to wave at them as Zivoin barks his address at the driver.

'Do her parents live here too?'

'On the other side of town. We'll see them at the wedding.' He drums his fingers against the car door as they drive through his home town, scouring the streets for indications that things are not right. It is a short drive. Zivoin does not see anything out of the ordinary. Unlike Belgrade, Nikšić seems untouched – the shops are still open, the cafés are still running, the bakeries are putting out their signs advertising fresh loaves for two hundred dinars. But still, after he pays the taxi driver he does not hang around in the courtyard of his parents' grey apartment block. He keeps his head down and carries rather than drags their suitcases into the building to avoid any unnecessary noise. If Alegria has noticed the change in his demeanour, she does not address it. The bulb in the lobby has blown; this is a good thing. They wait in darkness as the lift rattles its way down.

'They know we're coming, right?' she whispers as they ascend. Much like the building, the lift is so dilapidated that Zivoin has to hold the manual door in place to avoid it springing back open.

'Of course they know.'

'And they're . . . happy about it, yes?'

'Of course,' he repeats.

'You're hiding something,' she says. But by now they have reached the seventeenth floor and Zivoin puts a finger to his lips.

The apartment is at the opposite end of the corridor. They creep towards it and he taps on the door softly, ignoring the bell. He catches a glimpse of Alegria's worried face in the reflection of the brass knocker before the door is flung open by his father. Drago is so tense, he doesn't smile as he reaches out to pull his son into his chest. 'Dobro došli, dobro došli . . . welcome, welcome.'

Alegria nervously introduces herself as they're directed into the small kitchen. Her first glimpse of Zivoin's mother takes her by surprise – Milenka is even shorter than she is, her thick, dyed hair so much lighter than her son's. Drago is tall, imposing, slender. He limps slightly as he tries to help with their bags.

'Sit, Tata. I can do it.'

All Alegria's worries that his parents might not like her melt within minutes. They fuss over her, asking her so many questions through Zivoin that he starts to protest. 'At least let us eat first!'

Milenka is already making preparations for lunch, even though it is barely nine. The kitchen table is set with breakfast – freshly baked bread, a tin of sardines, boiled eggs, sliced cheese, a tub of feta swimming in brine, a string of small Njeguši sausages. Zivoin looks at his mother lovingly as she busies herself kneading filo dough on the kitchen counter. 'I'm making cheese and spinach pita for later – does she like those kinds of things?' Milenka asks. She watches Alegria sit with a nervous smile, and gestures towards the bread, the cheese, the eggs. She goes out of her way to try and make her feel welcome, filling her plate with food, resting a hand on her shoulder, offering her first coffee, then yogurt, then fresh blackberry juice. Zivoin is grateful for her efforts. His father is silent next to him as he flips through an address book. He bounces his good knee relentlessly. Drago is in problem-solving mode, because of the news he got yesterday – the news that he now has to break to his son.

'I need to talk to you.'

'Can't it wait until after breakfast?' Zivoin asks through a mouthful of home-made bread.

'There's a problem with the registrar, sine.'

Now Drago has his full attention. He puts down his fork and swallows his mouthful. 'What problem?'

Next to him, Alegria senses the change in tone and looks up from her plate.

'When you registered in Belgrade, they found out she's a foreigner. Now he says he can't do it without a translator present,' Drago says quietly, glancing over at Milenka. 'Not too much cheese in the pita this time, my stomach can't handle it.'

'Why not?'

'No way to guarantee she can understand what she's agreeing to.'

Zivoin sighs heavily and rubs his face with both hands. 'Where the *fuck*,' he says in a low voice, 'are we going to find a Serbo-Croat–Portuguese translator? If one even exists?'

'What's going on?' Alegria asks, her eyes flicking between the two men. 'I can tell something's wrong.'

'We might not be able to get married tomorrow.' As he fills her in, Alegria seems to deflate, slumping in the chair.

'I can't believe this – what do we do now? Can we find another registrar?'

'I'm not sure.'

Drago leans forward to get his attention. 'I think we need to go pay them a visit – I'll reason with the registrar, sine, don't worry. I know him. He's your grandad's neighbour – good man.'

'And if he won't change his mind? The wedding is tomorrow.'

No one answers him, because no one knows what to say. The situation is deteriorating; the streets are emptier than they have ever been. He should have considered this.

Alegria is quiet, biting her bottom lip again. Milenka

pours coffee and observes her son. This is who Milenka is: fearsome, small at barely five foot, with very short hair and a large mole on her chin with several hairs sprouting from it. She rarely leaves her kitchen. She is a woman from the mountains, a perpetual frown on her face as she stokes the fire, bakes the bread, curdles the milk. When her son called to tell her that he would be getting married, she'd cried angrily down the phone to him – her only son, marrying a foreigner who doesn't know their customs? Who will have foreign children that will speak broken Serbo-Croat and know nothing about her world? She'd planned to be reserved, cold even, when he came back. But she'd seen the joy all over him and her resentment had fallen away at once. Now Milenka has met the woman he plans to marry, and she understands.

'If it's a question of translation, surely *you* can just translate,' she says. She sees a smear of dried blood on her son's jaw where he'd cut himself shaving, licks her thumb and grabs his face with her other hand to steady him as she wipes it away. And he lets her do it even though he hates it. Privately, Milenka is surprised the town hall has even remained open, that they agreed to this wedding in the first place. She worries about the attention it will attract in this small town. There have been stories of men who vanish one day and haven't been heard of since. She even knows some of their mothers. She wishes he had not come.

Zivoin pushes his plate away and stands up. 'OK. Let me show Alegria where we're sleeping. And then we go.'

Alone in their bedroom, he pulls her into his arms and sighs into her hair.

'How bad is this, do you think?' she asks, her voice muffled against his chest.

'I don't know,' he admits. 'I really didn't see it coming.'

'It's seriously because they need a translator? Couldn't you just translate for me?'

'Dad and I are going to go down there and see if that's an option. But I think it would be better if you didn't come with me.' He's relieved when she doesn't question this, and merely nods.

From the bed, where she now sits cross-legged, Alegria looks up at him. 'How long will you be?'

'Could be a few hours.'

She yawns. 'I slept pretty badly on that train.'

'You should rest – I might be back by the time you wake up.'

'Do you think you can get them to change their mind?'

Zivoin's hands shake from the effort of trying to be calm in front of her – so much so that he considers stepping out onto the narrow balcony of the cramped seventeenth-floor apartment to smoke a cigarette. But then it occurs to him that he's supposed to have quit. He turns and bends to kiss her, cupping her cheek with one hand. 'Of course – it's probably just a misunderstanding. I'm sorry to leave you alone with Mum . . . but Kajo said he'd come round for a coffee later.' Svetlana is meeting old friends to catch up in Café Tropicana on the main street. She hasn't thought to invite Alegria, and this irritates him.

'Don't be sorry. Your mother is amazing – I still can't believe *this*!' She holds up the hand-knitted cardigan his mother has made for her in coffee-coloured wool. Milenka had given it to her before they'd sat down to eat, in a very matter-of-fact manner that Zivoin knew was hiding a great deal of emotion. Alegria's reaction had been perfect. She'd reached out and hugged Milenka close, kissing her cheek. It was a moment that could have easily gone wrong – Montenegrins don't hug. Brazilians hug all the time. But her genuine, simple joy had, in Milenka's eyes, transitioned her from an outsider and an interloper to her daughter-in-law. 'It's so *warm*,' Alegria says now, putting it on over her T-shirt and dark green sweatpants. 'Don't worry about me, I'll be OK.'

He shuts the bedroom door softly behind him, wincing as its metal hinges creak. Zivoin has always seen this flat as the thing that saved his family. After nine miserable winters of sleeping on cramped hotel floors, this place is paradise. The kitchen is narrow but long, with a small table and concrete balcony at one end. The wooden floorboards creak no matter how carefully one walks across them, especially in the living room. His parents have not changed a thing there, from the navy velvet sofa to the metal shutters that have to be manually cranked open and shut. He hears the loud hum of the water heater as it surges with power next to his old bedroom, and smiles. This is the sound he fell asleep to as a teenager. He has always loved this flat. But now, Alegria's presence has made him notice, with an uncomfortable twinge, the broken bathroom ventilator, the cracked tiles near the kitchen sink, the stained yellow wallpaper from a decade ago when the flat above leaked, the strange grey stain at the bottom of the toilet that was there when they arrived and won't budge no matter how much Milenka cleans it. What was once a kingdom has become a village.

Drago is already standing by the front door, his coat in his hand. Milenka hovers next to him, gripped by a sudden thought. 'You have to tell her not to go out alone,' she says sharply.

This catches Zivoin off guard. 'I don't think she will, but so what if she does? No one's going to bother her.'

'Sine,' she says, and then stops. How can she put into words what is happening here, to her son who left this place years ago but thinks he fully understands the situation? She is afraid that his wife will draw attention to herself, like a beautiful tropical bird at the zoo that has accidentally flown into the wrong enclosure. She worries people will talk about this lost bird. *Did you hear? That's Zivoin's new bride*, they'll say, and the whispers will reach the military police, who will come storming into the concrete block of flats, hammering on every door, looking for men to steal. If she says the words out loud, they will sound ridiculous. The paranoid ramblings of an old woman. She wants to tell him that he was a fool to come back here, but Milenka is a woman with bones made of steel, and she will not show her fear. Besides, Zivoin is her son, and he will do what she says.

He meets her eyes. 'Just a moment.' Drago and Milenka fall still as they hear him open the guest bedroom door and say something to Alegria.

'What did you say?' Milenka says anxiously, the second he reappears.

'I told her not to leave the flat . . . and not to go anywhere without her passport.' Zivoin bends to kiss her cheek. His face is calm, blank. When he and Drago depart, Milenka exhales and sinks into her chair with a soft groan.

Back in the little bedroom, no space to even open up a suitcase, Alegria lies back, looks out of the window and takes a few deep breaths. Just a few minutes ago, she was relaxed. But this new development is concerning. How many days can they stay here, if they need to? She rolls onto her stomach and reaches out a hand to check if the radiator is on. At least the flat is warm – she was astounded when Zivoin told her his parents had been given this home for free, *and* had their heating bills covered in the winter. An entire flat, theirs to own until the day they die, no strings attached. She could never imagine this happening back home.

She has to stop herself from checking on the flowers Zivoin bought her in Belgrade. She has snipped off a few of the buds and pressed them between newspaper and books, hoping to preserve them. Alegria badly wishes she could call Si. She's certain her whole family would have meshed seamlessly with Zivoin's – she can already picture Adelina and Milenka in the kitchen together, Toninho and Drago smoking palheiros and playing checkers, like all the old men in Brazil do. Simone would make Drago laugh, and he would grow a soft spot for her – just like everyone else. Their absence from this next step in her life still makes her ache.

Before she left, she had asked Si if she was still planning to stay home for a while. After all, her sister often changed her mind, jumping from idea to idea depending on what mood she was in. But this time, she'd seemed resolute. 'I think I should stay here for now,' she'd said whilst stroking Alegria's hair. 'Hang out with Mãe and Pai for a bit. I think they'll need time to adjust to you not being here.' It worries her that Simone doesn't seem to have any real idea of where she will go next, or what she wants to do. Alegria doesn't like the suggestion that by leaving, she is condemning her sister to live with their parents indefinitely. She will have to talk to Si about it the next time they manage to speak on the phone. She tries to sleep, but the worries – about the registrar, about whatever Zivoin is hiding from her, about her sister – swim around her head like sharks.

Eventually, Alegria climbs off the bed and walks into the living room in search of her new mother-in-law. She wants to help with the cooking. Alegria has seen – the way only a woman can – the amount of work Milenka does in the kitchen, churning out meal after meal for her family. She is in a state of perpetual chopping, boiling, roasting, baking – for the current meal, for the next meal, for the wedding that may or may not take place.

Milenka is hovering by the breakfast table. She's wondering whether or not to clean up when Alegria enters, wearing – to her satisfaction – the cardigan she made for her. It took her three weeks of knitting late into the evenings to make it on time, and she is pleased to see it being appreciated. Milenka knits for everyone – socks, mittens, waistcoats, vests, scarves. But she only crochets for a handful of people. She is almost done with her son's wedding gift.

She beckons Alegria to sit with her – makes yet another pot of Turkish coffee, which Alegria sips at politely. They can exchange fewer than six words between them, but they find small ways to communicate. Mostly a lot of smiling, a lot of pointing. She has so many questions for her son's soon-to-be wife; she wishes she could reach over, grasp her hand and see directly into her mind. Alegria makes a point to pick up the used plates, carrying them to the sink and washing up. Milenka protests at first, but gradually she relents and allows Alegria to creep into her space. An hour later, the women have figured out a way to cook together. The pita dough has been placed on the centre of the kitchen table, now scrubbed clean and sprinkled with flour, and Milenka teaches Alegria how to slowly stretch it out in a clockwise direction, centimetre by centimetre, until what was once a thick mound becomes flat and wafer-thin.

They have just covered it with a damp cloth to allow it to rise when Kajo arrives. As Zivoin's best man, his role requires him to carry out certain duties, including paying respects to the groom's parents. He staggers slightly under the weight of an entire crate of grapes, a box the size of a dinner platter filled with little cakes in the shape of walnuts, a bag full of sour plums, and, most impressively, an entire leg of smoked Njeguši ham, weighing seven kilos. Alegria watches carefully as he greets Milenka, trying to absorb as many of the customs as she can. Zivoin has taken her through the basics of his culture: three kisses on the cheek to greet someone – no hugging; never show up empty-handed; feed your guests to the point of sickness; never refuse a drink or a meal in someone's home . . . The list goes on. She had not realised how much tradition this country held, and watches curiously as Milenka orders them both to the living-room sofa and then brings out a spherical glass bottle with a long, narrow neck. 'Oh!' she gasps when she sees what's inside. A whole, perfect pear floats within the clear liquid.

Seeing the look on her face, Milenka turns to Kajo: 'Explain it to her.' She hands the bottle to Alegria for her to turn back and forth. The pear nudges against the glass with a wet thunk.

'This is rakija,' Kajo says, 'pear brandy. Our national drink – we take it when we come off the mountains in the winter and we're frozen from the cold, and we take it with guests as a welcome, so that our house makes them feel warm in here.' He thumps his chest with his fist.

'But how does the pear get in the bottle?'

'The bottles, with the brandy inside already, are placed over the pear blossom before it grows. So the flavour slowly infuses the bottle – first the sharp bitterness of the young pear, then the honey of the old one. It takes up to two months to make.' Sensing Milenka's eyes still on him, he adds, 'Most families have a special, secret way to make it, not just with pear but all kinds of fruit – this is her family recipe.'

Looking satisfied, Milenka pours three shots of the rakija and hands one to each of them. 'Živeli,' she growls, and Kajo echoes her. In synchronised movements, they down their entire drinks, not breaking eye contact. They place the empty glasses down, unfazed.

For Alegria, it's a different story. The smell hits her before the taste does. She inhales unintentionally, then almost chokes as the liquid lands on her tongue and slides down her throat. She had expected it to taste like sherry, sweet and thick. Instead, it smells like rubbing alcohol and although she senses a faint whisper of pear, the strength of it overpowers everything else. It's like Alegria has swallowed a small ball of fire. She gasps as she feels the heat travel through her oesophagus all the way to her stomach – it's the most intense thing she's ever tasted. They're both watching her – Kajo in amusement, Milenka in concern. 'Ha-ha-*hvala*,' Alegria splutters, tears now streaming out of her eyes. Suddenly the three of them are howling with laughter, Kajo pounding the sofa with his fists as she doubles over, struggling for breath. Milenka, still clutching the bottle, laughs the loudest, great full-throated bellows flying out of her mouth like missiles. It is the first and last time Alegria will ever accept rakija.

After she composes herself, Milenka brings out syrupy slices of baklava and serves more Turkish coffee. Alegria settles back, content to watch the two of them speak for a while. Milenka crochets as she and Kajo fall into rapid-fire conversation. The frown has returned to her face, all traces of elation gone. Kajo tries his best to translate what he can, and Alegria, aware of how tiresome this can be, tries to make it clear how appreciative she is. After a while, though, she disengages and stares instead at the small television with the slightly fuzzy screen. She watches the local news footage with interest – something about a bear – maybe roaming somewhere it shouldn't be? A suited man shaking hands with another suited man, both standing at lecterns. A demonstration of sorts, mostly made up of old women wearing triangular headscarves. A group of armed men clad in black camouflage, patches of red, blue and white on their biceps. They patrol a street wearing helmets and bulletproof vests. Alegria realises that the room has gone quiet. Kajo and Milenka are staring at the screen. Milenka's arms are folded. She has sucked her lips into her mouth, her chin jutting out. Kajo's face has not changed, but the TV set has his complete attention. Alegria feels a flutter of annoyance at Zivoin for keeping her in the dark, like a child. *What is going on?*

Milenka picks up the remote and turns off the TV. She looks at Alegria's bewildered face.

'How much does she know about what's happening?' she asks. When Kajo shrugs, avoiding her eye, she snaps, 'How much has Zivoin told her?'

'Not much, I think. She knows about the soldiers in Croatia, she knows things are very tense at the moment.'

'Does she know about the police?'

'I don't think so.'

'The border?'

Kajo shakes his head and Milenka does something very rare – she curses her son. 'What is he *thinking?*' she cries furiously. 'He's walked her into a situation she knows nothing about.'

'Tetka Milenka, I think he's trying not to scare her. They're here for barely a week, and all of this happened as she was up in the air on a plane! What was he supposed to do – send her back?'

'She's not a piece of luggage!' she snaps. 'I kept thinking how strange it was that she seems so calm – this whole time, she had no idea? You tell her! Tell her everything, right now!'

As they argue, Alegria's eyes flicker between them curiously. Finally, Kajo sighs. Looking uncomfortable, he says, 'Zivoin asked us – Svetlana and me – not to talk to you about it because he knew it would scare you. But this thing that happened in Croatia – it was very bad. Very, very bad. Many people are saying it was a provocation. To start a war.'

'I know this,' Alegria says, feeling her heart rate increase. 'I already know this.'

'The thing is,' Kajo says, 'there are already some parts of

Croatia that kind of *are* at war. Like, a small, regional kind of war. Not serious. But that is why your bus took so much time – it had to go around Croatia because the Yugoslav Army has closed the border.'

'OK.' She wishes he would get to the point.

'So, there is a lot of confusion at the moment. Things like this have happened before – some drunk idiots attack soldiers, and the soldiers kill them, and everyone says, "OK, now it is war," but it never is. And the president – him, on the screen – is saying that the people involved in killing the soldiers will be shot, that Yugoslavia is strong, all these things. But at the same time, there are rumours that he will also announce a state of emergency, expand the army and close all our borders.'

'All the borders,' Alegria repeats, her eyes wide. 'So . . . we can get stuck here?'

'Not you,' Kajo says, more sharply than he intended to. '*You* will be allowed to go. It's us – Montenegrins, Serbs, Bosnians – who won't be able to leave if a war does break out.'

'And Zivoin,' she breathes, looking from Kajo to Milenka. She suddenly remembers something he said in one of his letters to her. *These days, every Yugoslav I know is walking around with a pit in their stomach.* Once again, Alegria feels foolish for not having pieced things together sooner. She should have been quicker – she should have demanded that Zivoin spell it out for her, instead of letting herself get lost in the elation of being back with him.

'Yes, and the other problem is the military police.'

'What do you mean?'

'They have been out of control lately. Not so much in

Belgrade or the big cities, but down here it's been very bad. Sometimes they arrest men with exemption papers who haven't been around much – students, overseas workers, people with minor health issues – and beat them, or send them to the front lines. To remind them who's really in charge.' Kajo's voice is bitter as he delivers this. 'They're thugs with guns.'

'What do you *mean*?' Alegria's voice rises to almost a squeak. She immediately looks at her watch, wondering where Zivoin could be. What if he is being arrested as they speak?

But Kajo is not done. He is speaking quickly again, as though unable to stop. 'We have a distant friend, Bato,' he says in a low voice. 'A few days before you came, he was arrested at his son's birthday party. We don't know if it was just by chance, or if his name was on a list, or if someone was angry and reported him. He had a medical exemption but they took him anyway. Him and another guy. They put them in the back of a truck and said they were being sent to do some routine military training. Instead, they took them across the border into Croatia and they were given gear and rifles and sent on patrol.' His voice rises as he speaks, and Alegria has the childish urge to block her ears so she can't hear what comes next. 'Almost immediately, the group he was with were ambushed by Croatian paramilitaries. A grenade went off near him.' Alegria covers her face with her hands, but Kajo ploughs on. 'The shrapnel embedded in his chest and thigh. He's still in hospital – the surgeons can't remove any of it because it's too close to his heart and to the – the big vein in this leg.' He touches his right knee. 'We think he's going to be OK, but who knows? And Zivoin, he thinks they don't know he's back because he came through Serbia. I told him to be careful – you know what we trained as, in the army?'

'Machine-gunners?'

'It's a pretty important position – only the snipers are in higher demand.'

Everything slots neatly into place. She understands now why Zivoin and his whole family have been so strained, why he's been in a rush to leave ever since arriving. She heard him vomit last night, and he told her it was just travel sickness. Alegria realises she's on her feet. 'We have to go,' she says somewhat wildly. 'Zivoin can't be here!' She thinks of where they might be able to go unmarried. Greece? Back home? Portugal – her passport would get them into Portugal! Perhaps they could marry there.

Kajo has both hands raised, as if trying to settle a spooked horse. 'This is why he was going to tell you all of this later. He knew it would scare you.'

'He's an *idiot*. Of course it scares me!' she retorts, and turns back to Milenka, who is on her feet too. 'Please can you tell her I'm sorry?' she asks Kajo. 'Tell her I'm sorry for being the reason her son is back where he shouldn't be.' She feels sick with guilt.

Kajo starts explaining, but Milenka waves the words away, shaking her head as though offended. Although Milenka's eyes are still wet, she smiles and gestures at Kajo to translate. 'She's asking you to stay calm – to trust her son. She says she's never seen him this happy before, and that there have been times in her life when she's been scared for him – for the decisions he makes – and he has asked her to trust him, and he has always been right.' Looking a little embarrassed by the intimacy of the conversation, Kajo pauses to listen once again to Milenka, who has laid a hand on Alegria's arm. 'She's saying that Zivoin never would have – her son never would risk his life if it wasn't worth it. That it would be an insult to his love for you if you don't trust him now, at the final step. She's asking you to sit down and trust him.'

What can she possibly say in the face of that? The only other woman in the world who has more of a claim to fear, guilt and grief than she does is asking her to have faith. She knows how to do that. Alegria takes a long, trembling breath. She sits down and tries to act normally, even though there's a ringing in her ears. The border, the police, the war. She does not know this world – but Zivoin does, and if he is not afraid enough to stay away, then she will force herself not to feel any fear either. 'What about you?' she asks Kajo eventually. 'Are you exempt from the army?'

'I'm not exempt, but I've got a little more protection than Zivoin. I paid a few people to keep my name off a list. But Svetlana and I are thinking about leaving too, actually.'

'What kind of protection?'

Kajo tries to shrug, but it comes across as more of a twitch. 'Many things. My family is well connected. But Zivoin's . . . well, he's from the village. No one's going to step in to vouch for him if he's caught.'

When Zivoin and Drago arrive back at the flat several hours later, they find Alegria and Milenka sitting side by side on the sofa, crying silently. Kajo is awkwardly perched on the other end. He is clearly relieved to see his friend, jumping up with a slightly panicked look on his face.

'What's going on?' Zivoin asks, alarmed. 'Why are they crying?'

'I couldn't tell you, brate. Something about her mother.' Kajo makes a face at him, as if to say, *Women*, and turns to Drago.

'Whose mother?' But Kajo is busy greeting Drago, so Zivoin turns to Milenka and tries to meet the moment with a joke. 'Majka, what did you do? Attack her?'

'Oh, *don't*,' Milenka says indignantly, wiping her eyes. 'You moron. I'm crying because – because – I'm thinking of her mother, so far away and unable to attend her daughter's wedding, and how devastating that must be for her.'

'I see.' He looks at Alegria and switches to English. 'Are you all right? What's wrong?'

'I'm crying because she's crying,' she says simply, reaching out to grasp his mother's hand. She looks up at him and Zivoin can see in her face that she knows everything. All the shit he's tried to absorb for her: the danger, the lack of time. He can see it in the clench of her jaw. He gestures to the balcony, and picks up a blanket lying on the sofa.

'What did they say?' Alegria asks the second the door closes behind them. 'Any luck? Please tell me it's good news.'

He wraps the blanket around her shoulders, puts his arm around her and presses his mouth onto the top of her head, exhaling softly. It's evening, but the sky is still bright, barely starting to purple. The sun sets late here. 'The registrar is refusing to marry us without an official, certified translator. Apparently, you might not understand what you're getting into.' He laughs, tries to gauge her reaction, but Alegria says nothing. She is looking out at the view. To prevent birds coming in and making nests in the corners, Milenka has attached chicken wire to the entire balcony. They see the city through a chain-link fence, the sky scissored into small diamonds.

'But it's going to be OK?'

'It's going to be OK. I think. I've found the last possible official who can marry us – he's just able to fit us in.'

'The last one? What does that mean?'

'It means they're going to stop issuing wedding licences from next week. But I've paid him extra – I've bribed him, actually – to marry us before that happens. As long as I can translate on your behalf, as long as he thinks you understand, he'll do it. So you better just nod at everything I say, OK?'

'I can do that.' She exhales and relaxes against him. 'So we still marry tomorrow?'

'I'm sorry, Peach, this new guy has another wedding in Kotor – lots of other weddings, in fact. It turns out many people are frantically marrying foreigners. Three days from now.'

'Three days.' Given everything she now knows, the wait feels like a threat. 'There's a lot that can go wrong in three days. There's a lot that's gone wrong already.' Zivoin thinks of the way she looked up at him when he arrived and starts to apologise, trying to find the right words to explain himself. But she stops him with a single shake of her head. 'We won't speak about it, because it will not happen again. We will not treat each other as though we can't handle the truth. Deal?' She tilts her head up to look at him and forces out a smile. 'I'm braver than you, after all.'

'Are you now?' Though he's aware of his family on the

other side of the glass door, Zivoin can't help it. He stoops to kiss her. 'Braver *and* smarter.'
'Don't forget better-looking.'
'Always.' He kisses the tip of her nose.
'But it's not safe for us to stay here right now.'
'We aren't staying here – we're going on our honeymoon. I called the hotel in Budva – I'm taking you there tonight.'
'*Before* the wedding?'
'Before the wedding.'
Zivoin tells her about the first time he swam in the sea, during summer's sweaty peak. It had taken seventeen years for him to see the rich green and blue hues of the water, despite living a couple of hours away from the coast. As the sky darkens, he talks about the astonishment he felt when he first set eyes on the never-ending sea, how he couldn't understand how it could expand left, right and ahead, with no end point. How he didn't know about the water's saltiness until a wave had pushed a mouthful down his throat and he'd choked and gagged, trying not to empty the contents of his stomach. The way he learned to smell salt in the air and know how far the tide was. How cold and clear the Adriatic was. He could look down whilst swimming and see the sunlight catch mother-of-pearl and old glass bottles half buried in silt. If he put his head under the water and held still, he could catch the brown flash of a sea snake zigzagging across the seabed towards patches of grass. Zivoin describes the feeling of deep contentment he'd had, looking at the way the mountains met the sea and the sea met the sky, knowing that his place in the world was fixed and safe, that his existence made sense. 'Everyone says Croatia is the most beautiful part of Yugoslavia, but actually, it's the

coast of Montenegro. I'm going to take you there, so we can make that feeling ours.'

Alegria is quiet as he speaks, feeling the chill of the concrete through her socks. She's never heard such longing and awe in his voice. 'In Brazil, we never hold the party before the birthday. It's asking for something else to go wrong.'

'Peach, things have already gone wrong.' He shrugs, kisses her forehead. He thinks about the way she pushed him down onto the hotel bed, that night in Belgrade. If they leave after dinner, they can be there by nine. 'We're just going to have to make our own luck from now on.'

CHAPTER 23

Nikšić, April 1991

Day 7

On the morning of her wedding day, she wakes up before he does, and discovers they're holding hands. She can't remember if they fell asleep this way or if they found each other during the night. Alegria wants to check the time, to get some water, but she does not want to let go of Zivoin's hand, nor is she willing to disturb him. He has been sleeping badly since they left Belgrade, often waking up during the night, shouting in fear. He dreams of people standing at the foot of their bed, preventing him from leaving. Alegria is luckier. These days she does not remember her dreams. She lies on her back and stares at the patterns on the ceiling made by a weak sun filtering through the metal shutters. A good omen. She makes a list of all the different things she feels: excitement, of course, for the wedding. Nerves, for the same reason. Relief that they've made it to today; peace with the choices she has made leading up to this moment. Fear – that one makes sense. And grief, that her family will not see her – that one carries the sharpest sting. As it has many times over the past few weeks, the enormity of Alegria's decision rolls over her yet again. She really did leave them. She really did go. The version of herself from half a year ago – inflexible and highly strung – is unrecognisable to her now.

With her free hand, Alegria rests a palm on her abdomen and feels it rise and fall with her breath. They speak about children all the time, she and Zivoin. Of course, now would be too soon. They have so much to learn about each other still, so much life to build between them. And yet, she remembers the first time he showed her his bedroom in London, the pride in his voice as they went through photos of his nieces and nephews, and she thinks about how neat and romantic – and inconvenient – it would be if she were to discover she was pregnant the same day they married. But she isn't, she already knows that. Alegria is on the pill. She hasn't ever missed a dose.

Eventually, her thirst becomes too much to ignore. She puts on one of Zivoin's jumpers over her pyjamas and pads into the kitchen, trying not to make a sound. To her surprise, Drago is already sitting there, balcony door open as he finishes off a cigarette. She pauses, a little awkward, and he freezes momentarily, then waves at the empty seat next to him. Alegria has spent almost no time with the patriarch of the family. He is silent most of the time, his tinted glasses making him hard to read. She has heard plenty about him from Zivoin, all of it respectful, but not all of it good.

She notices Drago has no cup of coffee and decides she will make some for the both of them. After watching Milenka make Turkish coffee ten times a day, Alegria's pretty sure she knows how to do it too – she just needs to figure out this wood-burning stove. From the pantry, she finds the coffee, matches and a small packet of brown sugar, then fills the dzezva, the coffee pot, with water. She crouches down by the cast-iron base of the stove and examines it, trying to look confident as Drago watches her curiously. She pulls open the hatch and stares at its soot-smeared walls, wondering what next. An image of the room on fire, smoke pouring out of the balcony, makes her pause. And then Drago is bending down next to her, his knees clicking as he settles into place by her side. 'Ovako,' he says, and shows her how to make a woodpile: two small strips of wood stacked on top of two more strips in a square formation. He hands her a sheet of newspaper and mimes a tearing motion with his hands. Together, they place balled-up wads of paper in the centre of the woodpile and Alegria sets it alight. They watch in satisfaction as the fire catches immediately, hissing and popping as it consumes the black ink. The coffee is not quite as strong as it should be, but it will do. She adds a spoonful of sugar to her coffee and offers some to Drago, who shakes his head quickly, as though repulsed by the idea. They drink without speaking, smiling at each other occasionally.

To make space for the events later that day, someone – maybe Drago – has pushed the table up against the wall. It is covered with decorative plates: two diagonal rows of them, each with a different pattern. They don't particularly match, or even go well together, but she likes them all the same. It's something different in an otherwise dark and austere flat that displays almost no personal touches or quirks apart from the room they're in now. This kitchen is the only artistic part of the home, Alegria realises. She glances around and notices other small details. An old plastic toy car, missing its two front wheels; white crocheted chair covers; a tea towel with a small yellow hen on it; an ashtray filled with multi-coloured beads, the remnants of a broken necklace. She likes that someone – Milenka – has gone to the trouble of making this part of the home feel lived-in. No wonder everyone gravitates here.

As she makes these observations, Drago watches her, and feels nervous. His hand twitches towards hers at one point, as though to pat it, but the gesture goes unnoticed by Alegria as she lifts the cup to her mouth. This is almost enough to make Drago give up altogether, but he is painfully aware that she will leave tonight with his son, and this may be his only chance. As soon as she sets the cup down again, his large hand closes over her own, and he squeezes it gently, trying to convey, in a single movement, how grateful they are for her presence. 'Heppy,' he says, and points at himself, hoping she gets it. Drago still does not understand how his son could ever find happiness with someone so different from himself, but some things don't need understanding. They just need embracing. Alegria smiles her wide smile at him, places her other hand on his for a moment, nods. He lets go, relieved. Offers her a cigarette, and when she says no, goes outside to smoke it. The television remains off.

Milenka appears, looking shocked at herself for sleeping in, followed by Zivoin, already dressed, visibly excited. There are just a handful of hours before they must get ready and make their way to the town hall. It will be a simple wedding: no flowers, no hairstylist, no make-up, no cake. She and Zivoin are already wearing their plain wedding bands. He's promised her a diamond ring one day; she's told him she doesn't care about any of that. Privately, though, Alegria is glad that some of her wealthier extended family members aren't standing in this kitchen with them.

Zivoin touches her shoulder. 'We should go sooner rather than later.' She nods and vanishes into the bedroom.

'Are you going somewhere?' Milenka asks, trying – and failing – to keep the reproach out of her voice. 'Can't it wait?'

She sees irritation flash over her son's face for a second before he pauses and then says, his voice gentle, 'She needs to call her family before the wedding.'

'Oh.' What can she say in the face of that? 'But we have a phone she can use . . .' Milenka's voice fades as Zivoin goes to her and envelops her in a hug. There is a heavy black rotary phone in the corridor with a deafeningly loud ring, but they cannot make international calls on it. She knows this. He has told her a hundred times, every time she complained about the number not working when she tried to call him in London. But Zivoin does not remind his mother of this today. He just holds on to her until they hear the bedroom door open. Alegria is back, swaddled in a hat, scarf, gloves, coat. Milenka almost laughs at this – it's April, after all – but she remembers what Zivoin told her about how it does not snow in the city she's from. 'Be careful' is all she ends up saying. The words hover in the air after they leave.

In the building's rattling lift, the yellow light bulb casts a urine-coloured glow. Alegria leans against him and smiles. 'Hello, husband.'

'Don't say it yet!' he protests, using his foot to keep the

doors from opening prematurely. He wraps his arms around her and says, 'Isn't it bad luck?'

'I thought we were making our own?'

The post office is not far, but Zivoin insists on taking a taxi. Although Alegria would prefer to walk, she complies, knowing he is still wary. She observes Nikšić from the car window instead. She knows there's an abandoned church at the top of a hill that you can reach by walking a path through a forest – she would have loved to see the town from above. To her, everyone looks completely normal. The streets are occupied, shops open. If there's tension in the air, she cannot feel it. In the post office, Zivoin points her to one of two little booths and hovers before she goes in. 'Can I say hello to them?' he asks.

The question surprises and thrills her. 'Of course! Let me catch up first – I'll call you in.'

Apart from one brief call in Belgrade, she has not had the chance to speak to them. Toninho picks up, and Alegria exhales in relief. 'I caught you before your shift,' she says happily, her eyes already filling with tears. 'Oh, I'm so glad.'

'Filha!' Toninho's voice lifts when he hears her. 'Wait, let me call everyone . . .' He assembles the family, and as Alegria hears them fussing over how to turn on the speakerphone, she starts to both laugh and sob.

'. . . No it's this one.' Si's voice is suddenly much louder in her ear. 'Ale, can you hear us?'

'I can.'

'Great – Mãe wants to say something. Go on. Why are you pausing?'

'Can she hear me?'

'I *just* said—'

Alegria dissolves into more laughter as mother and daughter argue, fierce longing pumping through her chest. She misses them so much it feels like part of her has been left back in Brazil with them. 'Si – I only have about twenty minutes. Have this argument later.'

'Oh, sorry, sorry. How are you? Excited?'

'So excited.'

'Nervous?'

'*So* nervous.'

'I bet.'

'Are you wearing the peach dress, my love?' Adelina asks, sounding hopeful. 'Will you take lots of pictures?'

'Not this time, it's too cold here – just a few days ago it snowed!'

'And how's the situation there?' Toninho cuts in, his voice laced with worry.

Alegria glances back at Zivoin, forgetting momentarily that he cannot understand her anyway. 'Very safe,' she lies. 'Nothing to worry about.'

She tells them about her honeymoon and how lovely it was, despite the cold. Although Alegria has never seen Croatia, she has already decided that she agrees with Zivoin's declaration that Montenegro is better. They'd stayed in a hotel overlooking the Adriatic, sleeping with the curtains open to watch the stars dot the sky and the sun fill the room. They had walked through the Stari Grad, a great stone citadel built on the cliff face that once defended the inhabitants from pirate attacks, and they had eaten plate after plate of grilled, freshly caught squid. The beaches were glorious and wild, untouched by tourists, and the sea changed colour from hour to hour. At sunrise, it was clear, faintly purple. As though the sea hadn't quite woken up yet. On their first morning, Zivoin took her to a beach hidden around a cliff face, navigating a secret path through the rocks. By the time they arrived, the water had become stronger, darker, a perfect crystalline blue, and then it was green, clear enough for her to see fish darting in and out of rock pools. By late afternoon, the water was a dark navy, almost menacing, before it took on the colours of the sunset and transformed, once again, into the kind of beauty that made her stand still and reach for Zivoin, unable to move in the face of something so much bigger than the two of them.

'It's a different kind of beauty, more rugged than our beaches back home,' she tries to explain. 'But there's no sand! It's all stones, little round stones. Can you believe it?'

Simone is disdainful as she responds. 'Sounds painful.'

'It was, actually – and the water! It was so *cold*! It hurt my bones!'

'Did you swim in it?' Adelina asks anxiously. 'During the snowstorm? You shouldn't have done that. Did the snow melt when it landed on the water?'

'Of course not, Mãe.' She has forgotten how much she laughs when she's with her family and how, when one of them laughs, the rest of them do too, as if they're programmed to mirror each other's joy.

The conversation slowly turns towards the wedding, the subject they've all been dancing around. Adelina sighs and says, 'I still can't believe so little administration is involved.

Isn't it strange? You just show up, get the licence and marry this gringo.'

Toninho sounds amused as he says, 'How is that different from what we did here?'

'It feels very different – over there she's a foreigner. What about your passport? When will you get a new one?'

'After I marry, we'll pick up the international licence in another city, the same one we fly out of. And then we'll pay for an expedited passport.' To be legally recognised as married, Alegria will have to register her marriage with the Brazilian Embassy and request a new passport, erasing her former self from Britain's borders. She does not allow herself to think about all the things that could go wrong with this plan.

'Why the rush? Why don't you stay there for a bit?'

'We . . .' Alegria thinks about the borders. Of the possibility of her being allowed to leave but her husband being forced to stay, vanishing into the front lines of a war she still doesn't understand. This is a conversation for a different time, when they are far away enough from it. This is what Alegria tells them instead: the money is running out. They need to find jobs again. Zivoin can't afford to keep renting his room in London unless they return, and without both a job *and* a fixed address, his indefinite leave to remain will be invalidated. She cannot even apply for a visa without him sponsoring her. Their return tickets are already bought, and just two days from now, she hopes they will be back on the streets of London, searching for jobs once again. She has two hundred dollars in her bank account, and that's it.

'I still don't see why you have to change your name,' Toninho says softly when she finishes speaking. The family grows quiet. Brazilians typically keep their own names when they marry. She will cease to be Alegria Dias in a few hours' time.

'I need a new passport, with a new name, so I can try to enter the United Kingdom again.' She has told them all of this before, but her father's sadness is an open wound. She sees Zivoin waiting outside the booth and waves him in, seizing the distraction. 'Someone wants to say hello!'

She smiles encouragingly as Zivoin takes the phone and says a hesitant 'Good morning' in Portuguese, his emphasis in all the wrong places.

Simone, who, of course, has met him many times before, gives a scream of delight. 'Good morning, Cricket!' She dissolves into giggles as Alegria hides a grin with her hand and Zivoin closes his eyes, mortified. He tries valiantly to connect with her family, nodding with satisfaction when Toninho tells him, politely, that he's the nicest gringo he's ever met. Never mind that he's the *only* gringo her father has ever met.

The conversation goes back and forth like a ping-pong game, everything repeated twice, sometimes three times, and Alegria and Simone translate in a blur of stops and starts. Eventually, she thinks of the cost and forces herself to bring the call to an end. 'Let me just say something to Si quickly – alone.'

Zivoin steps out of the booth and she hears her sister breathing down the line. 'I'm really going to find it hard, being here without you,' Simone says, gently. All the humour is gone from her voice. 'I don't know how to exist all by myself.'

'*Si.*' Alegria is sobbing before Simone even finishes her sentence. 'Don't – you're acting like I'll never see you again!'

'Oh, I know you will!' Simone, too, is crying. 'You'll come back to visit, or I'll come to see you. You've changed, irmã. The sister I knew a year ago would have never dared to do half of what you've done. This is who you were always meant to be, before you were forced to grow up and take care of us.'

'I wouldn't have chosen any other path.' Alegria wipes her cheeks with her free hand and tries to get her emotions under control. Her voice is gluey from the tears. 'Si, you need to promise me that you won't step into my shoes, OK? I want you to live your life the way you always do – not for anyone else.'

'Don't worry about me, irmã. You know what I'm going to do next? I'm going to find a rich man to whisk me off around the world. Maybe I'll marry one of those European princes who has more money than brains. I'll fly you out for the wedding.' She laughs, and in the background her mother laughs too. Alegria closes her eyes and tries to memorise the sound. 'I have to go.' The air grows heavy once again. Her parents will not watch her marry, will not hold her hand, will not hug her. She wishes with her whole body that things could be different, and promises them she will visit soon with Zivoin, to show him the home she loves so much.

'Go with Deus, filha,' Adelina says, her words tender. 'We're all thinking of you today.'

'Be safe, my daughter.'

'Call us when you get to Belgrade, irmã!'

'I love you! I love you!' she slams the phone down and takes a great, shuddering breath. Laughs away the tears.

Zivoin slips back into the booth and draws her into his chest and starts to whisper how sorry he is, but she waves away his guilt. Alegria pays over ten thousand dinars for just twenty-five minutes – that might as well have been twenty-five seconds – and finds Zivoin's hand with her own. 'Come on, Cricket,' she says, her eyes red. 'Let's go get married.'

Back at the flat, Alegria looks at herself in the bathroom mirror, peering through the steam. She is still brown from the sun, freckles stronger than ever. She smiles, then peeks out to see if the coast is clear and slips into the bedroom. Zivoin is waiting in the front room, wearing his father's old double-breasted suit. Her hair is wrapped in one of his old cotton shirts to protect it from the water. Just before she left Brazil, Alegria had it cut into a short, asymmetrical French bob. It had taken a lot of persuasion from Simone – Alegria was used to her curls defying any attempts to tame them. Yet her sister had been right, as she was about many things. The cut suits her. She looks more glamorous than she feels.

Alegria glances one last time at the silk dress and reluctantly folds the tissue paper back over it. Not today. The only other option that feels remotely suitable is a short-sleeved red dress that falls just above her knee. It cinches in at the waist, flares out at the hip. She pairs it with black heels and her gold hoops, leaves her neck bare, and adds red lipstick to top it off. Checking her reflection one last time, Alegria takes a deep breath.

Zivoin waits by the door, Drago and Milenka by his side. He's fiddling with his watch strap when he hears the click of heels and looks up to see her standing in the hallway nervously. She's a vision in red. He glances quickly at his parents. If they're surprised by her choice of wedding attire, their smiles don't show it. Good. She's perfect.

'You look unbelievable,' Zivoin says quietly, drinking her in. 'The most beautiful woman in the world.'

'Don't lie!' But Alegria can't contain her smile as she walks to him, her cheeks glowing. He gently pushes one of her curls off her face, caresses her cheek with his thumb, then takes her hand.

'Ready?'
'Ready.'

CHAPTER 24

Nikšić, April 1991

Day 7

In the end, all the tension gives way to laughter.

They leave the flat and end up walking because there are not enough taxis to accommodate Zivoin's family congregating outside, and because a sense of giddy excitement imbues the group. Zivoin weaves through the crowd, introducing Alegria to his aunts and uncles, his cousins and their children. She soon loses track of all the names, but greets these new relatives of hers with as much warmth as she can – even when they do not reciprocate. The air is crisp and delicious; neither of them can stop smiling. It is a small town: they walk past two or three high-rise buildings and the giant concrete bunker from the Second World War, wire fence rattling in the wind. She searches for good omens and they come easily: the bird fluttering above their heads, wings flush against the lemon-yellow sun, the green of the trees, the lace table runners fluttering on the tiny balconies like veils.

It's a short walk. People stare. Zivoin holds Alegria's hand proudly, careful to keep his pace slower than usual so she can take her time in her heels. He drapes his military coat around her and feels bulletproof. He thinks: so this is why people write love poems. He looks at her, and she catches him looking and winks at him real quick, then stares down at the uneven concrete ground, watching her steps. Zivoin has only ever seen a functional example of love; his parents seem well beyond whatever passion they might have once had for each other. A mutual tolerance. He does not want that to happen to him; he wants to fall in love with her all the time, for all of time.

Alegria repeats two words in her head over and over: Da, razumijem. 'Yes, I understand.' These are the words she will need to say confidently, clearly, in front of the registrar. She wrote them on a piece of paper and now, as she walks, she realises she has left it on the bathroom sink. No matter. She feels so light and carefree that she could laugh from the thrill of it all.

They walk on. And because the town hall is in the town square, they hear the echo of the crowd before they see it. A swell of at least two hundred people waiting for them outside, blocking the way into the small, squat building. The flag of Yugoslavia hangs above it, blue, white and red fabric, stiff and dignified. Alegria wonders how they got it to stop flapping like that. She feels Zivoin's hand tighten around her own and he scans the scene with narrowed eyes, assessing the ratio of familiar to unfamiliar faces.

Drago appears at his shoulder and mutters, 'They've sent a local news reporter to cover the wedding.' He looks worried, and Zivoin can see his own concerned face reflected back at him in his father's tinted glasses.

'How did they even know about it?'

'You really thought that people wouldn't find out?'

'They shouldn't have done that,' Milenka says, joining them with a stony look. 'How vulgar – I'll make them leave.'

But Zivoin stops her. His eyes are still darting from face to face, calculating, keeping a smile on. 'No, it's good reporters are here. The police will leave us alone – and look...' He nods towards the group of people standing right by the entrance. Out of everyone, they look the most curious. They are craning their heads to get a look at his bride, talking quickly amongst themselves. 'I've never seen them at one of our weddings.'

'What's happening?' Alegria asks. 'Why are there so many people?'

'I think they've come to see you,' Zivoin tells her, and she wrinkles her nose in disbelief.

'That can't be it.'

'It's true. No one here has ever seen a Brazilian woman before.' Kajo is on Alegria's right-hand side now, Svetlana hovering behind him in a blue tea dress.

Alegria wants to say something about feeling like a zoo animal, but she's still translating the sentence in her head when Svetlana jumps in. 'You're famous,' she tells Alegria, watching her carefully for a reaction. 'The Gypsies have come to claim you. It's tradition for the groom to pay a dowry – they must think they're owed money.'

'They what?'

She wants to probe Svetlana for more details, but Zivoin gets in between them and snaps something at her and she melts away. He puts an arm around Alegria's shoulders. 'Ignore her. She's trying to scare you...' He trails off, looking uncertain. 'They probably think you're a relative, or something.'

'I can see why,' she says pointedly. These men and women are smaller, darker-skinned and darker-haired, just like her. They watch her with open interest, smiling, waving at her. She takes in the women's long hair and hoops glinting in their ears, their full skirts and coloured headscarves, the men's bright waistcoats and nylon sports jackets. She looks like she belongs there with them, not in the sea of slender, grey-eyed Montenegrins, many of whom stare back with open dislike. 'Should I be worried?' she asks, and is unsure who the question is directed towards.

Zivoin kisses her cheek. 'No, of course not. Unless you're planning on running away with one of them?'

'Well, I like the beard on him,' she says, nodding at a man so old he is bent double, supported by two relatives. As Zivoin follows her gaze, the man gives them a smile speckled with missing teeth, and they both laugh.

They push through the crowd, and Alegria feels eyes raking over her face and her body. She pulls the coat a little tighter around herself. The dark-eyed men and women at the building's entrance smile at her, speak to her in a language she does not recognise. As she passes, they stretch their arms out, only just stopping short of touching her. It feels like a blessing of some kind, though the tension between them and Zivoin's family is palpable enough to make her keep her gaze low. A camera follows them, rhythmic whirring makes her jump, *flash flash flash*. When she closes her eyes, the rectangular light is burned into her eyelids. She hears two of Zivoin's cousins speaking quietly to each other behind her, their voices clipped and sharp. He has his arm around her still, holding her close to him. Alegria is not afraid, necessarily, but there is something disturbing about the way everyone's eyes are glued to her. The bodies around her close in. *Like a prized animal on its way for slaughter*, a voice says in her head. She's waiting for yet another thing to go wrong.

They pass the steps and file into the building's slim hallway, and much of the crowd follows them into the small, sparsely furnished room. There is only a single desk in the corner, a navy and gold coat of arms hanging above it. There are no chairs for anyone to sit on, and no windows either, but the room quickly fills with people: neighbours, locals, strangers, family and friends, who examine the couple loudly and unashamedly. Alegria closes her eyes for a moment. She suddenly feels detached – from this room, from the man next to her, from her own body. None of it seems real. This is a sitcom playing out back home on Globo, she thinks, and when she opens her eyes again, she will be back on the plane, heading to London for the very first time.

'Peach.' She feels his hand take hers. 'You OK?' Alegria wants to open her eyes, but she cannot just yet, she needs to figure out the answer to his question. She wants to say, 'I want my mother.' But this feels like a pathetic response at her age, and there's nothing he can do about that, anyway. He asks again, quieter now, and then she feels his lips on her temple, gentle, calm. 'We can leave right this second,' Zivoin whispers. 'Go and do this in Belgrade. Me, you and two strangers I drag off the street.'

And for some reason, this image of two confused people witnessing them marry makes her smile, brings her back to herself. She feels her feet pressing into the floor and her high heels pressing into her soles, and bears down on them a little to increase the pressure. Squeezes his hand back and takes in his steadiness. 'A solid plan B. But I'm OK.' And she is.

'I love you,' he says, and Alegria says it back to him, and feels present again.

Zivoin helps her out of his coat and feels her wince when silence falls. The crowd takes in her bright red dress, short sleeves, bare legs. He hears the whispers, timid at first, but then louder: red, to a wedding? What is she thinking? Who does she think she is? *What kind of woman* – this last voice he recognises as a distant cousin of his, a woman he hadn't invited, hadn't even known was coming. He rounds on her. She falls silent, but Zivoin looks her directly in the eye and addresses the room at large. He has already had a few shots and realises now that he's verging on drunk. 'If I hear one more thing about my wife,' he roars, 'or one more opinion about what's happening here today, I will *personally* escort you out. As a matter of fact, most of you weren't invited here in the first place – but I'll be hospitable. Shut up, or fuck off.' Although his words are met with a shocked rumble of displeasure, the spectators quieten. His immediate family have pushed their way through to them by now and gather around protectively.

'I didn't think this many people would turn up,' says Nada, the only cousin in the family who is exactly his age. She surveys the room indignantly. 'They're like vultures.'

'They are, but you didn't have to be so rude,' Jelena, her mother, mutters. 'We're the ones that have to live here after you go.'

'With husbands that could get drafted any second.'

'No one is getting drafted,' Milenka says firmly. 'And no one,' she shoots her son a warning look, 'is shouting at family. If anyone says something they shouldn't, *I* will deal with it.' Her face softens as she reaches out to rub Alegria's shoulder. 'Tell her she looks beautiful, sine.'

'I *have*—'

They are interrupted by the registrar, an impatient-looking man in a black wool suit who enters the room already scowling. After a quick handshake, he introduces himself, glances at the swollen room, then checks his watch. 'We start, yes? I have other weddings...'

'We're ready,' Zivoin confirms, and finds Alegria's hand again.

The registrar nods and directs them to the desk. He slides a piece of paper towards them. 'She will need to sign this first, to say she waives her right to a state translator.' As soon as Alegria's hand rises from the paper, the ink still wet, he launches into the procedure without preamble or warning. The room becomes still, silent.

Alegria had expected this part to feel like a blur. In fact, it is almost painfully slow. The registrar intones sluggishly, looking first at Zivoin and then back at her as Zivoin translates. She smiles and nods when Zivoin struggles through something about inheriting property in the case of his – or her – death, barely pausing to listen. As if he would want the little house in Uberlândia with lizards living in the roof tiles. As if she would ever try and lay claim to Milenka and Drago's flat on the seventeenth floor, which Zivoin alone stands to inherit as the family's only son. None of it means anything, anyway. Between them, they will forge their own understandings of their marriage. Without moving her head, Alegria glances around the low-ceilinged room and sees a hanging strip of yellow paper, covered in the bodies of dead flies. Surely someone could have removed that before their arrival? Her stomach rumbles, and she shifts a little, the wooden floor creaking underneath her.

The registrar starts saying something complicated. More property law. He speaks for so long and in such convoluted terms that Zivoin loses all sense of what's being said. Even when it's in his native language, he realises he doesn't understand it. But the registrar, Luka, is watching him expectantly, and he remembers the conversation they had over the phone. Luka had warned him that whilst he didn't particularly care whether or not the people he married could understand what they were doing, the state very much did. 'There are so many foreign marriages happening at the moment – everyone's trying to get out of here. These days, if anyone refuses an approved translator, they have to send people from the Interior Ministry to make sure it's a legitimate wedding. So, no hesitating, no skipping any translations.'

The two men who followed the registrar in are watching Zivoin too. He turns to Alegria and tries his best. He trips through something incomprehensible as she stares at him with her face blank. He sees her glance towards the officials too, and knows two things. One, that she hates lying, and two, that she hasn't understood a word he's said. Zivoin tries again, and he can feel the room tensing, leaning towards them. The crowd holds its breath. Once again, he tries to explain – something about perpetuities, something else about right of way, adverse possession. These are words he does not know the direct translations for, so he simply makes them up.

'Do you understand?' the registrar asks.

Alegria hesitates, looking from him to Zivoin, before she says, 'No.'

As one, the spectators gasp, and frantic whispers break out behind them. Someone takes a picture. He imagines the headline: *Foreign Girl Rejects Local Boy*. It is all so absurd, so ridiculous that despite everything, Zivoin cannot help but laugh. It bursts out of him, full-throated and loud, and a confused silence falls. He feels a mild pain – Milenka has stepped forward and smacked the back of his head. '*Behave*,' she hisses grimly, looking scandalised. All this does is make him laugh harder. Beside her, Drago is shaking his head in confusion.

Alegria looks back at them, and then at the crowd. 'Why are they all looking at us like that?'

'They think,' Zivoin wheezes, holding his ribs, 'you've just changed your mind.'

'*Oh*,' she breathes, and then addresses the room, wide-eyed. 'I understand,' she cries, 'I understand! I understand!' A collective sigh of relief, more flashes – someone whoops loudly – applause so thunderous it drowns out Zivoin's laughter. Aware of his mother glaring at him, he composes himself. It is a wedding, after all.

And then, just like that, it is done. Knowing the first kiss is important to her, he shocks the room by taking her into his arms. Alegria squeals in surprise, but kisses him back ferociously, her arms wrapped around his neck. They sign a piece of paper like it has cost them nothing to get there, like it's easy, like they would do it every day if they could. Svetlana makes them pose for a photo, swearing that they will want it one day, and he will always be grateful that she insisted. The photo will come out well. Him: lanky, brown-suited, ears sticking out. Her: golden and glorious, head resting on his shoulder, her chin tilted upwards. Their hands are entwined. For the first few years, he will carry the photo with him in his breast pocket whenever they are apart, before relenting and framing it in their kitchen.

They exit to huge cheers. The sky is a passionate blue now, the sun shining down on them in the best and most beautiful way possible. Alegria is blinking in the new light, finding her bearings, when she hears them: the gunshots. She reacts instinctively, crouching down low on the ground, one hand over her head, the other groping sideways, searching for her husband's hand. She isn't sure if the people around her have recognised the sounds – but then again, how could they not? They are so loud. She thinks: the military police have come, just like everyone said they would. But, no – shooting into a crowd makes no sense. She thinks: war? But the idea of this feels impossible to grasp, so archaic and ridiculous that it leaks out of her brain immediately. The shots keep going; her hand still frantically searches for her husband. She thinks: robbers. A gang, maybe? Like the ones that run some of the poorer neighbourhoods back home, that must be it. Fine, there's nothing of value on her. She tries to pinpoint the direction the bullets are coming from. She can hear them behind her and on both sides, which means the only way to run is forward. Everyone around her is shouting now – at last, realisation and panic have crept in.

And then Zivoin is lifting her by her arm, the bullets *still* flying – she doesn't want to stand. He tilts her chin up, forcing her eyes to meet his, and Alegria realises he is laughing. 'It's OK!' he shouts. 'I should have warned you!' He points to a few of his cousins, all men, all aiming revolvers in the air and firing. 'It's a tradition – I completely forgot.' Everyone around them is cheering, she realises. And the people around her, who have seen her dive to the ground, are either gaping at her or laughing at her bemused face. She stares at the guns in shock for a moment, brain and body still catching up. She has been taught that the sound of guns means: *duck*. Means: *panic*. Means: *run*. She flinches with every bullet, and then, at last, the noise stops. No longer laughing, Zivoin searches her face. 'Are you all right?' he asks. 'You've gone pale.' She is, in fact, grey from shock.

'I'm OK,' she says, forcing a laugh, and tries to ignore the people still staring at her as if *she* were the insane one. Someone switches on a boom box, someone else starts passing around cigars. Friends descend on them with bottles of beer, wine, shots of rakija. By the time they get back to the flat, they are both pink-cheeked and wine-soaked, and the incident has relaxed into something even Alegria can joke about, poke fun at herself for. One day, whenever she retells the story, she will laugh.

As they walk back, most of the strangers peel away without even saying congratulations. Milenka busies herself serving the tiny walnut cakes, plates of grapes with bitter skins, and tray after tray of oily, flaky pita as guests cram into the kitchen and living room. Her nieces chase after children to wipe their noses, persuading them to swallow mouthfuls of food, scooping up dirty plates and used tissues and overflowing ashtrays. The men smoke and opine and shout 'Ojha!' as Drago pours drinks, makes toasts, thanks people for coming, and Zivoin and Alegria accept little envelopes of cash, thanking guests until their cheeks ache.

After a fourth round of toasts, they escape to the balcony with Kajo, Svetlana and a handful of his old school friends. They ask Alegria questions about Brazil, talk about teachers they hated, people they once knew, and then, inevitably, about her arrival. Kajo tells the group the story of how they stayed up until the early hours of the morning, working out where Alegria's bus would end up. He exaggerates it, of course, and she – sleepy, tipsy – gasps along with them as if hearing it for the first time. Zivoin strokes the back of her neck, massages her scalp, and feels heavy with contentment.

'I have to be honest with you,' Kajo tells her, throwing an arm around Zivoin, 'there's no way a girl like you will stick with this grumpy old man – I give this marriage two months.' He's red-faced from drink, leaning against his friend for support. The group falls silent, Zivoin glances at her, but Kajo isn't finished. 'The first month,' he mumbles, 'is for you to find out what kind of budala my friend here is. The second is to get rid of him!'

To everyone's surprise, Alegria laughs good-naturedly. 'I'll make a bet with you,' she says, her tongue coated with red wine. 'If we're still together two years from now, you meet us in, let's say, Paris, and take us out for dinner.' She sticks her hand out. 'I choose the restaurant, though.'

'Deal,' Kajo grins, and they shake on it.

'I like steak, so you better start saving up your money,' she quips, and the group dissolves into laughter.

Delighted, Zivoin turns to Kajo and claps him on the shoulder. 'That's why you don't mess with my wife!'

'She's terrifying!' But Kajo isn't quite done yet. 'You know,' he tells her, 'Zivoin told us how you first met.'

'Really?'

'We all thought you were crazy!'

Alegria raises her glass of wine, as if toasting them, and says, 'Well, what sane woman would marry him?' This earns her a shout of approval from his friends, and they drink. She briefly rests a hand on his lower back, her way of apologising for making him the butt of the joke, and Zivoin loves her so much for it in that moment that he wishes they were alone.

When she first arrived, he had worried she would misinterpret the blunt way his people spoke, and the jokes they made. 'Everyone messes with everyone,' he'd told her, multiple times. 'It's just our way – don't take it to heart.' And she'd rolled her eyes at him, told him not to worry. He realises now he was a fool to think she couldn't handle it. He grins as Kajo keeps prodding, and Alegria coolly spars with his poor, drunk friend. He cannot stop watching her, and he cannot stop smiling.

'Wait,' Alegria says suddenly. 'What's that sound?' They fall silent, and a woman's voice filters through from inside. Zivoin recognises it and opens the balcony door. They slip back into the flat in silence. Milenka is standing in the centre of the living room, her small frame surrounded by guests, her own mother-in-law in a wheelchair by her side. She is singing a slow, sorrowful song, her hands clasped in front of her. Her voice is thin, and she cannot hit the high notes, but still the room is moved, still the men and women are silent, pierced.

The room is gripped with melancholy. Milenka sings with her eyes closed and her head bowed, and after a while, people join in. First Zivoin's aunt, reaching for her sister's arm, and then, to Alegria's surprise, Svetlana, whose eyes are wet. Eventually, the whole room is singing. Though Alegria cannot understand it, she feels an immense sadness radiating from the people she now considers her family. She thinks, once again, about her parents and sister, and wonders if all the people she and Zivoin love will ever be in the same room at the same time.

Later, she will ask Zivoin about it, and he will tell her it's an old mountain song people sing after first harvests, weddings, funerals, a song about how the only certainty of life is death. 'It's become a song about our country,' he will say, 'a plea for spring to come and renew the earth.'

'And why,' Alegria will ask, 'did she choose to sing that?'

'Because our country is dying, and though we can all feel it, today something new has grown out of its poisoned soil,' he will reply.

For now, though, she says nothing and simply listens, her heart contracting. The spell over the room breaks when the song ends; it seems clear that the festivities are over. People start to filter out of the door, and there is a final toast, a final round of kisses, clasped hands, congratulations.

And it is indeed time for them to go – the night train looms. Tomorrow evening they must fly back to London. Milenka's eyes are wet, Drago kisses Alegria's forehead and then holds his son a little too hard and Zivoin inhales mothballs and brandy and tries to close the gap between them. Just before they leave, Milenka thrusts a heavy bag into Alegria's hand, and she looks inside to see a white crocheted blanket, the one her mother-in-law has been working on endlessly since their arrival. Alegria presses her face into the blanket. It smells of Turkish coffee, lavender and – she grins into the twisted threads – pear rakija.

When they board the train, Alegria observes her husband's profile as he stares out of the window. The town pulls away from them in a rushed blur. 'What now?' she asks. The question means many things at once, they both know. It means: will things get easier? It means: will we be all right? It means: are you scared?

'Now,' he says, lifting her hand to his lips and kissing it softly, 'now . . . we can actually start dating.' Alegria's eyebrows arch in surprise and she begins to laugh, her head thrown back, throat exposed. Zivoin looks at her and thinks, yet again, about how beautiful she is. He stands and pulls her – still laughing – to her feet to kiss her, and Alegria presses her body into his. They kiss, they break apart, they kiss again – not tenderly but impatiently, breathlessly. They laugh into each other's mouths.

Seventeen hours later

The fear of yet another thing going wrong follows them like a stray dog. They arrive at Heathrow Airport with a few hundred pounds between them – all the money they have left – and the whole performance begins again: documents confiscated, interrogations, first separately, then together. Finally, they are locked in a room and told they must wait – as though they have a choice in the matter. Not for the first time, Zivoin contemplates the many exhausting moments he and Alegria have had to perform the immigrant's dance. Shuffling from town halls to notaries to embassies to waiting rooms, all whilst clutching stacks of papers to prove they are who they say they are – both together and apart. The process has made him feel like a lesser version of himself, a mass-produced object in a factory like the one his mother once worked at. He wishes the city that brought them together would just leave them be, that love across borders could be given the same chance to bloom as every other kind of love. He is tired of begging for the door to open. It never ends. The bony hands of exhaustion grip at them. Long minutes pass without them speaking, because it feels like there is nothing to say. The waiting has begun; a wire stretched so tight it threatens to snap at any moment.

'What's wrong?' he asks, pointlessly, half an hour later. He already knows, of course – no one has come to update them. It's taking far longer than it should. Alegria is agitated, jiggling her foot up and down as her eyes dart around the room. She's barely registering him.

'It was raining when we boarded the aeroplane.'

'Yes, so?'

Alegria shakes her head and continues to jiggle. 'Bad omen.'

'What makes you say that?'

'Because rain, grey skies, all of that is bad.'

'Not really.' Zivoin is aware of how petulant he sounds, arguing with his sleep-deprived, stressed-out wife about superstitions he knows she doesn't really pay any attention to unless she's paralysed with fear. But her pessimism feels too much to bear in that moment. 'Without the rain there would be no crops. Without the rain our rivers and lakes would eventually run dry. The heat would never break. Who says rain is a bad thing?' She doesn't reply.

The room smells like bleach; that is the most overpowering thing about it. It's the sort of room someone could glance at and conclude that nothing is amiss, but that feeling changes once the door of this room is shut and its claws dig in. For starters, there is almost no natural material to be found. Almost everything in there is made of plastic. It is an unpleasant and dehumanising thing to realise. There are no windows, so the chemical stink lingers and coats their airways when they breathe it in. They can taste it. But the bleach has not extinguished all life: a spider has made its home in the back corner of the room, between the sink and the wall. It stays very still. Perhaps it is resting. The walls are white, blank, made of a cheap plaster that leaves a powdery residue clinging to the clothing of anyone unlucky enough to lean against them.

On closer inspection, Zivoin realises there are various

miscellaneous stains on the walls. Not many, but enough to be off-putting – especially the faint, yellowing ones around the toilet. The fact that the room is both bleached and dirty is disconcerting. Clumps of grime, hair and dust have become smeared together and pushed into the corners, where they lie like black worms. There is a stain on the rickety wooden table too, a ring of what must have once been coffee. Also on the table is a plastic jug and two cups that they do not drink from, an unspoken agreement. The underside of the table should be avoided at all costs – old wads of gum are stuck along it in various states of elasticity. Some have clearly been there a while – his hand accidentally brushed against one so hard, he at first mistook it for a plastic rivet. He'd momentarily explored it with his fingers before whipping his hand away in disgust.

The bed, which is positioned directly opposite the door, is bolted to the floor. A single bed, with a mattress only two or three inches thick. The white sheets on it are flimsy and papery, ripping after just a few minutes of Zivoin lying down on them, an arm flung over his face to shield his eyes from the strip lighting directly above. In what must be a serious design flaw, a shiny metal toilet has been installed half a metre from where someone occupying the bed would lay their head. Neither of them has used the toilet yet in front of the other – an act of humiliation they will not allow. They are still in that careful stage of love where there is no room for things like blood and excrement and smells, only soft skin, brushed teeth, plucked eyebrows.

Alegria is sure it is the same interrogation room she was in the first time round. There is a familiar staleness to it that feels a lot like hopelessness. In the hours they have been there, Alegria has become utterly convinced that she already knows what the outcome will be, and her despair has temporarily immobilised her. She wonders if the cameras in the room are switched on, if they are secretly being recorded. She thinks about the promise she made herself, the one about never relying on the mercy of the British immigration system again, and wonders how she still has room for naivety after everything she's gone through. By her side, Zivoin is still, quiet. Hunger has driven him to the point of nausea, and every breath in is an attempt not to bring up bile. All that would do is make the room smell even worse. He had anticipated this, after all. It is not surprising: newly married, a country on fire, only one, tenuous visa between them.

As they had walked through passport control, their passports had been seized, bags searched, documents scrutinised with enough suspicion to make them both nervous. They were brought in and told to wait and see if Alegria would be granted the right to enter. Alegria's fresh passport with her new, married name in it is less than a day old. If the border control computer system connects it to her old passport, everything will fall apart in the most spectacular way. *These things take time. These things cannot be rushed. No news is good news.* All of this he relays to her as she becomes more and more agitated. He wills her to believe him. But something about this white, sterile room pushes her to the edge of reason.

Alegria watches the clock face above the door and thinks

about happy endings and who gets to have them. This is what will kill me, she thinks, the endless repetition of airports and passports and bureaucracy and begging. This is what will kill me. She leans forward until her forehead is pressed against the table and wraps her arms around her head. Lets out a long, loud groan, as if she's in physical pain. 'I can't keep doing this,' she whispers, 'I can't keep doing this.'

'You can,' Zivoin says immediately, and begins to rub her back. He feels stiff and a little clammy – the uncomfortable feeling of having been in the same hoodie and jeans for too many hours. He wonders what life will be like when they aren't constantly on the verge of breaking down, whether there will be enough hope left for him to still be tender. They're doing it again, of course: as she inches closer to resigned helplessness, he leans the other way and insists that it will be all right. Isn't that what partners do to comfort each other when things are uncertain? One panics and the other reassures? You *must* keep doing this is what he wants to say as he makes slow, gentle circles between her shoulder blades. The back of her neck is a little paler than her shoulders, protected from the sun by her hair. He strokes the exposed strip of skin and then massages her scalp. 'Is that nice?'

'Sure.' Alegria takes a big breath, and blinks rapidly to avoid tears. 'Another hurdle?' she asks the empty room, her voice muffled by the table. 'Really? Every time we think we're doing OK, something else comes along to complicate it, sucking away all our time, our money, our happiness.' Her voice gets louder as she speaks, and by the end, Alegria is almost shouting. 'Is this the rest of our life – a constant battle? Never able to relax? I can't do it. *We* can't keep doing this.'

Zivoin could, in this moment, misinterpret what Alegria is saying and take it as an expression of doubt about their relationship instead of panic. And this is his first instinct – here she is, telling him their life together is too hard. But he refuses to give in. 'Peach,' he says. 'Have I ever told you about the time I saw a bear?'

She laughs into her arms and shakes her head, then rocks slowly from side to side as he tells her the story of the mountain. He watches her breathing slow down; her grip loosens. When he finishes, she lifts her head off the table, curls obscuring her face. Says, 'I don't know how you stayed so calm – the fear alone would have killed me. I would never climb a mountain again.' And then she adds, 'You're crazy.'

'I was terrified – you should have seen how I ran away. I'm only brave when other people are looking,' Zivoin admits, thinking of how close he's come to breaking down in front of her in recent days. 'The point is that I did climb that mountain again – many, many times. The point is that I was afraid, but I kept going. The point is, I would do this all over again with you. You're the only person I want to go through this nightmare with, the only person I'll give up everything for.'

Alegria's lips twitch into a smile. She straightens and rolls her shoulders back, as if gearing up for a round in a boxing ring. 'That's a lot of points.'

'We just have to keep going. What's that thing the English are always saying?'

'Punching and rolling? No – rolling with the punch?'

'No, keep calm. And then carry on. If they can do it – these soft, arrogant people – then we can too.'

She laughs properly now, tipping her head back to look at the ceiling. An image from their first few weeks together unexpectedly pops into her brain: Zivoin dancing in his bedroom, naked apart from a pair of socks. They'd been doing that thing new couples do for hours at a time, making silly jokes, asking ridiculous questions, competing to make the other laugh, performing for each other. She knew he'd once loved to dance, knew that if she played her cards just right, she'd get him to show off a few steps. It was a test – yes, you shouldn't test people, sure, whatever, but she'd wanted to know if he was the kind of man who could make a fool of himself in front of her. If he could be vulnerable. She'd expected him to refuse, or fob her off. But he jumped up immediately and goofed off for her, delighting in making her belly-laugh until it hurt. The memory comforts her. Here is a man who likes himself enough to look like a fool, just to make her smile. Who shuns tradition for her. Who puts his freedom, maybe even his life, at risk for her. Men like that do not abandon people just because life gets complicated. She strokes his stubbled face and notices how tired he looks, how dry the skin is. Says: 'You're not drinking enough water.'

'Neither are you.'

'But I washed my face this morning.'

'What does that have to do with anything?' he asks, and then they both laugh and things feel a little more normal at last. They talk about where they might live, and what they might do in the mornings they have free together, and who will make breakfast, and who will clear up. They envision houses with plenty of windows and streets lined with trees that will grow big and green in the summer, painting the pavements with shadows. Parks with duck ponds, wide, open fields for picnics, open-air swimming pools and gardens with banana shrubs and walls that are low enough to chat to their neighbours. Maybe by the time it's summer, things will be all right again. They debate where in this hopeful new city of theirs might be best to raise children, what sort of children they might have, and how they will tell this story to them years down the line.

'I bet,' Alegria says, 'they'll ask us if we were afraid. I wonder what we'll tell them.'

'Obviously we'll tell them the truth.'

'Which is?'

'We were fucking terrified.'

She lets out a burst of nervous laughter. It sounds like a machine gun. 'We can't tell them that!'

'Then we'll lie. We'll say we knew from the start that it was going to work out.'

'Urgh,' she moans. 'I *wish* that were the case.'

'It'll be all right,' he tells her, for the hundredth time. 'All we can do is control what we can control. The rest has already happened, or will happen, or isn't going to happen. If this doesn't work out, we'll figure something out – there's always another way. Your country, or mine, or somewhere else in the middle.' Zivoin keeps his voice light and says it like it's the most obvious thing in the world. She nods, and he runs his hands through his hair to try and hide how shaky he feels. Sometimes the only way out is through. They hear footsteps coming their way and look at each other quickly, urgently.

It feels like something is about to change. 'The point is, there's always a bear on the mountain, and we have to climb it anyway,' Zivoin blurts out, with as much conviction as he's got. His knee jiggles furiously under the table, his teeth are clenched.

Her hand finds his and grips it with extraordinary force. 'Brace for impact,' she says. The door opens. Someone is calling out her name.

Epilogue

Strangerland *is a true story, though certain names, dates and small details have been changed. Yugoslavia partially closed its borders in May 1991, making it virtually impossible for men of fighting age to leave. A series of horrific civil wars swiftly followed, finally ending in 2001. Yugoslavia became a country marred by brutal war crimes, including genocide and mass rape, claiming around 140,000 lives. The wars resulted in 2 million internally displaced people and 2.4 million refugees. In 1991, the phrase 'ethnic cleansing' was used in print for the first time in history. The country was split into six entities: Croatia, Bosnia and Herzegovina, Slovenia, Serbia, Montenegro and North Macedonia. Montenegro was annexed by Serbia until it declared independence in 2006. That same year, the real Alegria and Zivoin had their third and final child, a son. They live together in west London to this day, and have visited each other's countries – and families – many times. Although Simone never left Brazil, she lives a beautiful life. Alegria and Zivoin's eldest daughter works with young children. Their youngest son has just become an adult. Their middle daughter became a writer. Eventually, she asked her parents for their blessing to write this book. And they said yes.*

Acknowledgements

Growing up, I listened to my parents talk about how they met as though it was the most mundane thing in the world. It took until I was in my early twenties, falling in love for the first time, for me to realise how incorrect that perception was. It felt like too important of a discovery to keep hidden.

In a surprising twist, as I began writing about their journey, I ended up embarking on one that was eerily similar. I consider myself lucky, therefore, that I could tap into their courageousness whenever I lacked my own. Thank you, Mãe, thank you, Tata, for giving me your story and trusting me to tell it. Thank you for reading the early drafts. Thank you for giving me the most insane expectations for romantic love. Thank you for being my parents.

This book is also a testament to my grandparents, three of whom left us too soon. I wish I'd had more time with you – there is so much I would ask. To Simone, thank you for being our witch auntie and for being completely brilliant. I know the readers will love you as much as we do. To Lara and to Luka, I love you both so much! And to my wider family, sorry for being so absent whilst I figured out how to write this thing.

To Jamie, my love. Thank you for your unwavering support and for understanding me in profound ways.

To my wonderful friends, who have listened to me whine a lot, and who are kind enough to still ask how the writing is going – I love you all and I'm so grateful for you all. Thank you to my writer friends, a special and gifted bunch. And also, thank you to the people who I may not know as well, but who spent

ACKNOWLEDGEMENTS

their precious time and money on my work simply because you wanted to. That's a far cooler act than any of the people I'm about to mention, to be honest.

Thank you to Catherine Mayer for believing in me. To Cindy and James, thank you for your political views and your opinions about space, in that order. Simone, Myra and Alice – you were the reason why I clung onto my day job as long as I did! And I really needed that! Thank you, Masuma, for feeling things as strongly as I do. Thank goodness for our conversations. A special thank you to Helena, for being extremely hot and funny. And to everyone's ray of sunshine, Becca, for reading an entire manuscript of mine on a plane ride instead of napping – no higher honour. Also to Kylie, because I'm in awe of you all the time, and because you are the self-assured 21-year-old I wish I'd been. To Jamie (again) for ghost-writing all my work, it's so crazy that no one has figured it out yet. Thank you, Simi, for your love. Most especially, thank you, Ruby, for reading the first draft of *Strangerland*. You are so generous and *so* talented – please become an editor/agent and please let me be your only client.

Oh – to everyone who asked if I would be writing sex scenes into the book, thank you for keeping me humble.

Thank you to Millie, my agent, for your reassurance and excellence. Thank you, Amy, for your editorial skills. You are so good at gently guiding me down the path, it's easy to overlook how vital your role has been in shaping this book. A huge thank you to Caroline Johnson for copy-editing this manuscript. My grasp of commas is shaky at best, so I appreciate your magic. Thank you as always to the #Merky/Cornerstone group, Cameron, Alice D, Laurie, Helen. Thank you to Kirsten, Emily, Alice G, Anna and Barbora for making this book sellable (important!) and Zahraa for your artistic flair. And to those names I don't know – the artists, designers, assistants, sound engineers, publicists, marketing coordinators, typesetters and

ACKNOWLEDGEMENTS

many more, thank you. I'm always grateful for your part in this work, you have no doubt made it better. Thank you, Abi, for the years we worked together.

I also thank you, the reader. To have made it into a moment of your complex and beautiful life is an immense privilege, and I am deeply grateful for it. Thank you for reading this story.

And now to the most important bit. I think all writing – especially, fiction – is about truth telling. We live in an age of distortion and falsification, where the meanings of truth, suffering and empathy are up for debate and purchase. We are witnessing a genocide being carried out against Palestinians by Israel, under the false flag of freedom and security. We have seen the callousness and complicity of many state leaders, Prime Minister of the UK included. Yet, those who express outrage and despair at this most profound injustice are labelled as threatening, dangerous or hateful. Truth has been distorted beyond recognition. What are we doing? As a writer, but more importantly, as a human being, I am horrified.

As I wrote *Strangerland*, a novel which touches on, albeit briefly, the impacts of war, discrimination and poverty, I watched the people of Palestine be ethnically cleansed, dehumanised, and murdered. The record of their existence has been reduced to that of suffering, a cultural genocide as well as a literal one. Thousands of stories have been extinguished – generations of writers, journalists, poets, storytellers and artists gone for ever. The world has failed Palestine, and we will look back at the last hundred years with deep shame. That is the truth. I cannot be a writer without talking about Palestine, but others with far larger platforms than I have done the heaviest lifting. To list them all would be impossible, but I thank Isabella Hammad, Arundhati Roy, Selma Dabbagh, Ibtisam Azem, Naomi Klein, Clementine Ford, Jia Tolentino, Mahmoud Muna, Sally Rooney and all the others who do not flinch.

Free Palestine, always.